fLUX Runners

By:
William Joseph Roberts

16 + suggested. Mature subject matter and situations. Yeah, if you need a safe space, put the book up now and just forget about it.

Aliens + Pew Pews will always equal violence of some kind. Plus, some good old fashion torment.

Humans go to space, humans meet aliens, what the hell do you think is going to happen? Remember, Kirk was the first man-whore in space.

Let's face it, these guys are space miners. They cuss, a lot.

Yup, you guessed it there, Sunshine. They smoke, they drink and even talk about or use other substances.

Contains probably way too many "hold my beer moments" and uses of duct tape.

Yup, you guessed it again. People die, creatures die, aliens die. Lots of shit dies. Hey, we have to have a body count of some kind.

This is a blank page.

Why you ask?

Just because that's just the way that it all laid out. I couldn't help it. I had to toss something in here.

OMG, you have a problem with blank pages, don't you? Are you prejudice against a page being blank? Sometimes it is what it is and there isn't anything you can do about it.

Shhhh, just let it happen. It's all good, man. Nothing but rainbows and butterflies….

(Just for you, Tata. ☺)

dEDICATION:

To Meg, my loving, patient, and very tolerant wife; who has put up with my crazy caffeine induced ramblings over the years. You have been my rock, my sanity, and my voice of reason while I found my way through the darkness of self-doubt and fought my demons. Without you, I may never have completed any of my works. Without you, I would have been lost… er well? I'd probably be missing a few fingers or limbs by this point if it weren't for you.
Thank you for believing in me when I didn't believe in myself.

Le grá go deo

Also, a thank you to my friends and family that have been there to support me through all of my craziness, and to help spur the ideas within this book. (I know by now a few of you are sick of hearing about it and just want me to be done.) A few of which I will list, namely our lovable crew. Y'all know who you are without last names, ya' goofy bastards:

Meg, Doug, Krista, Wes, Kara, Pat, Amanda, Leah, Mel, Andy, Trae, Tiff, Cammie, Janey, Jenny, Denise, Cara, Danny, Chris, Flip, Bob, Richie, Rachel, Jamey, Ben, Camille, Steph, Becky, Perry, and all of the others that I'm forgetting in the wee hours of the morning.

Also, a huge thank you goes out to Project Gutenberg for allowing me to mention them and to make their efforts a huge part of my backstory. Check out the actual Project Gutenberg page here: https://www.gutenberg.org

Last but not least, a great big thank you goes out to some of my fellow authors. To those who have been there to bounce ideas off of and offer input, no matter how painful it might have been. Thank you to Dan Hollifield, Christopher Woods, Taylor Anderson and especially to Benjamin Smith and R.J. Ladon. You two have probably heard more of my insane mind squirrel ranting than anyone else. Thank you, guys. Thanks for putting up with my sorry ass on this crazy ride

pREFACE

This novel, along with so many of my other stories have been a long, drawn-out labor of love. I have conquered, or at least temporarily vanquished those evil demon voices of self-doubt that we all must deal with when completing the first novel of what I hope will be many more to come.

This particular story began life as a nifty idea back in 2010 or so. The thought was how could a crew of asteroid miners pirate another vessel and get away with it. It was jotted down and tossed into the slush pile for later use. Well, this one didn't take too kindly to just lying around collecting dust. It nagged at me. It beckoned to be heard. So, I started adding to the thought, a note here, a scribble there and the story grew. After piddling around for the better part of a year with the outline I sat down in September of 2018 and punched out the raw meat of the story in a few months' time. It has been one hell of a learning and growth process, which I think has paid off tremendously. I have grown on many levels as an author with this particular work. I'm relieved that it is done, but the story isn't finished yet. I have another 6 or so books to write in this series, time and life-permitting.

Part of the inspiration for fLUX Runners comes from what is, in my opinion, the best space opera game to date, _**Starflight**_. It may not have had the best graphics, but what game really did in 1986? It was the gameplay and the emersion into the universe that I loved. The feelings of adventure and curiosity that it evoked overwhelmed me at times. I discovered new worlds, hidden mysteries, and alien races. I learned so many things about elements from the periodic table and how to physically measure a cubic meter because of this game. Hell, I still have my notes from all those years ago. I'm sure that I played way too many hours of this game like many others on my ancient, dual floppy drive Franklin 2000 personal computer. If I think hard enough, I can almost hear the drives grinding as they processed the massive amounts of data for this game; (everything for this game was contained on two 360K diskettes.)

So, needless to say, this story has brought back a bit of nostalgia for me. I have laughed, I have cried, and I have gotten pissed off along with these characters as their lives have been fleshed out into something for all to enjoy.

Also, as a thank you and a bow down of my unworthiness to all of those who have inspired my thoughts and my style, you'll find more than a few Easter eggs laced into the pages of this work of fiction. Good luck finding them all, because I've started missing them myself at this point.

I hope that you truly enjoy fLUX Runners and fall in love with these characters and this universe as much as I have.

Prepare yourself for an adventure with a lovable crew of degenerates and misfits as they dive into the dark unknown....

pROLOGUE

Bolton Street
South Boston, Massachusetts, USA
October 5, 2178/ 1942 hrs local time

Misty rain drifted down from the dark October sky. The scent of urine mingled strangely with the acrid smoke that rose from a burn barrel at the end of the South Boston alleyway.

"Note to self," Doug mumbled. "Do *not* let Lizz talk you into picking up new recruits at the start of winter when you live in an underground bunker in the desert." Frosty breath escaped his cupped hands as he blew warm air into them. Shifting his weight, he leaned against the opposite side of the doorway. He produced a small silver case from his black leather trench coat. Retrieving a cigarette from the case, he lit it, took a long draw and let the thick white smoke roll from his mouth, inhaling it into his nostrils. He slicked back the dampened strands of iron black hair, wringing out his ponytail in one smooth motion.

Angry squeaks drew his attention to the dumpster on the opposite side of the alley. He watched as a small family of rats emerged from behind the bin. They chittered and bicker over a half-eaten slice of pizza that the largest of the black rats had freed from the rotting dumpster.

A figure stopped at the far end of the alley, along Bolton Street. He could see that she was an Asian woman in an overcoat and bowler hat of all things. She pulled up the left sleeve of her coat and tapped at her forearm. The light from her Subdermal Aethernet Personal Portal illuminated her young face. She slid her finger across the screen of her SAPP, shutting off the device, then pulled her sleeve down and continued into the alley.

Doug stepped out of the doorway and into view. He looked up, making sure to stay under the awning that covered the entrance.

"There were three ravens sat on a tree," Doug said. He took another long drag from his cigarette, letting the smoke out slowly through his nose.

The young woman stopped in mid-stride. She warily looked over her shoulder toward Bolton Street, then back to Doug.

"They were as black as they might be," she said.

"Think you have what it takes to be a pioneer?" Doug stepped into the street, his hands extended to his sides, palms open.

"I do, but it would have been nice if Uncle Danny could have told me more."

"There are reasons for that and why we're meeting like this," Doug said, motioning to the cold dark alley that surrounded them. He took one last drag from his cigarette then field stripped the filter. The red glowing ember of burning tobacco hissed against the damp pavement.

"Before you agree to anything, you deserve to know what you are getting yourself into. To start with, there is no guarantee that you can come back to Earth any time soon. The Independent Alliance and the Martian Reich have both issued bounties for all known crew and ships. More than a few people would turn in their grandmothers for less coin, so we have to be careful.

"Careful from what, exactly?" She winced, taking a step away from Doug. "Are you running guns or drugs or people? I love my Uncle Danny, but if that's the sort of thing that he's gotten wrapped up in, then I want no part of it."

Doug laughed under his breath. "No, it's nothing like that, I promise you. But we're still enemies of the state."

She nervously rocked back on her heels. "Well, go on already. I'm listening."

Doug thought for a moment, then cleared his throat. "Do you know why we listen to two-hundred-year-old music or watch ancient videos?"

"Yeah," she said. "It's because it costs entirely too much for any regular or sane person to access any of the latest media."

"It isn't just a matter of cost," Doug said. "It's a matter of privilege. At least on Earth, it is. You have to be given permission by the I.A. before you can even pay for the privilege to watch or listen to their brainwashing dribble. We have what we have only because someone way back in the day had saved everything in the public domain and kept it safe for the decades that followed. What do you know about the war and the Hell years?"

She tilted her head with a look of odd consideration on her face. "That the world went to shit, but that's really about it. They don't teach history in school. We are too busy training in our assigned job fields."

Doug grunted a laugh. "That's because they don't want you to know the truth. They don't really like anyone who can think for themselves, either. They want mindless drones to do their bidding. See, about a hundred years ago after the world went to shit and the hell years were over, the I.A. formed from the scraps that remained of the old United Nations. Somehow, they became the overseers of the newly formed powers on Earth. The American Confederation, The Australian Peoples Republic, and The New Britannia Empire. Eventually, they colonized the solar system and controlled everything, until the people of Luna and Mars revolted. Since then they have taken direct control of everything that they could. World media, corporations, even farms have been absorbed into the conglomerate that is the I.A. Not everything, mind you, but most things are directly controlled by them. There are a few independent operators out there besides us, but they are dwindling away."

"Why don't the people just revolt like the other colonies and overthrow them?"

"Because mankind as a species is inherently lazy and on the whole, they would rather be told what to do and how to live their lives."

"And exactly what does any of that have to do with me joining you and my Uncle in becoming fugitives from the law?"

Doug smiled. "We basically told the I.A. to go fuck themselves and started our own colony. We are completely independent of any government and have already established a few powerful allies should the I.A. or the Reich decides to come after us. Your uncle is one of our lead engineers that we have working on our mining operations in system. You'd be proud of him and the work he's done for us." He retrieved another cigarette and lit it.

"And you? She crossed her arms impatiently. "Who are you exactly?"

"I'm the second in command, only to our Overseer, Lizz."

"That still doesn't tell me who you are," she said in a perturbed tone.

"My name is Captain Douglas Rackham. I see to the day to day operations of the colony."

"How do I know that Uncle Danny sent you? How do I know that I can trust you? For all I know you could just be some creep that learned about this meeting just so you could take advantage of a helpless girl."

"Well, first off, I know you aren't helpless. Danny has told me how he trained you to box. Second, you could ask him that question yourself if you wanted to."

"Wait? Uncle Danny is here?"

"Yeah, just down the street," Doug said as he turned away from her and started walking down the alley. "It'll only take about twenty minutes to get there from here."

She ran, catching up and walking alongside Doug. "Okay…," she said with a tone of nervous curiosity. "So how exactly did my uncle get wrapped up with you and running from the law?"

"Well, you see. That's a bit of an interesting story, depending on how far back you go. Where should I start?"

"At the beginning," She said.

"Fair enough," Doug said. He smiled at the young woman, then took a deep breath as they continued down the alley. "Once upon a time…"

Peachtree Street
Atlanta, Georgia, USA
April 13, 2168 / 2112 hrs local time

"I must be *bat shit* crazy to have followed you back here." Krista shifted her weight from foot to foot, warming her hands over a rusted burn barrel. "Dammit, Doug. I'm cold, I'm hungry and I just wanna go to sleep." She coughed from the acrid smoke that wafted into her face. "And, oh my God, I wish they would shut off that music." She flipped her raven hair with twist of her head then brushed away a loose strand that clung to the side of her nose. The orange glow of firelight from the barrel flickered, casting an eerie shadow across her strong Native American features.

The distant thump of heavy bass from a nearby club reverberated over the pavement. "Why are we even back here? I thought we had left Atlanta for good. You said no looking back. Your buddy Max won't take kindly to finding you back on his turf since you turned your back on the crew."

"We did and I did say that, but things change." Doug leaned against the brick wall of the ancient playhouse and lit a cigarette. He closely watched the eastern entrance of the old midtown Emory hospital. "You see the old hospital over there?"

"Yeah. It's an old hospital. So what," Krista grumped.

"See, it was abandoned over a century ago and became a beacon to refugees after the world fell apart and before the hell years began. It served as the original home base for the American Confederation. A new country literally formed in that building in the years following the war. Once the capital of the newly formed American Confederation moved to Wichita Falls, Texas, the old hospital took on a new life and became a community all in itself. Some of the original guards stayed in Atlanta and turned it into low rent housing that included protection from the assholes outside. Merchants, craftsman and the like set up shops in the lobby and office areas while the old hospital rooms became apartments. Its layout and construction made for an easily defendable community complex, all in all."

"And what exactly does any of that have to do with us coming back to Atlanta and me freezing my ass off?"

"You insisted on coming with me, so I don't want to hear it."

"It was a better option than staying with those *weirdos* in Cartersville while you committed suicide," Krista huffed.

Doug looked back over his shoulder and down the alley, then shrugged at Krista. "You could have handled them," he mused.

"Well, this seemed the better option at the time."

"One of the traders that came up to the compound in Cartersville last week kept going on about this narcissist from South America that showed up. He said the guy came up from Florida and insisted that Max add more mirrors around the Emory complex."

"Sounds like an asshat to me," Krista said.

"Oh, he is," Doug laughed. "Trust me. Samuka is a complete asshat, self-absorbed, and a *narcissist* to the extreme. But he's also the type of person that could sell ice to Eskimos."

"Can you get to the point already?"

"Samuka is loaded and he owes me big time. He may be an asshat, but he's an *honorable* asshat. He'd rather pay up than to have the tiniest amount of unfinished business that could tarnish his reputation. With what he owes me, we could go west to Denver maybe and get a fresh start."

"Let go of me," a voice shouted from down the street.

Doug stepped to the corner of the building and peeked out from the alley. "That doesn't look good."

"What?"

"There's this lady being harassed by a couple of guys down at the corner by the club. She can't be from around here. The jacket she's wearing looks way too expensive for anyone on this side of town."

Krista tucked her hands under her arms and huddled against Doug's side. She peered out from the alley. "Yup, sure looks like it to me. I used to have a coat just like that. Oh my God, it was so warm, too. Sucks to be her." She snuggled her head against his side.

He pulled Krista away from his side and glanced down at her with an unsure look.

"*What?*" Krista said defensively. "Mommy and Daddy always bought me anything that I ever wanted. I told you before they were loaded from their shares in the casinos up north."

Doug shook his head. He smiled at his bedraggled companion. "The life you lead now must be like night and day." He took a step forward but stopped abruptly, jerked backward as Krista latched onto his arm.

"*Doug,* no. It's not our business. There's no telling what those guys might do. Besides, it took disappearing to get away from the street crew. Do you really want to chance Max catching wind that we're back in town before you can talk to this Samuka guy?"

"I can't stand by and do nothing. It just isn't right," he said as he brushed her away and stepped out of the alley.

"Dammit Doug," she forcefully whispered down the street after him. "You'd better not go and get yourself killed and leave me all alone out here. I swear I'll never talk to you again if you do."

Doug nonchalantly made his way toward the street corner, keeping his eyes averted as he approached. Two large men laughed and made lude comments toward the woman as they shoved her about. They passed her back and forth between them.

"You think we should sell her? She looks healthy enough," the larger of the two men said. "She's pretty, but she doesn't look like the type that Max would want." He snapped his fingers in a moment of inspiration. "We could take her to Whitaker and his crew. I bet they'd take her off our hands."

"Would be easier to just strip her and toss the body," the other man said. "Less bullshit to deal with.

"You'll regret this if you don't let me go," the woman growled. She struggled against the larger man's grip.

The larger of the two men let out a deep, bass-filled laugh. "I bet this one just got herself turned around and doesn't even know where she is."

"Ya know, I bet you're right," the other man said with a snap of his fingers. "I bet that's exactly what she's doing on this side of town." He looked her up and down, hungrily licking his lips. "It would be our civic duty to help her find her way. There are a lot of *unscrupulous* people on this side of town," he said sarcastically.

"It is such a wonderful sight to see citizens of this wonderful city taking an interest in the elderly," Doug said as he walked past the scene.

"*Elderly?*" The woman squeaked. Her blonde curls flew outward as she snapped a scowl in Doug's direction.

Doug leveled the barrel of his antique Judge revolver at the man who held the woman. He cocked the hammer back. "How about I play, boy scout and take her off your hands?"

The two men calmly raised their hands, releasing the woman.

"How about we leave these two gentlemen to their evening?" Doug nodded for her to join him. She slipped behind him; her hand pressed against the back of his shoulder. He took a step backward, "I do hope that you gentlemen enjoy the rest of your evening. Don't do anything I wouldn't do." He continued to back away slowly, the revolver aimed at the larger of the two men.

"She's probably a dead lay anyways," the smaller of the two men shouted.

"Yeah, all them rich white girls are the same," the larger man added.

"We'd better not see your mug out on the *peach* again, punk."

Doug decocked the revolver and tucked it into a pocket. "Are you okay," he asked. He turned; taking her hand he quickly led her back to the alley.

"Are you freaking crazy," Krista berated.

"Thank you so much," the woman interrupted in a thick Australian accent.

"My pleasure," Doug replied.

"Your pleasure my ass!" Krista slapped him across the arm. "You could have got yourself killed and left me all alone out here. Then where would I be? Hu?" She slapped him again.

Doug's jaw muscles flexed. He stared at Krista through narrowed slits. "Could you really just stand by and do nothing, knowing what they were about to do to her? Would you want me to leave you to the same kind of fate?"

"No, not really," she reluctantly admitted.

"Thank you," he said to Krista. "Come on, let's get out of here just in case those guys change their minds about letting us escape."

Doug hurriedly led them down the alley three blocks over to Currier Street. They arrived at a small diner that was set in the corner of a partially crumbled building. The back half of which had collapsed, littering the street with bricks and debris. A bell jingled as Doug opened the door to the small diner for Krista and the other woman. They immediately slid into the first open booth just inside the entrance of the building.

"What'll it be," a waitress said in a gruff tone as she approached. She produced an order pad and pen from her apron and began to scribble as she arrived at the table. She looked up from her pad at Doug and immediately curled her nose with disgust. She examined their worn and filthy appearance then turned to the well-dressed woman. "Is everything alright ma'am?"

"Yes, actually," the woman said. "Everything is actually more than alright." She smiled at Doug and Krista, then looked back to the waitress. "Please bring us three house specials and three beers." She turned back to Doug and Krista. "If that's alright with the two of you, of course."

The two of them looked to each other in disbelief. Doug shrugged. "Sure," he hesitantly slurred with a chuckle. "I won't turn down a free meal and a beer. Something preferably dark and chewy, not chilled piss, please."

Krista elbowed him in the ribs, then nodded at the waitress. "Yes please, but cider instead of beer, if you have it."

The waitress scribbled the order on her pad and stepped away. "Coming right up."

Krista elbowed Doug in the ribs once more. "How do you know that she isn't going to kill us and take our kidneys or something?"

"Really?" Doug scowled.

"My name is Elizabeth Trower. You can call me Lizz." She extended her hand in friendship. "Again, thank you for your help back there."

Doug shook the proffered hand. "So, what's the deal? You don't look like you belong on this side of town. In all truth, it's probably one of the worst parts of the city that a woman can walk around alone."

"I was told that there are a lot of starship crews that hang out at the bars on this side of town when they come planetside." Lizz removed her heavy coat and straightened the jacket of her gray business suit.

"Yeah, a lot of them do," Doug admitted. "But a woman like you out here alone on this side of town is just asking to disappear without a trace. What's so important that you'd risk being out here alone like this?"

Lizz closely examined the filthy pair seated across the booth from her and smiled wide. "I recently *retired* from my position as the head of marketing for a large corporation in Sydney Australia. After selling my shares back to the company, I decided that I should do something new and do that something quickly."

"That's great and I am *so* very happy for you, I really am, but that still doesn't explain why you're here," Doug said.

"Because I have already done it all," Lizz said. "I accomplished everything I had set out to accomplish. The job was no longer a challenge. So, I decided to reinvest my windfall quickly and try something few have done successfully. I purchased a ship and plan to run an independent operation without any corporate attachment. The crew will be independent contractors working directly for me. No union or spacer guild allowed."

"Okay...," Krista said with a disbelieving tone.

Doug sniggered to himself as he picked at his fingernails. "You do realize how hard that is going to be, don't you?"

"I do," Lizz admitted. "Which is why I want to attempt it."

Doug shook his head then smiled at Krista. "You're basically painting a great big target on your back for the Independent Alliance to take potshots at. You *do* realize this, don't you?" Doug snapped his gaze back to Lizz. "There's only a snowball's chance in hell that you could succeed at a plan like that."

Lizz leaned forward and smiled. "I do, and I could use a *go get em* guy like yourself to run the day to day operations for me."

"What exactly's in it for us," Krista interrupted.

"Are you two a package deal?" Lizz glanced from Doug to Krista and back again.

"Yes, we are," Doug answered. "She brings up a very good point though. What's in it for us?"

"Well for starters, you get to be captain …"

cHAPTER 1

The Nunnery,
Northeast Atlanta, Georgia, USA
May 12, 2176 / 1643 hrs local time

"**P**lease make yourself comfortable, Mr. Smith," the well-endowed hostess said. "Your *counselor*," she giggled, "will be with your momentarily. Should you need anything, merely press this button." She gestured with a slender finger as she held out a small keychain fob with a single red button in the center. The hostess seductively arched her back as she bent at the waist, leaning down to unlock the door.

Animalistic lust welled up within him. His eyes bulged and his pulse raced at the sight of her tender pale flesh, ever so delicately wrapped in an almost nonexistent leather skirt. She swung open the door and stepping aside, motioned for him to enter. Rich red velvets and golden accents stood out in the dimly lit room.

"Please, enjoy your stay, Mr. Smith."

"*Yes*," Mister Smith anxiously hissed. "I do believe I will," he said with a slight stutter. Nervously he wiped away beads of sweat from his balding head, then wiped his hands across the back of his rotund girth. He entered, slowly closing the door behind him. Various instruments of pain and pleasure hung on the gaudy, gilded walls. Large tapestries hung about the room as decoration, but he could see a partially concealed restraint system hidden behind one with images of a great forest stag.

A quiet, girlish giggle emanated from the shadows of the room.

He gasped, turning in the direction of the sound he sucked in an anxious breath.

"Don't you just *love* the energy of this place, Mr. Smith?" The voice from the shadows said in a soft, Australian accent. "They have everything that you could ever need to accommodate even the darkest and wildly imaginative of fantasies. The owners of this establishment have taken virtually all possible wants or desires and gathered them all neatly under one roof. An absolutely brilliant business strategy if you ask me."

"You are wise beyond your years, Mistress," he blurted with nervous anticipation.

Seductively slow steps echoed over the tiled floor as a petite figure emerged from the shadows. Her hips swayed with each measured step of her thigh-high stiletto boots. She strode into the brighter, but still dim overhead light at the center of the room. She wore a black velvet mask with accents of colorful blue feathers. The shadows accentuated lines of maturity on her face that peeked out from the edges of the mask. Her hands rested casually behind her back as she paced. Her full tightly curled locks teased along the tops of her breasts but did nothing to hide her naturally voluptuous curves stuffed into a strapless corset. The intricate bronze-trimmed latches that decorated the garment looked strained and at the maximum load limit of their design, barely able to contain the naturally large breasts.

Mister Smith gasped, struggling to swallow a dry breath.

"Do not look at me, Maggot!"

He looked away with a quick reflexive jerk and lowered his head. He attempted to hide a nervous grin that crossed his face. "Yes, Mistress," he said submissively.

Her arms relaxed and fell to her sides. She uncoiled a thin, yet sturdy looking leather whip that fell to the floor about her feet.

"Undress yourself, Maggot."

In one blindingly quick motion, she cracked the whip and unlatched the simple belt buckle that he wore.

"Yes, Mistress," he nervously replied. Struggling to remove his clothing he stumbled over himself. He stumbled forward but caught himself and regained his footing.

She approached him with confident, heavy-heeled strides. She double wrapped the whip around his neck with the speed of an experienced cougar and forced him to his knees. "From this moment on, you *are* my property. You do *what* I say, *when* I say, and *how* I say, or the punishment shall be severe."

"Yes, Mistress," he groveled.

"Perfect," she purred. "Very good, my little maggot. There may be hope for you yet. Now on your *feet*!" She tugged hard on the whip-like a horse's reins and lead him to the rear of the room. She turned slowly to face him, examining her prey. With the tip of a finger, she traced the line of his thick, bulbous jowl to just under the ear where the jaw attached to the skull. She pinched his ear lobe then pulled him downward. He pulled him closer to her and whispered. "Do you like pain, Maggot?"

His breath came in shallow, excited gasps. He dryly swallowed, stuttering his reply. "Yes, Mistress."

"You do not impress me, you fat maggot! You are a sorry excuse for flesh. No! You do not even rate as high as meat. You are not flesh. You are now, *nothing*. You will bleed for me and beg for more! *Then* you may rate as something tangible."

"Y...y...yes, Mistress," he said with a confused but excited stutter. A line of drool formed at the corner of his mouth.

She tore back a heavy, red velvet curtain to reveal a small anteroom. In the center of the anteroom stood a highly polished, articulating examination table. Four restraint arms protruded from each corner of the table. With much more strength than he thought she was capable of, she shoved him toward the table.

"Lay down," she commanded. She landed a forceful kick to his rump. He flopped face down atop the table without hesitation. It groaned and creaked from the strain of his shifting mass. His entire body quivered with anticipatory shudders. She paced around the table with deliberation and closed the restraints over his limbs with four satisfying metallic clicks. "Are you ready for the *fun* to begin?" She chortled. "This is the part where most people begin to panic. They think that they have made a terrible mistake, and they let fear take control. But not to worry, you are in good hands. I promise you that."

She let out an amused snicker as she inserted a rubber ball gag into his mouth and secured it around his head. "It would be best if you were to stay calm. We wouldn't want you to hyperventilate yourself into *unconsciousness,* now would we? That would just ruin all of our *fun.*" She leaned down from the waist and crossed her arms on the edge of the tabletop. She rested her chin on her arms and gazed contemplatively into the eyes of her subject. "Where, oh where, to begin? So many choices, so many *possibilities.*" She let out a contented purr as she seductively stretched, her hips swaying hypnotically. He whimpered between spasmodic breaths of excitement.

"It seems that you have been a very naughty boy, Mr. McGill." He tensed at the mention of his real name. "And now, you seem to have found yourself in a compromising and inescapable predicament." She smiled at him and stretched as if she were a cat that had just awoken from a nap. Languidly, she rolled and stood upright, then began to pace around the table. "You see *Senator*, there is something about cornering a creature that brings out the worst in its temperament. Even more so if the species is doomed for extinction. There is nothing that an endangered species will not do in order to continue breathing for one more day or to put food in its belly. Some of those recent bills that you lobbied for and helped to pass are a perfect example. Bills like those hurt people like myself and my family. They take even more credits out of our already threadbare pockets. They will make it that much harder for us to make a living as independent operators out in the black. We are a dying breed thanks to *great* and *powerful* men such as yourself, Mr. McGill." She slapped him briskly across his exposed rump.

He jerked; muffled words foamed from around the red rubber ball gag.

"The Madam has kept a very detailed record of your visits to this establishment, Mr. McGill. It seems that there are very few services offered by the Nunnery which you have not partaken. It surprises me that a Senator of the Independent Alliance must frequent a house of ill repute in order to satiate his desires." She returned to his field of view as she continued to circle the table. A conniving, yet seductive grin colored her face.

She snickered to herself. His sad, chubby countenance resembled a trussed-up suckling pig, apple in mouth and ready for the fire. The look in the senator's eyes begged for merciful release.

"You, Senator McGill have some very important information locked away in that disturbed mind of yours, and I want it," she said with a snarl. "I intend to leave here with that knowledge, or the video of this session and all previous sessions will go viral across the Aethernet, uploaded to every connected intranet server and appear simultaneously on every active screen across the globe." She nonchalantly leaned her hip against the table and sneered. "However," she paused, pushing her hair back as she leaned down. "By the time this particular session is over it would be more embarrassing than all of your other visits, combined." Her crazed glare bore into his soul. She stood and continued around the table, one slow, seductive step at a time. "Physical torture would only be a pleasure to you. I know because I have studied you for quite some time, Mr. McGill. Humiliation wouldn't do the trick either. It would only be enjoyable for you. So I said to myself, how will I be able to coax the information that I want from this man when he would thoroughly enjoy almost anything that I could come up with short of cutting off body parts. Then it hit me. I had this brilliant idea. A vice that up to this point, even you hadn't tried. At least not that I could find any evidence to the fact in my extensive research of you. So, a plan blossomed in my mind. Something that would be painful on so many levels that you cannot even fathom what it will be like. It's something that must be experienced. The musky, distinguishable scent of the encounter will forever haunt your soul once I am finished with you, Senator." She guffawed at her own inner thought.

Panic washed over Senator McGill's face. He thrashed to the extent that the restraints would allow. The table suddenly doubled over, lowering his feet and head so they nearly touched the floor.

"You, my good Senator McGill, are about to experience the most pain that you could ever endure on a physical, mental or emotional level." Her footfalls grew quiet, out of sight. Pops and squeaks of what sounded like old rusted hinges rang out in the circular room. The very distinctive clip-clop, clip-clop of hooves on the tiled floor accompanied her as she re-appeared within his field of view. Following closely behind her was a dappled gray horse led by a long leather tether.

"Mr. McGill, I would like to introduce you to my friend, Bruce. Bruce, this is Senator John McGill," she tittered. "Bruce here is the Madam's prize stallion. He has made the Madam quite the small fortune in breeding fees alone over his lifetime. And of all the mares over all the years, he has never once had trouble mounting his quarry. To be honest the stable hands have had more trouble in keeping ol' Bruce here from mounting anything he can get hold of. Too bad men aren't as reliable," she sighed. "A good mounting can be hard to find."

The Senator whimpered. His eyes bulged with confused disbelief as he struggled against the restraints.

"Excuse me, I digress. Just trust me, Senator. You have never and may never again experience pain such as that which you are about to receive." She continued her slow stride around the table, leading Bruce out of the Senator's range of vision.

Muffled screams of panic erupted around the ball gag in the Senator's mouth. Large veins pulsed across his reddening face as he struggled against the restraints.

The room exploded into a flurry of smoke, fire, and motion. The main entrance flung open as soldiers in full riot gear flooded into the room and surrounded the trio. Their submachine guns trained on the scantily clad dominatrix. She tugged against Bruce's reigns as he reared to escape.

"Friends of yours Senator?" She smiled at the soldiers. "Oh how I do love a challenge," she purred. She stroked the side of Bruce's neck, soothing the scared beast. "You'll be alright, big guy. Did these bad men scare you?" She dropped the tether and stepped toward the nearest soldier. The entire room resounded with the clatter of rounds being chambered. She stopped. "Aw, too bad, and I had such high hopes of a good *mounting*," she chortled.

A new figure, a sergeant by the rank on his sleeves entered the room. He tucked his helmet beneath his right arm as he produced a piece of paper from a pocket. The sergeant unfolded the paper and began to read. "Elizabeth, *Lizz*, Trower, you are under arrest. The charges against you will be presented at the time of your processing. Any resistance will result in immediate execution without fault or liability against the Independent Alliance. What say you?"

She glanced back over her shoulder toward the quivering form of Senator McGill. "I am so sorry that our time has been cut short, Senator. It looks as if I have a more pressing engagement. Another time perhaps? And to think of all the fun that we were about to have," she cackled.

The Vortex,
Atlanta, Georgia, USA
May 12, 2176 / 1735 hrs local time

"There is absolutely nothing like being back home," Captain Douglas Rackham said while entering the song code into the jukebox. "Well, maybe not *home* exactly, but besides *the Betty*, Atlanta is the closest thing any of us really have to a hometown." He returned to his table and happily forced his mouth around a massively oversized burger. Small dribbles of bacon grease glistened across his chin as he chewed. His gaze darted from an odd antique on the wall to the ancient BMW motorcycle suspended from the ceiling to a fake shark's head, mounted high on the wall behind the bar. "Huh, I wonder where Joyland Park actually was?" He pondered a sign that hung just a few feet away, then looked back at his science officer, Wesley Skaggs, a tall, husky framed fellow. "Hey, I just don't get it. I thought you were supposed to be the grand wizard of all things tech. You do call yourself *The Geek* for a reason, don't you?" He dove at the burger once again.

Wes looked up from the SAPP implant in his forearm, his eyes wide with an ecstatic cherubic grin. "Indeed, I am, my captain, but in this case, even a wizard needs the help of a thief." He pulled the sleeve of his gray-green flight suit over his forearm, then brushed back his shaggy blond hair from his eyes.

Doug scowled at Wes with a sidelong glance. "Explain," he murmured around a mouthful of masticated meat. Impatience colored Doug's face.

"Think of it like this." Wes paused abruptly as he glanced around the room. "See that three-foot-tall penis by the door? Consider that wooden dong as the documents we want to acquire, and this restaurant is the server that they're stored in.

When you crossed the state line into Georgia you had to show your ID papers. To get through the Atlanta regional defense system, *you had to show your ID papers another three times.* Which all in all isn't such a big deal, but this place, this place is some super-secret squirrel shit right here. Even looking in the direction of this place will draw attention, not to mention trying to get in the door will most likely get you killed. You have to have the password, no way around it. Like that super-secret squirrel handshake that you have to know to get into the Nunnery over on the east side of town. Oh my God, that place was just phenomenal, the things I learned that night." He blankly stared into nothing as memories flooded his mind. He shook his head. "I digress, where was I again?"

"Super-secret squirrel handshake," Doug said, then squeezed the remainder of the sandwich tight with both hands to better fit it into his mouth. Greasy drippings mingled with egg yolk and the spicy house sauce escaped to the plate below.

Wes grabbed a napkin and dabbed at a splatter of burger juices from the table. "Right, that's it. So without that passcode, you can forget about ever getting into this place or getting to glimpse, let alone stroke the dong of destiny," he said, pointing toward the wooden phallus by the main entrance.

"You know, I worry about you sometimes."

"Hee-Hee, yup." Wes grinned, then took a sip from his beer.

"So if Lizz manages to get that passcode, we're in, no strings attached?" Doug wiped grease from his fingers on a napkin.

"Exactly! Though we'll have to be quick about it. Once the informant is found it won't take long for the code to be locked out of the system."

"Excellent." Doug leaned back in his chair. He let out a long, groaning stretch that ended in a loud belch. "Ugghhh… God, that was good," he said as he retrieved a thin silver case from his jacket pocket. "Four months in The Belt eating rations really makes you appreciate those little things from home," he said with a half hiccup-burp. "Excuse me." He pulled one of the hand-rolled cigarettes from the case, checked it, then took a long satisfactory draw as he lit it. "I'll inform the customer as soon as the code is in hand so they can transfer the contracted funds. Are you sure that this can't be traced back to us?"

"That depends. I have everything covered on my end. All trace of my presence will be wiped clean once we have the files. As long as Lizz doesn't give herself away we should be golden."

"Perfect," Doug said. He took another long drag from his cigarette. "The payout on this gig will set us up for a few months and give us a chance to do a few upgrades to *Betty*."

"We need a new ship, Cap! For fuck's sake, I feel like I need a tetanus shot every time I step foot on that old rust bucket."

"Naw," Doug said dismissively. "*Betty* is broken in and reliable. She may not be the prettiest ship in the sky, but she does the job and doesn't give us too many problems. You can't argue that she wasn't built well, especially when she's as old as she is. And besides, she has style. She's sexy. All of those newer flying boxes just look like the same old shell without a soul. *Betty* has a soul and a personality to boot."

"Uh-huh. And parts are getting harder and harder to find for her" Wes tapped at his forearm and projected a holographic image of a circuit board on the table.

"Alright, that's one of the ship's main processors, isn't it? What of it?"

"You are correct," Wes said. "That is one of the main processor boards. One of twelve processor boards, mind you, that the ship originally came with. They were designed to run the primary, secondary, and tertiary systems with a serious focus on redundancy. We are down to one primary board and one backup. All of the others are fried, and I've had to reroute all of the ship's functions through the two remaining boards."

Doug loudly sighed. He stared off into nothing for a moment. "Ok, I gotcha. So we need a spare board just in case one goes down. How much will it cost us?"

Wes chuckled. "Do you really want to know?"

Doug closed his eyes and took a deep breath. "Ok, hit me with it."

"Six million credits if we're lucky. And that's because this is the only processor that I've found that isn't in a museum."

"Dammit. Couldn't you use your wizardry and build one out of newer hardware?"

"Oh yeah, I absolutely could. But are you going to give me about six months to build, install, and retrofit all of the ship's systems so it can all still communicate? We need some serious downtime, Cap."

Doug leaned back and forcefully rubbed at his eyes and temples. "Shouldn't you be able to plug and play everything? That was one of the major changes to ship designs when *Betty* was built. Modular systems that were all plug and play."

"True, but that's all hardware." The Geek chortled. "See, the programing language of this original hardware compared to the modern tech would be like trying to explain the true function of the Aethernet and how it all works to a dark ages nun without her claiming that I'm a heretical witch and burning me at the stake, or dunking me until I drown to prove whether I float or not," he squeaked out on the last remnants of a breath.

"Breath, Geek," Doug said. He reached across the table and slapped Wes on the shoulder. "It's okay, man. No need to get so excited about it."

"I'm not getting excited," he said. "I'm just explaining the truth of the matter."

"Well, hello. What do we have here?"

"What," the Geek asked in a confused tone.

"We can talk about upgrades later. How sure are you that this plan is solid," Doug asked. His gaze locked on something behind Wes.

"Why?" Wes's voice cracked in a panicked squeak.

"Oh, I don't know. It just seems a bit odd that there are three guys in expensive suits at the far end of the bar staring over this way."

"Oh shit," Wes excitedly whispered. He stretched, stealing a quick glance back at the trio as he did so. "That's not good, Cap. Not good at all. Should we get out of here or what?"

"Just chill. There's no reason to get yourself all worked up, just yet. They could just be a couple of businessmen having some dinner and a drink. It is Atlanta after all."

"Yeahhhhhh, good point," Wes said, stabbing a finger in Doug's direction. "You're probably right. I'm just getting myself worked up over nothing."

"Exactly." Doug retrieved another cigarette from his case and lit it with a deep draw and a long, exhaled sigh. He chugged the remainder of an inky dark stout and slammed the glass on the table. "And ya know what, Geek? I can also be wrong at times too," he said as he quickly stood and donned his black leather trench coat with a flourish.

"Oh shit. What? Are they coming this way?"

"Um-hum," Doug hummed around the cigarette hanging from his mouth. He closed his eyes as smoke from the cigarette rolled up his face and straightened the collar of his coat. Reaching into the left pocket he loosely gripped the heirloom Judge magnum revolver that rested in a hidden holster.

"Are we going or what, Cap," Wes forcefully whispered as he put on his jacket.

Doug glared at his science officer, his head tilted slightly to avoid more smoke rolling into his eyes. Otherwise motionless, he glanced about the room, then back to the men in suits. *These guys look like pros,* he thought. There was only one way out of the diner, and it was past these guys. He took another long draw of his cigarette. *If I pull my gun, those guys will open fire and unload in this direction. Won't work. Wes is between me and them. Not an option*

"Stay, Geek."

"What? Why?" Wes impatiently waited for a reply.

Doug took a deep breath, then let his hand casually drop from his coat.

"Just wait," he said with a grin. "It's too late because they are almost here." He took the last drag from the cigarette and dropped the butt into his beer glass.

"Captain Douglas Rackham?" A short stocky man in an expensive-looking black suit. He stood a few paces behind Wes with his hands behind his. His two larger and heavily muscled companions looked uncomfortable in their dark suits and stood a few paces behind the short stocky man.

"That depends on who's asking," Doug replied. "And I'll tell you what. I'm in no mood for innuendo and beating around the bush at the moment, so I'll be upfront. Four long and lonely months in The Belt can do that to a man." He reached across the table and grabbed the beer glass from in front of Wes and finished off the warm amber liquid in one glug.

"Hey, that was my beer," Wes fussed.

"Too late now," Doug said. "Besides you let it get warm. Bad Geek." Doug smiled wide and placed the glass back onto the table.

"What the fuck man, seriously?"

"Sorry. You snooze, you lose." Doug laughed as he lit another smoke.

"Ass," Wes replied.

"Sometimes," Doug returned.

"Eh hem." the short man in the nice suit coughed.

Doug returned his attention to the trio of men in suits with an annoyed glare. "I'm sorry, what was it that you wanted again?"

"I think he wanted to get your name or number or something," Wes said. "You do look lovely and dapper in that coat. Like Brandon Lee in *The Crow* kinda cool."

Doug's head drunkenly jerked in the direction of the suited men. "Ohhhhh. I'm sorry about that, I didn't mean to totally ignore you." He grossly exaggerated a wide, teeth bared grin. "You do look very handsome in that shiny black suit and all but you just aren't pretty enough to take home to Mother. I'm sorry. Nothing personal. I'm sure that one day, you'll make someone a great housewife. Just be patient and never give up on your dreams. You'll find your place one day."

The two muscled men coughed, fighting back the urge to laugh at the last comment.

The dapper dressed man let his arms drop forward and relax. He straightened his suit, then produced an envelope from one of the jacket pockets.

"I will only ask nicely once more, sir," he said as he fumbled with the envelope. He unfolded the letter contained within, cleared his throat and began to read. "Captain Douglas Rackham, I am hereby authorized by order of the director, W.J. Lepetomane, of the Independent Alliance to detain and arrest you and your crew, as well as impound your ship by any means which shall be for an unspecified amount of time as deemed necessary. Immediate capital punishment has been authorized for any individual that resists arrest."

"Well that was a mouthful, now wasn't it?" Doug smiled as he slowly exhaled a thick cloud of smoke.

"I think he's serious, Cap," Wes said. He looked up at Doug.

"Now, *Captain*," the fine dressed man said in a sarcastic tone. "Are you Captain Douglas Rackham?" The suited man placed his hand on the Geek's shoulder, "And are you, Wesley, *The Geek*, Skaggs?"

"I am," the Captain said with a confident scowl.

"I am, too," Wes sighed as he buried his face in his hands. "Fuck my life."

The short man took a step back from the table and motioned toward the door. "If you would please follow my associates, we will be on our way, gentlemen." He nodded with a shit-eating grin across his face.

Doug's neck cracked with a loud pop as he leaned his head at an odd angle. "Ok, let's do this." He smacked his hands on the table. The three suited men flinched, each of them with a hand in their jackets.

"Let's go, Geek, I have things to see and people to do."

"Yeah, yeah, I'm coming," Wes said as he reluctantly stood and followed the captain out the door.

cHAPTER 2

Independent Alliance/American Confederation Consulate
Facility
North Atlanta, Georgia, USA
May 12, 2176 / 2015 hrs local time

"**A**ndy! Would you please just sit your ass down, relax, and get the hell out of my way. There's no way out of this room and they are watching our every move through this two-way mirror." Big Willy anxiously thumbed at the mirrored wall to his left as he continued to pace the length of the room. The mountain of a man barely fit into the sleeveless, grease stained green coveralls that he wore.

"But I'm on the other side of the room," Andy said. "And besides, I might have an idea if I can just reach that vent up there." He climbed onto the large metal conference table in the center of the sterile white room. He dug around in the multitude of empty pockets of his utility vest in search of something. "I'll be damned if they didn't even leave me so much as a pair of tweezers."

"Better listen to Big Willy, man. You know he doesn't like to be cooped up," Trae added. The large man leaned the cold metal chair back against the wall, crossed his muscular, tree trunk sized arms and pulled his gray beanie cap over his eyes.

"Just one second," Andy said. "Let me look at…"

"Dude! What the hell is wrong with you?" Tiffany nervously fidgeted with the tips of her nails. She blew out from the corner of her mouth at a loose wisp of hair, then chewed and blew a decent sized bubble with her gum that popped and covered the tip of her button nose. "Do you want them to come in here and hogtie every freaking one of us? Just sayin', ya know. Cause that's what they do, isn't it?"

Big Willy closed his eyes and drew in slow, deep breaths. His fists clenched with the pace of each breath, knuckles white with each contraction.

"Calm down big guy," Krista said. "Contain the bear, become the butterfly."

"Andy!" Melanie shouted from beneath her reproduction superman baseball cap, then lifted it, glaring in Andy's direction. "Get your ass off of that table and sit down right now!" She quickly stood, straightening the blouse of her nurse's scrubs, her self-imposed cafeteria uniform and began looking around for something to throw at Andy.

"Since Cap ain't here, that puts Willy in charge," Fergus said matter of factly. He scratched at the two-day's worth of stubble along his neck, then straightened his thick brown 70's style mustache. "Violation of a direct order is a punishable offense per the ship's charter." He gently stroked the mousey brown hair of the ship's pilot, Rachel, who lay napping in his lap. He adjusted her brown leather flight jacket that covered her still form. "Now, sit your ass down before you wake Rachel. You know she gets bat shit crazy if she doesn't get her rest. Do you really want to send her spiraling off down a manic rabbit hole?"

"Fine." Andy jumped down from the table and stumbled against the wall. "Don't come asking me for help when they come to execute all of us."

"EVERYONE JUST SIT DOWN AND SHUT UP!" Big Willy slammed both of his ham sized fists down on the metal table, leaving two distinct indents on its surface.

"Tansy cakes with peppermint cream," Rachel said. She snorted and jerked awake from her light doze.

A crying scream erupted from the corner of the room. "It'll be alright, sweetie," Maggie, one of the witches three said soothingly as she hurried past Big Willy. Her multicolored skirt flowed in a flurry of motion and jingles as she rushed to

Amanda's side at the rear of the room. She pulled the young crewman close, cradling her to her bosom.

Kara, quickly finished re-tying her curly dark locks up in a head scarf, then sandwiched Amanda between herself and Maggie. "It's okay baby. Willy is just a big mean bully," she said in a coddling baby tone. She adjusted her button downed shirt to cover her otherwise normally displayed cleavage.

"Oh, my Jesus fucking Christ, people," Krista huffed. She stood and looked around at the others. "We are all good, no one is hurt, and nearly everyone is here. Once Doug finds out that we've been arrested, he'll come to bail us out. It isn't like this is the first time any of us have been thrown in a lock-up."

A loud humming clack emanated from the room's heavy-duty steel door. It swung open, thudding against the concrete wall and bounced back as Doug stumbled headlong into the room.

"Cap!" The group stood simultaneously.

"You'd better watch yourself; I like it rough," Doug said. He grinned and winked at the guard who shoved him further into the room.

"Hey now!" Wes stumbled through the doorway just as a guard began pulling the door closed.

"You could have at least left me my smokes! Assholes!" Doug kicked at the door as it latched closed.

"Oh my God! Wesley!" Kara squeaked. She dove into Wes's arms, latching onto his husky frame. "My dear sweet *teddy bear*, they didn't hurt you, did they?"

Doug scanned the room, mentally counting heads. "Missing Lizz." He flashed a look of concern at the Geek.

"Don't look at me," Wes said defensively. "It wasn't my fault. She knew what she was getting into when we set up this plan."

Doug rubbed his chin slowly in thought. "Just gotta hope for the best at this point I suppose..." He suddenly sighed, eyes fixed on the two large dents in the table. "Um. Do I even need to guess what happened to the table?"

"That's in the past," Krista said with a wave of her hand as she walked up to Doug. "All done and over with. Nothing to worry about now."

"Have they said anything to any of you, yet?" Doug looked to Willy.

"Nothing ye…," Willy started but was abruptly cut off.

"None of us have been charged with anything," Krista said. "We were hauled in one by one and tossed into this room." Her eyes narrowed as she looked from Doug to Wes and back again.

"I'm as clueless as you," Doug said. "The guy in the suit that brought us in just said that the ship was impounded, and we were all under arrest."

"Hell, that's a lot better than what happened to me," Trae said. "The last thing I remember, I was on my last set of squats and boom, I went black. Next thing I know, I wake up here on the floor with a killer headache and Amanda crying in the corner."

"Is everyone else okay?" Doug scanned the faces of the crew. He saw no obvious sign of injury or harm to any of them, then looked directly at Willy. "How're your fists?"

"They'll be fine, Cap," Willy said reluctantly.

"Can't say as much for that table." Doug pulled out the nearest chair and sat. The crew gathered around him. "Anyone hear from Lizz before you were arrested?"

Mumbled no's accompanied head shakes of the crew.

"Good, maybe she'll be able to work her magic from the outside and get us released."

Fergus sat on the edge of the table. "So, what's the plan, Cap?"

Doug leaned the chair back and placed his hands behind his head. He closed his eyes in a brief moment of contemplation.

"There isn't one, Doug said. "It would be suicide to try and escape this compound. We haven't been charged with anything yet and Lizz is still unaccounted for. The best plan that I can see is that for now, we wait. Let the Alliance goons play their cards and we go from there."

A loud humming clack emanated from the door once again. Four heavily armed and armored guards entered the room followed by a small balding man in a black suit.

"Speak of the *devil*," Doug hissed. He leapt to his feet and turned to face the balding man.

"How are all of you this evening?" The small man asked, his voice soft and timid. "My name is W.J. Lepetomane, Director of the Independent Alliance. I hope that your stay hasn't been too unpleasant."

Doug shook his head in disbelief, "Did you just say, Director of the Alliance?"

"Yes, I did," the Director said with a matter of fact smile. "And unless I am terribly mistaken, you would be Captain Rackham, I presume? Hmm."

"I am," Doug replied. He glanced over at the Director. "Why are we being held without charges?"

"My dear boy." The Director laughed under his breath as he reached for one of the occupied seats at the table. "May I?"

Doug nodded for Fergus to move and sat back down in his seat at the table.

"You see Captain Rackham," the Director continued as he took the seat. "That is one reason that I admire you. You are direct and methodical, but you easily sway with the winds of change as the landscape begins to shift." The Director held his right palm over his shoulder. The nearest guard produced a small holo-scroll that he extended as he placed it in the director's hand. The director cleared his throat and held up the clear sheet. Digital text scrolled upward with a swipe of his finger. He tapped the page with his finger to stop the scrolling, then began to read.

"I, W.J. Lepetomane, Director of the Independent Alliance, its subsidiaries, and all non-entity subcontractors, to be referred to as the Independent Alliance as a whole from this point forth, hereby charge the following persons with crimes against the Independent Alliance, its employees, its property holdings and/or possessions, equipment, or infrastructure."

The crew all shifted nervously as an angry awkwardness permeated the room.

"Captain Douglas Rackham, you are hereby charged with smuggling, the selling of classified intelligence to an enemy, misuse of an Independent Alliance communications network, espionage, and malicious intent toward the Independent Alliance."

"Wesley Skaggs, aka *The Geek*, you are hereby charged with hacking, misuse of public Independent Alliance communications & data networks, espionage, illegal collection & storage of classified documents, pirating of copyrighted material, and malicious intent toward the Independent Alliance."

"Rachel Coram, aka *Cheezy*, you are hereby charged with flying into restricted airspace, failure to comply with orders of Independent Alliance officers, failure to comply with submitted flight plans, failure to adhere to port speed regulations, and unauthorized flyby of earthside control towers at illegal speeds."

"Andy and Melanie Kleszinski, you are hereby charged with the illegal salvage, sale of Independent Alliance property, and damage to Independent Alliance property."

"Trae and Tiffany Crowley and Fergus Coram, you are hereby charged with illegal salvage and sale of Independent Alliance property, theft of Independent Alliance property, damage of Independent Alliance property, illegal trade of class 9 weapons, and illegal trade of classified military grade targeting systems."

"William Murphy, aka *Big Willy*, you are hereby charged with illegal salvage and sale of Independent Alliance property, and damage to Independent Alliance property."

"Krista Weet'A igMOO wahTOEgluh," the Director struggled with the pronunciation and smiled. "That is a mouthful, isn't it?" He glanced about then turned back to the holo-scroll. "Now let me see, where was I, ah yes, here we go. Krista Weet'A igMOO wahTOEgluh, aka New Moon Cat Untamed, aka Moon Shadow, aka *Goddess*; Margaret Tasarla, aka *Maggie* and Amanda Maeer, aka *Giggils*. You are hereby charged with the illegal production and distribution of narcotics, opiates, and hallucinogenic substances; smuggling of illegal substances into and out of Independent Alliance borders, and illegally writing a prescription to an Independent Alliance citizens without medical licensure." The Director produced a handwritten script in a plastic bag from his jacket pocket. He held it up for all to see for a brief moment, then placed it back into his pocket and returned his attention to the holo-scroll.

The sound of hard heels on tile echoed through the open security door from the hallway beyond the room. The Director relaxed in his chair. A large smile crossed his face as he closed his eyes.

Lizz stepped into the doorway and stopped in surprise. Whispered gasps of *Lizz* leapt from each crew member's lips. A look of concern painted her face as her gaze darted around the room to each member of the crew. Her expression melted to utter surprise at the sight of the bald man seated next to Doug. She leaned against the door frame, the curve of her hips accentuated by her stance. She crossed her arms and nearly pushed her breasts out of the black leather corset. The uniformed men that surrounded her were visibly distracted, a stolen glance here, an uncomfortable bulge there.

"Why go to so much fuss, W.J.? It has to be something

insanely dangerous or equally stupid for you to drag the entire crew in like this."

The Director remained motionless in his seat. He took a deep nasal breath as if coming out of meditation.

"Hello Elizabeth," the Director said. "I see that you still favor cinnamon and cedar."

"Don't go getting all mushy and nostalgic on me," Lizz said. "I asked you a question W.J."

The crew gawked at Lizz with looks of utter disbelief painting each of their faces.

"Wait, the two of you actually know each other?" Doug turned in his seat to face Lizz with a look of surprised confusion.

"It's a very long story, but yes," Lizz said.

Director Lepetomane sat up straight, then turned sideways in the chair. "You look as lovely as ever, Elizabeth." He admiringly smiled at her.

"Don't try to butter me up, W.J. What gives?"

"Can a man not bask in the memories of what once was?" The Director smiled a knowing smile.

"I know you better than that, *Director*," Lizz said with pointed emphasis. "You want something and on top of that you know that I am the only one that can give it to you." Lizz glared at the director.

"On so very many levels, my dear," he said in a soft tone.

"Cut the shit, WJ," Lizz growled. "What do you want with us?"

The Director sighed. "Very well, Elizabeth. If that is the way that you would prefer it." He turned back in his chair and resumed reading the holo-scroll.

"Elizabeth Judith Trower, aka Lizz, aka Deborah Hickman, aka Tracey Johnston, aka Ava Tudor, aka Brianna Weis, you are hereby charged with extortion, kidnapping, attempted assault with a farm animal, tax evasion, defamation, espionage, and treason against the Independent Alliance." The Director handed the holo-scroll back over his shoulder to the nearest guard, then laced his fingers together. He callously examined the crew. "We have enough charges against each of you for *immediate* execution, for which I just happen to have the execution orders right here." He reached into his jacket and produced an order of execution that he handed over to Doug.

Doug glanced over the document then placed it on the table. He leaned forward, his face in his hands he vigorously rubbed his eyes, then looked up at the Director. "So what's the catch? If you wanted us dead, we wouldn't even be here. Your goon squads could have picked each of us off without any of this dog and pony show. You want something."

The Director laughed with joyous delight. "I do so love that about you, Captain Rackham. Direct and to the point, even in the face of utter destruction. Misdirection, tedium, or shall I say, fluff, are in no way part of your personality. You are a very unique man, Captain, and you are also correct. My men could have easily taken each one of you out and you would never have known what had happened."

"Then to the point, if you would, please," Doug said.

The Director smiled wide, then turned in his seat back to Lizz. "Please, my dear, would you grace us with your presence? You know how I dislike speaking over my shoulder, and this does involve you quite a bit, I do believe." The Director looked to the soldier by the door. "Sergeant, if you would be so kind as to leave us and close the door behind you, please."

The Sergeant scowled at the Director. "I'm not so sure that is a good idea, sir."

"Rest assured, Sergeant. I am in no danger," the Director said. "Isn't that right, Elizabeth?"

"*Fine*, W.J., whatever suits your fancy." She strode into the room and took a seat on the edge of the table.

"Mmmmmmmm, my dear…" The Director beamed as the hum of the magnetic locks re-engaged behind the soldiers leaving the room. He breathed deeply of her uniquely spiced perfume.

"Eh hem, *Director*," Doug prompted.

"Oh yes," the Director said, composing himself. He straightened his jacket and turned his attention back to Doug. "I am terribly sorry. To the point then, shall we?" He creepily smiled at Doug and continued. "We have gathered intelligence on a new prototype technology that the Martian Reich has been developing for some time. However, we are not certain of that technology's current stage of development. My offer is simple: gather all information, schematics, and details that you are able to obtain and eradicate all data that is in the hands of the Reich on this technology by any means necessary."

"Ha! Oh my god, really? That's it? That's all that you want?" Trae chuckled. "It's a *freaking* suicide mission, Cap. Just shoot me now and get it over with."

"Hold on, Trae," Doug said. "You still haven't answered my question, Director. Why us?"

"Government is nothing more than a method, Captain Rackham," the Director said. "It is a dirty and corrupt business scheme. And as you very well know, information is the key to any good business strategy. We must stay ahead of our competitors, defend our holdings, and use any means necessary to keep our razor-thin edge in the game. That being said, there are few people within any organization that can be fully trusted. A person can easily change sides with proper motivation. I tell you this now because I would trust Elizabeth with my life. She is the primary reason that you are all here. The second reason is that you and your crew have very little reputation with any faction or government. You are truly independent in the sense that you don't care where your pay comes from. If your ship and your crew were to enter Martian airspace with a load of cargo for a potential buyer, you would be less likely to raise suspicions than one of our undercover operatives who have potentially been… compromised. According to my analyst's, you and your crew also possess most of the skills that they deem necessary to successfully execute this venture. You choose the cargo, which will be free of charge, along with fair compensation for your time and efforts upon completion of the assignment and we will strike up a contract."

The director stood and straightened his suit. He turned and smiled at Lizz. "You are all temporarily free to go, pending your *decision*. The guards will show you out, momentarily. Elizabeth, please contact me with your decision within the next twenty-four hours. You know where and when. I will be impatiently awaiting your answer. Otherwise, Captain, it has been an absolute pleasure to meet you. I wish it were under better circumstances, but such is life."

The Director stepped toward the door and stopped in midstride across from Lizz. His gaze lingered on her for a long moment before he pointed toward the door. The electric hum of door locks reverberated once again. "I bid you all, *adieu*." The Director turned and briskly walked out of the room.

cHAPTER 3

The *Betty*, Nova star class mining transport / Witches quarters
Atlanta International Spaceport
Atlanta, Georgia, USA
May 13, 2176 / Noonish, local time

"**B**y bluster of wind, and healing of rain, down deep within the earth or seared by white-hot flame. I call for power, for healing and pain. I call for knowledge, for insight by name. I call upon the sisters and the powers that be, I call for the wisdom of the *witches three*." Kara's sing-song-contralto echoed throughout what was once the ship's grand mineralogical laboratory.

"Oh, hey Kara." Krista's head appeared through the curtained doorway of a side room. "We'll be out in just one second," Krista said and vanished behind the curtain.

"Not a problem, good sister. Take your time," Kara said with an unconcerned wave. She looked about the ancient lab that now functioned as the living space and workshop for the ship's resident healers. Bottles and jars covered nearly all available shelf space. Dried herbs hung from the upper bulkheads throughout the room and hid abandoned test equipment. A well worn and massive red velvet couch dominated the center of the sitting area.

"Oh my God, that looks like it'll hurt," Amanda said in a concerned tone from behind the curtain.

"It's okay, sweetie. This won't take but a few minutes and it'll be over with. *Trust* me, it'll be so worth it in the end," Maggie said with a giggle. Her tone was comforting and motherly.

"Are you sure? It doesn't look like it'll fit," Amanda said.

"Suck it up, *buttercup*," Krista ordered. "You said yes and I'm all ready to go. It's too late to turn back now. Shhhhhh, just let it happen, man." Krista giggled.

"*Oh*, that, *no*, ouch," Amanda cried.

"Shhhhhhh, it'll be alright *sweetie*," Maggie said soothingly.

"All right, are you ready for the big *push*?"

"No, not really," Amanda whimpered.

"Well too bad," Krista said. "Ready or not, here we go."

"No! I changed my mind. Oh God, that hurts."

"Shhhhhhh, I went through this too, sweetie," Maggie said. "It's not so bad after the first time. I promise it gets so much better after the first time."

"Oh *God*, I can't breathe," Amanda said. "That *hurts* too much." Amanda began to breathe heavily.

"One more second, we're almost there," Krista said.

"*Please* stop," Amanda demanded through ragged and raspy breaths.

Kara stared at the curtain in horrid fascination. "What in the hell," she whispered to herself.

"Happy thoughts sweetie, happy thoughts," Maggie said soothingly with a motherly shush. "It's almost over. Just let the Goddess finish and it will be all over."

"Why won't you stop," Amanda said as she began to sob. "Oh God, it hurts."

"Come on! Just a little bit farther. It's almost there. Just a little harder," Krista growled.

"God damn you, Krista," Amanda cried. "Ohhhh, ahhhhh...Uhhhhhhhh!"

"Wheww! There we go. All done," Krista said. "Now just leave it where it is and don't fiddle with it. You gotta give things time to stretch and settle into place however they need to."

"See, sweetie? It wasn't all that bad," Maggie said.

"You weren't the one at her mercy!" Amanda sobbed and gasped for breath. "*FUCKING SADIST*!"

"But I have been, sweetie," Maggie said. "I have been there. Krista helped me my first time just like she helped you and it has been one of the most wonderful things in my life ever since."

"But it hurts like my insides are a jumbled mess," Amanda said between sobs.

"Oh shit, I forgot Kara," Krista said. "We have a customer to take care of, ladies. Just put some ice on it, you'll be alright."

Krista exploded from the curtained doorway. She fought with loose wisps of hair, pulling her thick dark mass of hair back into a loose ponytail.

Kara stared at Krista with a worrisome look. "Is everything alright back there?"

"Oh yeah," Krista said. "Absolutely. Everything's just *peachy*. Nothing but fairies and rainbows, man, just fairies and rainbows. Nothing to see, just pretend that any of what you might have heard didn't happen even happen." Krista flashed a mischievous grin at Kara.

Maggie emerged from the side room, gingerly leading Amanda toward the couch.

Kara peered over Krista's shoulder and stared at the slow-moving pair. "Are you sure? She doesn't look well."

"Oh absolutely. A little tenderness and sensitivity are to be expected after what she just went through. She will thank me in a few days when things stretch, and the soreness wears off."

"FUCK YOU, SADIST!" Amanda glared in Krista's direction.

"We're almost there, sweetie," Maggie said softly as she guided Amanda to the couch. "Slow breaths, it'll be alright."

"I can barely breathe," Amanda whimpered as she tugged at the brown suede corset that hugged her torso.

"Oh…," Kara said, wincing.

"She'll be fine, no need to worry," Krista said with a dismissive wave. "So what can we do for you today?"

"Well, you see, Wesley and I will be celebrating our five-year anniversary next week. Seeing as how we'll most likely be stuck on this ship at that time, I have no idea of what to do to make it amazing and special. I am at a total loss of what could be amazing and special while trapped in the bowels of this rotting beast." Kara angrily stomped her foot on the deck plating. Her eyes glistened with tears of frustration.

"Hmmm, well, we have a few different things to prolong, enhance, or totally alter the experience," Krista said. "It really just comes down to what you want." Krista tapped her lips as she pondered, then ran toward a shelf near the rear of the room.

Amanda gasped. "I know things are a bit pressed for time with the whole I.A. death threats looming over our heads and all. But why not just ask the captain for some extended shore leave the next time we're Earthside?"

"You could go all out and explore each other in deep, sensual detail," Maggie suggested. "Lots of candles, wine, massage. Have you ever heard of tantric massage?"

"Oh, hell no! That takes too damn long, and it's too slow," Krista retorted. "What you two need is a good old-fashioned sex fest. Here," Krista shoved a dark, unlabeled bottle into Kara's hands. "Give him this in a drink, then in about ten minutes you can jump on and ride till he begs for mercy." Krista laughed as she excitedly arched and swayed her hips.

"Excuse me," Maggie said. "It isn't too slow. It's sensual and deeply romantic."

"And can be very overrated in my opinion," Krista said. "So, mix ten drops of this into something with a heavy flavor—"

"I beg to differ," Maggie interrupted. "It is not overrated! It is a way to deeply learn and explore your partner on a whole new level of understanding."

"To each their own, sister. To each their own." Krista grinned.

"And how many pieces of furniture have you destroyed with your sex fests?" Maggie scoffed, she crossed her arms and directly confronting Krista.

"I don't see where that is any of your concern," Krista said. "It's not like any of your furniture has broken *yet*."

"Wait. *Yet*? You mean to tell me that you've been having sex on my bed?" Maggie fumed.

"Why do you two have to argue about everything?" Amanda began to cry. "We were supposed to be a family!" She rolled to one side and pushed herself off of the massive couch and slowly shuffled away.

"See what you've done now?" Maggie scowled at Krista. "Her tears are on your hands," she said then hurried after Amanda.

"What I've done?" Krista turned back to Kara. "Hey, where did Kara go?"

The ship's intercom crackled to life with a pop of static. *"Attention all personnel,"* Doug said over the intercoms. His voice echoed as if he was speaking through a tin can. *"Report to the wardroom immediately."*

"Well shit, what now?" Krista huffed. "Come on, girls, Doug needs us."

cHAPTER 4

The *Betty*, Nova star class mining transport
Atlanta International Spaceport
Atlanta, Georgia, USA
May 13, 2176 / Afternoon, local time

Krista whistled a light tune as she skipped onto the bridge, her skirts billowing around her as she flared them back and forth with each skipped step. She pushed her way through the rest of the crew gathered at the massive wardroom table at the port rear side of the bridge, adjacent to the Captain's quarters.

"So, what's up big boy?" Krista smiled. "What's all the fuss about?"

Doug glanced up from the datapad in his hand. "Good, the witches are here," he said. "Wait...," he began then paused, glancing past the gathered crew at Amanda as she made her way slowly onto the bridge with Maggie's aid. He turned back to Krista with a look of concern. "Is she ok?"

"Oh, she's just *dandy*, nothing to see here, moving along now." Krista grinned as she innocently rocked on her heels.

"Fuck you, sadist!" Amanda shouted.

"See, told ya." Krista smiled wide with a quick nod. "She's just dandy. It's all rainbows and butterflies from here on out. Nothing but love, man, nothing but love."

"O-ohhhh-kay then." Doug leaned against the wardroom table and loudly cleared his throat. "Listen up, folks. I know none of you like the idea of working for the Independent Alliance, especially considering the circumstances by which we've been *employed*." He frowned at the taste of the word. "Thanks to the electronic wizardry of The Geek, we've managed to find out that the tech the I.A. wants is a new propulsion system. Come to find out that this tech is actually well past the design and prototype phase. The Martian Reich has developed a new class of heavy frigate built around this new drive system and is currently conducting shakedown runs out in the asteroid belt. Considering this new information, Lizz has spent the last two days in, um, intense *negotiations* with Director Lepetomane. They will resupply our fuel, ammo, and provisions at no cost. They have also agreed to supply us with sixty thousand liters of Bavarian Weizen, Bock, and Pilsener as cargo for our cover story. Lizz has also been working to find us buyers in the Martian colonies and out on some of The Belt stations.

"Holy shit balls, Cap," Trae interrupted. "Seriously? Sixty thousand liters? I mean, hell, that's what—" Trae's fingers flicked at the air in front of him as he did the math on his mental chalkboard. "One gallon is three-point seven nine liters … which is fifteen thousand eight hundred thirty-one gallons at, let's say, ten pounds per gallon since beer is denser than water and round up for safety's sake. Sooooo … that's roughly one hundred and sixty thousand pounds of cargo."

"That shouldn't be a problem. *Betty* has carried double that before," Doug responded.

"The weight isn't the issue, Cap. The possible problem is volume." Trae scratched his head and stared off for a moment in thought. "It all depends on how they package it for shipment. Is it going to be in bulk storage tanks, cases of bottles, or steel kegs? Normally when we're out in The Belt, mining, we process the ore and make ingots that stack nice and neat into the holds."

"I don't know, but that's a damn good question for Lizz to find out," Doug replied with a nod at Lizz.

"Got it," Lizz said as she scribbled on a small note pad.

"Trae, Fergus, and Andy," Doug continued, "I need you to make getting us loaded and ready for launch a priority."

"Will do, Cap," Trae responded.

"Willy," Doug called on next. "You and Cheezy take care of refueling and any repairs or servicing that you can get done in the next two days. We need to be airborne and on the move ASAP," Doug urged.

"You betcha, Cap," Rachel replied.

"Does that include grease, anti-seize, hydraulic fluid, stuff like that?" Big Willy asked.

"Yes, absolutely. Put together a requisition list and give it to Lizz. She'll handle it from there. *Betty* needs to be in the best shape that we can muster. Tiff and Kara, you're on ammo duty."

"Will do, Boss," Tiff said with a raised thumb.

"Ammo duty again, but I just had my nails done," Kara whined.

"They are nails, and they'll grow back," Doug said. "Mel and the Witches," he looked around for Melanie.

"Back here, Cap," Melanie replied from behind the others. She waved her hand in the air for Doug to see.

"I see you, Mel. I need you to make a full restock manifest and submit it to Lizz before the day is out. Standard ration packs for half of the restock, fill the rest of the pantry with fresh foodstuffs. Make sure to pick up some good pepper cheese for me and dark chocolate for you ladies. Add in a little something special for everyone else and whatever standard medical supplies that we need for a six-month run. Get it ordered and stocked, and no wishlist items this time, Krista."

"Oh, what the hell," Krista said. "I still don't see what all the fuss was about the last time. It was only a few baby ducks and chickens."

"That would have shit anywhere and everywhere they pleased. No livestock on my ship, got it?" Doug said with a stern gaze.

"That's just perfectly fine there, *Captain Dougie*," Krista said. "If that's the way you want it, don't come crying to me the next time you want a little somethin' somethin'." Krista crossed her arms and glared in Doug's direction.

"And we're moving on," Doug continued with a swipe of his finger across the screen of the datapad. He reached beneath the large table and retrieved two large boxes. "Wes, I know you'll know what to do with these as soon as you see them. Before you go all nerdgasm and start humping my leg, you have to know that Lizz is the one responsible for pulling this off." Doug made his way to the operations station and handed Wes the boxes.

"Oh, sweet," Wes squeaked. "It's like Christmas came early." He ripped open the first box like a kid unwrapping gifts on Christmas morning. "Holy shit, Cap, how… where… Oh my God, this is so freaking awesome, Cap! How in the hell did you manage to get a main processor?"

"Open the second one," Doug said with a nod of his chin.

"Woohoo! Two freaking processors! How in the hell is this even possible?"

"Don't ask me, ask Lizz," Doug replied with a smile. "I told her what we needed, and she found a way to make it happen."

"Oh my God," We said. "Thank you, Lizz! Thank you! Maybe now I can get some of the systems up and running simultaneously again." He hugged the boxes. "Thank you, thank you, thank you."

"You're very welcome, Wes," Lizz replied.

"So get those processors installed and any upgrades that you can manage before we leave port," Doug said.

"Aye, Captain," Wesley replied. He turned in his seat and popped a two-finger salute in Doug's direction.

"Now as a surprise bonus, our lovely quartermaster," Doug said with a wave toward Lizz, "has managed to get a contract in writing from the I.A. for this assignment. It states that any and all physical property of Martian origin that we happen to acquire while on this run is solely ours to do with as we wish. No taxes, customs, import embargoes, nothing. It's a privateering commission with full salvage rights that comes from the Independent Alliance being at war with the Martian Reich, even if it is just a cold war. So while we're in Martian space, each of you please work your magic and pick up any goodies that we can easily move when we get back Earthside. As per normal, see Lizz for all final decisions on transactions. Until we get all of the details on the target. We are keeping the plan loose and fluid. When we get into Martian airspace, we'll make a few transactions, offload some cargo, and get ourselves set up for the endgame."

"And pray tell, my Captain," Krista said with a sarcastic tone. "What is this grand endgame of yours?"

Doug leaned back and cracked his neck with a loud pop. "The endgame," he said with a long, deep sigh. "The endgame could kill every one of us or it could square up a few old debts and set us up for years to come. Each of you has a hard choice to make in the next few days. You can either stay on as crew with the ship or tender your resignation prior to launch. No hard feelings from anyone if you chose to stay behind. You'll be released from my employee and released from any retaliation from the I.A. Lizz has already seen to that, considering the nature of our assignment. So, the endgame."

Doug circled to the far side of the large table and pressed a few keys on the control panel. The table came to life as a three-dimensional hologram of the solar system hovered above its surface. A dotted line shot out from the Earth in a wide arc and entered the orbit of the Martian moon, Deimos, then continued to the second moon, Phobos and finally stopped in a high orbit around Mars itself.

"Our first stops will be the Deimos and Phobos security platforms, then to the Hund shipyard in Mars orbit. Lizz has already arranged buyers for over half of our cargo while at the shipyard. Once there, Wes will be able to hack their systems without any lag or signal degradation and dig out the info that the I.A. needs. From there we'll head for mining outposts *Zurich* and then *Nuremberg* since it's a relatively short hop to reach them from Mars orbit. Per the shakedown schedule that Wes found, we know that the prototype ship, the *Hans Landa*, designation Z62, will be near Nuremberg in fifteen days. With a little fudge time thrown in to make sure that we're in place at the right time, we launch in two days." A dead serious look washed over Doug's face as he manipulated the hologram display.

"My plan is to place a Trojan horse in their path, here." Doug pointed at the hologram as the view quickly zoomed in. "We'll park the *Betty* in the asteroid field near the flight path of the *Landa*. Wes, I'll want you to modify our transponders to make it look like we are a civilian Martian mining vessel. We shut down everything but the most minimal life support in the upper crew compartments, internal comm systems, and passive sensors. Once we pick up the *Landa* on sensors, we turn on the distress beacon and wait. If all goes to plan, they will come to assist with repairs or rescue and that's when I mean to board her."

The crew gasped and muttered under their breaths.

"Well there we have it, people," Krista said with a slap to her thighs. "It has finally happened, people. The captain has lost his ever-lovin' mind. Seriously, are you fucking crazy? What in the hell would possess you to want to become a pirate? Not to mention to take the *Betty*, a hundred-plus-year-old mining transport, up against the Martian Reich's latest prototype frigate? Exactly in what realm of insanity did the little guy in robes tell you this was the path to success? Did you hit your head or did you just go stupid all of a sudden?"

"I have my reasons," Doug said with a growl to his voice. His eyes narrowed to slits as he stared back across the table at Krista. "As I said before, this is entirely up to each of you. You each have the free will to make your own choices. I do not own any of you. Therefore, I will not order you to do something that has a high risk of death attached to it."

"Umm … Cap. We kinda risk our necks every day out there in The Belt," Trae said plainly. "I signed on to do the job and that's that, I'm in."

"Hell, we're at risk even when we're in port, Cap," Big Willy added. "There's always someone out there looking to take advantage of any Independent. I can't tell you how many times I've caught some corporate shitstain messing with the *Betty*. So really, how is this any different than any other day? I'll keep her flyin' as long as I can, Cap."

"Ok, so Willy and Trae are in," Doug said with a smile.

"If it wasn't for all of you, I'd still be begging for scraps on Luna station," Amanda said tearfully. "You took me in like I was family and family shouldn't abandon family. I know I don't know much yet, or that I even do much of anything yet, but I'm staying, and I'll do whatever I can to help."

"Are you kidding me, Cappy?" Rachel said with a laugh. "This isn't even a choice for me. You let me fly however I want to fly. If I could find a job with one of those big companies, they'd make me follow … um … those ... things … um ..."

"*Rules*!" Wes said beratingly. "Really, Cheezy? You couldn't remember the word, *rules*?"

"Yes! That thing! Rules! They'd make me follow *ru-uuules*. Me no likey rules," Rachel finished with a stupid smile.

"Oh my God. Why was it again that you hired her, Cap?" Wes shook his head.

"Because she's damn good at what she does," Doug said. "What about you, Geek?"

"Guess I'm in," Wes said. "Who the hell else is going to keep her squirrels in line?" He said, thumbing toward Rachel.

"Oh no, Wesley," Kara whined. "This is a big decision. You can't just willy nilly make this choice without considering me."

"Wait… After all that we've been through together, you want to just quit?" Wes turned to Kara with a stern gaze.

"No, I suppose not. I guess we're both in," Kara said reluctantly.

"Not like I have anything else better to do," Fergus added. "I mean, who else is going to keep Trae from blowing himself up with one of his contraptions? And besides, if Rachel stays, I kinda have to stay. Ya know that whole *marriage* and death do us part stuff." He motioned with air quotes.

"I guess I should hang around since things would probably fall apart without me," Lizz laughed. "Which reminds me, when was the last time that you got any rest, Doug?"

"Or ate anything for that matter?" Melanie added. "Without me, all of y'all would probably starve to death. Hell, I sat there and watched Andy have a fifteen-minute argument with the microwave one day because he couldn't figure out how to turn it on."

"Now hold on just one second," Andy argued.

"Andy, just shut up and say yes already," Melanie said with a look of absolution.

"Fine, whatever. I guess I'm in. Just don't come blaming me when we're tied up and being tortured by the Martians."

"Well, that's almost everyone," Doug continued. "What say you, Tiff?"

Tiff slapped the table with an open palm. "As long as I might get the chance to shoot at some real targets, then hell yeah, I'm in."

"Good," Doug acknowledged. "That just leaves Maggie and Krista. What say you two?"

"I couldn't just up and abandon everyone," Maggie replied. "Besides, where else would I go and who would be there to help Amanda through the hard times or keep Krista out of trouble if I just left?"

"Then I suppose we're down to one," Doug said as he looked to Krista.

"I don't know what in the hell has possessed you to take all of us with you on this insane path. We made a commitment to each other all those long years ago and I'll be damned if I'll let you down after all the shit we've been through. I promised to always be there and support you the best that I could. I don't know what bug has crawled up your ass to make you suicidal, but I've got your back as best as I can have it."

"Good…," Doug started but was interrupted.

"But I'll tell you one damned thing, Captain Douglas Rackham," Krista said as she jabbed a finger in Doug's direction. "You just remember. If you're going to this insane mission for the wrong reasons, I promise you, it will come back to you threefold. Maybe not this lifetime, but the karmic debt will be paid back in one form or another. So you'd best be doing this for the right reasons."

Doug solemnly looked around the table at each of his crew — his family — and proudly smiled. "Alright then, it's settled. All in. Let's get to work."

cHAPTER 5

The *Betty*, Nova star class transport
Sol system, en route to Mars Orbit
May 19, 2176 / Early morning (Betty Time)

"Good Morning Miss Melanie," Wes crooned as he walked into the ships mess hall. It was one of the blander areas of the ship. The walls and bulkheads had been painted a dark pea green at some point in the ship's distant past. Coolers lined one side of the room while storage compartments lined the other. a long room. At the opposite end of the room was the cooking and serving area of the mess hall. It was dominated by a buffet-style chow station situated on the far end of the room. Behind that was the counter space and gadgets used for meal preparation and the domain of the ships cook, Melanie Kleszinski. She spent most of her duty days prepping meals for the crew. "What culinary surprise do you have in store for us today?"

"Ain't none of you getting shit from me today!" Melanie threw a spatula into the galley's dishwasher. "I swear every damn one of you keeps making messes just for me to clean up! Don't you think that if I wanted to have kids, that I would have had them by now? I swear to God, when I find out whoever has been wiping snot boogers under my tables, I'm gonna throw them out of a damned airlock!"

Wes quietly slipped into the ships head, the restroom at the forward end of the Mess hall. "Oh my God, she's on a rampage today," he whispered to himself as he lifted the toilet lid. "Oh, what the fuck! Really? Skid marks again! Seriously, people." He sighed.

"Are you shitting me, Wes?" Wes could hear Melanie's heavy footfalls on the deck plating as he made her way toward the head. "Are there skid marks in there again? I just scrubbed that bathroom yesterday. I swear I'm gonna feed every damned one of you laxatives one day then lay duct tape on that seat to make sure you people remember to clean up after yourselves! That's it! I am so done! Every damned one of you are on your own today!" The distinctive sound of a metal pot clattered to the deck plating somewhere out in the mess hall.

"Don't worry about it, Mel. I've got it," Wes said. "Who seriously still does this outside of elementary school?" He quickly sanitized the room, then took a seat and accessed the SAPP implant in his left forearm.

"So, what's the latest and greatest in tech news this morning, I wonder?" He hummed to himself as he browsed the latest articles on nano processors.

The ship's intercom system crackled, popped, and buzzed to life. "

Shit, that's not it, where did you go, you little bugger?" Rachel's voice whispered through the tinny intercoms. *"Ah-ha! There you are!"*

The classical sounds of Mozart that played in the background were suddenly replaced with the electronic beats and whip cracks of Devo's *Whip It,* wrapped snugly inside of a metal coffee can.

"Huh, Cheezy's up early, but good choice of songs to start the day," Wes mused. He continued to browse the articles and hummed along with the beat. "Hmmm ...indeed..."

"Dammit! Not that one, the other one. Stupid fingers," Rachel fussed. The song suddenly changed to the heavy base fueled punches of Marilyn Manson's cover of *Tainted Love.*

"Oh, what the hell does she think she's doing messing with my playlists? Devo was a classic, but this crap has got to go," Wes mumbled to himself. "Cheezy! Get away from my station!" His frustrated shouts vibrated off of the inside walls of the small restroom. With a quick flick of his wrist, the holo display vanished and he hurriedly finished his business. Moments later, Wes stumbled onto the bridge, gasping for breath as he rushed to his station.

"Geek on the bridge," Rachel announced. "Isn't this such a *touching* song, Wesley," she sarcastically snickered. "Oh, come on Geek, let it play man. It gets so boring with your *old* people music playing in the background."

"To hell with that," Wes said. "The Captain put me in charge of communications and the intercom system is part of communications. That means I own the intercoms!"

He tapped his access code into the control screen followed with an audible, *"BLEEERP! Access denied,"* from the computer.

"You locked me out of my console again? Dammit, Cheezy! How the hell do you keep doing this? You do not mess with a man's tunes or his computer. It's sacrilegious!"

"To a nerd maybe," Rachel laughed.

"Oh my, God! There is such a huge difference between a geek and a nerd. Unlock it now!" Wes pointed at his console with a serious, eye-bulging stare.

"Why should I? Hu? I happen to like this new playlist. It doesn't sound so much like *old* people music. Why can't we have something new for a change every now and then? Huh? Huh? Are you afraid of change or something?" She propped her feet up on her console and relaxed, lacing her hands behind her head.

"Look now," Wes said, jabbing his finger in Rachel's direction. "If it weren't for the time I spent downloading and backing up all of those files, you wouldn't have anything at all to listen to in the first place. You don't realize how hard it is to come by some of those files, do you? The corporations have anything considered entertainment locked down so tight that free is almost extinct. If Project Gutenberg hadn't saved everything from before the world went to shit, none of this would even exist. We'd just be shit out of luck and stuck paying a king's ransom just to hear some music. They have had to keep moving the files and changing servers to keep the corporate asshats from deleting them and leaving people with no choice. And with every move, some of the files are lost or are no longer accessible. Total failure and loss are inevitable. A file can only be copied so many times before it becomes corrupt."

I already waste too much time hacking around your half-assed shit pranks like this," Wes fussed. "Somehow this time you managed to lock me out without a problem. Quit wasting my time and unlock it, Rachel! Now!" Wes reached for Rachel's foot and a large, well-worn pipe wrench suddenly appeared in her hands as she rolled from the pilot's acceleration couch and leapt to her feet.

"Hey! Turn it down," Doug shouted from the doorway of the captain's quarters at the aft of the bridge.

"I can't Cap. She locked me out of the system," Wes shouted, turning back to face Doug.

"What?" Doug replied as the music suddenly stopped.

"I said, she locked me out of my station again!"

"How dare you shout at the captain like that, Geek. He's going to keelhaul you for your insolence." Rachel grinned; her expression was that of innocently guilty.

Doug yawned. "Don't get me wrong, you two. I do love the tunes, Cheezy, but not so early and not so loud. Okay?"

"Not a worry, Cap," she replied.

"What's our status? I don't even know what time it is," Doug said through another yawn.

"Nothing really to report, Cap," Rachel said. "It is just after 0400 hours and we're still on course. ETA to Martian space is approximately twelve hours, forty-two minutes."

"Ok, good then. I'm going back to bed for now," Doug said through another yawn. "Let me and everyone else sleep in unless an emergency pops up."

"What the *hell*? That's it? No punishment? She locked me out of the system again, Cap," Wes growled.

"It isn't my *fault* that you make it so easy to access your console." Rachel stuck her tongue out at Wes with a *Plibbtt!*.

"Both of you, just chill," Doug said. "Seriously, do I need to be a hard ass and toss you guys in the brig or something? Don't lock him out of the system anymore, Rachel. What's going to happen if you lock him out and then disappear? How are we going to get back into the system then?"

Doug cocked his head to the side and stared at Rachel with a confused but quizzical look. "Why do you have a pipe wrench?"

"Not my particular flavor, but to each their own, I suppose," Lizz interrupted as she strode onto the bridge. "Can someone please tell me what the hell is going on and why the speakers are blaring this dreadful music all over the ship before Willy goes on a rampage? Metal does not soothe a sleeping grizzly bear."

Doug turned back to look at Rachel. "I thought you turned it off?"

"I just turned down the bridge speakers," Rachel said, then smiled. Rachel unceremoniously slid the pipe wrench to the deck on Wes's side of the console. "Wes did it!"

"Hell no, I didn't," Wes said, returning the wrench to Rachel's side of the console.

"Children!" Lizz glared at pair.

Wes turned around facing forward in his seat with a huff, "Fine."

Rachel slid back into her seat with the best straight face that she could muster. Full-on laughter looked as if it were ready to burst from her seams. "Oh shit, he looks pissed," she whispered across the center console to Wes.

"Hu…" Wes said as he turned to look behind himself toward the rear of the bridge.

"Did it happen to occur to anyone that some horrible music is blaring from the intercoms throughout most of the ship," Big Willy said as he angrily stomped onto the bridge.

Wes pointed with both index fingers at Rachel.

With the reflexes of a cat on its twelfth life, Rachel passed the wrench over the console to Wes's side once again, letting it clatter to the deck.

"Oh no, you don't," Wes shouted. "Willy! Rachel has your wrench again!"

"Not me, Geek did it," Rachel said defensively. "See, he's hiding it under his seat."

"No, I not."

"*Yes,* you did, now hush." Rachel shushed him with a chortle.

"What the fuck ever."

Willy stomped over to Wes and snatched the wrench from the floor. "Dammit, Rachel! If you move my tools, I won't be able to find them when I need them. I'm going back to bed, Cap," Willy grumbled as he stomped off the bridge.

"Snitch!" Rachel glared narrowly at Wes.

"Payback's a bitch, isn't it?" Wes smugly smiled.

From beneath the pilot's acceleration seat, Rachel produced a twenty-four-inch long double-headed dildo. In one smooth motion, she smacked Wes in the back of the head, twirled it like a baton, then tucked it away out of sight.

"Oh God! What … What in the hell … Oh my God … Really?" Wes looked from Doug to Rachel in complete confusion as to what had actually just happened.

"I dub thee, Sir Snitch-a-lot, the Knight of Tattle!" Rachel giggled, then turned back to the flight controls as she hummed a sigh of satisfaction.

"That girl may need to see a therapist the next time we're in port," Lizz said to Doug. She stepped over to the helm and quietly held out her hand.

Rachel looked up at Lizz with sad, puppy dog eyes. Her lower lip quivering. "But I'm still using it."

"Now, please," Lizz demanded.

"Dammit!" Rachel grumbled under her breath, then retrieved the neon pink phallus, handing it to Lizz.

"I'll be in my bunk for a few more hours if you don't mind, Captain. Beauty does have its price," Lizz said with a smug smile as she sauntered off the bridge.

"You might want to give that thing a good wash, Lizzy, it smells a bit off," Rachel said loudly.

As suddenly as before, a rubber snake arced through the air struck Wes across his midsection.

"Alright! Enough, stop already," Wes said pleadingly.

Doug yawned loudly as he scratched his chin. "Both of you stop it or I'll send you to your rooms, on Earth, through an airlock. Turn the music down and get back to work."

"Yes, Dad," Wes and Rachel replied in laughter-filled unison.

"Good. It's time to get serious. We've got a lot of work to do today, but not before I get some coffee," Doug said with a smack of his lips.

"Are you coming back to bed, Doug?" Krista's voice pleaded from the open door to the captain's quarters.

Doug smiled wide with a grunted giggle. "Hmmmmm, methinks coffee can wait."

cHAPTER 6

Nuremberg mining station
Sol system asteroid belt
May 22nd, 2176 / 0746 hrs local time

"So's ya see, I says to him," Big Willy said as he leaned heavily onto the metal countertop of the dock master's duty desk. He pulled up his pants and adjusted his stance. "No sir, I said. I did not go out drinking last night. I was just too damned worn out, I said to him. And at that particular moment when I was talking with my buddy, Randy Stalnaker, he'd only been home for about ten minutes or so. Hell, he hadn't even sat down at that point and you could tell that he was worn slap the hell out. The poor guy worked his ass off. He was working three jobs just to make sure that his wife, Amber, and his daughter, Pam, had everything that they could ever ask for. Now at that particular time Amber's sister, Raquel, had had a string of horrible relationships and she'd managed to get herself kicked out of her boyfriend's place for the umpteenth time, so she was staying with them, too."

"Full refuel and …" Hanns, the dockmaster, impatiently interrupted with a thick German accent. He tapped an impatient beat on the metal countertop.

"I just need a top off of the protium and coolant tanks. The old girl has so many leaks, it's almost like I fix one and three more lines start leaking."

Hanns unenthusiastically looked up from his screen. "The only fuel currently available on the station is CL42. How many cubic meters do you need?"

"What? There's no chance of fueling her up with some hot sauce, Hanns? Some deuterium or tritium, I'd at least prefer some protium if nothing else? It's so much easier to tune the old girl when she's got a belly full of the good stuff. There's gotta be something you can do."

"I am sorry, Mister Murphy, but no," Hanns said sternly. "The mining convoys departed for the asteroid belt last week. All available fuels are running short at the moment."

"Hell, man, she was topped off with hydrogen nitride back on Luna station," Willy fussed. "You know what would happen to my storage tanks and injectors if I fueled up with CL42 without a full system scrub down? What else do you have available?"

"We do have a large quantity of helium-3 available, but it is very expensive."

"How expensive is expensive?"

"One point four million Martian Marks per metric ton, Mister Murphy," Hanns said coldly.

"You have got to be fucking shitting me. Are you serious? How in the hell is a man supposed to eat and refuel his rig?"

"Then buy the CL42," Hanns said. "It makes no matter to me, Mister Murphy. Or you can wait around on the station until other fuels become available."

"I don't have that much time to waste, Hanns," Willy complained. "Alright, fine, I'll take a full load of CL42. I'll just have to tell Cap that we're stuck here overnight while I scrub the systems. Dammit, man. I just got the injectors realigned, too. I'll tell you what, that's just my damned luck."

"I am sure that you will make short work of it, Mister Murphy," Hanns said blandly as he entered the order into the computer. "Merely page the refueling crew once you are ready to fill your tanks."

"Well, what about the remaining hydrogen nitride?" Willy asked. "Don't tell me I'll have to dump it. I'd prefer to sell it back for at least something."

Hanns briefly glanced back to the datapad, tapping the screen as if cycling through a list. "I am authorized to purchase hydrogen nitride at a rate of one thousand and twelve Marks per metric ton."

"Damn that's a loss," Big Willly said with a sigh. "Alright, it is what it is I guess. Not like I have much else of a choice. It'll be at least late tonight before I can drain and flush the systems.

"Very well," Hanns replied. "As I previously stated, just page the refuel crew once you are ready for either the defuel or refuel."

"Will do, Hanns. So's anyways," Willy continued. "This was all going on just after I had graduated high school and got a job working at the same place as my buddy, Randy. He talked me up to the bosses and got me in the door. So since the job was almost two hours away from my hometown, he let me move in with him, but we ended up on opposite shifts. Well, he worked like 16-hour days, 7 days a week. The man was a machine. With him being gone so much, one thing led to another and before you know it, I was dating Pam and became her mom and her aunt's dirty little boy toy anytime I'd find myself alone with them. The hardest part was keeping it all under wraps so that none of them knew I was doing any of the others all while keeping Randy from finding out any of it. I tell you what, family dinners were some stressful times," he chuckled.

Hanns unmovingly stared at Willy, then sucked in a quick breath. "You do realize that you have told me that same story at least the last dozen times in all of the years that you have visited this station?"

"Huh, really?" Willy looked away in thought. "I guess I've told that story so many times, that I just lost track of who I told it to." Willy chuckled. "Anyways, full fill-up of the tanks in the morning. It'll take me most of the night to purge and scrub the systems. Cap isn't gonna be happy," he said as he turned to leave, then looked back to Hanns. "You're sure there's nothing else you might have squirreled away anywhere?"

"I am sorry, Mr. Murphy, but the CL42 and the helium-3 are the only fuels currently available."

"Alright. It'll have to do then. I appreciate it, Hanns. You take care and I'll catch you in the morning." Big Willy turned, heading back toward the station's point of entry airlock. It was the single point of access between the station proper and the individual docking ports spaced along the stations primary docking ring. All spacer traffic entered the station through this portal with the exception of Martian military vessels, which docked at separate points from civilian craft.

"Do not move," Hanns ordered. Un-holstering his sidearm, he pointed it in Willy's direction.

"What the hell, Hanns? I just said take care. Is it offensive or something in German?" Willy asked with a sarcastic laugh as he slowly turned and raised his hands.

"Not you, Mr. Murphy. Please step aside and do not interfere." Hanns held his weapon steady as he sidestepped and aimed at a target beyond Big Willy.

"Okay, Hanns? I don't get why…"

"Andy Kleszinski! Surrender yourself and no harm will come to you."

Willy spun around to see Andy blankly staring at Hanns. "What in the hell, Hanns? On what charges? He's one of our crew."

"He is to be arrested on sight if he boards this station," Hanns said coldly. "I have also alerted station security that there is a possible situation and they will arrive momentarily."

"On what charges, Hanns?" Willy asked.

"On charges of sabotage and the destruction of Martian Imperial assets."

"Wait…" Andy said in a questioning tone. "I fixed a bunch of stuff the last time we were here, not break it. I spent like two days helping Fritz to bypass and reroute lines because of a faulty relief manifold."

"Unfortunately, I must inform you that you did *not,* in fact, fix anything, Mr. Klesenski," Hanns said coldly.

"Well, hell, let me get down to engineering to talk to Fritz and see what's up. Maybe we can figure something out," Andy said as he started down the few steps from the airlock.

"This is your last warning, Mr. Kleszinski. I do not want to shoot you, but I will if I must. You will be arrested if you step foot off of your ship."

"Whoa, now hold on Hanns," Trae shouted as he exited the hatch. Cautiously he put his hands up and turned to Andy. "What the hell did you do this time?"

"If Andy steps off the ship, Hanns has to arrest him," Big Willy said.

"But I need to go see Fritz down in engineering," Andy argued.

"Ha! Um … How about, *no,*" Trae said, laughing. "I suggest you get back on the ship."

"Hanns! Old buddy, old pal!" Tiff cheerfully shouted. She ran over to Hanns and wrapped her arms around his neck, giving him a big hug. Her eyes went wide and locked onto the gun in his hands. She took a slow step backward. "Hey, Hanns, um, what's with the gun, man?"

"If you would please, Mrs. Crowley, take a step back," Hanns requested. He brushed Tiffany aside to clear her from his line of sight. I am afraid that Mr. Kleszinski must be arrested if he steps off the ship."

"What the hell, dude," Tiff said, fussing at Andy. "Not even off the ship yet and you're causing problems? Dude, that shit just ain't cool."

"What's up?" Rachel said as she exited the airlock. She stopped and looked from Hanns to Andy. "What did you do?"

"Hanns is going to shoot Andy," Tiff replied.

"Hanns isn't going to shoot Andy," Willy said. "Are ya Hanns?" He crossed his arms and looked back at the Martian dock master.

Hanns dryly swallowed. "That has yet to be determined, Mister Murphy," he replied.

"Ha! Hell, go ahead. No one will miss him anyways," Fergus laughed. He sidestepped Rachel and exited the airlock. "Hey, Hanns!" Fergus waived. "Am I good to go?"

"Yes, Mr. Coram. You may disembark."

"Okay, cool. Good luck Andy," Fergus said. He slapped Andy on the back as he passed then turned and extended his arm to Rachel. "Dear?"

"Why I'd be honored, good sir." She half curtsied and wrapped her arm into his. "Toodles." Rachel waved to Andy with her free hand as they walk out of the customs office.

"Okay, so are me and Tiff good as well, Hanns?" Trae asked.

Andy shifted uncomfortably. "So, you're all just going to leave me here?"

"Pretty much." Trae smiled over at Andy. "If you did go and put your nose into other people's business you wouldn't be in this predicament. I'm going to assume that me and Tiff are good," he said, turning back to Hanns.

"Yes. The both of you may disembark, Mr. Crowley."

"Good, let's go, Tiff," Trae directed as he walked away from the airlock.

"Aww, but I wanted to see what happens," Tiff said.

"Andy does something stupid. Hanns shoots him, Andy dies, then end," Trae said. "Now let's go."

"Andrew Raymond Kleszenski!" Mel's voice echoed from within the depths of the airlock.

"Oh hell," Andy cringed. "Hey, Hanns, it was just jail, right?"

"Don't do it, Andy," Big Willy said.

"What the hell have you done now, Andy?" Melanie shouted as she stepped from the airlock. "We haven't even gotten off of the ship and you have a gun pointed at you. Seriously, what the hell is wrong with you that you bring this sort of thing on yourself?" Melanie waived with a quick salute toward Hanns. "Hey, Hanns." She promptly turned and slapped Andy in the back of the head. "What the hell did you do, Andy?"

Andy rubbed at the back of his head. "I'm not even entirely sure yet."

Melanie gritted her teeth, glaring at Andy. "What are the charges, Hanns?"

"Sabotage of the station's main power relays, sabotage of the station's environmental systems, and destruction of imperial property."

"What in the hell, Andy? Really?" Melanie slapped him across the back of the head again.

"Don't reset his brain too hard, Mel," Willy said. "You might knock him forward and Hanns will have to shoot."

"So…?" Melanie shrugged.

"Hanns has to arrest him if he steps foot on the station," Willy said.

"And what happens then, Hanns?" She crossed her arms and braced herself for the answer.

Hanns cleared his throat. "Incarceration until he can be transported to the prison mining facility."

Melanie snapped her gaze back to Andy. "Well, hell. That's actually kinda tempting."

"You *wouldn't* dare," Andy said.

Doug emerged from the airlock and stopped abruptly. He looked from Hanns to Andy and back to Hanns.

"Hey, Hanns," Doug said with a wave. "We're still cool to dock, right?"

"Yes, sir, Captain Rackham," Hanns said.

"Okay, good. Just making sure. So what's with the gun then?"

"Andy's dumb ass broke their station the last time we were here and now he isn't allowed off the ship," Melanie said.

Doug tilted his head with a quizzical look at Hanns. "Why haven't you just arrested him then?"

"Per the inner system trade agreement, your ship constitutes sovereign soil. My jurisdiction ends at that point of entry. I cannot cross the border to issue or carry out a warrant without the trade consortium's approval.

"Oh, okay," Doug said then looked back toward Andy. "Get back on the ship, dumb ass. Don't step foot off of it unless you want Hanns to shoot you." Doug turned back to Hanns and waved. "See Hanns? Problem solved." Doug slid his hands into his pockets and walked down the corridor toward the station's promenade.

"He's all yours, Hanns. I don't know what to do anymore. I'm so over it," Melanie said, following Doug down the corridor.

"Um…Mel," Andy said. "You aren't going to help me?"

"Nope," Melanie shouted over her shoulder. "Just do what Doug said. Turn around and you'll be helping yourself."

Andy stared at Hanns.

Hanns stared at Andy.

Andy slid his foot forward as if to take a step off the ship and onto the station.

Hans pulled back the hammer on his pistol.

The sound of running footfalls echoed from the corridor that led to the station's promenade.

"Security is almost here, Mr. Kleszinski," Hanns said.

"All right, all right. Fine, I'll stay on the ship," Andy said. Reluctantly he turned, making his way back onto the ship.

cHAPTER 7

The *Betty*
Sol system asteroid belt
May 23rd, 2176 / Early Morning (Betty time)

"To...*Carry on!*" Wes bellowed as he strummed at an imaginary guitar. The tinny tune blared power chords over the bridge intercoms. He lurched and swayed around the bridge to the rhythm of the tune.

"Wes! Hey, Wes! Geek!" Doug shouted through cupped hands.

Wes jumped with a start.

"How in the hell are you supposed to monitor the scanners when you aren't even at your station?"

"Sorry, Cap, I just got sucked into it. It's such a good song that I couldn't help myself."

"You'd better, or you won't be sailing anywhere anymore," Doug said. "You'll be floating away."

Wes's eyes bulged wide. "Aye Captain!" He rushed to his station and turned down the volume.

"Good, now what's our status?"

"Um...one sec," Wes turned down the music to a lower level. "Nothing on infrared. Standard radio chatter. Active scanners are offline and passive systems show a pair of class J martian mining vessels parked on a rock just over sixty thousand klicks away. But… Huh, that's weird." A perplexed look contorted his face.

"But what?"

"There's another transponder signal out there, but no data attached to identify the ship. Just like, hey, we're here, don't run into us, but we aren't going to tell you who we are."

"That could be our target." Doug excitedly looked over Wes's shoulder at the console readout.

"Or it could be a pirate," Wes added. "Well, another pirate ship besides us, I mean."

"It's possible," Doug admitted. "Are they close enough to get a visual?"

"Maybe. Hang on, let me see." Wes switched the main viewscreen to an image of the expansive asteroid field. Rocks of all shapes and sizes tumbled and rotated within view.

"Where is it?" Doug leaned against the back of the Geek's chair.

"The camera is pointed right at it. It should be about eight hundred klicks off the port side and thirty degrees nose high."

"Just behind that big rock then, I'd guess. Dammit." Doug slapped the back of the chair.

Wes turned in his seat to face Doug. "Most likely, Cap. The only reason we know where they are is because of the repeater beacons out in the field. They relay transponder data so you aren't temporarily blinded because your line of sight is blocked."

Doug straightened and let out a frustrated breath. "How close is that rock to us?"

"I don't know. I'd have to power up the radar to tell you. But if we do that, then they might pick up the signal and our cover will be blown."

"Well if it were pirates, they'd be running completely dark," Doug said.

"Most likely," Wes said. "Any corporate or independent ships would be broadcasting to keep themselves legit. Even if their comms had been damaged, there are ways to transmit and let others know where you are."

Doug took a deep breath. "Let's do this thing then," he said as he walked back to the captain's chair.

"Wait, what if it isn't them?"

"It has to be them. Who else would be running legal but silent?" Doug sat back in his seat and flipped on the ship's intercom. "All hands on deck! Target in sight."

"Arrrg, Yo ho," Wes sang.

"Stop *it*!" Doug glared at Wes.

Wes lowered head, looking abashed. "Sorry, I just couldn't help myself."

Doug sighed. "I know…," he said, then grinned and pressed the comm button again. "Sail on the horizon!"

Wes giggled then excitedly turned back to his station.

"Willy, lock her down and muck up the engines enough so it looks like we're dead in the water. Don't let her get cold though. I want to be able to go full throttle at the first sign of trouble."

"Trae, Fergus, get prepped and on standby at the airlock. Cheezy to the bridge." Doug released the comm button with a flourish. "Wes, you're with me."

"Oh my God, I get to be part of the boarding party?" He nearly squealed, barely able to contain his excitement.

"Yes. But just remember that we have to take that ship quickly," Doug said. "Keep your head down and take control of their systems once you get on board. Now turn on the distress signal as soon as Cheezy relieves you and go get yourself ready."

"Aye aye, Captain!" Wes saluted. "Yo ho ho!"

cHAPTER 8

The *Betty* / Airlock Docking port
Sol system asteroid belt
May 23rd, 2176 / Morning (*Betty* time)

"*C*ap.*"* Rachel's voice cracked over the intercom. Doug pressed a button on the airlock corridor comm panel. "Go ahead, Cheezy."

"*Bogey is about to knock on our door, Cap*," Rachel said. "They keep trying to hail us, but I did like you said. I mucked up the signal and gave them an ear full of noise."

Doug turned back toward the airlock door. Trae and Fergus stood at the end of the short corridor. They prepared themselves, checking over their own and each other's weapons and gear.

"Are you two ready?" Doug asked

"Yup," Trae said without looking up from the display on his odd-looking weapon.

"You betcha," Fergus said.

Doug proudly smiled at the two crewmen. "Good. Keep your eyes and ears open. Should be any time now."

"Copy that, Cap," Trae acknowledged.

"So where the hell is the Geek?" Fergus asked, making air quotes with his fingers.

"Hell, I dunno. I thought he was with the two of you."

"I'm right here," Wes said proudly as he strode into the docking port.

Trae snorted a laugh. "Really man? Oh my dear God. We're all going to die, aren't we? That's the only explanation. We're all going to die and the Tallyman decided to have a sense of humor about it today."

"Hu, what the hell are you going on about?" Fergus turned and suddenly choked on a laugh. *"Or ...* we'll go down as the worst space pirates in history."

*"Um ...*Wes ..." Doug scratched his head as he took in the image before him. Wes wore full pirate regalia, complete with a red velvet jacket, dark wig and an oversized feather in his wide-brimmed hat. Doug stifled a laugh. "Um...What's with the pirate outfit, man?"

"This may be my one and only chance to be a pirate," Wes said. "So, by *God*, I'm going to do it right!" He planted his hands on his hips and stood proudly, smiling a wide, cheesy grin.

"Oookay then." Doug shook his head in disbelief and turned back to the other two. "Trae, Fergus, you two sweep the ship and secure engineering. Wes will stay with me and we'll head for the bridge." Doug's eyes narrowed at Wes with a stern, questioning gaze. He reached into his coat and produced an odd-looking gun that he tossed at Wes, which he barely caught. "Do you know how to use that?"

Wes held the gun like a delicate butterfly in his left palm. He caressed the lines of cold black steel with the tip of one nervous, chubby finger. "My little *friend*," he lovingly said the gun.

"Cap," Rachel chimed in over the comms. *"Hard dock imminent, they are on final approach."*

Doug quickly scooped the gun from Wes's palm with a frustrated huff. "Look." Doug pointed, then opened the breach of the pistol. "You have four rounds." He held out the weapon for Wes to see then closed the breach. "Flip this lever and it'll be hot and ready to go. Just point and click. Whatever you do, do not, I repeat, *do not* touch whoever you shoot unless you want to get zapped yourself." He handed the weapon back to Wes.

"Oh, okay, cool." Wes longingly stared at the odd pistol.

"Hey, have you tested this yet?" Fergus asked as he fiddled with a strange flashlight shaped object mounted under the barrel of his tactical shotgun.

"Nope, not yet," Trae said. "I haven't had the time or a brain-dead *sucker* willing to be a lab rat for me. I considered just finding a random mouth breather, but that seemed too cruel. This will make for a great test run, though. Just remember that at max power, you should have about a thirty-foot range."

"What does this one do?" Fergus asked as he looked over the odd weapon.

"It's my latest variant of the original incapacitator," Trae said. "There should be an almost instantaneous reaction." He held up his beloved auto-shotgun and pointed to an odd pear-shaped object mounted under the barrel. "And this is my new and improved brown sound emitter. A two-second burst within forty feet and the target's insides will be outside." He chuckled with a gleeful grin.

"Wait, what?" Fergus shook his head with disbelief.

"You made a *shit gun*?" Wes laughed.

"Yup." Trae smiled proudly. Fergus held up a fist to Trae, who bumped it without even looking.

"What the hell does this do?" Wes asked as he looked over the thick pistol in his hand.

"It's a taser pistol," Doug said. "Four rounds of fifty-thousand-volt hell. You will hit anything that you point it at up to twenty feet."

Wes sighed, then clasped the gun to his chest. "Thank you, Cap. I love it."

"Cap," Rachel chimed in over the intercom.

"Go ahead Cheezy."

"Hard dock in five."

"Lock and load *bitches*!" Fergus cheered and pumped his shotgun in the air over his head.

"Yup." Trae chambered a round and let the slide move forward with a loud metallic clunk.

"*Four.*"

Apprehensive, Doug turned to Wes. "You ready?"

"*Three.*"

"Yup," Wes said. Sweat beaded on his forehead. He flipped the prime switch on the taser pistol and drew his Cutlass. "*Avast* ye scurvy dogs!"

"*Two.*"

Trae and Fergus glanced at one another, then broke out into hysterical laughter.

"*One.*"

"I'm owning this, dammit!" Wes scowled, "I am the pirate! Arrg!"

The ship rocked with the dull metallic *thwunk* of hard dock. A green light illuminated on the small control panel of the airlock. Cold silence muted the echoed mechanisms of hard dock as the light hum of charging capacitors resonated within the confined space.

Pressurized air hissed as it was released, and the airlock doors slid open. Two unsuspecting crewmen stood in the doorway. Their bland gray flight suits a perfect match for the muted gray of their ship's interior. Perplexed confusion painted both of their faces.

"Was zur Holle ist das?"

"Throw the hooks and board her, lads!" Wes shouldered his way ahead of Trae and Fergus. His pistol pulsed with the sound of instant electrical discharge. The crewman on the left convulsed violently to the *tick, tick, tick* of tased electrocution. Ozone and burnt hair permeated the atmosphere of the confined space. As if with practiced ease Wes's arm floated right, pistol cocked sideways. The second crewman doubled over in a knot of spastic muscle contractions. Wes roared in a fit of unadulterated geek rage. He lunged forward, leaping with all of his might over the twitching figures and onto the Martian ship.

"Well hell," Fergus said.

"I know, right?" Trae turned and looked over to Fergus. "He just took all the fun out of it for us. Screw it!" Trae aimed at the crewman on the right.

"Let's test them anyways." Fergus aimed at the one on the left. Binaural tones undulated as multicolored LED lights flickered from the under-barrel attachment of Fergus's weapon. Both crewmen wretched and writhed in fetal-like balls.

"Oh god that stinks," Fergus said through a heaving gag.

"What the hell is that?" Trae sniffed at the air, then dry heaved.

The scent of digested sauerkraut laced the small compartment with the sick sweetness of raw sewage that viciously enveloped the occupants.

"Oh my, God, that's *nasty*." Fergus chuckled between gasps of breath.

"But they worked," Trae said proudly.

"Guys! Enough! Get moving and sweep the ship," Doug ordered. "I'll catch up to the Geek and get him to the bridge."

"I think that worked pretty damn well, overall." Trae held out the weapon at arm's length and admired the craftsmanship.

"Yup, I'd say so." Fergus laughed as he shouldered his shotgun. The pair cautiously tip-toed their way over and around the mess, onto the Martian ship.

Doug pressed the intercom button on the wall panel. "Willy, Andy, Kara, Clean up at the airlock, please. You can thank Trae and his tinkering this time. Tie these two up and toss them into a holding cell while you're at it. Switching to my personal radio." He released the intercom button then cautiously stepped over the unconscious crewmen and onto the Martian ship.

Panel labels and small strips of trim in red accentuated the dull grayness of everything else in the corridor of the Martian frigate. Deck plates, wall panels, and exposed conduits were painted the same drab gray of the Martian crewman's flight suits. He turned left and jogged down the corridor toward the forward section of the ship. At the end of a long hall, the dullness made an immediate right. Doug rounded the corner where a glimpse of red silk, feathered hat, and taser pistol pointed in his direction grabbed his attention. He dropped to the deck just as the sound of electrical capacitors discharging filled his ears.

"*Down* Geek!"

"Sorry, Cap." Wes tucked the pistol into his waist sash and knelt beside a closed hatchway. He turned his attention back to a dislodged control panel that dangled by a multitude of wires.

"They locked down the bridge, didn't they?" Doug checked the starboard corridor for defenders.

"Yup, but not for long," Wes said. "Give me a few more seconds and we'll be in." Wes firmly grasped a single wire from the wire bundle and yanked it loose from the back of the control panel. He stripped away the insulation from the metal conductor with his teeth, then producing a pair of wires with metal clips from his pocket he connected the clips to the bare wires. Wes probed the exposed circuit board with the opposite end of the wires, glancing every so often at the screen that still displayed, *Sichern,* in bold red letters.

"*We've got a problem Cap*," Rachel chimed in over the radio. "*Someone is transmitting a distress signal. I'm doing my best to jam the signal, but they are modulating the frequency.*"

"Copy that, Cheezy, we're on it. Can you hurry it up a little, Wes? We can't let them call for help."

"Will you back off already," Wes said. "It's bad enough as it is without you breathing down my neck." A tiny blue spark leapt from the circuit board as he poked it once again with the probe. "Oh, well hello. That might just be the spot." A bright blue electrical arc leapt from the wire to the circuit board. The control panel beeped, and Doug could see the display change to, *Entsichern.* "Ha, I think I've got it." He flipped over the panel and pressed the green button displayed under the lettering. The door slid open with a whir of electrical motors. "*Hazzah!*" Wes shouted as he stumbled to his feet.

Doug instinctively raised his pistol at the open doorway and cautiously stepped forward. He swung his sights left, then to the right as he entered the bridge. "Wes, get in here and secure the controls." Doug cleared a storage compartment to the left of the hatchway, then continued clockwise around the bridge.

"On it!" Wes rushed over to the helm station. "Oh shit. We have a slight problem, Cap," he said over his shoulder as he looked over the controls.

"Get your ass on the ground now!" Doug shouted.

"What the hell? It's not my fault! Everything is in German," Wes said, putting his hands in the air.

"Not you Geek."

Wes turned but remained seated. Doug stood at the rear port side of the bridge; pistol aimed at an open storage closet. Wes keyed his radio. "Cheezy, do you know any German?"

"*Um...bitte ein Bit, Dummkoph, Bratwurst. Why?*"

"Because everything is in German," Wes said.

"*Well, yeah, what else would you expect? They are primarily Germans, ya know,*" she said sarcastically. "*I don't know what to tell you, bud. I guess you're just kinda screwed, now aren't ya', Mister Wizard?*"

"Wes, get over here and give me a hand with these two," Doug ordered.

Two crewmen in gray flight suits emerge from the closet with their hands in the air. Doug keyed his radio, "Cheezy, see if anyone in our crew knows any German." He motioned with the gun at the two crewmen to get onto the ground.

Wes rushed over as the pair laid flat on the deck, their hands on the back of their heads.

"Tie them up," Doug ordered.

"With what?"

"I don't care, find something. Use your pirate sash if you gotta," Doug said.

"But my pants will fall down."

"I don't *care* if your pants fall down. Just do it. You either tie them up or they kill us while we aren't looking, understand? Now tie them up. We don't have time to find something else."

"Fine," Wes grumbled. He fumbled with a knot in the silk material for a moment then stood straddling one of the crewmen and bound the man's wrists behind his back.

"Cap..oh shit. Hey, Cap!"

"What the hell now." Doug keyed the radio again. "Go ahead Cheezy."

"We have a problem. Two patrol ships are inbound and hailing us."

"Shit, shit, shit," Wes said as he quickly bound the second crewman's hands. He raced back to the helm.

"Cap," Trae shouted bellowed over the ship's comm system.

"Oh my god," Wes said with a gasp. "The base and definition of those speakers are amazing." He looked about the bridge with a wide smile of pleased astonishment on his face.

"Snap out of it," Doug said, snapping his fingers at Wes. He sat in the Command chair and stared at the confusion of controls on the command chair's display screens. He keyed his own radio. "Go ahead Trae."

"Engine room and lower decks are secured. We found two more crewmen down here hiding at the back of the main engineering space."

"At least something is going right," Doug said. "We have two more crewmen up here. You want to come get them and lock them away with the others?"

"Copy that, Cap. We'll be there in a sec to collect them," Trae replied.

Doug keyed the mic again. "Cheezy, did you find out if anyone over there speaks German?"

"If they do, no one has fessed up to it yet, but I've got an idea."

"Anything is better than nothing at this point," Doug said.

"Hey, Wes."

Wes keyed his radio. "I'm all ears, Cheezy. What ya got?"

"Tell me what you see. What sort of flight control system do they have, ya know? Describe it all to me," Rachel said.

"There's the manual flight control yoke, throttles, and what looks like engine output data."

"Okay, well, what about thruster outputs? Do you see anything that might look like thruster controls?"

"It might be this global display thingy on the left. *Maybe,*" Wes said hesitantly. "It shows the ship in 3-D on the inside of a sphere in wireframe. But there's this weird red squiggle just ahead of the ship and two red triangles off to one side. It sort of looks like their distance is being shown. There are numbers under each triangle that is slowly counting down like they are getting closer."

"Does anything look similar to the controls for the scrambler drive on the Betty?"

"Well...hold on." Wes tapped a finger to his nose as he glanced across the wide array of digital screen controls. "There is a big red button under a cover here on right side of the console."

"That's it," Rachel cheered.

Doug keyed in, "are you sure, Cheezy?"

"Where's the meat cap," Fergus interrupted as he and Trae entered the bridge.

"Geez man!" Wes jumped in his seat and turned toward the shouting. "Can you be any louder? Your wife is trying to help me figure out these, *stupid* controls."

"Yes I can," Fergus shouted. "Hey, honey!"

"That was my freaking ear, man," Trae fussed. He cleared his ear with a wiggle and pop of his pinky finger.

"You gotta key the radio to talk to her, you ass," Wes said with an emphasized middle finger in Fergus's direction.

Fergus keyed his radio. "Hey hot stuff, can I come back over and plunder your booty?"

"Not right now, dear," Rachel replied playfully. *"I have a headache and I'm kinda busy saving your asses, again."*

"Damn," Fergus disappointedly said with a snap of his fingers. He keyed the mic again. Raincheck?"

"Sure Ferg, um, remind me later," Rachel said dismissively. *"Um ... Hey Cap. These guys are getting way too close for my liking. We really need to get out of here, quick. And I mean like, Speedy Gonzales quick."*

Doug pointed toward the trussed-up Martians laying on the port side of the bridge. "Secure all of them in one of the quarters or something for now," he said to Trae and Fergus. "Hurry up and get ready for a jump."

"Will do Cap," Trae replied.

"Cheezy, disengage the Betty and get out of here. Rendezvous at Luna Station, four."

"On it Cap."

Wes fumbled with his radio. "Cheezy are you sure about the big red button?"

"Um...Yeah pretty sure."

"Pretty sure? That's it? No warm fuzzies or anything?"

"Yup."

The ship shuddered.

"The Betty has detached and is clear, Cap," Wes said. "Should I hit the button?"

"We don't have many other choices. I say go for it. Hit the button Geek," Doug ordered.

"Shit, okay then. Hold on." Wes tapped at the display console. The image of Earth's moon appeared on the helm screen. "Course set, I think," Wes said nervously.

"Good, punch it," Doug ordered.

"Aye aye, Cap." Wes shoved the throttle levers forward, then flipped open the cover and slammed his hand down on the big red button. Red warning lights flashed in time with the blaring roar of a klaxon.

"What in the hell is that?" Doug shouted over the alarms.

"What the hell did you do Geek? You guys are putting off all sorts of weird emissions and lots of radiation," Rachel said over the comms.

"I don't know," Wes said as he looked over the readouts. "The readings are weird. Main power is maxed out and doing this weird pulse, thingy."

"Captain! Anomaly dead ahead!"

"What the hell." Doug keyed his radio, "hang on tight, everyone!"

"Something is forming directly ahead of us, Cap," Wes said over the sound of the alarms. "Holy hell! Is that a freaking wormhole?"

"Did you just say wormhole?" Doug looked over the captain's readouts. "How the hell is that even possible?"

"I have no clue, Cap," Wes said. "The helm isn't responding. We're being pulled in. Crossing the threshold in three."

"Cap...," the radios squelched.

"Two," Wes said.

The radios exploded with static and variable EM noise. *"We're being pulled ..."* Rachel began but was cut off by static intertwined with high pitched electronic squeals.

"One ..."

cHAPTER 9

Martian Frigate, *Hans Landa*
Asteroid belt
May 23rd, 2176 / Morning (Betty time)

The viewscreen suddenly blinked to black and flashed back to life with a slow electronic hum. A new warning alarm joined the cacophony of the still blaring klaxon.

"Now what?" Doug shouted over the noise.

"I don't know!" Wes tapped at the controls. "Oh shit, hold on!" He grasped the control yoke and pulled back hard while slightly rolling the ship to the right. The scene of a vast asteroid field faded to life on the viewscreen. One very large and uncomfortably close rock slid downward across the screen and disappeared from view. "Okay, we're in the clear, Cap." He wiped his brow. "That was freaking close!"

"Alright," Doug said, letting out a restrained breath. "Get us up-spin of the ecliptic just to make sure we're clear of any other rocks. Did we take any damage?"

"If I'm reading this right," Wes said, "it looks like the main engines are offline, but otherwise I don't see anything. Oh hey," he said, jabbing a finger at the control panel. The warning alarms subsided, and the ships emergency lighting returned to normal.

Doug keyed his radio. "Trae, Fergus, you guys still with us? Cheezy, are you out there?"

"*Yup, we're still here,*" Trae replied.

"*Hey,*" Fergus said, chiming in over the comms. "*Did you know that these guys shipped out with beer in the fridge? I kinda like the way these guys think.*" He chuckled over the comms.

"We're here Cap," Rachel said. *"Just pulling back alongside you. What in the hell just happened?"*

"Wes said something about a wormhole," Doug said.

"I thought wormholes were supposed to tear ships apart? Or at least that's how they always show them in the movies," Rachel said.

Wes keyed his radio. "Theoretically we should be stretched out to an infinitely fine string, but that's nothing but pure theory. No one has ever documented an actual wormhole that I know of."

"Hu," Doug laughed. "Then we got damn lucky, I guess. Any sign of those patrol ships?"

"I'm still not even honestly sure what I'm looking at here, Cap," Wes said, motioning at the console. "The controls are all in German to start with and their layouts aren't exactly *Earth* standard."

"No sign of them on my end, Cap," Rachel said. *"It's really weird. Like they just disappeared."*

Doug stared at the viewscreen, momentarily drifting off in thought. "Can either of you get me a fix on our position?"

"Already working on it, Cap," Rachel chimed in. *"So far nothing makes sense. I'm not sure if the nav computer got scrambled or what. I'm not picking up any of the communications relays or navigation beacons that should be in range. It's like everything just vanished. Maybe we blew a relay or something in the sensor suite? Just hang tight though, I'm on it. But ...,"* she mildly hummed, *"I am picking up a strange signal. Looks like it's an extremely high band, modulated frequency. Shit, we don't have a reference point. Um... The signal is coming from forty-two degrees nose right and ten degrees nose high."*

Doug tilted his head quizzically, changing his relative view in relation to the viewscreen. "Hey, Wes, is there something wrong with the view screen? The color seems a bit off. Everything has a reddish tinge to it.

"Hold on," Wes fiddled with the console controls. "That looks like a camera icon." He tapped the icon that exploded to a series of new icons arranged around a silhouette of the ship. The image on the viewscreen panned slowly to the left. "Oh, what the hell? We aren't in Kansas anymore."

"That's something new," Doug added, mouth agape. "Are you seeing this Cheezy?"

"Of course not," Rachel replied. *"The damn view screen is on the fritz again."* A loud crash followed by the sound of something heavy and metallic clattering to the deck echoed over the comm system.

"Rachel," Wes said. "What was that?"

"What was what? I don't know what you're talking about," Rachel said. *"Give me one sec and let me get to a porthole."*

"Look to Port, Cheezy," Doug said.

"Holy mother of the Great old ones. That looks like a red giant!"

"I think I figured out the ship's comm system Cap," Wes said.

"Good, patch us through to the Betty."

"Alright, go. Your live, Cap."

"That's what it would appear to be, Cheezy," Doug said in a calm and concerned voice. "Wes, Rachel, patch me in ship-wide on both ships, if you two would please."

"You're on, Cap," Rachel reported.

"I think you're good on this side, Cap," Wes added.

"Listen up," Doug said loudly. "It appears that we've somehow gotten ourselves a little lost. We are no longer in the Sol system. Off of our port bow is what looks to be a red giant star. It may take Cheezy some time to get our position. Until then we need to prep both ships for the long haul. Geek, Cheezy, find us a safe harbor until we can get our bearings.

And check out that odd signal you found earlier but do it carefully.

Trae, Fergus, check out this new hulk. Let's get an inventory of everything on board. Mel, witches, for the time being, we are on minimal rations. Make the necessary adjustments and make all of our stores last as long as you can. Big Willy, Andy, once we get to a safe harbor, I want you over here to help Wes figure out this ship's systems and make sure to re-label everything as you go. For right now, cut off all nonessential systems for max power conservation. We have no idea how long we'll be here or how we'll refuel without a spaceport. Captain out."

"Wes, Cheezy, get on it."

The bridge comms chime to life with the short blast of an old-world bosun's whistle. *"This sure is a fancy new ship you got here, Captain,"* an unfamiliar voice said over the comm system. *So much nicer than, the Betty, don't you think? She even has that new ship smell to her,"* the unknown voice audibly sniffed at the air. *"But it looks to me that the reactor is near to going cold. Better get one of your boys down here to tend to it."*

Wes spun around in his seat and stared at Doug with a look of utter disbelief. "That can't be possible."

Doug's brow furrowed. "What the hell? Was that the Chief? I thought we got rid of him with the bug bombs?"

Wes's eyes bulged with astonished surprise. "I thought we did too. Holy shit, that signal came from the engine room. How the hell did he get on board?"

Doug keyed the intercoms. "Trae, Fergus, get back down to engineering. That stowaway that calls himself The Chief is loose down there somewhere. Toss him in with the Martians when you catch his crazy ass."

The short, high pitched whistle sounded again over the intercom, followed by the clatter of something plastic dropped to the metal deck plating. *"Um ... Cap. If I'm not mistaken that signal isn't exactly high band. It's a multilayered and highly compressed transmission."*

"How the hell does he do that?" Wes stared at the helm as the controls took on a life of their own. He held his hands in the air and clear of the console. "I just lost helm control."

"Adjusting course by three point one four degrees to port. Here, listen to the difference," the Chief said. Suddenly the modulated sound of static cleared and gave way to an odd, angelic sing-song. The voice flowed with a smooth and unbroken intonation of syllables like the flow of water in a Zen garden fountain.

"Ya see, Cap," the Chief continued, *"we were just picking up the distorted fuzz along the edge of the transmission. So, I got us aligned with the signal and ran it through a decompression algorithm. You're welcome, Chief out."*

The comms went silent.

"How the hell does he do that?" Wes turned in his seat to look back at Doug. "It's like he's a secret wizard of everything tech."

Doug sighed, "I don't know, but I suppose I owe him a ration pack for helping us out."

cHAPTER 10

Martian Frigate, *Hans Landa*
Red Giant system asteroid belt
May 23rd, 2176 / Late evening (Betty time)

"Holy frijoles Cap!" Trae exclaimed. "The basic sensor package on this thing is way above any civilian system that I've ever seen. This is a state-of-the-art military spec sensor array."

"No shit," Fergus added. "I could shove a BB up a gnat's ass from ten thousand klicks with these targeting systems. See, check this out." He fiddled with a control console on the port side of the bridge, then turned and looked up at the viewscreen. The alien asteroid field, backlit by the glowing red giant appeared on the viewscreen. "Are you ready?" Without a response, Fergus tapped the panel and the view screen zoomed in at a sickening rate. It halted its advance and focused on a very clear image of dust particles surrounded by what looked like snowflakes.

"Wow," Doug gasped in surprise. "What's the distance?"

Fergus snorted, suppressing a laugh. "Ninety-seven hundred klicks."

"Damn," Trae gasped then whistled.

"What else have you figured out?" Doug asked.

"Oh, I've got this," Fergus said with a wide grin. He quickly tapped away at the controls. "Once I figured out what all of these buttons did on this console, I fired off a probe to get a full layout of the system. It isn't finished, but we have a good start."

The viewscreen zoomed out and tilted to display a top-down view of the red giant system. Large sections of the image were displayed in a washed-out gray. Three blinking dots, in the colorized area of the image actively blinked. Trae stepped in front of the viewscreen and pointed at the green and orange dots positioned near the lower half of the screen with his trusty laser pointer.

"The green dot is the *Betty* and the orange is this ship, the *Hans Landa.*" Trae motioned about with a widespread of hands, then turned the pointer back to the screen. "The probe that Fergus launched earlier is the blue dot. So far we have found that there is an extensive debris field at just over one hundred and five million klicks from the star's center. Roughly the distance from the Sun to Venus. We've also found a total of five planets with over twenty moons and a substantial debris field in this system's Oort cloud that is at least four times as dense as the one surrounding the Sol system."

Trae sidestepped to the tactical console, glancing at the readout he nodded to Fergus and continued. "Okay, so nothing really out of the ordinary. Well, nothing other than we are now in an alien star system. We also know that there is an alien transmission. After we backtrack the path of that signal, go ahead Fergus," Trae said with a nod. His laser pointer blazed to life again and pointed to a yellow line that zig-zagged it's way across the screen.

"We first sent the probe to check out the transmission, represented here by the yellow line. It looks to be a guidance signal that works its way through the asteroid field along a series of repeater probes, leading us back to this planet." Trae pointed at the small image of a rocky brown world displayed on the screen. "Along this path, we did manage to find small bits of wreckage and what may have once been a field mining station built into one of the larger asteroids. The interesting discovery thus far is this ..." Trae grinned at Fergus and nodded.

"With pleasure, my friend," Fergus said.

An image of the rocky brown world filled the screen.

"This is the second planet of the system," Trae continued. "Spectral analysis shows high concentrations of oxygen and nitrogen with traces of helium, argon, and carbon dioxide in the atmosphere. Assuming that these clouds," he pointed the laser at the screen again, "contain water and not some acidic or poisonous compound, we may have ourselves a safe harbor. That in itself is very good, considering Willy needs to get the *Betty* on the ground to replace a few of the main coolant lines. He decided to err on the side of safety and not risk killing everyone on board by venting all atmosphere from engineering while he makes the repairs. Next image," Trae said with a nod to Fergus.

The view screen suddenly zoomed in and refocused on a dull bronze-colored object. Symmetrically shaped, like the wide ends of two cones glued together by a green glowing seam.

"What in the hell is that," Doug asked, his jaw dropped in astonishment.

Trae snorted a laugh then smiled. "We don't have a fucking clue." He smiled wide. "But," he said, extending his index finger, "we have a theory about it. Now mind you, what you are seeing are just long-distance images from our probe."

Doug gawked at the strange object on the screen. "Can we get that thing into one of the cargo bays?"

"Yes, it should easily fit into the *Betty's* main bay, but there is a slight problem." Trae nodded to Fergus again.

The image suddenly zoomed out to redisplay an image of the planet, overlaid with a grid of golden dots that surrounded the planet.

"There's more than one," Doug said with a sigh.

"Precisely," Trae said. "We don't have an exact count yet, but there are possibly thousands of these things in orbit."

"Any idea what they are for?"

"Not yet. Earth is surrounded by its own cloud of satellites and junk. These could be for communication, weather, defense, or any number of other things. There's no way to tell for sure until we get hold of one and get a good look inside."

A warbled klaxon alarm roared to life. Trae sprinted to the helm station.

"What the hell is that?" Doug shouted over the alarm.

"We're being painted boys and girls," Fergus said.

"If I'm reading this right, we're being heavily scanned, Cap," Trae added.

"Hell, we're being more than scanned. Something is trying to get into our computer core," Fergus shouted.

A new alarm sounded and mingled with the klaxon, but with an offbeat timing.

"Bogey inbound," Fergus shouted.

"What the hell, from where? Get me a visual," Doug ordered.

"It's the satellite grid! They're powering up. Bogey impact in ten seconds," Fergus reported.

"It's a defensive grid," Doug mumbled to himself.

The bridge of the *Betty*
Red Giant system asteroid belt
May 23rd, 2176 / Late evening (Betty time)

"**P**ut it in your mouth and suck big boy," Rachel said. She leaned across the center console between the helm and operations stations. She stretched, reaching to place the compressed energy bar into Wes's mouth.

"Absolutely not." Wes leaned away and glared at Rachel.

"Come on, just a little lick," Rachel said. "Open up for *Mommy*, here comes the rocket ship."

"Oh, my, God." Wes gasped. "What the hell is wrong with you? Are you demented or something? Get away from me."

"But Wesley, be a good boy and take a great big bite. You want to grow big and strong, don't you?" Rachel waved the half-eaten snack bar toward Wes's tightly clenched mouth, tapping him on the side of the face.

"Stop," he mumbled through the corner of his mouth. He cringed at the smell of the pickled fish bar. "Oh my God, that's just disgusting." He visibly clenched with revulsion with the beginnings of a dry heave.

"Come on man," Rachel begged. "I swear you can taste a sweet honey flavor after you get past the pickled herring bit. I need a second opinion. How the hell am I supposed to write a proper review on these things if I don't collect all of the data I possibly can? Now open up," she said as she fumbled for the closest nipple.

"Help! Rape! Someone! Please! Someone get her off of me! I need an adult!"

"Hey now, seriously," Krista yelled from the open door of the Captain's quarters. She clapped her hands together as she emerged from the doorway, wrapped in a silk robe. "That's enough, both of you. Aren't you two supposed to be doing something or another? And where the hell is Doug? Shouldn't he be back by now?"

"I'm trying to work, but she keeps trying to force-feed me these freaking nasty ass pickled fish bars."

"Meat candy," she growled. "Get it right, Geek. *Meat candy.*"

"Blegh," Krista gagged. "Oh God, that's just …" she took a deep breath and dry heaved again. "I'm good, it's all good. Rainbows and butterflies, man. Rainbows and butterflies. Oh God, that's just nasty. What the hell is wrong with you, Rachel? Really, who would eat that sort of thing willingly?"

"See! What did I say?" Wes shouted at Rachel as he pointed to Krista.

"Now Rachel," Krista began to explain but gagged once again. "I'm alright. Now, a little fishy somethin' somethin' every now and then is all right, but not all the time, and especially not like that. That's just wrong on many many levels."

"Nope, it doesn't count. Taste it, Geek!" Rachel shoved the bar back into Wes's face.

"Children, enough!" Krista clapped her hands together and glared at the unruly pair. "You're going to sit your asses down and do your work or so help me God …"

"But it's…," Rachel looked away then back to Krista with a doe-eyed gaze. "It's only a honey herring bar."

"Blegh," Krista gagged.

Wes exploded with chortled curses.

"It ain't funny," Krista said. "Just the thought of that is freaking gross, man." Krista scraped her tongue across her teeth in an attempt to remove the imaginary taste. "Just get back to whatever Doug had you working on or whatever. It's late and I don't fucking care anymore. Just be quiet. I'm going back to bed." Krista shuffled back into the Captain's quarters, slamming the door closed behind her.

"How about trying an eel smoothie," Rachel shouted. "I think there's one left in the freezer."

"Blegh," Krista gagged from behind the Captain's door. "I can still hear you!"

Wes and Rachel quietly snickered at Krista's discomfort like a pair of mischievous imps. Rachel shoved the honey'd herring bar back into Wes's face.

"No!" Wes glared at her.

The bridge door slid open with a mechanical hum.

"Wesley, when are you coming to bed?" Kara pined, shuffling her way onto the bridge.

Wes sighed. "Not any time soon at the rate that I'm going," he said without taking his eyes off of Rachel. "Doug has me trying to figure out what that signal is for."

"But ... the bunk is so *cold and lonely* without my big teddy bear," Kara said in a soft, innocent tone. She appeared behind Wes and began to massage his shoulders. "Come on to bed my big bull mastiff, I'll make it worth your while." She leaned in close and nibbled at his ear lobe. Dainty fingers skittered across his chest, teasing with an ever so delicate touch.

"Hey, Kara would you ...," Rachel started.

"No," Wes interrupted. "She doesn't want to try it either. Go away, Cheezy."

"Okay ...," Kara's gaze darted between the two with confusion.

"Just ignore her and her imaginary friends, my dear," Wes said, taking Kara's hand and kissing it gently. "They are nothing but a bunch of ruffians and insane lunatics," he said in his best high society voice.

"Hey, I'm right here, and Bob doesn't care much for that comment," Rachel argued. "He says that it's offensive and he doesn't like you anymore."

Kara stepped around the chair and straddled Wes's lap. "So, you're *coming* to bed, right?" She lovingly massaged his face and scalp.

"Um ...," he hummed as he drifted into massaged bliss.

"Are you even listening to me, Wesley?" She pinched his ear lobes.

"Ouch, what the hell was that for?"

"Are you coming to bed or not?" Kara asked. "I'm ready for bed and you've been up here on the bridge all day long. I've been *lonely* all day." Kara snuggled herself closer and buried Wes's face into her cleavage.

"Oh my God. Get a room you two." Rachel tossed the half-eaten fish bar into Wes's face.

"Dammit, Cheezy! Do you mind? We're having a moment here and I happened to be enjoying that." Wes shot her a look of disdain before turning his attention back to Kara. "No, I can't come to bed yet," he said softly. "I have to figure this out and help Cheezy find us a place to set down."

"But *Wesley*," Kara whimpered.

"No, but Wesley," Wes said. "I have a job to do and if I don't do it, we could all wind up dead."

Kara huffed. "Fine, I guess I'll just have to *warm* up the sheets all by myself then." She thrust out her lower lip and dismounted. Her bare toes brushed against the control console as she swung her leg wide. Electronic beeps and blurbs rang out as her toes engaged the controls.

"Holy hell!" Wes pushed Kara aside and checked the console. "Dammit, Kara! You sent a reply message."

"I wonder why I even try sometimes!" Kara stormed off of the bridge in a furious huff.

"Hey, incoming signal. Data only," Rachel said with a surprised glance to Wes.

"What do we have here?" Wes mumbled with an intrigued tone. He brought up the signal on his console. A series of angular glyphs appeared on the screen. Below this were two selections in the same odd glyph-like language.

"It's asking you a question," Rachel guessed.

"I have no Earthly clue," Wes said. "It would help if I knew the language."

"Well, it kinda looks like one of those survey, thingies. Like, did you enjoy your stay, yes or no," Rachel said mockingly in her best infomercial voice.

"Possibly, but I have no idea," Wes said. "For all, we know it could be demanding our surrender or asking for parking fees." Wes tapped at the console. "Well, that's not good."

"What?"

"It won't let me cancel the message. It's like it has the comm system locked until I answer the message."

"So, then answer it, Duffus."

"Dammit, Cheezy," Wes said. "Don't you get it? It isn't that simple. We could all die if it happens to be the wrong answer to the wrong kind of question. We won't know which is the right answer to the right question until it's done, and it could be too late to save any of us from utter annihilation by that point." He sucked in a breath.

"So, then how would you go about clearing it?" Rachel asked. "You can't just close it and reopen it so you can access the comm systems again?"

"I'd have to shut down, and hard boot the entire operating system to be absolutely sure."

"So, then the answer is yes," Rachel said.

"No," Wes growled. "I'm not answering yes. I don't even know if that's what it actually says or not. I *can't* read it, Cheezy."

"Yeah, it does. See," Rachel said pointing at the first selection on his screen. "This is yes and this one is no. I don't care who you are, yes always comes before no."

"And exactly how the hell would you know? Met any nice aliens before?"

"No, but that's beside the point. If I'd have met aliens before now, I'd be a queen and you'd be on your knees, eating fish bars, and begging for more."

"Why do I even bother?" Wes mumbled to himself. "You're not right, you know that?"

Rachel's right hand slowly extended toward Wes's console. He quickly smacked the back of her hand. "Stop it."

"Stop what?" She reached for the console again. Her eyes locked onto him, unblinking.

"Stop that!" Wes shouted. "Stop before you get us all killed."

"Both of you stop it before I come back out there!" Krista yelled from the Captain's quarters.

"See what you did? You pissed *Mom* off," Rachel said, laughing.

"What? I did?" Wes shouted. "You're the one trying to kill everyone."

"No, I'm not," Rachel said. She reached for the console again, yanking her hand back just as Wes swatted at her with all of his might. His palm planted firmly on the face of the console. An electronic tone *bleeped* back at his touch. He moved his hand to see the suspected *yes* button flash, then disappear.

"Shit," he said with a panicked squeak. "See what you made me do?"

The console chimed with an odd warbling jingle as a new series of glyphs appeared on the screen along with the same selection buttons as before.

"See, I told you it's a survey," Rachel said proudly. "You'll have about four or five of them and then you'll have to give it a star rating or whatever symbol these guys use for ratings and surveys," she said then turned back to her console as if nothing odd or out of the ordinary had happened.

"It's not a survey!" Wes wiped a hand down his face in frustration.

"Yes, it is. See, watch this," Rachel excitedly said. From the depths of her flight suit, the neon pink double-headed phallus appeared once again and struck a mighty blow against the unsuspecting control console. With a flourish of her martial skills, she twirled her weapon of choice, grazing the tip across Wes's cheek, then the other and quickly returned the phallus to its previous hiding place.

Wes sat motionless. His left eye twitched spasmodically as a look of perplexed disgust varnished his face. "I'm not even exactly sure what the hell just happened." He let out a long sigh.

The console replied with a short sequence of electronic beeps followed by another series of glyphs.

"Dammit, Cheezy!" Wes shouted. "Why? Why do you always go on these psychotic trains of thought when our lives are possibly hanging in the balance?" He hovered over the control console to protect it from another strike. "Are you that *insane*? Or do you just not care if any of us live or die?"

Rachel rolled her eyes and sighed. "But, *Wesley*, I do care," she sobbed. "Why does everyone think that I'm crazy? I'm not crazy." A single tear rolled down her left cheek. "I just want to be loved, man. That's all. Nothing more, nothing less. Just love ..."

"Oh shit," Wes said apologetically. "I'm sorry, Cheezy, I didn't mean ..."

"Gotcha!" With a blinding dash of speed and skill, Rachel produced, struck and returned her weapon to its holster in the span of a heartbeat.

Wes flinched as she snatched for her arm and fell atop the console. An oddly loud *beep blerp* replied to his caress of the console. Warning alarms ignited across the bridge.

"What did you do Geek?" Rachel shouted over the alarms.

"Me? You're the one that's trying to kill all of us," Wes shouted. He turned down the volume on the alarms. "We're being targeted. Munition Inbound. Contact in five."

"I swear to all of the Gods that I am going to feed you both laxatives until you crap yourselves to death!" Krista shouted from the now open door of the Captain's quarters.

"Hi, Mom! Wes did it! It wasn't anything to do with me." Rachel flashed a quick smile back at Krista.

"Four," he shouted. "And no, I didn't!" He turned in his seat and looked to Krista. "We have a missile or something locked on and heading right for us."

"Oh shit." Krista ran for the Captain's seat like her ass was on fire. She strapped into the five-point harness and pressed the ship's intercom button. "Everyone listen up! You have two seconds to bend over and kiss your asses goodbye. Tweedle Dee and Tweedle Dumb up here are getting us shot at!"

"Three."

Rachel slammed the throttle forward and pulled the control yoke to her chest. "I am Tweedle Dee," she crooned. The ship rolled to the right as the nose pitched upward. The positive g-force pushed them all into their seats.

"Firing countermeasures!" Wes furiously tapped at the controls. "Two!"

The ship nosed over into negative G's and side slipped to the left as her massiveness gently rolled to the right. Rachael cut the throttle and pulled the yoke back hard. She quickly keyed the comms. "Willy, I need full burn now!" She released the yoke, slid the harness straps over her shoulders then slammed the throttle forward and smacked the big red button that was mounted to the side of the throttle quadrant.

Wes turned to Rachel with a look of horrific shock. "What the hell, nothing happened. One …"

"Willy! I need full burn now!" Rachel pounded her fist down onto the big red button.

"That's it! Been nice knowing y'all," Krista said as she curled into a seated fetal position, her eyes squeezed closed in anticipation.

A heavy metallic thud impacted the lower hull and resonated throughout the ship as the alarms went silent.

The intercom chimed to life. *"What have you run into this time, Rachel. I'm going to put you in a suit and make you fix the damage,"* Willy said.

"Oh my God! We're alive!" Wes jumped from his seat and did an odd truffle shuffle happy dance.

"Not exactly by the numbers, but we survived. Looks like the thing was a dud," Rachel said.

"Doug had better damn well not leave you two alone again," Krista said. "You two cause nothing but trouble. Now, are we *done*? Can we *please* be done, now? Cause if you're *done*, then I'm taking my ass back to bed."

Wes snapped his fingers. "Numbers! That's it!" He stared off into the space of deep thought. "Those glyphs were numbers!" He leapt back into his seat and began tapping away at the console. "If I have the computer do a comparison on those series of glyphs, assuming that they are numbers and the alien race that created those satellites used a base-ten numbering sequence then …" He watched the screen as the known glyphs ran through a sequence of number matching. "If we get at least two out of ten numbers to lock into place then we just need to send a message again in order to gather more data and decrypt at least the numbers in their language." He excitedly squirmed in his seat like a child waiting for a bowl of ice cream.

The ships comms chimed to life. *"Hey Wes,"* Doug yelled. *"What the hell just happened? Is everyone alright over there?"*

"Come on baby, come to daddy." Wes crossed his fingers as he watched the numbers cycle across the screen.

Rachel keyed the comms, "The Geek may be about to have a geekgasm. I don't think there's any blood left in his brain at the moment."

"No, I am not. I think I figured out what went wrong after Rachel almost killed us all. We accidentally started what I think is a security passcode."

The console beeped as two numbers locked into place with the existing glyphs. "Hell yeah!" Wes shouted with a fist pump to the air. "That's two, just one more and I'll be able to figure this out."

"And all of that means just what exactly?" The frustration in Doug's voice was heavy and thick.

"If I'm right, when this algorithm finishes, we'll know the numerals for this alien language. Then I send another signal to the satellite grid and run the additional glyphs that come up in the data message. Once I have an idea of what we're dealing with, then I might be able to figure out how to bypass the defense system."

"Cheezy, do you think you can outrun one of those missiles if they launch again?"

"As long as Willy is ready for a burn, then yeah. Shouldn't be a problem."

"Okay then," Doug continued. *"I'll get Trae to park us behind one of these big rocks. You do the same with the Betty, just in case. We can transmit our comms through the probe that Fergus launched."*

"Gotcha, Cap. Will do," Rachel said.

"Three, four, woot! We just got four numbers!" Wes did his seated happy dance.

Rachel backhanded Wes across the shoulder. "Hey, did you catch any of that, Wes?"

"Yup, and it looks like we have four of their numbers to work with." Wes brought up multiple software windows on his screens and tapped the comms. "I'm tied into the probe Cap. Tell me when you're ready and I'll send the signal."

"The *Betty* is in position," Rachel said.

"Same here," Trae came over the comms. *"Secured for station keeping."*

"Send the signal, Wes," Doug ordered.

Wes tapped the controls. "Copy that, Cap. Signal sent."

"Incoming data stream," Rachel announced.

Wes worked his electronic wizardry and accessed the signal. Four new glyphs appeared on the screen with the same selections below as before. "We're in, running decryption software, now." Wes tapped at the console. The known glyphs appeared on the main viewscreen, aligned with four of the numbers on a number line. Below this, the new glyphs appeared with numbers cycling through the sequence beside them. Slowly, the numbers locked into place, filling in the empty fields. "One, seven, six and four. Woo! Now we have an idea of what we're looking at."

"*Okay, Geek, but what does it mean?*" Doug asked over the comms.

"I have no Earthly idea," Wes said. "But I started another piece of software to see what the numbers may relate to. It might take a little while to process, but the more data we have the quicker it'll be."

"So hit the button Geek," Rachel said.

"What? No. Do you really want to get shot at again?"

"You have a fifty-fifty shot at being right. Considering everything else against us, those are pretty damned good odds."

"*Just hit the button Geek,*" Doug said. "*Considering there aren't any signs of patrol ships, and the fact that the last shot was a dud, I think it's safe to say no one's home and haven't been for a while. Hit the damn button, Geek.*"

Rachel giggled. "Ooo … Ooo, I wanna do it." She reached across the console to Wes's touchscreen. Her finger hovered just above the screen as she pointed back and forth at the two selections. "Eeny, meeny, miny, moe," she sang as she pointed.

Wes swatted at her finger. "Are you seriously making a decision like this based on a grade school rhyme?"

"Yup." She smiled wide and jabbed her finger at the first selection. "Mo!"

The console beeped and the display changed to a new series of glyphs.

"I'll be damned," Wes gasped. "You didn't kill us." He eagerly shuffled the data from the new selections to his decryption software screen.

Rachel poked at the same button again and the console beeped.

Wes smacked her hand away. "Oh God, we're gonna die."

"Will you two pull it together," Doug ordered. *"What's going on over there?"*

The screen flashed with a message written in the strange alien text that scrolled vertically down the screen. Abruptly the screen changed to a rendering of the asteroid field with a list of coordinate points to one side.

"I think we've been allowed safe passage, Cap," Wes said. "This looks like flight path guidance to something planet-side." He studied the data with fascination.

Rachel craned her neck to look at his screens. "What the hell do you mean flight path? Let me see, Geek."

"If you would wait just two seconds, I'll send it over to your console." He tapped at the controls.

"God, *Geek*, come on already." Rachel rolled her eyes, slouching in her seat.

"There," Wes said. "Are you happy now?"

"Yes, now shut up." Rachel stuck her tongue out at him. "Hey, Cap. Somehow the Geek's right. This looks like flight path guidance. It lands us in the northern hemisphere of the second planet. I can't make out anything except the numbers yet, but that's what it all looks like to me."

"Set a course and stick to the flight path," Doug said. *"That defense system could power up again if we deviate from the course. Let's get these birds on the ground, do a few repairs and get our bearings before we do anything else."*

cHAPTER 11

Unknown Red Giant star system
2nd planet, Northern Hemisphere
May 25th, 2176 / Midday (Betty time)

Doug sat silently against the seat of his rat-rod like hoverbike. He leaned over, reaching for something deep within the starboard saddlebag. The bike's landing gear foot sank awkwardly into the loose sand. He retrieved a datapad, then shifted his weight to where it was before, relaxing against the bike once again. The red giant loomed low in the sky, partially hidden behind the remains of the ancient, but dead metropolis that surrounded him. Low in the sky before him, three large moons hung brightly in what he guessed was the evening sky. Long shadows stretched across an expansive canyon that lay before him.

"There has to be something good out of all of this," he sighed. He scrolled through a list of ships supplies on the datapad.

Three months worth of freeze-dried rations, one month of perishables and just over ten thousand liters of freshwater in reserve, he thought. *We shouldn't have a problem with water rations as long as the recyclers don't break down again. Four months of supplies can be rationed to five or six if we really try to stretch it out.*

He tucked his head inside of the vintage looking vest that he wore to light a cigarette. Ragged strings of the roughly cut vest fluttered in the dry breeze. Small holes and thread-bare spots peeked out between a myriad of pins and patches that covered the gray corduroy garment. The sharp grating crackle of the flip lighter disturbed the serene silence as he struck the flint over and over again.

"Fucking, *hell*!" The datapad soared out of sight over the canyon's edge. "Can't I get a break!?"

He took a deep breath, then tucked his head once more. A small, blue flame flickered to life within the lighter's chimney. Quickly he took a long drag from his cigarette. He took in the scenery that surrounded him. The ancient monoliths of a long-dead society stood tall and proud against the ravages of time and the elements. Across the dry, abysmal canyon lay more of the same structures that surrounded him here. The strangely shaped skyscrapers jutted from enormous sand dunes along the wide canyon, stark white against the dark brown dunes of fine sand. The structures resembled the tall slender stalk of asparagus with their bulbous tops stretched high above the ground.

This must have been a sight to see in ancient times, Doug thought. *I bet it looked something like those old pictures of New York city from before the Hell years. Three moons over the bay with the city lights reflecting in the water.* He stood and shielded his eyes from the glare of the red star. The structures of the opposite shore had silently defied the eons, but they fought a losing battle. Foundations of those closest to the edge had crumbled in places. A number of the ancient alien skyscrapers had fallen victim to gravity, collapsing into the precipice. The scars of time showed on the surface of all of the surviving structures. Sections had crumbled away in spots while the remaining walls had been scoured smooth by sand and wind.

No telling how long any of this has been here, Doug thought. *There might even be some decent salvage left lying around or buried in these ruins. Things in the deserts and pyramids back on Earth were preserved for a few thousand years.* "Makes sense to me that the same would hold true for this desert." He grunted a laugh then took another long drag from his cigarette. The smoke rolled slowly from his mouth into his nose. *The first order of business is food and water. There's no telling if or when we can get back to Earth. We might be stuck here permanently. Not a sign of life anywhere, yet. Wouldn't that be something? An entire star system to ourselves. How the hell do you put a claim on an entire star system?*

The radio on the bike crackled to life. *"Hey Doug,"* Krista said. Concern laced her voice.

He turned and hit the radio switch on the bike's dash. "Go ahead."

"The kids think they've got something figured out and need you to take a look. Will you be coming home soon?"

Home, He thought. He took another slow drag and let the thought linger. *I guess that rusted bucket of bolts is the closest thing any of us have ever had to a real home.* He hit the switch again. "Yeah. I'll be there in a bit. I'm about twenty klicks South of you."

"Okay, I'll let them know."

"Hey," Rachel interrupted. *"Ask him if he's going to take that windscreen off and ride that bike like a real man or not."*

"Will you shut up and get back to whatever the hell it is that you're supposed to be doing," Krista said.

"Tell her not to worry about it unless she's going to ride with me. I'll be back shortly, packing up now," Doug responded.

"Copy that," Krista's tone was resigned.

He lit another cigarette from the smoldering stub of the previous one, then strapped on his helmet. The pulse drive rumbled to life with the push of a button and the bike immediately hovered inches above the ground. Doug mounted the bike and rolled the throttle. His metal steed leapt forward an instant later. A rooster tail of sand blossomed and rose high into the air behind the bike as he cruised through the dead streets of the alien city.

cHAPTER 12

Unknown Red Giant system
2nd planet, Northern Hemisphere
The Betty / Nova Star class mining transport / Machine shop
May 25th, 2176 / Midday (Betty time)

"Okay, I've got a good one for you. Do you know what the meaning of relative humidity is?" Fergus asked with a stifled snort.

"Really?" Trae laughed. "I need to get this pulse relay rebuilt and you want to tell bad jokes?" He pressed a button on the hoist control, lowering the rigging hook. "Hey, reach over there on the wall and grab me the inch and a half wrench while you're doing nothing."

"That one?" Fergus pointed at a series of wrenches hanging on the back wall of the workshop.

"No, the one on the other side of the toolbox," Trae said, pointing to the port side wall of the compartment. "It has an odd bend at the end of it. The thing is perfect for getting to those lower actuator bolts on these things. Alright, relative humidity. Knowing you, it has nothing to do with the pressure or temperature of water vapor."

Fergus chuckled as he grabbed the wrench and handed it to Trae. He climbed onto a stool near the worktable and opened a package of crackers. "How did you ever guess that?"

"Hey Willy, can you pull those chains around and hook them in?" Trae asked.

"No problem," Willy said, reaching for the chains above his head. "Bring it on down." Willy hooked the thick shackle over the hook.

"Awesome. Thanks, Willy." The hoist clicked and hummed to life once again. Chains clanked as they tightened, and the relay slowly rose from the dolly. "Alright, be careful, but give it a little push this way, please."

Willy set his shoulder into the side of the massive gauss relay and shoved it slowly toward the worktable.

"Ok, Fergus. So, what is your definition of relative humidity?" Trae grabbed one of the chains secured around the relay and guided the dangling mass so that it hung squarely over the table. "That's good Willy. Hold up right there."

"It's the bead of sweat that rolls down your sister's back when you're banging her doggy style," Fergus said, then chuckled.

Trae lowered his gaze, shaking his head in shame. "See, that's exactly the sort of thing that I expected from you."

"Yup, you love me. I know it." Fergus laughed and offered Trae a cracker from the sleeve.

"No, thank you." Trae lowered the relay onto the worktable and removed the chains.

Willy pulled up a stool next to Fergus and took a handful of crackers. The pair quietly munched, or as quietly as one can munch, on the dry crumbly wafers.

"Okay. Give me one sec, I've got one for you," Trae said. He removed the last chain from the relay and set the hoist to lift the mass out of the way. "Hey, Willy. Can you hand me that impact wrench behind you?" He pointed in the general direction of the workbench behind Willy.

"Sure, no problem man." Willy shifted on the stool to reach the workbench behind him. "Here ya go," he said, handing Trae the tool.

"Alright, here we go," Trae sighed. "Three Georgia Tech engineering students were gathered together in a heated discussion of who must have designed the human body. The first one said, "It was a mechanical engineer. Just look at all the joints." Another, an electrical engineering major said, "No, it was an electrical engineer. The nervous system has many thousands of electrical connections." The last one said, "No, actually it had to have been a civil engineer." The other two engineering students looked at him, perplexed. "Who else would run a toxic waste pipeline through a recreational area?"

Big Willy chuckled, coughing on a mouth full of crackers.

"Are you kidding me," Fergus huffed. "That one is as old as dirt. I've got one that'll make you piss your pants."

The impact wrench whirred to life as Trae removed four bolts from the side of the relay. "Whew, that stinks," he coughed, waving a hand at the air-driven tool. "Might be a good idea to purge the compressed air system, Willy. It smells nasty. Stale and moldy like." Trae threw a rag at Fergus. "Alright then. Let's hear it, Mr. Comedian. What else you got?"

"Alright, here we go. You ready?"

"Spit it out already, will ya," Willy said.

"Alright. What does the sign on an out-of-business brothel say?"

"No clue." Trae shook his head as he continued to disassemble the relay.

"I've got nothing," Willy said.

"Beat it. We're closed," Fergus delivered.

Trae let out with a light chuckle. "That was absolutely horrible. Horribly true, but horrible none the less."

"Well wait, I've got more," Fergus said. "What's the difference between a tire and 365 used condoms?" He looked from Trae to Willy, then continued. "One's a Goodyear. The other's a great year."

Willy laughed and choked on the cracker he'd just bitten into.

Andy descended the ladder at the aft end of the workshop. "What's so funny?"

Fergus grinned wide as he glanced to Willy, then to Trae. "Hey Andy, can ya lick it?"

"Lick what?" Andy's face twisted with uncertainty.

"Ignore him, Andy." Trae waved, "Trust me, it isn't worth hearing again."

Andy stared at the trio for a moment, then shrugged. "Okay. Have any of you seen a half-inch brass pipe coupler? It's the one with the triangle stamped on the side of it. I had it set aside so I could finish this thing for Mel and now I can't find it."

"There's a whole stack of couplers in the drawer over there," Fergus said through spurts of cracker crumbs.

"No, I need the one that I sat on the workbench," Andy argued. "Did any of you use it for something? Did it get tossed back into the drawer?"

The three men simultaneously shook their heads with a unanimous, "nope."

Andy rummaged around on the work counter, searching the small metal hardware drawers that lined the bulkhead at the back of the workspace.

"If anything disappears around here, Cheezy is usually the one to blame," Willy said. "I have my big wrench under lock and key now because of her. What is the world coming to when a man can't leave his tools out on the workbench?"

Fergus chuckled then munched another cracker. "I must just be lucky then. As much as she likes to play with my dick, she still hasn't made off with it yet. Guess that's one bonus to being hung like a church mouse." Cracker crumbs flew from his mouth as he laughed.

Trae dropped the impact wrench onto the worktable and caught himself on its surface. His knees buckled as he exploded with laughter. "Really Fergus? I'm trying to work here man. I do not want, nor do I need that sort of *visual*," he stressed.

The deep bass rumble of a pulse drive resonated from the deck below.

"Oh shit, the boss is back." Andy quickly closed the parts drawer that he was searching through, then scurried away through the aft hatch of the compartment.

"I guess he was supposed to be working on something else," Trae said. He shrugged, then picking up the impact gun returned his attention to the relay.

"Yeah," Willy laughed. "Cap put him to work purging the reclamation system before he went out scouting."

The low rumble of the Captain's hoverbike ceased, followed by the sound of boots on ladder rungs. Doug's head appeared from the lower deck hatch. "Come on you apes. I need everyone together in the rec room."

"Oh sweet, movie night," Fergus cheered.

"Not quite Ferg," Doug said. "Though I wouldn't mind kicking back for a few and becoming a vegetable." Exhaustion and worry showed on his dusty face. He rubbed a hand over his face and shook the dust from his hair. "Willy, get on the horn and call everyone upstairs," he ordered, then continued up the ladder.

"Can't, Cap," Willy said hesitantly.

Doug stopped and hung from the ladder. "Why the hell not?" He glared from Willy to Fergus, then to Trae.

Trae cleared his throat as the trio passed looks to one another. "Wes is rebuilding the master control panel."

"What? Why is it broke? It was fine when I left."

"Something about manually bypassing the lockouts on the intercom," Fergus said between bits of cracker.

"Seriously?" Air whistled through Doug's sand caked nostrils as he banged his head against a ladder rung. "Run and gather everyone to the rec room." His grip on the ladder suddenly weakened, he slipped but caught himself before he could fall.

Willy leapt forward. "You okay, Cap?"

"Yeah, just felt a little dizzy for a second there. Maybe a little too much sun."

"Yeah," Willy mumbled, glancing at Trae. "Might just be too much sun."

"Get everyone together, I'll be there in a bit," he ordered then disappeared up the ladder.

"Aye Cap," The trio replied in unison.

cHAPTER 13

Unknown Red Giant system
2nd planet, Northern Hemisphere
The *Betty* / Nova Star class mining transport / Recreation room
May 25th, 2176 / Afternoon (*Betty* time)

Alright, so where in the hell is Doug?" Krista perched herself on the edge of the pool table of the rec room. "I've got important shit to be doing.

A large screen that displayed a first-person view through crosshairs dominated the aft wall of the compartment. A home-built weight bench sat on the starboard side of the compartment, while oddly random couches and chairs dominated the port side of the compartment, near to the door that led into the mess hall.

"Who cares man, I'm kicking some serious ass on this game." Tiff crouched low; her head leaned oddly to the side from the weight of the virtual reality helmet. "Ha! This is so freaking easy man. That's right y'all, PeAcHyCrEeCh is in the house!" The game monitors on the wall displayed a zoomed-in view of a uniformed soldier, rifle crosshairs centered between his eyes. "*Just the tip,*" Tiff whispered to no one in particular. The enemy figure's head suddenly exploded in an exaggerated spray of blood and gore.

"Rrrg," Trae grunted through a heavy exhalation. Veins bulged across his arms and face as he pushed the bowed bar of weights upward.

"Come on you, *wussy!*" Rachel shouted as she hovered above Trae, spotting him as he lifted. "Push the damn bar already! You're killing me, man. My grandma has bigger balls than you!"

"She ain't lying either," Fergus said as he jabbed the cue stick forward. Balls clacked and scattered across the table. "The old broad showed me this one time. Like down to her knees and shit."

"Ahhhhh!" The bar shivered in Trae's grip but slowly it ascended. He dropped the heavy bar into the rack with a heavy clunk.

"About damned time, *wussy*." Rachel flung herself down onto a nearby recliner and kicked the footrest out.

"Dear fucking god, man." Trae sat up and laughed into his hands. "Visuals man. Oh my God, we've had this very discussion before. Visuals I do not need, especially when I'm lifting. What ..." He turned on the bench, "Four, eight, twelve forty-five-pound weights plus all the other shit Cheezy tossed on there."

"Ah, sure you do," Willy added as he took his shot at the table. "That way you know what you have to look forward to, later in life." Willy and Fergus chuckled.

"Hey! Y'all spaz down," Krista shouted.

"Oy! Maybe all of you bloody bogans should calm down," Lizz said, directing her words toward Krista as she strode into the room.

"Hey now, that's not very nice," Krista pouted.

"You'll get over it, honey," Lizz said. "Now where is Doug?"

"I'm right here," Doug said as he entered the room from the engineering access on the aft wall. He waved a long metallic probe about, that was tethered to a device slung across his shoulder.

Fergus set his pool stick down on the table. "What's with the rad detector, Boss?"

"We have a slight problem," Doug said as he examined the detector display. "It looks like we're alright inside the ships. The hulls are built well enough to keep the radiation out, but if you go outside in the open for prolonged periods, you're going to get a light dose of radiation."

"Bloody hell," Lizz said as she took a seat on the home built sectional sofa.

Maggie gasped.

"It can't be lethal if the alarms aren't going off," Trae added.

Krista slid from the edge of the pool table and took a step backward. "Wait, what the hell are you doing in here if you're radioactive?"

"Don't worry," Doug said. "I hit the decon chamber and took a dose of Radiodine and a RemyRad. I'll be queasy for a bit, but otherwise fine."

"Okay, so we're stuck in here," Andy said. "No foraging I suppose?"

The room erupted in panicked questions and speculation.

"Shut it you bunch of bloody bogans!" Lizz glared at the crew. "Let Doug finish."

Doug sighed. "This is just one more nail in the coffin."

Amanda began to sob. Maggie pulled her close and cradled her to her chest.

Doug took a deep breath and continued. "I know that we can overcome all of this. Now, this does assume a lot. But if the ship's systems hold up, then yes, we'll be safe inside. We could stretch out our supplies for about six months by my figuring. And as long as the recyclers are functioning, water won't even be an issue."

He paused in thought, "If we haven't figured out that new drive system on the other ship by the six-month mark then we'll either need to forage or grow what we need."

Everyone went silent. The low pulsing hum of the main reactor in the next compartment overwhelmed the uncomfortable silence.

"Andy," Doug barked. "Did you finish maintenance on the recyclers?"

"Um … Well, you see."

"Oh, what the hell, Andy?" Mel slapped the back of his head. "We're all about to die and you get sidetracked again?"

"Melanie!" Doug glared at her. "It's okay. We'll get it done, but we need options. Like Trae said, if the radiation was lethal the alarms would have sounded on both ships by now. Long term I'm sure it would be lethal, but for the short term, it's an annoyance to deal with. It doesn't feel much worse than being stuck on a rock in the Belt during a solar flare."

"I could calibrate the sensors on both ships," Wes said. "It might give us a better idea of the amount of exposure."

"Okay, good. What about the ship and its systems, Willy?"

"I'd say at this point, it's best to leave well enough alone. Swap out filters and such, but otherwise, I wouldn't do anything. If we start messing around with some of these old systems, they're liable to break on us."

"Fair enough," Doug said. "Get with Lizz for any inventory items you need. See what you can do to make the filters last a bit longer too. No modifications or repairs to anything without going through me first. Got it, Andy?" Doug questioned.

"Yeah, whatever you want," he mumbled as he picked at a fingernail.

"We might could use the suits for any outdoor activities," Fergus suggested. "They work well enough on spacewalks."

Trae stepped forward and propped a foot on the wooden cable spool that the crew used as a coffee table. "It might not even be an issue with anything but exposure to the sunlight. Until we can do a little research, we won't know exactly how much of that red giant's radiation is getting through the atmosphere. If the air isn't irradiated, we might get away with just covering up and de-coning our clothes."

"Good thought," Doug said. "You and Ferg can work on that and see what you can come up with. Mel, I want you to cut rations and see what you can do to stretch everything out as far as you possibly can."

"Um, hello," Mel waved her hand in the air. "Does that also include the Martians locked up in the other ship?"

"Shit," Doug huffed. "I totally spaced on those guys."

"I'd say float their asses out an airlock if we get to live that much longer," Kara said, interrupting.

Wes pushed Kara off of his lap. "Kara," he said, shocked. "What the hell? Really? You'd float them?"

"Yes, *really*," Kara said. "Why should we waste our precious resources on them? They are just *Martians*, after all. They'd do the same to us without a second thought."

Doug glared at Kara. "No one is to lay a finger on them. I'm the Captain. It's my call. Got it!" Doug looked about the room to each of them, daring anyone to say otherwise. He continued, "Tiff, help Wes to calibrate the sensor systems and start gathering data on this place. Rachel, I want to know where we are. If we need to get back into orbit, we can plan a launch later. Do what you can for now from here and see if you can get me a fix on our position." Doug caught himself on the back of the sofa as his knees buckled. He straightened, then continued. "Witches, we are going to need more Remeys or whatever you can come up with to flush the contamination from our systems. Also, dig into your supplies and see what supplements you can come up with, so we won't become vitamin deficient. Then I want any vegetable seeds you might have stashed away turned into Lizz for inventory."

"We have some basic seeds, I'm pretty sure," Krista added.

Doug nodded to Krista then adjusted his weight and leaned on the back of the sofa. "I found what looked like a set of hangar doors sticking out of the sand on the northside of this spaceport. I need to get back out there and check it out as soon as I possibly can. If it is a hangar, we could get ourselves underground and out of direct harm for a while." He leaned forward over the sofa as his knees gave way again.

"The hell you do," Krista and Lizz shouted at the Captain in unison as they ran forward. Each one put a shoulder under an arm and held him upright.

"I don't give a shit what you *think,* you're going to be doing," Krista said. "I'm here to tell you right now that your ass is going to bed. That's what you're gonna do," Krista ordered.

"I'll get your med kit," Maggie squeaked as she ran out of the room.

"All of you get to work," Lizz ordered. "I'm in command until Doug recovers. Trae, Fergus, check out that possible hanger after you two figure out where the radiation is coming from. And take Andy with you. If he isn't here tinkering, then he can't break anything."

cHAPTER 14

Unknown Red Giant System
2nd planet, Northern Hemisphere
May 26th, 2176 / Early Morning (Betty time)

Andy cleared his throat to break the awkward silence. "Ya know the Brits back in the day really knew how to build a beast of a vehicle," he said, his voice muffled and tinny through the suit speaker.

He bounced and rocked with the movement of the pieced together transport as the trio raced north across the sand-strewn surface of the starport.

"I mean, look at this cross-bracing on the roof frame. This thing could probably land on its top and not even get a dent."

"Really, Andy?" Fergus shouted. "Are you kidding me? If we could have found an old deuce and a half in decent enough shape to convert, we would have," Fergus said. "Those things were *beasts*. I'd bet we could jump that thing at least three hundred yards in lunar gravity with a good run-up."

"Hey, Andy," Trae broke in. "That's like saying that Lamborghini, Ferrari or Porsche knew how to build a good family vehicle back in the day. There are reasons that companies like those didn't survive the Hell Years. They didn't know how to do but one thing and one thing only."

"Unlike us," Fergus added with a chuckle.

"Exactly," Trae said.

"We took this busted ass hulk and turned it into something usable," Fergus continued. "She was dinged, missing the powertrain and the rear wall. Trae here somehow managed to scrounge parts from six other heaps to build her," he said, thumbing toward Trae

"Yup, that we did. The power plant and rear hull I picked up from a class three mining shuttle. Tranny and axles were out of an old Mark V lunar transport tug. Solid wheel assemblies from an old excavator that we found abandoned south of Atlanta."

Fergus chuckled. "We even stripped out a busted-ass C-130 for the wiring harnesses and the seats. Sensor and communications package from an abandoned," he said using air quotes, "Russian communications satellite. Thrusters from an old Chinese launch capsule. Um...The gyro from an old World War 2 sub," he said as he tapped at the gyro display mounted in the center of the dashboard. "Oh, and the best part. We've got the hood ornament from a 1934 Rolls-Royce Phantom II that we came across on a cargo run to Switzerland."

"Oh God, that was a sad moment," Trae said. "The hood ornament…"

"Yup, the hood ornament," Fergus said with a sigh.

"Why's that?" Andy asked, leaning forward between the front seats.

Trae and Fergus looked to each other then both laughed.

"Ya see, we were sent to this old warehouse for this particular delivery. The place was a disaster," Fergus said.

"Oh God, yeah," Trae said. "I'm surprised the two walls that were still standing didn't collapse on top of us."

"The warehouse," Fergus took his hands off the steering wheel momentarily and air quoted," had partially collapsed. Apparently, it had taken a few hits from artillery fire from during the Great War that started the Hell Years way back when. Well, we were there waiting for hours. So, when we got a little bored, we started to look around for any good scrounge. You can't turn down good usable scrounge that might come in handy somewhere, ya know. Well, the back section of the joint had taken most of the damage. Looked like a few mortar rounds had gotten to close or a few small bombs. The craters that were still there weren't all that big. Someone at some point in the past had gone through and added supports to sections and tried to salvage part of the structure, but the main roof beams had collapsed. And wouldn't you know it, one of those roof beams had landed a little off-kilter but more or less longways on top of this classic Rolls-Royce Phantom."

"The hood ornament was the only thing worth salvaging from the mess," Trae said. "And that was the moment that we decided to name this heap, *Lazarus*."

"What were you hauling to Switzerland?" Andy asked. "I thought those borders were completely locked down decades ago?"

Trae coughed. "Don't ask."

"Nope, don't." Fergus snickered. "We'd have to kill you if you knew."

"Um … *Okay*," Andy said nervously.

"We need some music," Trae demanded.

"Yes, we do, my brother from another mother," Fergus said. He leaned forward and tapped at one of six touchscreens mounted to the dash.

"Unbroken!" Heavily distorted harmonics shook the cabin from the hodgepodge myriad of speakers mounted throughout *Lazarus* interior.

"Hey, you got anything in there like Metallica or Kiss?" Andy asked.

Trae turned in his seat and awkwardly reached into the back seat, fumbling for Andy. "Stop the fucking truck!"

"Okay," Fergus giggled. *Lazarus* slid to a bumpy stop in the dusty sand.

"Get out," Trae demanded.

"Better do what he says," Fergus calmly said.

"Get the fuck out now!"

"What? Why?" Andy leaned to his right and out of Trae's reach.

"Because those two are some of the most overrated corporate sellouts from back in the day, Trae said. "I wish to God that the Gutenberg project hadn't saved those files. They lost sight of the passion and the soul of the music." Flecks of foamy spittle clung to the inside of his helmet. "To them, it was all about the all mighty dollar, not the music! For Christ's sake, Andy, Kiss turned to disco!"

"Let it go, brother," Fergus said calmly. "Breath, man. Just let it go. Cap won't be too happy if we leave Andy out here. It's all good. Lean back, take a deep breath and just soak in the rifts, man."

Fergus turned the volume dial to eleven, which was marked on the dash console in bold, dark marker. "Yeah, baby!" He pumped his fist in the air then swung and missed Trae's shoulder. "That's what I'm talking about!"

Fergus slammed the pedal to the floor. *Lazarus* slid sideways once again as a fountain of dust erupted in an expansive cloud behind the rover.

The rover lurched forward, sliding to an abrupt stop. "Oh hey," Fergus said. "I think we're here."

"I'd say so," Trae said. "That sure looks like a set of hangar doors to me."

"Are you sure?" Andy leaned forward between the two front seats. "Just looks like some rock sticking out of the sand to me."

"Look at those dark spots peeking out from behind that sand dune," Fergus said, pointing.

"Yeah?" Andy leaned further forward to get a better view. "It just looks like a rock to me."

"Well it looks like a corroded blast door to me," Fergus said. "Like that time, we were doing that job in Sarajevo and we got lost in the desert."

"Exactly," Trae added. "Man, that was an interesting trip."

"Well, maybe not as good as the trip to Thailand," Fergus said.

"Are you kidding?" Trae chuckled. "Oh man, Thailand. That's been well more than a minute ago. That harem we rescued in Sarajevo didn't hold a candle to the girls at Mother May I's."

"Nope," Fergus sighed. "Contortionist college girls, what's not to love?"

"What happened in Sarajevo and Thailand?"

"Don't worry about it," Fergus demanded.

"We wouldn't want to have to kill you," Trae finished.

"Good times man, good times," Trae said.

"Yup!" Fergus chuckled. "Welp, let's go ladies. Times a wasting." He flung open the driver's door and slid to the ground. "Holy fucking shit! There's something in the sand!" Fergus let out a blood-curdling scream.

Trae stared at the open door as Fergus clawed and grasped for something to hold onto. He turned to Andy. "Get out!"

"Oh my God, it's got my leg!" Fergus shouted.

"What? No," Andy said. "Why should I get out? You're the one that's attached to his hip."

"AH! Ah! Ah! Why me? I'm too young to die," Fergus said sobbing.

"Get out of the fucking truck!" Trae drew his sidearm and charged the bolt.

"Hell *no*! I'm not going to get eaten by some Venetian sandworm."

"No, no, no! It's crawling up my pants leg! Oh my God it's in my pants leg!"

Trae pointed the gun at the open door, fired, then aimed the pistol at Andy's crotch. "Get … out … of … the … truck," he growled in a low tone.

"Oh shit. Okay, okay, I'm going," Andy said as he leapt from the transport and unceremoniously tumbled headfirst into the sand.

Trae pushed open his door and stood, leaning out of the cab. "Quit laying there trying to get a suntan. Won't do you no good, no how. Now get over there and check on Ferg." Trae aimed the pistol at Andy.

Fergus screamed.

"I'm going, I'm going, geez man!" Andy scrambled across the deep dusty sand and jogged around the front of the transport to the driver's side. "He's not here."

"Bullshit, he has to be there."

"I'm telling you, he ain't here," Andy said.

Trae reached across the cab through the driver's door and grabbed the door handle. "Did you look under the truck?"

Andy leapt back, out of the way as Trae slammed the driver's door closed. "Oh crap. Um...Trae. I … I … I think I found his head."

"Where? What do you see?"

"His helmet is up under the truck, half-buried in the sand. Do you think his head is still in it?"

"Dammit," Trae grunted. "The hell if I know. Is the suit still there?"

"Um …," Andy glanced around the area. "No, I just see the helmet."

"Dammit to all the hells, Fergus!" Trae shouted. "You had to go and make even more work for me. Now I have to figure out how to make a new suit."

"Um … okay," Andy said. "But what about Fergus?"

"He's probably worm food by now," Trae said. "Better to just forget and move on. Grab the helmet and get back in here."

Andy crouched, slowly. The helmet lay silent in the shadow of the massive transport. Grains of sand tapped at the side of his own helmet as the wind picked up.

"Hurry the hell up, Andy. We need to check out this place and report back to the Cap."

"What if his head is still in the thing?"

Trae let out an exasperated sigh. "Then dump it out. How hard is that to figure out? My God man, it's just a freaking head."

"Sure, just *dump* it out," Andy mumbled to himself. "It's just a head. Nothing out of the ordinary at all about that." He inched to within an arm's length of the helmet and hooked the edge with one gloved finger. "Got it," he said and began crawling backward from beneath the vehicle.

The weight of something massive wrapped itself around his left leg and dragged him away from the transport.

"Trae! Help! Don't let the sandworm eat me!" Andy clawed helplessly at the ground as he slid backward, legs elevated, his face plowed through the sand.

"Nope, sorry man. No can do!" Trae shouted. "You're on your own. Gotta conserve the ammunition ya know. Really, it's nothing personal."

"Damn you, Trae! Get out here and save me!" The thing released its grip as abruptly as it had grappled his leg. "Open the door, Trae!" Andy stumbled and clawed his way across the loose sand to the transport.

"Nope, sorry man. Can't help you."

Andy beat his fist against the driver's door. "Open up!"

"Hey Andy, can I have my helmet back?" Fergus broke out into hysterical, snorting laughter.

Andy turned to see Fergus, red-faced and gasping for air between snorts.

The driver's door of the transport opened. "Are we good?"

"Oh yeah … We're … Good," Fergus sighed. "We're better than good, now, we're golden."

"Ok, good. Let's get to it then." Trae leapt from the cab to the ground next to Andy. "You good?"

"Ass."

Trae laughed, "Yup." He walked around the front of the transport toward the buried cliff face.

"Can I have my helmet back?"

Andy turned back to Fergus. "I hate you," he said, then trudged angrily in Trae's direction. "Get it yourself, ass."

"Admit it, you love me." Fergus chuckled as he picked up his helmet and trotted ahead of Andy.

"You're both a couple of douche nozzles!" Andy shouted.

<h1 style="text-align:center">cHAPTER 15</h1>

Unknown Red Giant System
2nd planet, Northern Hemisphere
The Betty / Captains Quarters
May 26th, 2176 / Mid Afternoon (Betty time)

Warm scents of lavender and vanilla mingled, filling the candlelit cabin. Slow, shamanic drumbeats resounded like the rhythm of a mother's heartbeat.

"I do not want to hear any argument from you," Krista said. Annoyance heavily weaved into her voice. "Shut your trap, lay still and just relax." She carefully tipped the vial of warm oil across Doug's back.

"Um, Krista, that's hot," he said, squirming away.

"Hush," Krista said soothingly. "It'll be good for you. Just let it happen, man. Just let it happen."

"Fuck you, Sadist," Doug sniggered.

"Maybe later, big boy. For now, just try to relax and forget all of your problems." She sat the vial back into the warmer on the side table.

"How am I supposed to forget that we're stranded on an alien world with limited supplies and no idea of how to get home?" Doug grunted as she leaned her elbow into the muscles under his left shoulder blade.

"You've got to let some of it go to start with." She worked the oil across his back in clockwise spirals then began to knead the muscles from his neck down. "This isn't your fault and you can't take it all on alone."

"How is that? I'm the Captain of the ship and they are the crew. Their lives are my responsibility."

"Because we all signed on for the job, that's how. Each one of us freely chose to be here, and in this moment. You didn't force us to be here. Every one of us could have just as easily walked away back in Atlanta, but we didn't."

"You might not be saying that in six months when the food runs out," Doug said.

Krista sat back on her feet and sighed. "Ya know, you're probably right. We should just go ahead and throw this big ass barbecue with what we have left, crack open the kegs of beer in the hold, and say fuck it all."

Doug stretched and groaned as he rolled over onto his side. "No, I didn't say that at all. I'm just not sure what we're going to do at this point. There are too many possibilities to calculate and too many unknowns at the moment."

"Well, start with what needs to be done first." She leaned forward and smacked him on his naked butt cheek, "Lay your ass back down, I'm not done with you yet."

"Yes, ma'am." Doug rolled back and laid flat on his stomach once again.

"The boys told me that they had figured out the radiation issue," Krista said. "They said that the levels dropped to nothing after the sun went down. There was only a residual reading when they went outside with that scanner of yours. They took off this morning in *Lazarus* to check out the thing you found. I made sure they wore their suits and had plenty of Remy's with them."

"Good," he sighed.

"So, we need supplies and shelter to start with, right? I had some vegetable seeds stashed away in the cupboard," Krista said as she continued with her massage.

"Good," he said through a grunt. "If we can get those to grow, then that'll help with the supplies. Make sure that Mel saves peels and eyes from the potatoes. If we can get those started, they may very well save our lives. Not to mention we can use any waste as compost."

"Well, what about shelter? Won't we be safe here on the ship?" She continued the massage, her fingers digging deep into his lower back.

"Yeah, we would," he said. "But how easy is it going to be to plant crops on board and keep them going. They will most likely do better in the soil if it isn't dead or can at least be conditioned. Has Cheezy had any luck figuring out where we are?"

"Not yet," Krista said. "She thinks she'd have a better chance if we launch one of the ships so she can start comparing the stars to our existing charts. Oh, and the boys think we might be able to do something with those satellites in orbit if they can get a closer look at one of them."

"As long as we shut everything down while planet side and run the solar collectors, we should be good for years on power. But that will also depend on the number of launches we do. Has Willy made any progress on the new drive system yet?"

"No, not yet that I know of," she said. "Lizz has been helping him translate everything until Wes can find the language controls." She slowly moved her hand down the back of his naked thigh.

"That tickles," he squirmed.

"Oh, really now?" Her fingers lightly scraped at the inside of his thighs.

Doug jerked away and rolled onto his back.

"And exactly where do you think that you're going, young man?" Krista giggled.

"That really tickled." He fought back laughter.

"It was supposed to." She purred, then leaned over and nibbled the inside of his quivering leg.

"Stop," Doug whined.

She nibbled at his quivering flesh with deliberate tenderness, moving upward one delicate inch after another.

"Oh god, you are sadistic."

"Yes, I am," she proudly purred. "Now hush and enjoy the doctor's prescription."

Unknown Red Giant System
2nd planet, Northern Hemisphere
May 26th, 2176 / Mid Afternoon (*Betty* time)

"*A*lright, back it up a little more!*" Andy shouted.

"What?" Fergus leaned out of the drivers' door; his hand cupped to his ear.

"*Dammit Andy, you don't have to shout,*" Trae yelled.

"*But he can't hear me,*" Andy said.

"*Then take off your damned helmet,*" Trae said with a frustrated laugh.

"*But ... What about the radiation?*"

"*It's still early, dipshit. Rad levels haven't gotten bad yet,*" Trae said "*Fine, you know what, never mind. You just stay in there and I'll take off mine, so I don't have to listen to you shouting in my ear.*" Trae removed his helmet and wiped the sweat from his face. He took a deep breath and immediately coughed, gagged and evacuated his stomach onto the dusty sand. He took another cautious breath. "I hope the entire planet doesn't smell like a fermented high school locker room."

"Stinks, don't it?" Fergus chuckled. "It honestly reminds me of a week-old jockstrap after summer football camp."

Trae glared back at Fergus. "No, it doesn't stink in the slightest. Smells like fields of wildflowers and sunshine."

Fergus breathed deep, then sighed. "Ah, the memories."

"Seriously? Sometimes you make me question your sanity," Trae said. He snorted and spit. "Just park it there and let's see what it does. We can move it again later if we need to." Trae walked over to the driver's side of the transport. "Hey Andy, you might want to move out of the way!"

"Oh yeah, that might be good, hu?" Andy scuttled to the side.

"Fire it up Ferg," Trae said.

"This is gonna be fun." Fergus sat back into the driver's seat and flipped a series of switches on the main console.

"Clear," Fergus shouted out the open door.

"Clear," Trae replied.

"Fire in the hole!"

The high-pitched whir of turbines buffeted their eardrums. Dust billowed into the air as the transport's primary thrusters spooled up to a steady-state idle. Trae replaced his helmet then motioned to Fergus and Andy to do the same.

"Radio check. You two got me," Trae transmitted.

"Check," Andy responded with a thumbs up.

"Breaker breaker one-nine," Fergus said. *"Any other old cooters out there got their ears on, come on back now. I got ya loud and clear good buddy.* Fergus slammed the driver's door on the transport. *"You copy me out there?"*

"Yup, loud and clear Ferg," Trae said. *"Change your pitch to zero degrees then take her to full thrust."*

"Copy that, moving to zero degrees pitch," Fergus said.

"Hey," Andy broke into the chatter. *"Don't you think we should anchor the transport?"*

"Naw, Lazarus should be plenty heavy in this gravity," Trae said.

"Nothing at all to worry about," Fergus added.

"Nope," Trae agreed. *"At least we hope. Alright Ferg, go to full power then start bringing the thrusters down slowly."*

"Gotcha, gotcha..." Fergus said.

Trae waved his hands in the air. *"Hold up, wait."*

"Der...Okay," Fergus said. *"I thought you just said go."*

"I did, just one second." Trae walked to the rear of the transport and slapped Andy in the back of the head. *"Andy! You dumbass! Get away from the back corner of the transport."* Trae turned and walked back to the driver's door. *"When those thrusters go to full throttle, you could get sucked into the jet wash."*

"Oh shit, hang on." Andy trudged through the fine dust away from the transport.

"Ok Ferg, clear!" Trae shouted over the noise of the turbines.

"Copy that. Clear," Fergus said. *"Thrusters coming up."*

The cyclic resonance of the turbines increased. Trae instinctively covered his ears, only to find his helmet in the way.

"It feels like my ears are bleeding," Andy shouted across the comms.

"That's because they probably are," Trae admitted. *"Now suck it up buttercup. Ferg, start rotating them down slowly. Give the jet blast time to carry the dust away."*

"Ten-four, good buddy," Fergus said. *"Coming down one degree every ten seconds."*

The sky darkened in the early morning light of the alien planet. Fine powdered sand roiled away over the top of the dune.

"Keep it coming, Ferg," Trae said. *"I can see the top section. It's a set of doors, alright."*

The thrusters dropped slowly as the dust cloud expanded, tripling in size.

"How's it look back there?" Fergus hung out of the drivers' door looking backward to get a better view.

"I think It's working," Andy said, unsure.

"Like a champ," Trae responded. *"If the doors run the length of this cliff line then they are massive."*

"Coming the rest of the way down," Fergus said.

"Gopherit," Trae replied. *"Max it out at forty-five degrees."*

"Copy that," Fergus responded.

The ground behind the transport exploded once again in a cloud of dust that raced away over the top of the cliff face.

"That's it, Ferg," Trae said. *"Shut it down. I can see the base of the door, now."*

The small turbines whined to a stop. Trae's ears continued to ring with a high-pitched shriek. Dust hovered in the air beyond the ridge of the cliff like a massive storm cloud breaching the horizon.

Fergus leapt from the cab and smiled. *"Well ain't that just pretty. Didn't think we could polish a turd so well."*

Trae removed his helmet. "Well alrighty then. I didn't expect to sandblast the door, but sure, why the hell not."

"Hey," Andy transmitted. *"What's that over there?"* Andy wandered into the newly made trench and kicked away sand away from something buried in the dune.

"What did you find?" Trae asked as he approached, Fergus following close behind. Andy picked up a smooth, white object from the sand, and held it out for Trae to see.

"Oh, sweet! A skull!" Fergus snatched it from Andy's hand.

"Doesn't look human, that's for sure," Trae said in a solemn tone.

"I got it!" Fergus poured sand from the skull and shook it clear. *"It's an alien!"*

"Well no shit, Sherlock," Andy sarcastically mumbled.

"I heard that," Fergus said, glaring up at Andy.

Trae took the skull from Fergus and turned it over in his hands. "Look at the canines," he pointed out. "And check out this short snout. Maybe something cat or dog like?"

Andy removed his helmet and knelt in the sand. "Looks like there's more of them over here." He excavated what looked like a leg bone, then a series of vertebrae and two more skulls from the sand.

"What the hell?" Trae puzzled over the scene as Fergus began to dig.

"Hey look, I found another skull!" Fergus cheered as he held the bleach white object triumphantly above his head. *"Oh shit, and another."* He tucked the skulls under his left arm. *"I got it! We can mount them to Lazarus!"*

"No."

"Aww, come on. It'll look cool," Fergus pleaded.

"Well, maybe one," Trae held up a finger.

"Sweet," Fergus said with giddy excitement as he continued to dig. *"I call dibs on the rest of them."*

Trae kicked the base of the massive door, which echoed with a hollow metallic thump. He examined the odd surface texture of the material. "I can't tell if this is pitting or just from the sandblast job we did to it," he mumbled to himself. He picked at the imperfections on the shiny gray-green surface of the door. "It sure as hell isn't any kind of steel alloy that I've ever seen before." He poked at a piece of scale that clung to the surface. His gloved finger penetrated the paper-thin surface of the massive door. "Oh shit. Hey Ferg, come take a look at this."

"What?" Fergus looked up from his excavation. *"Look what you did. You done went and broke it. Cap is gonna be pissed off at you ..."*

"Here," Andy said, handing Trae a large white stone. "Go all Trae the barbarian and open it up. I'll go get the flashlights."

"Hey, snag me a bag or something while you're at it," Fergus shouted over his shoulder.

"Get it your damn self," Andy said.

Trae tossed the large stone in the air to test the weight. "Barbarian it is." He swung the stone in a wide, whirlwind arch striking the door with a gong-like reverberation. Sections of the gray-green metal crumbled beneath the powerful strikes. "That should be big enough to climb through." He tossed the now chipped stone over his shoulder and peered into the darkness beyond the portal. He gagged. "Man, that stinks." He stepped closer to the opening and sniffed again. "Whew…Hey Ferg, I think I figured out where you left your high school gym socks."

Fergus stacked the skulls into a neat little pyramid of sorts, placing Andy's helmet on the top of the pile. *"It can't smell any worse than it already does. Hell, I think I'm starting to get used to it, honestly."*

"No, you're not, you brain dead retard. You still have your helmet on." Trae laughed and spat. "Trust me, it's worse than what we have been breathing." He stepped away from the opening and coughed. "It's dead air, man. No telling how long this place has been sealed up."

"Hell, send Andy in then," Fergus said jokingly. *"He'd make a pretty good canary."*

"I'm not so sure that it's safe. It could be like an old mine and full of poisonous or explosive gas."

Andy jogged up to the pair, snatching his helmet from the pile of skulls. "Awesome, you got it open." He handed Trae a flashlight then peered into the opening.

Trae replaced his helmet. The hiss of pressurization began as the helmet locked into the collar seal. *"Seal your helmet and go to your own air supply, just in case there's more than stale air in there."*

"Will do." Andy his helmet and clicked it shut. Seals hissed and expanded as his suit pressurized. *"Alright. Got it,"* he said with a thumbs up.

Trae peered through the opening as Andy slid through ahead of him. *"See anything in there?"*

"Yeah, the darkness."

"Oh, haha, asshole," Trae said. *"Anything else?"*

"I can see a wall to the left on this side of the door. Maybe more like a support bulkhead than a wall, but nothing in front of me or toward my right," Andy said.

"Cap might have been right then," Fergus said.

Trae leaned into the opening and flashed his light around. *"If this complex was an ancient starport, maybe this is a massive repair hangar like they have back in Atlanta."*

"Yup," Fergus said. *"I'd be willing to bet that you're right."*

"Hey Trae," Andy called. *"Do you think it's safe to go deeper?"*

"I don't see why not. Just keep an eye open," Trae said as he ducked and sidestepped through the opening.

"You guys have fun," Fergus shouted. *"I'm just going to stay out here and play with my new friends. I think I'll name them Moe, Larry, Curly and Hank."*

"You do that Ferg," Trae said. "Wait. Why Hank?"

"Just because," Fergus said.

"Hey while you're out here playing tea party with your new friends, tie us into the transmitter on Lazarus."

"Sure," Fergus said. *"I'll get right on that."*

Trae swung his light from side to side. The black nothingness around them absorbed their minuscule light beams.

"I think those are roof supports," Andy said. He swung his light to illuminate the massive pillar to the left of the opening. *"Hard to tell for sure though. Can't see the top of the thing. My light doesn't reach that far."*

Trae panned the light around, examining the structure. *"It would make sense. And if that support pillar went all the way to the top of the cliff, it would be roughly eight stories tall. So then if that's the case, then this way,"* he flashed the beam of his light down the length of the door, *"could run the full distance of the cliff face. Hell, that's a few hundred yards."*

Andy disappeared around the side of the massive support. *"Looks like there's a storage bay of some sort over this way."*

"Alright boys and girls, I've got the ship on the horn," Fergus said, chiming in over the suit comms.

"Got you loud and clear, Ferg," Wes responded.

"Okay, good," Trae said. *"You picking me up, Wes?"*

"Loud and clear."

"Awesome," Trae said. *"Looks like Cap may have been right. This is some sort of hangar. We aren't too deep in yet, but just rough guessing that we could fit both ships in here with room to spare if we can get the doors open ..."*

"Trae, over here," Andy abruptly interrupted.

"Over where? All I see is black," Trae said.

"Around the corner," Andy said. *"I found some strange looking containers on what I guess would be pallets. I mean, it doesn't look like anything we have ever used, but that's what the set up looks like."*

"Oh sweet, salvage," Ferg cheered. *"Hey, I'll give you guys some of the skulls if you let me in on the take."*

"No, Ferg," Trae grumbled.

"No thanks Ferg," Andy said in an annoyed tone. *"Oh, what the hell is this? Oh, man. That's just gross looking."*

Trae stopped, panning his light in the direction Andy had went. *"What the hell is what?"*

"Watch your step when you come around the corner, Trae. The floor is wet and slick with some kind of pinkish slime stuff."

"I copy on the pink slime, Andy," Trae said. *"You copy all of that Geek? Andy gets dibs on those pallets near the pink slime. He can come back and mark them later."*

"I copy," Wes said. *"That's at least some good news for a change. I've got Andy down for the main share. Just give me a count later."*

Trae laughed. *"Don't count it good yet. There's no telling what that slime might be without testing it. The water might not be potable, and the containers may just be empty."*

"Seriously," Fergus said. *"Why do you always have to be such a negative Nancy?"*

"I don't see you in here looking for body snatchers or anything."

"Um...Trae," Andy said, whispering into the suit comms. *"Still got your gun on you?"*

"Yea," Trae said curiously. *"Why?"*

Andy's breath shuddered as he whispered into the helmet mic. *"We are not alone…"*

"Don't worry Andy. There aren't any sandworms down here to gobble you up," Fergus said.

"Ferg, clear the line." Trae drew his pistol and continued slowly around the corner. *"What do you mean Andy? Please be very clear and very specific about what you are seeing."*

"I mean I am looking at something that is looking right back at me. Doesn't seem to like it when the light is shined directly on it, but it isn't moving. It's just crouched behind one of those pallets loaded with barrels."

Trae rounded the corner and spotted the stack of containers on pallets that Andy had mentioned. He aimed the beam of his flashlight downward. Iridescent hues of blue and purple glimmered across the pink surface of the vicious looking ooze. It spread out in a shallow puddle, approximately three feet across at the base of the containers.

"I'm at the slime, Andy," Trae said. *"I'm continuing in your direction."*

"What does it look like," Wes asked.

"It kinda looks like a cat or maybe a lemur in the face. Four fingers on the hand that I can see. It has really short black fur that sorta has this red tint when I shine the light at it. It has a really long tail that's holding onto the containers above its head."

"Christ," Trae murmured to himself. *"I hate to tell ya this Andy, but I think you are having your first alien encounter."*

Fergus laugh. *"Get ready to squeal boy! You gonna get probed!"*

"What the hell," Wes said excitedly. *"Why does that sound so familiar? I've heard that description from somewhere before."*

"Cool it! All of you," Trae ordered. *"Are there any more of them, Andy?"*

"Not that I can see. Just this one that's still staring at me and sniffing the air."

"Okay, slowly back your way out. I'm on my way to you."

"Oh shit, it's moving. It's standing up. Looks like it's nearly as tall as I am and wearing a skirt or kilt or something around its waist."

"Dammit! I know this," Wes said. *"What the hell. There's no connection. Dammit! There's no net connection here! Oh my god what do I do, I have no net, how the hell can I look anything up?"*

"Well no shit Sherlock," Fergus said. *"We aren't exactly near-Earth anymore, now are we?"*

"T...T...Trae," Andy stuttered. *"I think it heard you. It's looking back in your direction. I can see your light coming this way. I think it just pulled a knife from its belt."*

"Get back here, Andy. Run! Move it!" Trae began to run toward Andy.

"Trae," Andy said. *"It's on the move! It just took off and hauled ass back into the darkness."*

Casraownan soft padded forward through the Underdark labyrinth. He held his spear close and at the ready. Ahead in the darkness, movement flickered and glowed within his dark vision. Around the edge of a great pillar ahead, he could make out the long muscular tail of a Kaowla. A ravenous beast of chorded muscles and vicious teeth.

Casraownan let out a long, even exhale as he raised his spear to strike. One silent step in front of another, he stalked his quarry. Slowly, silent. Breathe in, slowly silent, breathe out.

The cavernous labyrinth suddenly resonated with a turbulent squall that buffeted his ears. He dropped his spear yowling in agony. The Kaowla sprinted away into the darkness at the start of the noise. The intensity increased, growing louder and higher in pitch.

Casraownan doubled over to the dusty labyrinth floor. His arms wrapped tightly around his head. His entire world dissolved at that moment. All that existed melted aways and became nothing to the enormity of the chaos that invaded his mind. He reached deep within and held on. The pain became everything. He was still alive if the pain existed. He yowled a sordid howl that could only have manifest itself amid the chaos that engulfed and absorbed him. Then there was nothing.

Like a warm and comforting blanket, the darkness enveloped him once again. Absolute silence absorbed the high-pitched vibration that continued to shake within his head. He felt a slight pain prick at his ear. Something warm and wet oozed down the left side of his head. Reflexively he wiped the side of his head and examined his palm. He could see the deep dark crimson shade of blood covered his palm. But, how? He could he see in the darkness. There were none of the glowing lichens in this part of the labyrinth. Light penetrated the darkness of the labyrinth.

How could there be light within the darkness of the labyrinth? This is not possible, he thought to himself. A thin beam of light penetrated the wall of the cavernous lair and struck the ground in front of him. Beyond the deafening ring in his head, a heavy thwunk preceded the expansion of light on the ground about him. His eyes followed the beam back to its source in the wall. Another heavy thwunk struck at something, more felt than heard, and once again the light expanded.

"By the blessed Morachao what could this be," he said softly, but couldn't hear his own words over the ringing in his ears. He felt another heavy thwunk and the spot where the light penetrated the darkness fell away. Something large loomed about the other side of the opening. He could see it reach in and grasp the edges of the opening. It ripped away large sections of the wall, allowing light to flood into the chamber. Casraownan backed away slowly. He cautiously moved deeper into the comforting embrace of the darkness.

cHAPTER 16

Unknown Red Giant System
2nd planet, Northern Hemisphere
The Betty / Mess hall
May 27th, 2176 / Mid-Morning (Betty Time)

"**D**idja hear, man? Wes said that they found an alien," Tiff said. "What if they're evil soul-sucking parasites or skin walking body snatchers?" She picked up a small orange from the mess hall serving bar aboard the *Betty*, then sat next to Kara at one of the many metal tables. "Or how about one of those face-huggers from that one movie?" The tangy citrus scent filled the compartment as Tiff dug at the peel with her nails.

"The way he told me, it sounded like they are big fuzzy pussy cats," Kara said. "Hmm," she purred, "I wonder if they purr like pussy cats when you rub their bellies?"

Melanie opened a cabinet below the serving bar and began sorting through its contents. "As long as they don't come on the ship and make a mess everywhere, I don't really care one way or another. But I'll tell ya' right now, the first one to poop in a corner is going to get a broom across its ass! I ain't cleaning up after some nasty assed cat alien if it ain't got the common sense to use a toilet." She slammed the cabinet door and stood, staring at Tiff. "What in the hell do you think you're doing? The Captain said to ration everything."

"What? I was hungry, man." Tiff popped a slice of orange into her mouth.

"No snacking," Melanie said. "Cap said to ration everything, so that's what I'm gonna do." She snatched the orange from Tiff.

"Aww man," Tiff whined.

"If you're both good girls and help me like the Captain told you to," she said, emphasized with knife-hand motions, "then I might let you have a treat afterward."

"Dude," Tiff whined. "That's just uncool man. It's not like I'm ten years old or some shit."

Kara glowered at Melanie. "That's just condescending and rude, Mel. We're all adults here."

"Well then, how about you actually act like it." She tossed a serving spoon into the washer and slammed the door shut. "Go over to the pantry cabinet and pull everything out so we can inventory it, then we can work up the menus."

Kara threw her hands up in frustration. "Alright, alright already. Fine, whatever."

"What the F ever, man," Tiff mumbled under her breath as she went to the pantry. "So, what do you think Cap is going to do about the aliens," she said, changing the subject.

"Don't know, don't care. We have other things to worry about right now, like surviving," Melanie huffed.

"I'm kinda torn on the whole situation," Kara said. "Do you really think we'll run out of food?"

Tiff opened the pantry and removed a box from a lower shelf. "I sure as hell hope not, man. Oh hey. What if we have to turn cannibal to survive? Who do you think would be the first to go? Or do you think the Cap would make us draw straws?"

Kara sucked in a breath. "Oh my God, that was abrupt. I would hope the Captain would come to his senses and it would be the Martians on the menu first."

"The Captain has already said there ain't nothing gonna happen to the prisoners," Melanie said. "Don't you even think about doing anything to them either."

"Oh, I wouldn't dare harm a hair on their precious little heads," Kara proclaimed. "Heaven forbid anyone goes against the *Captain's* order."

Mel glared at Kara. "Uh hu…"

"It could happen if things were to get bad enough." Tiff sighed. "I could do it if it meant survival, I guess. I mean, in the end, meat is meat, ya know. You just gotta picture it as a big fat honey glazed ham slice."

"Exactly," Kara said. "And if we added them to the menu now, then that's fewer supplies that they would use in the long term and be extra meat for our table."

"Alright, that's it," Melanie said, throwing a towel at the other two. "No one is going to eat anyone else. No one is going to kill anyone else. The Captain will figure it out. He always does. Have a little faith for a change, why don'tcha. For now, both of you get the hell out of my kitchen. I'm sick of hearing about it!"

Unknown Red Giant System
2nd planet, Northern Hemisphere
Alien Starport Underground Hangar
May 27th, 2176 / Mid-Morning (Betty Time)

"Geeze Doug, be careful," Krista said. "I just got you well enough to be out of bed. I don't need you slicing your head open on some rusty piece of metal."

"I'm fine, Krista." Doug sighed as he stepped through the opening in the ancient hangar door.

"You say that now…" her voice trailed off as she popped her head through the opening. "Oh wow, look at that. Dear God, does it ever stink in here."

Fergus held out a hand and assisted Krista through the opening.

Doug took in the sight. Large floodlights that were duct-taped to makeshift masts illuminated the area. Heavy roof beams arched across the roof span of the hangar entrance. Extending beyond the reach of the lights, the complex continued for hundreds of meters deeper underground. He continued toward the base camp area, joining Trae and Andy. "You guys weren't lying about this place. It's got to be about four hundred meters wide in this section alone." "Have you had any more sightings of the creature?"

"Not yet," Trae replied.

"I think we should arm up Cap," Andy said, sounding hopeful.

"I'm not so sure just yet," Doug said. "Just in case I'd carry a sidearm if you're down here, but no rifles and absolutely no grenades or anything else that goes boom." Doug gazed in wonder at the massive structure around them. "We don't want to provoke them if we don't have to. At least not yet anyway. They must be sentient if it was wearing clothing and holding a knife. So, it's not just an animal. Remember, we're the ones invading their territory."

"Are you sure Cap? Cause I can go back and load us up with a few things…"

"Andy," Doug barked, "No! Sidearms only. Got it?"

"Got it, Cap," Andy said under his breath as he returned to set up the floodlights.

Doug turned back to Trae. "You said something about salvage?"

Trae stifled a laugh. "Yup," he leaned down and scooped up a handheld floodlight. "You gotta see it to believe it though."

"Are you sure we should be in here," a meek voice said from the opening in the large door.

"It'll be alright sweetie," Maggie said. "Captain Dougie wouldn't have us here if he didn't think it was safe."

"Just watch your backside for the alien probes," Fergus said as his head appeared through the opening.

"Aliens?" Amanda squeaked and began to hyperventilate.

"Holy hell Fergus." Krista slapped his forehead. "It was bad enough for us to just get her off of the ship. Don't send her into a freaking panic attack."

Fergus's lower lip bulged in his attempt at a pouty face. He sniffled. "Well now, she can just put on her big girl panties and deal with it, can't she?"

"Fergus! Drop it and get Lazarus unloaded," Doug ordered.

Krista pulled Amanda close and patted her back while making a soothing, mother-like sound. "Maggie, come help me with her please." She stuck her tongue out at Fergus, then lead Amanda toward the center of the lit area.

Doug turned back to Trae. "Are we ready?"

"I'm ready if you're ready." Trae slung an overly stuffed backpack over his shoulder then tossed one to Doug. "Fergus will show the girls where we found water so they can get samples to test." He handed Doug a headlamp and a large piece of chalk. "No GPS to speak of here, so we'll have to map it out old school." He clipped a small datapad to a lanyard that hung from his belt. "So, we set our benchmark point, like this field transmitter," he said, pointing at a small box that bristled with antennas. He held up the datapad and synced it with the field transmitter.

Doug keyed his mic, "Geek you got me?"

"Loud and clear Cap," Wes replied.

"Set a timer for every thirty minutes if you would please, Wes," Trae said into his radio mic.

"Copy that and...you are set. Counting down one-half hour. Good hunting guys."

Trae switched on his floodlight and began to walk away, heading east, toward a large support column. "The container stacks that Andy found are about fifty yards this way. From what we could see there's a lot more stuff in here, but we didn't go much further. Without lights and markers, someone could get lost in here real quick. We figured it was safer to wait and get things set up the right way."

"Good thinking, especially since we know nothing about that alien you encountered," Doug said. "Any idea what's in those containers?"

"I have a thought, but I'm not absolutely sure. The containers that the cat thing was hiding behind are like the hangar door. It's some material that I haven't been able to identify yet. The face of the containers have been etched instead of being labeled. My guess is that the etchings are the standard kind of warnings and shipping information that we'd see on any of our hazardous cargo. I can't read a bit of it, but my guess is they contain or once contained deuterium."

"What makes you think that?"

"There's a symbol on the top corner of the markings that looks like a molecular diagram. Two elongated hexagons butted up against each other with a third off to the side on a dotted circle like the orbit of an electron. If it is deuterium, it could be worth a small fortune."

"It's only worth a small fortune if we can get back to Earth," Doug said. "But it does solve part of our fuel problem, though. That's less that we'll have to try and produce on our own for the short term."

"There they are," Trae said, pointed his light at a series of pallets with large metal cylinders stacked two high.

Doug studied the cylinders. Someone had recently wiped away the thick layer of dust that covered everything, including the heavily oxidized surface of the container. "You mean this symbol here?" Doug traced the lines of the symbol with a finger.

"That would be the one. The way that it's segregated from the rest of the markings makes me think it's for quick identification. I'd bet the rest of the info is warnings, hazards, the standard industrial gobbledygook."

Doug looked around at the stacks of containers around them. "There's at least a hundred of these containers right here. If they are still full we might be set for a while."

"We'll get a full inventory of everything later on after we get some lighting in here and make sure that it's safe."

"Which direction did the alien take off?"

Trae pointed his light down a long aisle of similar containers. Doug could see the odd footprints left on the dusty floor. "Who all did you say was over here?"

"All three of us were at one point. I wandered down to the end of this aisle. Looks like it opens up into a forklift path or something. Why?"

"If that's you and the other two's footprints, and that's the alien's, then what's that one?" Doug aimed his light at a group of smaller prints mingled on top of the others.

"Group of little aliens maybe? They look similar to the larger set." Trae knelt down and stared at the prints. "They all have claw marks like a cat."

"Maybe," Doug said under his breath. He pulled his revolver from its hidden holster. "Just keep your eyes open." He scanned the area with his light then stalked away into the darkness. "Let's get a perimeter marked out and go from there."

Trae brushed away dust from the concrete-like floor and marked an arrow in chalk that pointed in the direction they had come from. He powered on the datapad then pressed the icon to log the new waypoint. "Sounds good to me, boss."

Doug continued along the outer wall. A large section had collapsed in on itself at some point in the distant past, allowing sand to flood in and form a small dune. Movement caught his eye. Translucent tendrils protruded from the soil and dangled lazily into the darkness around it. Delicate frills vanished into the clear root stalks as his light shone upon the mass. "Trae! Over here, quick."

"Over where?" Trae's voice echoed. "Nevermind, I see your light," he said. He quickly appeared next to Doug, "What ya got Cap?" Trae leapt backward at the sight of the mass. "Oh shit! That's like something right out of a bad horror movie."

"Yeah," Doug said. "Mark it on your map. We can come back and examine it closer later on." Doug continued along the wall but gave the thing a wide berth.

"Hold on Cap," Trae said as he finished tapping at the datapad and let it fall to his side.

"Hold on, what?"

Trae picked up a small stone and tossed it at the mound. The stone landed on the dusty floor nearby with a light thud. The thing exploded into a flurry of motion. Hundreds of translucent tentacles sprung forth from the mound and stabbed at the motionless stone.

"Hu," Trae gasped. "It's like a jellyfish or anemone I bet. Stings its prey, then pulls it in and slowly digests it."

"Let's really keep our distance for now. Snag a picture for the database and mark the location on the map as extremely hazardous."

"Way ahead of you," Trae said as he updated the waypoint.

They continued silently for the next hour. Trae logged stacks of ancient trade goods, cargo containers, and skids full of what looked like personal luggage. Most of the containers were still intact, though a few had collapsed or broken apart.

Trae whistled a long breath. "Would you look at that, Cap?" Trae gasped in awe. "That I do believe, would be a jackpot."

"I'd say so," Doug said. "But they may be no better than scrap metal at this point." He panned his light across the surface of a small, one-man craft.

"True," Trae replied. "It all depends on what was wrong with them when they were parked and what time has done to them.

The upside is the environment hasn't been a bad one for long term storage. It's like the aircraft boneyard out in Arizona. There are airframes out there that are nearly two hundred years old and they are still in as good a shape as they were the day they were parked. The big question for me would be the tech. Can we figure it out in order to get them back up and running again?"

"I count four, wait maybe a fifth back that way to the east." Trae motioned with the beam of his flashlight.

"Maybe there wasn't anything wrong with them and they just ran out of pilots or fuel?"

"It's possible," Trae said. "That would be a sweet deal for us. There would be a better chance that we can get them functional again if that's the case."

"This one," Doug said, motioning, "looks like a light transport to me. Look at those engine nacelles. I bet this thing is set up for vertical takeoffs and landings. Easy loading and unloading through the lower cargo door. I bet it would be easy to drop and go. But with the cockpit so high up on that neck there, I bet it would be hell for the pilot to see anything on the ground."

"I'm sure there are cameras and proximity sensors all over the thing." Trae continued deeper into the hangar. "Ha!" Trae snorted a laugh.

"What's up?"

"I'm pretty sure I know exactly what this one is for. The design is nearly the same as the old Grayson and Ronin pusher tugs from back when the colonies were being established. See, that section sticking out there," Trae shined the light overhead as he backed away to see from a different angle. "Yup, that's what I thought. This outrigger station on the side here looks like it's the cockpit. With the cockpit offset like that, you can see around the load for docking and maneuvers. And hose mandibles there," he said, flashing the light over to his right.

"They would be used to lock onto a freight container module that could be stacked however deep they wanted to make it."

"And that one, my friend," Doug said with a tone of reverent awe, "looks like a warship if I've ever seen one."

Trae rounded the corner, catching up to Doug. He stopped suddenly and whistled. "Oh, no shit." He lustily gawked at the craft. "Would you look at that? Narrow body, small command deck, wings upswept like a hawk about to attack. I'd say your right, Cap. Looks like a warship to me, too."

"What do you suppose those are on the wingtips?" Doug pointed his light at the end of the wing.

"Not sure," Trae contemplated. "Antennas of some sort, maybe? I don't see anything that looks like an ammo container or feed system. It doesn't look big enough to be a mass thrower or any gauss system that I'm familiar with. Hell, none of this is our tech, so it's possible that those actually go pew, pew, pew."

Doug chortled, "Pew pew pew?"

"Well yeah," Trae said. "It's a technical term. Laser cannon or disintegrator beam just sounds a bit too far-fetched and hokey to me."

"Oh...kay," Doug fussed, "and moving on."

They continued toward a set of half-opened blast doors on the far side of the hangar bay. The nose and cockpit of a long slender craft sat parked in the way that blocked the doors from closing. A maneuvering tug and tow bar were still connected to the nose landing gear of the small craft.

"Hu, would you look at that, Cap."

"I'd bet that little bugger will move. That's a tiny space frame compared to those three massive engines on the back. I'd bet that its thrust to weight ratio is insane."

"Red on white paint scheme isn't usually military, maybe it's someone's personal transport. The equivalent of a Corvette or Lamborghini, maybe?"

"And that one," Doug pointed with his light over the nose of the trapped ship, deeper into the small side hangar. "I count four more of them back to the left," he tiptoed and peered over the small craft. "I can't quite see," he knelt down and crawled under the nose of the craft into the small side hangar. "Whoa, you gotta come see this, Trae."

Trae dropped to all fours and shimmied his way under the craft. "Son of a bitch." He quickly stood and shined the light back and forth.

"I'd say that's another fighter of some sort." Doug examined the larger group of the one seat craft.

"That would be my guess, too. Different design. Possibly an entirely different species altogether that made them. I mean those there," he said, shining the light back toward the smaller, three engine ships. Triangular engine layout, stubby atmospheric control surfaces. But these," he said turning the light to his right. "Four engines, much different frame construction and it looks like the wings separate." He laughed. "And I guess those four antenna looking thingys on the wings probably go pew pew, too."

"Still can't bring yourself to say it, can you?"

Trae sighed. "Nope. Not yet. At least not until I can examine them and prove or disprove. Regardless, we've hit the jackpot for sure."

"That's assuming that we can get them all operational again."

"Are you kidding? We now have our own squadron of fighters, a handful of rogue transports, and what do you think, over a half dozen shuttle pods maybe?" Trae shined the light through the open hangar door leading into the next bay as they quietly continued into the next area. "They kinda look like a hermit crab made its shell from an old bronze school bell or something. Even looks like claws on the front of the thing."

Doug laughed. "Yeah, I guess it does at that."

"Anyways, between me, Fergus and Willy, I bet we can figure out these systems and get at least a few of them operational again. It's not like there aren't spare parts laying around." He motioned toward the ancient spacecraft.

"That would be good. Then we'd just need to hire pilots. Maybe not for the fighters right off, but at least enough people to crew the transports."

"You could always get Wes to work his magic and put adverts out when we get back Earthside."

"That's not a half-bad idea," Doug said. "We could put out a blanket hiring ad for all positions and experiences. You never know who we might be able to pick up."

Doug continued and entered into the next small hangar bay through a set of vehicle doors that hung from corroded hinges. "Trae, come check this out." Doug shined his light upward and to the left of the doorway.

"Whoa," Trae said as he entered the bay. "Could be a pursuit or bomber craft, because of her size." Trae stepped backward to get a better look at this ship as a whole. "Four primary engines with what looks like dozens of thruster ports across the ship." He continued to talk as he walked around to see the ship at a different angle. "Looks like the cockpit is set up for a pilot and a gunner. And she has, one, two…" Trae continued counting to himself. "Eight total of what look like they may be some sort of laser emitter turrets. She's covered from any angle by multiple points."

"Wipe your chin. Hey, wait a sec. I thought you didn't want to believe that a true energy weapon was possible, yet."

Trae motioned at the ship. A slap-happy stupid grin crossed his face. "But look at her, Cap. She's so horribly ugly that she's beautiful. If any ship might have pew pews, that one would be the one to have them."

"Maybe Lizz was onto something when she mentioned psych evals for you guys," Doug said jokingly.

"Hu...hey, Cap. What do you suppose that is?" Trae held the beam of his light steady. Aiming it at an oddly lone blue box, that didn't seem out of place in the least.

"Shipping container maybe," Doug said, uninterested. He motioned toward a ramp that disappeared into the darkness of the floor above. "Looks like we found the way to the upper levels of the starport. It would be really nice if the control tower and all of its control equipment were still intact."

"We can take a look if we make it that far." Trae checked the time on his datapad. "We've been gone for a while already. Are you ready to head back or do you want to keep pressing on?"

"I've got nothing better to do. Let's keep going and find out what's on that upper level," Doug said.

cHAPTER 17

Unknown Red Giant System
2nd planet, Northern Hemisphere
Alien Starport
May 27th, 2176 / Afternoonish (Betty Time)

"I'm through, Cap," Trae yelled down through the hole. "If we're going to use this upper area, we'll have to clear out all of the sand and rubble from this opening. Not everyone is going to want to drag themselves through holes in the floor."

"I don't think that'll be a problem once we get some mining equipment down here," Doug said. He reached for anything on the other side of the hole to grasp. Trae reached down and pulled Doug from the hole with little effort.

"Damn man. Ever think you work out too much?"

"Nah," Trae said. He turned slowly, shining his light about and inspecting the area. "What do you think this area was used for?"

"Dunno right off," Doug said, slowly panning his light around.

The pair stood in a wide-sweeping corridor that arched gently to the left. Small alcoves lining either side of the path were cluttered with the desiccated remains of what looked like furniture or shelving.

"Look at the way the sand has filled in all of the rooms on this side," Trae said as he pointed to the right with his light. "If I had to guess, I'd bet that those spaces were once the outer wall of this place. The windows must have given at some point in the past and the sand flooded in filling everything up."

"You're probably right," Doug agreed. "It's as good an explanation as any, I suppose."

Doug's arm reflexively came up and blocked Trae's path. "Hold up. Look over there." He pointed to the right with his light toward an alcove. Sand filled the space and overflowed into the main corridor. Translucent tendrils extended from the alcove and hung nearly motionless at the edge of the corridor.

"Is that our little friend from below." Trae stepped to his left to get a better look at the thing.

"If it is, then it's massive," Doug said. "If not, then there might be even more of these things around. Just keep your distance for now until we can figure out what they are."

Goose flesh rippled across both of their backs. A strange guttural chittering resounded from the darkness ahead.

"That can't be good," Trae whispered from the side of his mouth.

Doug quietly drew his revolver and cocked the hammer. "Maybe, maybe not. Either way, we still need to find out what it is. We can't have a possible threat hanging around if we're going to temporarily set up shop in this place."

Trae sniffed deeply. "Do you smell that?" He followed Doug's lead and drew his pistol.

Doug sniffed at the air. "I can't smell anything but a fermented locker room.

"It doesn't take long, but you'll eventually get used to it." Trae sniffed deeply. "It's like...," he started, then sniffed again to be sure. "It's like the smell of a freshly squashed stink bug pickled in vinegar."

Doug stared at Trae with a look of perplexity. "That's really what you smell, or have you been smoking the good shit and holding out on me?"

A low growling hiss joined the strange chittering.

"Now that really doesn't bode well," Trae said.

Three pink-skinned *things* tumbled into the main corridor from the next alcove on the left. Each of the creatures looked to be roughly the size of a large house cat. Random tufts of golden yellow fur decorated their leathery pink skin. Each of the creatures stood on eight heavily muscled legs that dug into the dust as they scratched and growled at one another. Two of the creatures squared off with one another, teeth snapping. They growled in a mock attack. The third creature leapt upon the other two, its mouth wide, displaying impressive canines. None of them responded to the light being shone on them.

"Shit Cap, they're pups," Trae whispered.

"Maybe so, but look at the teeth and claws on those things. Pup or not, I wouldn't want to piss one of them off."

"They kinda look like the love child of a naked mole-rat and a wolverine. Just eight legs instead of four," Trae observed. "If these are the pups, then I wonder where the parents are?"

Something akin to the sound that a dolphin-rottweiler hybrid might make shrieked forth from the throat of one of the creatures. The third creature that had pounced on the other two rose up on its hind legs and sniffed the air, while the other two did likewise. They sniffed feverishly at the air. In unison, the trio let out an ear-piercing chirp mingled with a deep resonating growl.

"That might be our cue to leave and get back to the others," Doug whispered as he took a cautious step backward.

"I think you're right. Let's get out of here." Trae turned and found himself staring eye to eye with a much larger version of the alien pups. It sat back on its hind legs, sniffing feverishly at the air. Four tiny black dot eyes glimmered in the artificial light. A thick, faded brown tongue shot out of the thing's mouth and lapped at its leathery muzzle.

Thick black blood exploded from the creature's chest in time to the muzzle flash and pop of Doug's revolver. The thing roared; its upper claws struck at the emptiness in front of it. Trae took a step back and fired. The creatures left shoulder exploded in a shower of black ichor. It lunged forward toward Trae. Its gnashing teeth grazed across his chest.

"Get back," Doug shouted.

Trae fired again but missed. The creature leapt forward, one of its lower legs connected with Trae's right knee and dug in.

"Get clear!"

"I can't!" Trae punched the creature in the side of the head with his right fist. He pounded the creature over and over. Its teeth clacked as its massive maw snapped at Trae's face. The creature found purchase and clawed its way up to Trae's chest. He shoved his left fist, pistol and all down into the creature's open maw. Pop after pop repeated from inside of the beast as Trae unloaded the clip of .45 ACP rounds. The creature shuddered, violently convulsing as it fell backward, regurgitating Trae's arm and weapon from its insides. It lay motionless and unbreathing on the dusty, sand-strewn floor.

cHAPTER 18

Chinchassan Burrow

Casraownan looked about and smiled. Younglings played as mothers nursed those too young to join in the games. The clan had gathered once again, settling in before the time of rest amid the blue glow of cavern fungus that illuminated the clan burrow.

"What do you mean hairless?" Lilhanya gasped. She continued to brush and preen the calico fur of the youngling who sat on her lap.

"That is what I saw," Casraownan said. "They are nearly hairless, except for small tufts on the tops of their heads. I don't know how or what the thing was that opened the labyrinth to the outside, but it felt as if my head was about to explode. Then there they were. These beings entered the labyrinth on a beam of light from the heavens."

"Impossible! There are no such creatures." Gabhothi, the Chinchassa elder said as he shifted uncomfortably on his padded pallet. "You have been eating the wrong mushrooms again. There is nothing beyond us and the labyrinth."

Casraownan gave the elder a dismissive glance and continued his tale to the others. "I followed the large warrior and his companion into the eastern tunnels that lead to the above side."

"Isn't that where the Kaowla nest their young?" Ceiwo, the gray-haired elder shifted nervously. "You didn't continue to follow them, did you?"

"I did," Cass said. He held his head proud and defiant.

"We are so few already and you foolishly put yourself into harm's way," Gabhothi said. "Are you mad, boy? If any of this farfetched story is true, you foolishly endangered yourself as well as endangered all of us."

"I followed them and watched from a distance," Casraownan said. "I watched as the large warrior killed the Kaowla with his bare hands. I don't know why, but I wasn't worried. I had the feeling that if I were in trouble that the creatures would have come to my aid."

"You must be fevered," Ceiwo said, then spat. "You should rest and forget all of this nightmare or fever dream or whatever it was."

"I'm not making this up. Come and see for yourself and see that I speak the truth."

"Why," Gabhothi said bluntly. He scratched and preened the thick white fur along his jawline. "What difference would it make? Why would this happen all of a sudden? Nothing ever changes here. All is as it has ever been or ever will be. It would be a dangerous waste of time to venture into the labyrinth."

"Couldn't the tales of old be true, brother?" Fowembes shook, then turned to face Gabhothi. Matted gray braids swung as he shifted and adjusted himself on an uncomfortable stone. "Travelers from other far off lands once walked these sands. Back when the waters ran free in the open air of the above. Perhaps dear brother," he said with a manic chuckle. "Perhaps they have returned." He threw his arms into the air and shook his head wildly with an excited shout. Thick gray dreadlock like clumps of fur flew about haphazardly, striking anything within range without care. "The sins of the ancestors have been paid! May we once again dance among the stars, hand in hand with those of another kind!" The old gray creature knelt; his hands raised in praise. He bowed and placed his face upon the floor then blew out a deep breath that caused a puff of dust. "Oh my, the ancestors," he said in a worried tone. His thick matted dreadlocks flung about as he bowed and rocked in reverence.

"Shut it you old coot!" Ceiwo grumbled under his breath.

The old gray cat sobbed and scrabbled at the dust that covered the floor, drawing it toward him as if to bury himself. "The ancestors will protect me. They will keep me safe." Fowembes chuckled again. "Great, old stone beings protect me from the dangers brought upon us by my brother's evils," he wheezed as he let two handfuls of dust fall over his head.

"What if Fowembes is right?" All eyes turned back to Casraownan. What if the tales are true?"

"Enough!" Ceiwo glared daggers at Casraownan. "You are mistaken! Go see Olne for something to clear your head and never speak of this again! It is as it is and as it has always been except that you have become ill and must now be treated." Ceiwo shuffled away and kicked Fowembes in the side. "Come, brother, it is time to eat and to find less excited company."

"Yes, yes, oh yes, time to eat…" The old cat followed Ceiwo obediently as the pair shuffled down a dark corridor.

Lilhanya placed a gentle hand on Casraownan's shoulder. "Do not mistake Ceiwo's meaning. He may not understand what could be, but he does try to protect us." She breathed in a deep, worried breath. "Please do as he has asked and go see Olne." She followed in the direction of the elder brothers then stopped, pausing in thought. "If what you say that you saw is true, leave it be and do not interfere. Perhaps they will just move on." She flashed a sad glance back toward Casraownan, then continued after the brothers.

cHAPTER 19

Unknown Red Giant System
2nd planet, Northern Hemisphere
Alien Starport
July 1st, 2176 / Evening (Betty Time)

Sterile white light from the *Betty's* landing lights flooded the alien hangar bay. Ancient dust entangled itself with the scent of a heavy meat stew that cooked over an open fire between the two parked ships. Trae picked a twangy blues scale on an unplugged electric guitar. His fingers blurred at the intense heavy metal pace across the well-worn wooden fretboard. A black cross painted on the guitar with mother of pearl inlay at its tips stood out starkly against the wood grain of the instrument's body.

"Last call!" Melanie shouted, then slowly struck a metal drum with a hammer. "Y'all had best get over here and eat before it gets cold!" She set aside the drum and stirred the contents of the large stew pot that hung over the fire.

"Hang on, I can get this." Trae stretched his fingers then gripped the neck and continued fingering a difficult G# scale.

"You know, we should get you a new guitar for your birthday when we get back to earth," Krista said to Trae as she strode down the *Betty's* boarding ramp. "That poor thing just needs to be hung on a wall somewhere to look pretty.

Trae stopped instantly and glared in her direction. "This guitar will never be retired If I have anything to say about it. Do you have any idea who this once belonged to?"

"Nope," Krista said. "Don't care neither. A guitar is a guitar to me."

"My God woman! How could you say something like that?" Trae protectively cradled the instrument. "This guitar once belonged to the rock guitar god, the cowboy from hell himself, the one and the only…" Trae proselytized.

"Well if it's so damned important, then where did you get it from? Hu?" Krista glared at him, daring him to lie to her.

"Um…I found it in this place down in Texas this one time when me and Fergus were down there making a delivery."

"Uh hu," Krista nodded and smiled.

"Yup, that's how it happened."

"Alright, I guess that's as good an answer as any," Krista said. "So, how's the hand healing?" She grabbed a bowl from a stack near the fire and stepped toward the cookpot.

"Stiff and still hurts like a motherfucker," Trae said. He bent his hand backward at the wrist once again to fully stretch the tendons.

"It's been just over a month," Krista said reassuringly. "It'll take a little while to fully heal. It's a surprise that you even have a hand left after that dirt dog got a hold of you."

"Ain't that the truth," Fergus said as he walked into the light from the darkness of the hanger. "It's a good thing that she could save it. How else would you beat off without missing a lick." Fergus chuckled, slapping Trae on the back as he walked by, making his way to the pot.

Strange dolphin-like barks accompanied the clatter of pans falling to the floor. Three nearly hairless, eight-legged dog-like things circled Melanie. They leaned on her legs, reaching for a block of cheese that she held high over her head.

"No! Down! Trae! Get these damn things out of my cooking area!" Melanie snatched a spatula from her makeshift prep table and threw it at the three dirt dog pups. Noses raised, they sniffed at the makeshift table made from alien storage containers.

"Shwartz, Midna, Bear, go lay down," Trae ordered. The three creatures chittered irritably then fled to a ratty looking doggie bed placed on the outer edge of the camp.

Doug walked up to the serving line and nodded at Trae. "Looks like you've just about got them trained."

"Almost, but they are still pups," Trae said. "No telling how long their life spans are, so they could be puppies for a few more months or a few more years. We'll just have to see."

"Did you and Fergus finish setting up the solar panels?"

"Almost," Trae said. He leaned the guitar against a container table and shifted in his seat. "No!" He swatted one of the dogs away from his guitar. "Get your ass back to your bed." The pup whimpered and sulked all the way back to the doggie bed. Trae turned back to Doug. "We need to scrounge up a few hundred meters of cable to run it back here to the battery coils. Unless you'd rather have a base camp set up closer to the opening."

"No," Doug said, drifting off in thought. I think we're better off back here toward the core of the complex. There's less chance that we'll have any radiation issues down here. Do what you can to get it all set up. I don't want to launch and leave base camp in the dark."

"We could maybe get it done quicker if we strip the derelict ships in the other landing bays," Trae suggested.

"Um...no," Doug replied with a nervous laugh. "Let's not do that just yet. I want to keep those intact until we can really take a good look at them. We might be able to get them running. If we can, that would be some good salvage to take back with us."

"Hail to Miss Melanie, queen of stew and goddess of the famished," Kara loudly proclaimed as she made her way down the loading ramp of the *Betty*. "You have outdone yourself. This looks like a feast meant for royalty," she said with a flourish as she grabbed a bowl.

"Uh-huh. You just remember that tonight if the new mushrooms cause your insides to become your outsides," Mel warned.

"It smells wonderful Mel. Thank you," Wes said.

"Thank you, now eat," Melanie ordered.

"Yes, ma'am."

Tiffany ran down the *Betty's* loading ramp. "Where's my kiddo's? Puppies? Where's mommy's little babies?" The three little beasties chittered, barked and skittered their way over to her. Their thick claws scratched and scraped across the concrete like nails on a chalkboard. Tiffany crouched down to meet them on their level. Each pushed the other away as they tried to climb into her lap. "There's my babies," She scratched each of them behind the ear. "Are you all being good for daddy?"

"No, they aren't," Mel grumped. "If they don't stay away from my cooking area, I'm going to put them in the stew pot next."

"But they're just babies," Tiffany said with a whine.

"I couldn't care less. Keep 'em under control or they're fair game in my opinion."

"Trae," Tiffany said then stuck out her lower lip.

"Don't look at me," Trae said. "You're the one that wanted to keep them after they followed us back. I'd just as soon eat them as to keep them."

"Last one is a rotten egg!" Rachel suddenly sprinted down the loading ramp of the Martian ship.

"I'm too damn old to race, Cheezy," Willy shouted after her. "Hey Cap! I've got some good news for ya."

"Cool, Willy. Get yourself some grub first, then we can talk."

"I'm good right now," Willy said. He took a seat on one of the cargo containers and stretched. "I'll get something in a minute."

"Suit yourself," Doug replied.

"Andy! Where the hell is that man?" Melanie pounded three more times on her makeshift dinner bell.

"Smells good, Mel," Amanda murmured.

"Yes, it does. Thank you, Mel," Maggie said as she took a bowl. "It is very much appreciated."

"Hey Maggie," Krista said. "Did you get a chance to look over the possible garden area?"

"Yes. We went up and looked it over. It should be a great space as long as we can get water up to it. I don't see why it wouldn't work."

"Sweet," Krista said, rubbing her hands together. "We can get started on it first thing in the morning."

Lizz appeared on the loading ramp as she disembarked the *Betty*. "We got everyone?"

"Doug looked around, counting heads. "Has anyone seen Andy? He's the only one left."

"Andy!" Melanie pounded on the drum with all of her might. "Get your ass out here now!"

Doug took a seat at the table with Willy and spooned some of the stew into his mouth. "So, what you got Willy," he asked, sucking in air around a lava hot potato.

"I was right. It was the emitters that were the problem in that new drive on the *Hans Landa*. Everything kept checking out, then I decided to take one more look at the drive's main matrix. From what Lizz had translated for me, the Martians called it a faster than Light Universal Xcellerator or fLUX drive for short. It basically pokes a hole in the thin spots of the space-time fabric. So, it uses natural wormhole points to get us from one place to another without all that muddling about actually getting up to the speed of light or that warp drive idea that they never could get to work out."

"Okay, and? What was actually wrong with it," Doug asked.

"Well ya see, the drive is this gyroscope looking thing. Three rings that spin on different axis points that circulate this super saturated ferrous mercury slurry within the rings. Four EM emitters bombard this crystal matrix at the center once the gyro spins up to full speed. The best I can tell without taking a sample, the crystal is a Kyanite cluster. The gyro itself generates this field that I haven't quite figured out yet. But they use the crystal matrix as an amplifier and that creates the field around the ship to allow it to pass through these weak points."

Lizz took a seat at the table with Doug and Willy. "How are we doing today, gentlemen? Have you found out what was wrong?"

"Dunno yet, he was just starting to tell me about it," Doug said, taking another bite of stew.

"Oh, I'm sorry that I interrupted. Please, continue," Lizz said.

"Well anyways, when I got to really looking at this amplifier assembly, I found two of the four emitters were 0.0005 millimeters off alignment," Willy said. "But they were still within the design specs. The best I can tell, the thing works best when all four emitters are at the same declination to the matrix. If one is off 0.0005, they had all better be off by that much."

"Ok, but were you able to fix it?"

"Oh yeah," Willy said with a big smile. "It wasn't nothing to adjust. I'm just not sure yet what might have knocked it out of alignment or if it'll do it again on the next jump."

"That's just wonderful," Lizz said.

"I went ahead and made lockdown brackets out of some steel bar and duct tape for the time being. Hopefully, they won't move again before I can fabricate some proper locks for them."

"Willy fixed the drive," Doug said with a conspiratorial grin toward Lizz.

"That's some really good news for a change." She raised an eyebrow toward Doug. "I suppose this would be a good time to let everyone in on what we've been discussing."

"I suppose it would," he grinned. "Give it a few. Let everyone eat first." Doug continued to eat his stew in silence. He smiled at the scene before him. They may have vastly different personalities and get on each other's last nerve at times. But they were still one big dysfunctional family.

Once everyone had had the chance to eat, Doug stood and cleared his throat. He knocked his fist against the container he had been using as a table. "Listen up," Doug announced. The mealtime chatter went silent as everyone turned to look in his direction. "I'm not going to wait any longer. Someone can catch Andy up later." He looked to Lizz. She nodded back with a smile.

"We have some good news for a change. Willy has found the problem with the fLUX," he started to say then looked to Willy, who nodded back, "the fLUX drive onboard the Martian ship."

"Wait, what are you saying," Kara interrupted. "Does that mean that we can go home?"

"In theory," Doug said slowly, "yes."

Murmured prayers, chatter and hoots erupted around the encampment. Doug motioned for them to all quiet down.

"Well thank you I suppose, but it wasn't nothing," Andy said as he proudly strode into camp.

"Where *in* the hell have you been, Andy? Sit your ass down right now," Melanie said.

"Is dinner ready?"

"You can wait," Mel said with a huff. "Now sit and hush. Doug was talking." She turned her back on Andy and faced Doug.

"So why in theory?" Trae asked, getting them back on track. "Can't we fire it up and go back the same way we came in?"

"I believe so, but Wes and Rachel have been digging into the guidance systems among everything else. Better to be safe than sorry. Also, before we head back, I want to document everything we can about this system. As far as we know, we are the first humans to leave our home solar system, to actually encounter aliens and step foot on an alien planet. But beyond that, Lizz and I have been discussing other possible future plans."

Lizz stood and nervously smoothed the skirt of her jacketless power suit. She smiled at the crew with a sort of condescending motherly grin. It was the kind of grin, where you know that not everything, she is about to say will be pleasant. "What seems like a lifetime ago, I met Doug and Krista on the streets of Atlanta. At that time, I had lucked into the *Betty*, but I needed people to crew her. These two were young, homeless and damned near starved to death when our paths crossed."

"Wait. I thought the ship belonged to Cap," Fergus interrupted.

"Yeah, that's what I thought too," Willy said.

"Hey, shut your pie holes," Krista yelled. "Can't you see that she's having a moment? Let her finish already!"

The crew went silent.

"Thank you, Krista," Lizz said with a nod, then continued. "Since I knew nothing about running a ship and had no want to learn, I made them an offer. I would take care of the business side of things. Trade, sell, negotiations and the like. They would handle all of the day to day ship operations so I wouldn't have to. So, we came to an amicable agreement. I founded our operations; they ran it and we were all even partners in the venture. But it would be our little secret, so I didn't have to deal with personnel issues." She looked toward Rachel with a sidelong, motherly glance at a trouble-making child.

"What? I didn't do it," Rachel said defensively.

The crew laughed, then Lizz continued. "Shortly after, Wesley and Willy were hired on. They did an amazing job getting the ship space worthy and running again. Over the years other crew members have hired on, then went their separate ways. But all of you, you are the ones that have stayed on through the rough times and the good times. And there have been a lot of rough times, but still, you stayed," she said, fighting back tears. "However dysfunctional that we are, we have become a family."

smiled and swallowed hard as tears began to well up in her eyes. She sucked in an emotionally ragged breath and smoothed her skirt again, composing herself. She cleared her throat and continued. "That being said, Doug and I have discussed a great new venture and I would like to offer each one of you a true stake in it and in our futures. I want to offer each of you the chance to become full partners if we decide to pursue this opportunity."

"I am so confused now," Tiff murmured. "Is she about to try and sell us a condo on a beach in Utah or something?"

"Does that mean that we're not going home?" Kara asked in a confused tone.

Doug pursed his lips and blew out an ear-piercing whistle. "Calm down!" He glared at the crew. "Yes, we are going back to Earth one way or another, now that Willy has the flux drive fixed. The thing is, I think that we have an amazing opportunity here beyond any of our dreams. But it'll take a lot of work to set it up and get it fully functional."

"Whatever you think is good, I'm in Cap," Willy offered.

"Same goes for me Cap," Wes added.

"Wesley," Kara denounced.

"I'm in," Wes sternly glared at Kara. "You haven't steered us wrong yet," he said, turning back to Doug.

"Really Wesley," Kara huffed and slumped in her seat.

"Now just hold on," Doug interrupted. "Hear me out first, then take some time to think about it. It will be a life-changing decision for each and every one of us."

He straightened and stretched, then slid himself up onto one of the storage containers and got comfortable.

"For one reason or another, we have each made a fairly happy home for ourselves on board the *Betty*. And for possibly the first time in any of our lives, we have the opportunity to create something great. It will be of our own making, by our hands, and by our rules. No corporation or government will tell us what to do or how to do it. We call the shots and decide our own fates. So, my question to each of you. Do we fall back into line like good little sheeple or do we blaze our own trail on the new frontier?" He looked at each of the astonished crew before continuing. "As far as we can tell, this system is deserted. What life we have encountered has been feral to primitive. We know that there is another sentient species here, but other than Andy's sighting, we haven't seen any more sign of them. It makes me think that there are very few of them and that they aren't a real threat."

"So then, what are you thinking, Cap?" Trae leaned forward, intrigued.

Doug smiled a manically wide smile. "I propose that we establish a permanent base here in this hangar facility and establish our own colony, free from the control of Earth and the Independent Alliance."

The crew exploded in expletives to one another and murmurs of disbelief.

"By contract," Doug shouted over the din. "The Martian ship is ours. We fairly negotiated for information only to be returned to the Independent Alliance. Any and all salvage was ours, fair and square. When we go back, Lizz and I will fulfill that contractual obligation. But before that, Wes and Willy, I want you to make a special copy of the ships specs and schematics and do a little editing work to them. I really don't want the I.A. making their own drive and putting their nose in our business before we can get ourselves established." He pulled out his silvered cigarette case and retrieved the last smoke in it.

"Our plan," Lizz continued, "is to set up salvage and mining operations in this system. There is an entire planet worth of tech and salvage, plus the existing natural resources of the other planets and the asteroid belt. We would like for each of you as full partners to head up your own respective departments as founding members of the colony."

Doug cleared his throat once again, then continued. "I will handle the day to day operations as always. Lizz will continue with the overall business operations and negotiations. She'll take care of the books as always. Each of you will have your respective departments with people eventually working under you as we can bring them in. Wes will become department head for tech. Witches, medical. Willy, engineering, so on and so forth. For the short term, I want to load our holds to the brim with anything of value so that when we return to Earth, we can get the supplies, equipment, and manpower that we need to bring back and pull this off.

Any new hires that we bring back will be placed where they will benefit our goal best and will be your direct subordinates. Before we go back though," Doug added, "I have a number of tasks that I think we need to complete first. Cheezy, I need to know where we are. People aren't likely to hire on for a trip to the great beyond. But if they can put a finger on a map, it might help out. I also want a full survey of the system with the safest flight paths plotted through The Belt from the flux. We can set up beacons later as needed. But you'll be in charge of all system traffic. Nothing moves without your say so."

"Oh my God, oh my God, oh my God," Rachel said, frantically fanning herself. "You like me! You really do like me!"

"Yeah, something like that," Doug said then turn to Trae. "Trae, Fergus and Geek, I want those satellites operational. At a minimum, I want them functional for system-wide surveillance and communications. You can take *Betty* up, get a better fix on our location and capture one of those satellites. But really dig in and see what you can do to get those satellites functional and armed if possible, not to mention establish our own planetary intranet if their systems will support it."

Trae flashed a thumbs-up toward Doug. "You got it, Cap."

"Willy," Doug continued. "I want to know what it would take to duplicate that flux drive and retrofit *Betty,* or any other ship for that matter. If we reproduce the drive, can we control the drive? Also, pick a space down here as your workshop and we'll get you anything that you need to get started. The more ships that we have available with jump capability, the better. Which reminds me, Geek," Doug added, turning to Wes. "I want you to come up with a plan to hunt down and wipe any files that the Martians may have in the computer core about the ship or the flux drive. Let's not make it easy for anyone to reproduce the ship or drive should it fall into the wrong hands."

"Aye, Captain," Wes said with a two-finger salute.

"Hey, Cap," Trae butted in. "Here's a random thought. Have you thought about hitting up the major universities and such for funding? They might pay a pretty penny for their egg heads to have first dibs on an alien world. You know someone out there will want to study everything about this place. It could be a good bit of seed money for us."

Doug and Lizz smiled at each other. "I'll add that to the to-do list," Lizz cheerfully said.

"Great idea Trae," Doug said. "Keep them coming too. It will only benefit all of us in the end."

"While those of you space side are out of pocket, the rest of us will begin setting up base camp down here. This is cozy," he motioned to the little area they had built over the last month, "but in the long term, it's not very functional. If we are going to have a lot of traffic coming and going, we need to set it up as such before things start to get crowded. We need to move base camp further back toward the core of the starport. That'll give us direct access to the upper levels of the concourse and the smaller hangers as well. Eventually, we may even get this place looking like a functional spaceport again. But it'll take lots of time and lots of manpower."

"Well what about the rest of us, Cap?" Tiff shifted nervously from one foot to the other.

"I'm getting to that." Doug laughed. "Mel, I want you to head up general services. You'll be in charge of food, lodging, company store, that sort of stuff. When we go back Earthside we'll get you some help to run everything. Then once we have an idea on the number of bodies returning, I'll let you know so that you can set up bunks and make adjustments to meals. We'll need a temporary barracks area I suppose until we can set up permanent quarters for the folks coming in. We'll all have to pitch in where we can to make it all happen." He tapped at his lower lip as he drifted away in thought then returned with an abrupt breath. "Witches, you'll be in charge of our foodstuffs here. Plan to grow everything a small colony may need to survive and thrive on its own. And I mean everything. From fruits and vegetables to grains to flowers to even mushrooms and medicinals. I want you to really sit down and figure out what we will need, tools, seeds and supply wise in order to feed a small army with that garden of yours. Even if we need to hire a few gardeners and bring them back. Our survival will ultimately depend on you."

"Are you sure that you want to put so much faith into us," Krista hesitantly asked.

"Absolutely," Doug said, then turned to Andy. "When we get the extra manpower, you'll be in charge of a crew doing planetside salvage. For the time being, I want you to take a vehicle or one of the shuttles. Scout things out around here to see what's available and start mapping the place. We want raw materials, tech, and especially anything that looks immediately useful. Hell, we could even get down to stripping the wire and pipes out of wreckage if we get to it, but I doubt we'll need to do that any time soon.

"Ooo, Ooo, Ooo," Tiff grunted, holding her hand above her head.

"Yes, Tiff," Doug said.

"Can I be in charge of training and entertainment? I could set us up one badass gym with the VR systems and all.

"Um… Sure. You can coordinate with Melanie and take care of securing a perimeter while you're at it. Map out and lock down a defendable perimeter around the heart of the hangar.

"Sweet, I can do that," Tiff said.

"And what about me?" Kara crossed her arms and glared at Doug. "I suppose you want me to go dig for mushrooms or service the waste systems?"

"Actually, no," Doug said with a smile. "I want you to look through the derelict ships left in the hanger and pick one as your own. That ship will take priority for repairs and you'll be in charge of transportation around the system."

"So, you want me to be a taxi?" Kara huffed.

"For now, yes. Now, by the rights of the salvage charters, we can stake a claim to anything not already claimed and file it with the I.A. claims office."

"The only downside," Lizz interrupted, "is that to file the claim we would have to pay a fee of 0.001 credits per cubic ton listed on the claim."

Trae burst out in laughter. "That's a lot of upfront dough if you are going to stake a claim to an entire star system."

"No shit, ummm…," Fergus started. "This might sound retarded, but if we're here and they are there, why are we even bothering with filing a claim in the first place? It's not like they can come to take it from us or anything. I mean, we are the only ones in the known universe with a flux drive. Right?"

"He does have a valid point," Doug said looking over to Lizz.

"I say fuck the man!" Fergus proudly flashed both of his middle fingers at the universe.

"I second that. Fuck the man," Trae said. Unanimous murmurs and chatter erupted from the rest of the crew.

A deep baritone choir voice suddenly burst out in a singsong from seemingly nowhere. "Fu-u-u-uck the man, sooo-oo-o say we all…," Wes sang.

Everyone stared at Wes in disbelief.

"What?" Wes said defensively.

"Oh my God, Wes. That was amazing," Tiff squeaked. "I didn't know that you could sing."

Fergus chuckled. "So how many years did you work under," Fergus said motioning with air quotes, "the priest to learn how to sing like that?"

Rachel smacked Fergus in the back of the head so hard that he fell face-first onto the ground. "That was rude and uncalled for!"

"Shit, I'm sorry," Fergus said, rubbing his head.

"That was really beautiful Geek," Rachael said, her eyes becoming moist.

"Thank you, thank you, I'll be here till Tuesday." Wes bowed, then took his seat again.

"So, I take that as everyone is in?" Doug looked about at each of them.

The crew replied with nodding heads, Aye, Yup, Yes, and an enthusiastic hell yeah from Trae.

"Well okay then." Doug smiled. "We need to have a little talk with our Martian prisoners, then figure out what to do with them."

Wes chuckled, "Lizz as overseer, Doug running things, the Witches in charge of growing supplies and meds, and Mel in charge of services. Doesn't sound like a total disaster to me," he said.

A cacophony of alarm bells and sirens suddenly echoed from the distant darkness.

"What in the hell is that?" Doug asked Willy.

"Hell, if I know." Willy scratched his head. "It isn't any system alarm that I know of."

"It isn't coming from either of the ships," Ferg shouted.

"Oh shit," Andy jumped to his feet and sprinted in the direction of the alarm. "That's one of the traps that I set!"

The Labyrinth

"It is true," a youngling's voice excitedly whispered. Casraownan spun around, surprised to find his only son crouched down behind him, staring wide-eyed at the creatures. "By the light of the great flame, Jouqon, did I not tell you to stay with your sisters? The labyrinth is a dangerous place to wander all alone."

The young Chinchasan stared at his father. "But you come here by yourself all the time. And I wasn't alone," the youngling huffed as he crossed his arms," you were here the whole time with me, even if you didn't know it."

Cass inhaled as if to speak then stopped himself. "Your mother will have my head for this."

"Oh no father, it was her idea." The small Chinchasan said proudly. "She suggested that I should keep my eyes on you to keep you out of trouble."

"Then I must have a talk with your mother when we return."

"Oh," the youngling shouted with fright at the sound of multiple Kaowla's barking. He leapt for Cass's leg and tightly latched on.

"Calm yourself Jouqon, these beings have taken in the pups of the Kaowla mother that they killed after arriving. See there," Cass pointed, "that's the one that I told you about."

"Which one father?"

"That large one surrounded by the pups. That is the one that killed the Kaowla mother with his bare hands. Yet he took in the babes as if they were his own. A true warrior this one is. Honorable, kind, but deadly, nonetheless. Cass stared at the being in awed reverence.

"What do you think they want father?"

"I could not even begin to guess, son. Perhaps they are just passing through. Others of our kind have passed through before. Though it is extremely rare, it does happen once in a lifetime or so, but otherwise very few ever leave their home dens."

"Could they be like the ancient travelers that Fowembes spokes of?"

"Exactly," Cass beamed. "That is exactly what I think they are."

A loud banging and unintelligible shouts erupted from one of the creatures. Jouqon clung tightly to Cass's leg as they both ducked low.

"Have they spotted us, father?" the youngling shakily asked.

"I don't think so. It looks as if they are gathering for a meal. See, the one with dark hair," Cass said as he knelt down and pointed over Jouqon's shoulder. "She keeps checking that pot. She must be like your mother and be in charge of the clan meals."

"Ah, so that noise is her meal bell, like mother's?" Jouqon shifted and moved around to the left of the barricade that they crouched behind.

"Most likely," Casraownan speculated. "And look, more of them are coming out from the lights." He turned to see if Jouqon had looked at where he had pointed, but to his surprise, the youngling had vanished. "Jouqon," he loudly whispered. He looked back toward the encampment of creatures, then back to where the youngling had been just a moment ago. He quickly stepped to the left of the barricade and peered around its edge. "Jouqon," he whispered once more. His eyes caught a glimmer of movement in the darkness that surrounded the creature's encampment.

"Father," Jouqon whispered. "What is this?" The youngling sniffed at a strangely constructed thing. "It smells so delicious, Father."

Casraownan dashed forward at his full speed. "Jouqon, no," he loudly whispered.

"But, Father," the young Chinchasa said as he reached into the thing. "It smells so sweet and tasty."

Casraownan dove toward the youngling. He shoved Jouqon to the side as his momentum carried him into the strange alien construct.

A cacophony of noise enveloped and pummeled his senses.

"Father," Jouqon shouted.

"Run son! Run! Tell the others and do not return!"

cHAPTER 20

Unknown Red Giant System
2nd planet, Northern Hemisphere
Alien Starport
July 1st, 2176 / Evening (Betty Time)

Fergus grunted as he pushed against the makeshift cage. "You know, Andy, if you had built this cage just a little lighter, it might not be such a pain in the ass to move."

"It is what it is," Andy said, "I used what we had available. Just be glad that I welded on a set of retractable wheels. At least we didn't have to lift it or put it on a dolly."

"God," Willy said with a sigh. "Will both of you just shut up and push."

"Hey here's an idea," Fergus said. "Why don't we just shoot him and drag him out of the cage instead?" He pointed a finger at the creature. "Tap tap, two to the head baby." He blew on the tip of his finger as if it were a smoking gun barrel.

The creature trapped in the cage glared at Fergus and emitted a low growl-like sound. It swatted at Fergus's probing finger.

"Bad kitty!" Fergus shouted at the strange cat-like creature. He took a step back and kicked the makeshift cage.

The creature forced its face against the bars, grasping the inside of the cage it growled, baring its teeth toward Fergus.

"Oh, you really think so, do you?" Fergus unzipped his coveralls and stepped forward. "You won't growl at me again, ya little shit."

"Fergus! Enough!" Doug quickly approached from the base camp.

The creature hissed a laugh through its teeth as it lifted its kilt like covering and released a pungent stream that arced across the distance, onto Fergus.

Fergus immediately drew his pistol, racked a round into the chamber and aimed the weapon at the caged creature.

"Fergus!" Doug stepped in, nose to nose with Fergus. "I said enough!"

"But it pissed on me, Cap." Fergus growled through clenched teeth.

The creature hissed and again pressed its face against the bars of the cage. It glared at Fergus with deep, emerald green eyes. A low, growl rumbled in the creature's throat.

Doug drew his revolver from its holster and aimed at Fergus's head. "I will only say this once," Doug said. He drew in a deep breath and cocked the hammer of the .45 caliber weapon. "This is not the way that mankind's first contact with aliens is going down. Put down your weapon or I swear that I'll put you down!"

Both Fergus and the creature unblinkingly stared at Doug in astonishment.

"Cha baad'a," the cat creature said in a low murmur.

"If that's equal to fuck me running, then I totally agree, furball." Fergus uncocked and holstered his weapon.

"He can speak, that's at least a start," Doug said with a nod then holstered his revolver and stepped to the cage.

"My name is Captain Douglas Rackham," he said calmly, placing his palm on his chest. "I know that you don't understand a word that I'm saying, but no man deserves to be caged without a good reason. I'm going to open the cage and turn you loose."

Willy shifted nervously. "Are you sure about that, Cap?"

"Yeah, I'm pretty damned sure. I don't know about anyone else, but I'd rather not have our first contact remembered for abduction or imprisonment."

Doug held both hands out in front of himself, palms open for the cat creature to see. "Friend."

The creature stared at Doug, momentarily motionless as it pondered the situation. "Fff...Frr...Fr...end...Frend," the cat creature slurred and spit as it wrapped its lips around the word.

"I'm going to go out on a limb here and let you out." Cautiously, Doug lifted the locking mechanism and swung open the cage door open. He took a slow step away from the opening, palms open and exposed. "You see, we're all friends here."

The creature nodded at Doug in understanding and cautiously stepped out of the cage and stood before them.

It was easily six feet in height once it was out of the cage and could stand upright. Very feline-like facial features along with a long, lemur-like prehensile tail. Its fur was a thick black with a red iridescence that seemed to almost glow in the low light. It took another step from the cage and stretched, then turned its attention to Fergus. Its short fur stood on end as a low rumble emanated in the throat of the creature. It flexed its already impressive muscles.

Fergus instinctively leapt away, drawing his pistol and bringing it to bear on the cat creature.

"Fergus! I fucking said to stand down," Doug ordered.

The creature turned back, looking at Doug. It blinked rapidly, then turned back to Fergus and let out another chuckled hiss.

"Laugh it up, fuzzball." Fergus reluctantly holstered his weapon, again.

"Come, sit, eat." Doug motioned for the creature to follow as he backed away toward the camp.

The cat creature followed cautiously, one slow, soft-padded step at a time. Within moments, Doug and the creature had crossed the dark distances and entered the light of the base camp area. A red iridescent danced across the cat creature's otherwise charcoal black fur.

"Please sit." Doug sat at one of the makeshift tables and motioned for the creature to do the same.

"Mel," Doug said quietly without turning his gaze from the creature. "Please bring our guest a bowl of stew. We may have initially been rude, but we can still attempt to show our hospitality."

"On it Cap." Mel quickly made her way around the work table; she ladled the stew into a bowl and placed it on the table next to the cat creature.

Doug waved the crew back as they started to gather around. "Everyone give our guest a little room. We don't want to make him think we're surrounding or about to attack him."

"Oh my God, you weren't lying about them," Wes said as he approached. "He looks so damn familiar, but I can't place them." He intently stared at the cat creature. "Me...Wes...You," Wes said questioningly.

"What the hell, Wes? Are we playing space pirates and Indians now?" Trae laughed as he walked down the *Betty's* loading ramp. "The pups are all locked away, Cap."

The cat creature leapt to its feet and sprinted in Trae's direction. Sliding to a halt, the creature knelt before the large man.

Trae stopped in his tracks. "What the...well, um...okay then."

"Aguu araatan amitan. Bi bol Chinchassa Casraownan yum. Bi Tany sür javkhlangiin ömnö ööriigöö bökhiinö. Ööriinkhöö zamyg nadad zaagaach," the cat creature solemnly uttered, his head bowed in reverence.

"Um...Cap?" Trae looked down at the cat creature then back to the Captain.

"Hell Trae, while he's down there worshipping you and all," Fergus laughed with a grab at his own crotch.

"Um...how about, *hell* no," Trae said emphatically. "Hey, cat, dude, thingy. Come on, get up," Trae reached under the creature's heavily muscled arm and lifted him to his feet. He stood nearly as tall as the large man, and easily as broad across the shoulders. "No offense, but I'd rather you didn't do that, man." Trae placed his hand to his chest and patted it. "Trae."

The cat creature glanced down at Trae's hand then back up, a look of understanding blossomed across his face. The creature placed a clawed hand to its own chest, "Casraownan," it said with a bowed head.

"Casraownan, gotcha." Trae patted his chest again, "Trae," then pointed toward Doug. "Captain Douglas Rackham."

"Ca...pee...tan," Casraownan fumbled, then turned back to Trae, "Treee."

"Close enough for now. It's at least a start if nothing else."

"Agreed," Doug said.

"Wes," Lizz interrupted. "How adaptive is our translation software?"

"Um…," Wes pulled back with a perplexed stare. "Adaptive enough, I suppose. I know it has the option to manually enter slang and dialects."

"But what about adding an entirely new language?"

Wes reflexively tapped at his nose as he thought. "I don't see why not. I could copy one of the other database files and manually replace words that we know as we learn them."

"Do it, and make that your top priority," Doug ordered. "The quicker that we can learn their language, the better."

"Aye Cap," Wes slapped the table.

"I've always been good with languages," Lizz said. "I'm going to work with Wes and Cass for a bit just to see what I can pick up." She beamed with excitement.

"Sounds good to me. Get us a working dictionary ASAP, even if it's rough. Just start with the basics and start by making a list for now. Trae, Fergus, care to help me with interrogating the prisoners?"

Krista stood, excited. "I want to help. Can I help? Please?"

"You want to interrogate the prisoners?" Doug quizzically looked at her. "Exactly what experience do you have with interrogating prisoners?"

"You'd be damned surprised at what I've picked up over the years, big boy. Just go on doing what you gotta do and don't you worry yourself none. I've got this," Krista said proudly with a wink at the Captain.

cHAPTER 21

Unknown Red Giant System
2nd planet, Northern Hemisphere
Hans Landa (interrogation room 1) / Alien Starport
July 1st, 2176 / Late Evening (Betty Time)

"Commander Robert *'Flip'* Winston," Doug said as he scrolled through the crew roster on a datapad. Please specify your mission." He calmly began to pace about the small room. The prisoner sat backed against the wall at a small metal table. Wes sat opposite of him.

"Come on Cap, let me Zap him just once. Pretty please." Wes beamed with maniacal delight. His eyes bulged as a wide smile crept across his face. The smell of burnt ozone filled the small space as Wes clicked the button on the taser, causing a blue arc to jump across the probes.

The prisoner shifted on the cold metal seat. He scratched at his stubbled face and leaned forward, across the small table. "You never know big boy, I might just like that sort of treatment." He winked at Wes with a lusty smile.

Fergus sat stark still, across the small table from the prisoner. His face grew redder by the moment as he forced deep breaths through his nose.

"You see, when Fergus here hits his boiling point, he may decide to rip off an ear or maybe even just your pinky finger. But once it starts there's nothing that I can do to stop him."

"But I didn't do anything," the prisoner said pleadingly.

Trae sighed and disappointingly shook his head. "It's your funeral, man." Trae stood, uncrossing his arms and slipped out the door of the small room.

"So, I said to the guy, there's nothing that you can do. They're young and got to live their own lives."

"Exactly!" Willy shouted, bringing both open palms down upon the metal tabletop. "I don't know how many times I've told my sister, those exact same words. But nooo. In one ear and out the other. She's the kind that's got to have her nose in everyone else's business."

"Wasn't this supposed to be an interrogation?" Andy shifted nervously.

"Well...Yeah," Big Willy said, fumbling with the thought, then looked back to the prisoner. "What do you think Bob? Do you feel interrogated yet?"

Bob adjusted the size too small flight suit and leaned forward on the table, stretching the garments seams to their breaking point. He smiled at Willy. "You have done a very thorough job up to this point. And I must say that even though this has been the first and only time that I have ever been interrogated, I have found the entire situation a thoroughly enjoyable experience."

"Ooookay…" Andy said questioningly.

"Oh, and where are my manners," Willy interrupted. "Would you care for some sweet tea, Bob?"

"Why yes, I would Willy. That would be absolutely wonderful."

"Dieter, Johan, Captain. Martian Fatherland defense forces, 130-4752-6240," the prisoner said coldly in a heavy German accent.

Krista slapped her palms down on the small metal table. "Alright, that's it, we did it your way, Maggie. I am so sick and tired of waiting for him to talk. Let's just make him talk!"

"Please Captain Dieter, we just need to know if you'd like to stay on or go back to Earth," Maggie said pleadingly.

"Amanda, bag," Krista barked with a snap of her fingers.

Amanda glared at Krista. "Rude much?" She dropped a heavily laden duffle bag on the floor next to Krista and unzipped it.

Krista up at Dieter and smiled. "Now let me see what we have to work with here." She leaned down, rummaging around in the bag for a moment before producing a highly polished speculum. The fluorescent light of the room reflected from the chromed duckbill-like paddles.

A look of panicked concern washed over the prisoner's face. "Vas ist das?"

The jaws of the device expanded with a satisfying click as Krista squeezed the handle. She glanced back to Dieter. A mischievous grin danced on her face as she continued to work the handle. "What? This little ole thing? It's just something that I picked up at an antique medical auction. I've always wanted to try this thing out, but no one has ever been willing to let me. You're a prisoner. You don't have to *let* me do anything." She smiled wide.

"Really Wes," Doug sighed as he massaged the bridge of his nose. "No, for the last time you *can not* tase the prisoner. Just drop it!"

"Awwww," Wes said pleadingly. "Come on Cap. Just one little zap. Pretty please with sugar on top."

"Yeah Cap, just one little zap. Please? Right here," Commander Winston unzipped his flight suit, pulled up his undershirt then licked his finger and began to rub his left nipple.

The prisoner screamed out in pain. "I'll tell you anything that you want to know! Please! Just get him off of me!"

Trae grasped Fergus in a chokehold and leaned back. "Drop him, Ferg! Come on man, do *not* do this to me again. You don't know where this guy has been."

Fergus's jaw muscles flexed as he continued to gnaw on the prisoner's arm.

"Oh my, yes," Bob said. He took a satisfying gulp of his iced tea then set the glass back on the table and casually crossed his legs. "You see, I found that if you divide the injectors into clusters of five instead of the three large primary injectors for the intermix chamber there is a marked difference in response time and power output.

"But even if you divide the flow out into clusters that would cause turbulence in the system and the heat build-up would be exponential at that junction," Willy argued.

"Do you have the D-7 upgrade or the D-8?"

Willy chuckled under his breath. "Oh no, we're still on the D-3 system."

"Oh really? Well then," Bob gulped his tea. "That is just wonderful by the way, thank you." He snuck another light sip then returned it to the table. "But I digress. You see Willy, you just install new cooling coils around each individual injector and modify the stock coolers to encompass each cluster."

"But if it's set up the way that I'm picturing in my head, those injector assemblies would be at least two and a half meters in diameter."

Bob rolled his eyes in introspection, "Yes, that sounds about right."

"Won't work. There isn't enough space in the maintenance tube."

"She's a J model Nova Star transport, isn't she?"

Willy chuckled again. "Oh no. The Betty is a C model, tail number 82-0033. She was one of the first to be retrofitted for colonization duty."

"Oh my." Bob sipped at his tea for another moment. "I thought the last of the C models were decommissioned around 2120."

"They were, but we pulled her out of mothballs."

"Wow, that had to be an amazing feat in itself," Bob gasped.

Willy laughed at the memory. "Oh, it was."

"Well I hate to say it, but there isn't much you can do then without a full out retrofit, which includes structural modifications to accommodate the newer equipment."

Andy uncomfortably shifted in the corner. "Um...I'm just going to go ahead and go if you don't need me," he said interrupting.

"That's absolutely fine," Bob replied. "And thank you again for fetching such a lovely glass of tea," he said as he took another gulp.

"Dieter, Johan, Captain, 130-4752-6240"

"Do you think that we should use the ball gag or just an old sock to gag him with?"

Maggie let out a shocked gasp. "Why would you gag him?"

"Because I'm going to make him scream if he doesn't stop that incessant name, rank, serial number crap." Krista rummaged around in the duffle bag.

"That wouldn't be right of us as healers," Maggie said.

"There are all sorts of ways people can heal and sometimes that healing can be painful."

"Oh hey, what's this thing?" Amanda picked up an odd-looking two-handled contraption. A small motor was mounted to the rear of the device and an oddly shaped phallic like shaft protruded from the opposite end.

"Oh, that might be a little above your experience level, dear," Krista said with a, *you're not worthy* sorta wave.

"How do you turn it on?"

"Flip that little red switch by your thumb and pull the chord if you really think you're up for it."

Amanda flipped the switch and pulled the cord with all of her might.

Wes smacked his palm down onto the small metal table. "Stop it!"

Commander Winston smacked the table, perfectly mimicking Wes. "Stop it!"

"That's it you son of a bitch!" Wes leapt to his feet, sending his chair flying backward and pressed the arcing tip of the taser to the metal tabletop. Commander Winston convulsed to the rapid beat of high voltage electrical arcs.

"Wes! Out! Now," Doug ordered.

"But Cap, he wouldn't stop copying me!"

"Out!"

"Fine," Wes stormed out of the room in a huff.

Doug pressed the intercom switch on the wall near the door. "Medic."

"I am very sorry that you had to experience that Mr. Ward. I didn't think that my partner's PTSD's were as bad as they had presented themselves," Trae said apologetically.

"You people let that madman walk freely about on this ship?'

"I swear to you that most of the time he is perfectly fine." Trae leaned forward and looked around to be sure they weren't overheard. "You see, I know war trophies are illegal and all, but it's one of the few things that will calm him down. He will be back in his bunk finding his zen for the moment, so you have nothing to worry about."

"But what the hell is wrong with him? I mean, look at my arm." Richie held up his arm for Trae to examine. The flight suit material hung in tatters. "He tore the sleeve of my flight suit open and left teeth marks so deep that I'll need stitches."

"Do you really want to know?"

"Yes, I do."

Trae let out a long, reluctant sigh. "You see, Fergus was a smuggler back in the day during the Demios station revolt. He just happened to be in the wrong place at the wrong time. They took him prisoner and kept him on lockdown for over two years." Trae's gaze drifted off to his left in deep thought. He cleared his throat then continued. "He doesn't really talk about it too much. The things that they did to that man," Trae looked away and rubbed his sleeve across his eyes. "Well, that's all beside the point I suppose. One day he managed to escape his cell. Something about the locking mechanism failed or became jammed or something. Anyways, by his count, he had killed forty-seven guards and the warden of thc facility before he managed to steal a transport shuttle and haul ass out of there." Trae took in a few slow, deep breaths to recompose himself. "From each of the male guards that he killed; he took one testicle. And for the few females that tried to stop him, he claimed a nipple."

"Oh my God," Richie gasped.

"I know right?" Trae nervously rocked in his seat. "When the voices get the better of him, he goes down to his quarters and puts on his flesh necklace. It helps him to re-center and ground himself." Trae demonstrated with a deep inhale; his arms outstretched to either side. Then he let out a long exhale, palms inward, forefingers and thumbs touching.

"But what the hell set him off like that? I don't know him. I never did anything to him," Richie said.

"It wasn't anything that you did. It's just the uniform. He was trying to kill the uniform and you just happened to be the one wearing it."

Richie immediately unzipped his flight suit and began to undress. "You get me a change of clothes and I'll do whatever you tell me to do. I have no love for Mars or Martians, they did kidnap me, after all."

"Honestly, William. May I call you William?" Bob leaned forward, lacing his fingers together on the tabletop.

"Of course," Willy said.

"The more that I think about it, the more I realize that I really have nothing to go back to on Earth. I don't have any family and no real friends to speak of. The only thing that I'm really leaving behind is a small collection of business acquaintances." Bob sipped his tea slowly as he contemplated his next words. "Even when the Martians abducted me, it wasn't a difficult transition. It just seemed like a new opportunity with a bit of excitement and adventure tossed in for good measure." He tapped a nervous beat on the table with his fingertips.

"You still have some time to think it through," Willy said, reassuring him.

"Well... there isn't anything to think through. The reality is that my old job would have replaced me years ago. There was no reason for them to hold my position open. So I'd say that I'm in. Though I would like to return to Earth and tie up any loose ends that may still be dangling in the wind. I could possibly see if my landlord had saved any personal effects and such."

"I'm sure that the Captain wouldn't have a problem in the slightest with that, Bob." Willy held out his hand to shake.

Bob took his hand with a firm grip and smiled.

"Welcome aboard Bob."

"What in the world sounds like a two-stroke engine?" Doug opened the door to the small interrogation room.

"Don't do it, Amanda! You don't know the power that you wield in your hands." Krista moved the metal chair between herself and Amanda."

"Don't do it, sweetie. You don't really want to hurt the Goddess, do you," Maggie said pleadingly.

Dieter's face melted with hope at the sight of Doug entering through the doorway. "Captain! Please, sir! I beg you, unchain me and let me out of this asylum."

Amanda kicked the chair across the room and revved the small engine of the device. She lunged toward Krista. "Fuck you, sadist!"

cHAPTER 22

Unknown Red Giant System
The orbit of 2nd planet
The Betty / Cargo Bay
July 2nd, 2176 / 1152 hours (Betty Time)

Fergus sat perched on the edge of the *Betty's* open cargo bay. He kicked his feet in the open vacuum of space as if he sat on the edge of a swimming pool on a warm summer day. "Hold up, stop right there. That looks about even, hon," he said over the comm system of his spacesuit.

"Copy that, sugar buns," Rachel said. "Locking her down. *We are at station keeping."*

A bubbly empty slurp broadcasted through the open comm signal. "Dammit," Fergus said. "Goodbye, my sweet, savory goodness."

Trae threw his hands up into the air in frustration then laced his gloved fingers together behind his helmeted head. *"What the hell, Fergus. Did you fill your drink pack with that fruit punch mix again? You know that stuff is hell to get washed out of the suits water bladder."*

Fergus released a belch from the inner depths of his soul. *"Nope."* He smacked his lips together. "Oh, that does not taste the same coming back up. This time I got smart," He said with a chuckle. "I mixed a root beer and whiskey in it. All kinds of yum right there, mmhm."

"You're cleaning that suit this time if you upchuck in it."

"Yeah yeah," Fergus said. "Bla bla bla. You know, you're as bad as my wife sometimes."

"Um...Dear. I can still hear you," Rachel interrupted.

"Oh...um... Love you, Hon."

"Uh hu."

"Are you sure that you want to try this?" Trae pointed to an overhead hoist assembly. *"I've got the harpoon working again. It wouldn't be anything to set up and fire. And the magnetic grappler should do the job as long as there's some sort of iron alloy in that thing."*

"Are you fucking kidding me, man? Hell yeah, I'm sure. I am going to be the first person to free fall from orbit and capture an alien satellite with my bare hands. I am going to get my name into the freaking record books, biaaatch!"

Trae laughed with a moan. *"God love you, Ferg, cause no one else will. Alright then, it's your funeral, brother."* Trae walked over to a storage locker and retrieved a large fire extinguisher. *"Are you sure that you're ready for this? Last chance to back out, man."*

Fergus leaned over peering through the opening and sighed. "It may be as hot as a cajun country boil in hell and smell like a fermented locker room down there, but it's still gorgeous from up here." He swung his legs up and slid himself away from the edge of the cargo bay opening.

"Hey dumb shit," Rachel chimed in. *"You do realize that if you die, I get to finally play war with your miniature collection?"*

Fergus turned and looked up toward the ceiling of the cargo bay. "What the fuck will I care? I'll be dead." He chuckled, then clipped the shackled end of the tow cable onto the harness point of his suit.

"Here ya go Ferg." Trae handed him the overly large fire extinguisher. *"Safe journey Brother."* Trae punched him in the shoulder then made his way to the catwalk ladder.

"Awww. You better be careful with that shit. You might make me think that you actually care." Fergus stepped back to the edge of the open cargo bay and stared at the dusty planet far below.

Trae pulled a lever on the control panel for the overhead crane. *"Clutch is disengaged, Ferg. Cheezy, go ahead and shut down the gravity plating."*

The minute vibrations and background hum of the ship's gravity generator suddenly ceased.

"Oh wow," Rachel gasped.

Fergus looked up at Trae on the upper catwalk and shrugged his shoulders. "What?"

"The ship is eerily quiet without the Grav generators running."

"That's it? You'll get over that shit soon enough," Fergus said.

"Be careful space marine. Something from the deep dark may grab you and drag you out to deep dark space where it will slowly digest you over a thousand million years," Rachel said then moaned a sound similar to a cross of a tormented spirit mingled with the cry of a young bull moose at the start of mating season.

"That's it?" Fergus turned on his spot and looked upward at the ceiling in the direction of the bridge. "I'm about to make the record books and all I get is your moose in heat moan?"

"May...be."

"That's pretty damned disappointing," Fergus said as he knelt down at the edge of the portal. "Screw it, I'm out." He gripped the edge of the opening and let himself fall through the open portal. He clung to the edge of the outer door and dangled beneath the ship. "Hey y'all, look! I'm a dingleberry."

"We already knew that," Rachel said.

Fergus gurgled a wet burp. "Oh, blegh." He smacked his lips. "That tastes so damn nasty."

"You alright out there, buddy?"

"Yeah." Fergus swallowed hard. "Just enjoying the...hic..." Fergus forced the root beer froth back down his throat with a loud gulp. A small globule of foamy brown liquid drifted aimlessly across his view. "Well, that's probably not good."

"*What's not good? Hey, shit stain,*" Rachel said.

"Nothing."

"*Dammit Ferg, hold it in like a man,*" Trae said.

Fergus sucked in a deep gasping breath.

"*What the hell are you doing out there? All I can see is the top of your head around the edge of the opening.*"

He sucked in deeply once more and slurped in the floating brown globule. The bubbly brown liquid slammed into the back of his throat and cause him to violently cough. "Nothing, man," he said hoarsely. "Just breathing in the awesomeness of powerfully emotional moment."

"*Uh hu, right,*" Trae said suspiciously. "*Just go ahead and push off when you're ready. Remember, toss the extinguisher just before you get to the satellite and grab onto it like it's a greased pig.*"

Fergus snorted a laugh. "Soo-Ee!" He pulled himself around from where he dangled. Planting his feet on the outer hull he stood upright on the underbelly of the ship, fists on his hips. "In the name of all humanity, I declare myself the king of all that my eyes gaze upon!"

"*Really?*" Rachel laughed. "*Quit stalling like a little chicken shit and jump already. I have hundreds of mint condition packages to go start opening.*"

Fergus tucked the fire extinguisher under his arm and crouched down. He disengaged the magnetic boots of his suit and kicked off from the belly of the ship. "Off we go, into the pitch-black vacuum! Soaring high, over the sky," he sang horribly off-key to an old military anthem. He squeezed the trigger of the extinguisher and blasted forward, off course. "Whoa, Nelly!"

"*Let go of the trigger, you moron,*" Trae said. "*Short bursts! You know better than that.*"

"Yeah, yeah. Bite me."

"Don't tell him that, dear. He may take you up on the offer."

Fergus aimed the extinguisher nozzle to his left and tapped the trigger. "I think I got it. Looks like I'm back on course."

"Good," Trae said, releasing the breath he was holding. *"Stay on course and you'll be there in no time."*

"So, do you think Cap will let us call dibs on some of the salvage once we figure out all of the tech issues?"

"I have no idea, Ferg," Trae said. *"It would be pretty sweet though. Especially if those abandoned ships actually have energy weapons on board. That would so be worth hours of busted knuckles to get them operational again. Steady man, you're getting close."*

"I got eyes ya know," Fergus said.

"You're coming in a bit hot, don't you think? You might want to put on the brakes," Trae shouted.

Fergus swung the extinguisher from under his arm in a graceful overhead arc that continued to carry its momentum and Fergus in a backward somersault. "Um, well that's not good. Oh God, not good." The sound of muffled dry heaves permeated the comm signal.

"Almost there, Ferg. Hold it together buddy. You got this."

"What the hell are you two knuckleheads doing down there?"

"Um...Hey hun," Fergus said.

"Yeah, What?"

"My Magna XL tank is off-limits. Keep it in the package. Do...Not...Open it!"

"Wait, what?" Rachel shouted over the comms. *"Fergus, you get your ass onto that piece of space junk and back on this ship before I kill you myself."*

Fergus tapped the trigger of the extinguisher to slow his rotation. "Oh shit, this is gonna hurt." Plastic crunched and crumpled as he smacked hard enough into the satellite to be heard over the radio.

"*Fergus,*" Rachel shouted. "*Fergus! Dammit man. Trae, what's happening?*"

"*Well, he's on the satellite at least,*" Trae said.

"Uuug," Ferus groaned.

"*Hey, Ferg. You alright buddy?*"

"No. I'm dead. Asshole. But I think I tinkled a little in my suit."

"*Dammit man,*" Rachel said sobbing. "*I'm gonna break your neck when you get back here! Don't ever do that to me again!*"

"Love you too hun," Fergus gasped. "You did you get a video, didn't you?"

"*Yup,*" Trae laughed. "*And still recording. From start to finish including that fancy pinwheel maneuver thingy you pulled off and the horrible ass landing.*"

Fergus grunted in obvious pain. "It may have been horrible, but I did it, bitches! Woo, ouch. Note to self, ribs may be cracked."

"*Yes, you did. You are such a good boy, yes you are. You're such a good little Fergie,*" Trae said.

Fergus shook his leg and leaned to the left as if he were a dog being scratched behind the ear. "Oh yeah, right there, baby." He chuckled, then reached behind his back and detached the cable from his belt. He looped it through what looked like a mounting or lifting point on the satellite structure and clipped the end back to the cable. "That should do the trick. Alright, reel me in big daddy."

Trae engaged the clutch mechanism, slowly drawing in the cable slack. "*Hold on to something Ferg. It's going to jerk pretty hard.*"

"Spider monkey mode engaged! Become the monkey. Embrace the monkey. I am a spider monkey," Fergus sang in a sing-song tone. The cable drew tight and the satellite bucked.

Fergus slid backward across its bronzed surface, catching the edge of a panel with two fingers. "Whoa, shit Trae! Hold up!"

Rachel keyed the comms, *"Let the asshole fall."*

"Bitch!"

"Ass!"

"Now children," Trae said.

Fergus scooched his way up the side of the satellite and straddled it like a rodeo cowboy on a bucking bronco. "Alright, Trae, I'm ready. Let's try it again."

"Alright then, here we go." Trae reengaged the clutch. The cable drew tight once again and jerked the satellite toward the ship.

"Oh yeah, baby! I got it this time! Yee Haw!" Fergus threw a hand over his head like a cowboy out of the gate. "Holy mother Mary and the saints of whiskey. Rachel, check the sensors. There was just this massive flash of light. Umm...Shit. From my point of view, it was around the ship's ten o'clock at maybe eleven-thirty high. I just caught a glimpse of it over the edge of the hull."

"Okay, hang on," Rachel said.

"Hey Ferg," Trae said in a questioning tone. *"What kind of flash? Did it look like an explosion?"*

"Naw man. It was just this big white flash. It built up, got really bright, then winked out. It was bright enough out here that I had to squint, and the visor on this helmet is tinted."

"Holy shit guys," Rachel shouted. *"Contact! We have contact! Bogey bearing three two three-point four by seven two six upspin of the ecliptic and it's freaking massive."*

"Shit, shit, shit! Trae, dude," Fergus said. "Can't you make that winch go any faster?"

"Not if I want to keep it from crashing into the ship," Trae said.

"What's it doing hon? Shit, um...Shut down the radar? Go to passive sensors only so we don't ping them. See if you can get a visual on them. Whooo! We got ourselves a real live alien ship!" Fergus exploded in nervous laughter. "I sure hope they aren't the kind of aliens that probe on the first date.

"Shut up you freaking spaz, I got it under control," Rachel said. *"All systems running silent."*

"Watch your head, Ferg," Trae said. *"Hurry up and crawl around unless you want to be scraped off the side of that thing like a bug on a windshield. You're drifting too close to the edge of the bay and there's nothing I can do to steer it."*

"Aw crap, low bridge." Fergus scuttled around the circumference of the satellite. "What are they doing now hon?"

"Picking their butts and sniffing it," she said. *What the hell do you think they are doing, you freaking spaz."*

"Oh, ha ha ha. Seriously, what are they doing?"

"Whoa," Rachel gasped.

"Whoa? What whoa," Trae repeated. *"That kind of whoa isn't normally a good thing."*

"Just got a visual," She said. *"It isn't the greatest because they are way out there right now. Like, upspin of the ecliptic and near the inside edge of the asteroid field. Approximately fourteen million klicks distance. Whoa!"*

"Whoa what," Trae asked. *"We really need to work on your vocabulary Cheezy. Define this whoa."*

"Another whoa is never a good sign," Fergus added.

"I agree, it isn't," Trae added.

"They are transmitting on multiple frequencies across the band," she said. *"I think they are scanning the system. Hurry up guys, let's get out of here and back to base camp before they spot us."*

"Hang on Ferg," Trae disengaged the winch and removed a long pole that was attached to the catwalk handrail. *"Doors closing."* Trae pressed a button on the control panel. Fergus and the satellite continued to drift upward at a slow snail-like pace. *"Ready?"*

"Yup, ready," Fergus said.

Trae locked a leg through the handrails and pushed against the hull of the ancient device.

"I thought you said you'd never touch me with a ten-foot pole," Fergus said with a chuckle.

"For your information, this pole is twenty feet and I'm still not gonna touch you."

"Well, why the hell not?"

"Just no man, and I'll leave it at that."

"Awww." Fergus sniffed and whimpered. "Oh hey, almost there." He pulled himself along to the lower edge of the satellite and pushed off toward the deck. He landed on all fours gripping the grating. "Okay, come on down like another foot or two on the front."

Trae pushed the massive satellite with the thin metal pole. It drifted downward and contacted the now closed cargo bay doors.

"Alright, hon, turn the grav plating back on and get us out of here. We'll get it strapped down. The space turd has landed!"

Unknown Red Giant System
2nd planet / Alien Starport
The Betty / Workshop
July 2nd, 2176 / Afternoonish (Betty Time)

Lizz dipped her finger into the metal cup and swirled it about in the contents. She made a show of pouring the water into a clear glass for the cat creature. "Water," she said pointing to the liquid in the glass. "We call it water. What do you call it, Casraownan?"

Momentarily perplexed, Casraownan looked to Lizz, then to the glass of water. He smiled wide, in an expression of understanding. "Wa...Waterrr." He proudly nodded.

"But what do you call it?" Lizz pointed to the cat creature. He inhaled with a gasp of surprised joy and replied, "utss," followed by a barely audible purr. He then dipped his fur-covered finger into the glass and flicked droplets at Lizz. He propped his chin against his fist and leered at her with a mischievous smile.

"Hey Casanova," Wes said, interrupting. "Water," Wes held up his left hand, palm up. "utss," he said as he held up his right palm.

Casraownan blinked rapidly then nodded in understanding. "Waterrr, tiim utss," he said with a nod.

Wes entered the word into the translator database. "Alright, what's next?"

Lizz looked around the compartment. "I'm not sure what else to show him. What else on this ship would have a counterpart in his primitive, subterranean world?"

"Well, how about colors or numbers," Wes suggested.

"No." Lizz looked at Casroawnan in contemplation. "We can get colors and numbers at any time. What we need is to quickly get a large chunk of vocabulary in order to make some real progress. What is it that you bloody Americans say? A crash course cram session?"

"Okay...So how do you suggest that we go about it?

Lizz snapped her fingers and smiled. "We need to let him teach us. If we can get him to teach us his world, then we'll have a baseline that we can work with."

"And how do you suggest that we do that? We have body parts and water so far. Do you think he'll really take us to his home?"

Lizz turned to Wes, excitement beamed across her face. "That's bloody brilliant, Wesley." She stepped over to Wes and excitedly kissed him on the top of his head. "Pack your bags Geek. We're taking this show on the road!"

cHAPTER 23

Chinchassan burrow

"We should send someone to look for Casraownan," Mapharye said, pleading to Lilhanya. "If what Joquon says is true, Casraownan may need our help."

Ceiwo crossed his arms and hissed. "There are no such beings and we must maintain ourselves. Just because Casraownan has run away to sulk somewhere in the Labyrinth, does not mean that we should send anyone to search for him!"

Lilhanya hissed. "Ceiwo, calm down. If there is a chance that Casraownan is in actual trouble, then shouldn't we send someone to find out?"

"He was captured by the tailless creatures," Jouqon said, pleading to the others. "I saw them with my own eyes!"

"Silence child!" Gabhothi hissed. He leaned closer to the young Chinchassan. "Know your place, youngling. Our decision is final." He scowled at the child.

Jouqon straightened and squared himself off with Gabhothi. "I will not be silent. Casraownan is my father and I will see to his rescue myself if I must," the youngling said with a defiant growl.

"Jouqon!" Mapharye jerked him away from the clan elder.

Lihanya stifled a giggle. "Casraownan is most definitely your father, youngling. You have his fire in your heart."

"Jouqon is right, you know," Minyetyuh quietly added.

Gabhothi let out a low, throaty growl. His dark gray fur bristled with rage. "Silence you petulant girl!" He glared at the black-furred female.

"You should know by now that that will never happen, Father," Minyetyuh said then smiled at the elder Chinchassan.

"Nor I," Tesya, a young multi-toned female declared as she walked over to stand beside her sister, Minyetyuh.

"And what say you, Father," Olne asked gruffly, directing her question to Ceiwo. She joined the growing throng of frustrated young females. Her gray tabby-like stripes bristled with anger. "Isn't this something that we should all have a say in?"

Younglings joined the gathering of females. They latched onto their mother's legs or attempted to clamber into loving arms.

"He...he...he...he…" Fubar sang a laugh from his pallet along the back wall. "Insurrection is upon us, my brothers. The same as you started when we were barely grown ourselves," the malformed Chinchassan said in a hoarse whisper.

"Enough! Lilhanya, tend to your charges or you'll be the one to pay for this," Ceiwo ordered, seething with rage.

Lilhanya exploded with laughter. "Why should I? What if what Casraownan and Jouqon have said is true? What if there is a threat to us, to the younglings? Should we not prepare?"

Gabhothi spat. "Ha! If it were true, we would be exposing ourselves if we went looking for him. They could follow us back to our home."

"You do believe," Olne said. She stepped forward and stared into her father's eyes. "You're afraid, aren't you, Father?"

"Nonsense," Gabhothi said dismissively. Looking away he shuffled over to a stone and sat down.

"Then what is it that you fear, Father," Olne asked. "Do you fear for our safety?"

Gabhothi grumbled under his breath. His jaw muscles flexed as he chewed on the words that he did not want to speak.

"Then what? What is it that keeps you from sending someone to check on one of our own? What is it that you fear so badly that it paralyzes you," Lilhanya demanded.

"He fears change," Casraownan said. His deep voice boomed through the chamber.

All turned in surprise toward his voice. Casraownan stood tall and proud at the chamber entrance. Behind him stood three tailless and nearly furless creatures.

"Call the rest of the clan," Casraownan demanded. "We have much to discuss."

cHAPTER 24

Unknown Red Giant System
2nd planet / Alien Starport
July 2nd, 2176 / Afternoon (Betty Time)

"Ho...Ly...Shit Cap," Wes said with a gasp. "It's a monkey cat boobie farm!"

Doug and Lizz glanced back at Wes with confused looks, then back to the chamber full of alien cat creatures. The cavern was both wide and tall, and opened to least twice as tall as a man and illuminated by the blue glow of bioluminescent moss. Each of the creatures wore a leathery kilt like garment around their waist, similar to what Casraownan wore. Save for the fur that covered every inch of their bodies, they were all otherwise nude. The distinction between male and female of their species easily stood out in the gathered crowd of aliens. The females of their species proudly displayed their very human-looking breasts. Both large and small breasts protruded from their very human-like, though fur-covered chests.

"What?" Doug turned back to Wes.

"I know why Cass looked so damned familiar!" Wes's eyes bulged with excitement. "There was this old-world series called *Destroyermen* that had these kilt-wearing cat creatures who had evolved on this parallel earth instead of humans. Oh my god, they look exactly how I had pictured them!"

"Oookay then." Doug turned his attention back to the group of cats as the old, hunched gray one began shouting at Cass.

Lizz leaned over toward Doug and whispered. "What do you suppose that he's going on about?"

"Dunno," Doug said with a huff. "Let's just hope that it doesn't involve eradicating the invading aliens."

Wes leaned forward between Doug and Lizz. "What? Are you serious? You don't really think they would do that do you? We're the good guys."

"Think about it," Doug said, keeping his eyes on the cat creatures. "An alien species, unlike anything that you have ever seen before in your life has just shown up on your doorstep and you have no idea what they want. Wouldn't you get a little paranoid?"

"True, that's a good point," Wes said. "But Cass wouldn't let them hurt us. He seems interested in helping us."

Lizz laughed out loud. "What if he's the aluminum foil hat wearing conspiracy theorist that everyone ostracizes?"

"Oh crap," Wes blurted. "I didn't think about that."

"Yeah, that's it, exactly," Doug said turning to Wes. Movement in the corner of his eye caught his attention. A smaller, child-sized version of the cat aliens slinked about the edge of the chamber toward them. "Looks like someone might be coming to say hi." Doug nodded in the small creature's direction.

"Awww, would you look at it. It's so cute." Wes knelt down and motioned for the creature, "It's ok little guy, we're not going to hurt you."

Lizz smacked Wes in the back of the head. "Are you bloody stupid or something Wesley? You want to pet one of their children like it's a kitten?"

Wes thought for a quick moment. "Probably a bad idea, isn't it?"

"Yeah," Doug said. "It's probably the worst idea that you could come up with at this particular moment."

The small alien nimbly rounded the adults. It stopped in mid slink at the sound of a hissing growl that came from the older, gray furred creature.

"Oh shit," Wes said, pushing himself upward.

"Get up you bloody bogan." Liz's gaze darted from one cat creature to another around the room. "This could turn bad quickly if we aren't careful. We may need to run."

Casraownan bellowed a deep yowl that echoed throughout the chamber then turned his attention back to the old gray cat-creature. The old one straightened and said something in their native tongue to Cass. The small cat bounded toward Casraownan and leapt into his arms.

Doug leaned toward Lizz, "One of his children possibly?"

"It's possible. Did you see that gray and white female reach out like she was worried?" Doug asked. "Do you suppose that's his wife or mate or whatever they use?"

Cass approached the small group of humans, the child held close in his arms. He repeated the earlier exercise, hand on his chest, "Casraownan." He then pointed to the child he held in his arms, "Jouqon."

"He's introducing us." Lizz smiled with amazement. Cautiously, she held up a hand and reached for the child. "Jouqon?" She tickled the child's belly. It squirmed and laughed a laugh that sounded like it was hacking up a hairball. It curled over onto Lizz's hand and latched on, its claws lightly dug into the skin as a warning. "It's alright little one, I'm not going to hurt you," she cooed.

Cass eased each of the child's claws from Lizz's hand.

Doug rummaged in the cargo pocket of his pants and produced a ration pack snack bar. "Wes, do you think that they can eat our food, or do you think it might make them sick?" He removed the bar and tucked the packaging back into his cargo pocket.

"No telling for sure. But Cass here had one of those bars earlier and it didn't mess with him that I could tell."

Cass whispered something to the child, then its tiny arms sprung out, reaching for the bar.

"I don't think there's any worry over the food," Lizz said.

Jouqon took the bar, sniffed at it then immediately shoved it into its mouth. It open mouth chewed, cooing over the new delicacy.

Murmurs and bits of conversation flitted about from the other cat creatures in the room.

Doug's comm unit suddenly beeped. He growled with a nervous grin aimed toward Casraownan and the others. The device beeped again. Doug held up a finger then stepping away he keyed the mic.

"I'm kinda busy here, what's up," he whispered into the device.

"Cap, we've got a slight problem up here." Worry laced Rachel's voice. *"Something big just appeared out of nowhere while we were in orbit. The boys figured out how to tap into the satellite system using the one we snagged. The thing is massive and it's moving closer to us."*

"Alright, just hang tight Cheezy," Doug said, glancing back at the gathering of alien creatures. "We'll be back up there in a few. Have the boy's prep for a fight and get everyone ready to bug out if we have to."

"Copy that Cap, Cheezy out."

Doug turned back to Lizz and Wes. "Looks like we've got company."

cHAPTER 25

Unknown Red Giant System
2nd planet / Alien Starport
The Hans Landa / Bridge
July 2nd, 2176 / Afternoon (Betty Time)

"That thing has got to be nearly a klick in length," Trae said as he scanned over the data readout. "Ferg, can you get an accurate measurement with the satellites?"

"Give me just a sec," Fergus said. "The computer is moving a bit slow. It's having a little trouble translating the signal from the satellites." Fergus tapped at the control console.

Rachel pulled Big Willy's pipe wrench from beneath her seat. "Does it need an adjustment?"

"Dammit, Cheezy!" Willy let out a frustrated huff. He reached over and snatched the wrench from her hands. "Didn't I tell you to leave my tools alone."

"And no dear," Fergus added, "We don't need you to make any adjustments to this ship. We're on the Martian ship instead of the *Betty* because you made adjustments to the viewscreen over there. How about you just sit back and relax for the moment. It's okay. We've got this."

"Yeah," Trae said with a laugh. "Let's not make any unnecessary adjustments to this ship. It's still in mint condition. It even has the plastic still on the seats. Hell, if it weren't for the extra mileage, I'd bet the warranty would still be valid."

"Hey now," Rachel shouted. "All I was trying to do was to get the thing to stop glitching. Technically it did work. It stopped glitching out."

"Only because you threw Willy's wrench through the damn screen." Trae glared at Rachel as he shimmied out from under the control console of the port side auxiliary station."

Rachel scowled. "Don't you look at me in that tone of voice or I'll adjust your face the next time."

"Hey!" Krista shouted. "Shut it! Both of you!"

Amanda stormed off of the bridge amid an explosion of sobbing tears.

"Shit." Kara followed Amanda off the bridge. "Oh baby, she wasn't yelling at you."

Maggie furiously huffed. "See what you did? You made her cry again. Why do you always do that?" Maggie stomped her foot and followed after Amanda.

"Oh my God people!" Krista said, throwing her arms up in frustration. "Just stop with the bullshit arguing and let them get this figured out." She breathed deep, then continued. "It shouldn't be too much longer before Doug gets back."

"What did you do to Amanda this time?" Doug asked Krista as he entered the bridge of the *Hans Landa*. Wes, Lizz followed closely behind with Casraownan, and Jouqon bringing up the awestruck rear. Both cat creatures glanced about with looks of wonderous amazement.

"Praise the Lord!" Krista pushed her way past Doug and the others and rushed for the exit. "I am so fucking over it. The chaos is all yours big boy. It's your turn to babysit for a while. I'm going to bed."

"What the hell was that all about," Doug asked as he watched Krista stomp off of the bridge.

"Don't ask," Trae replied. "Wes, can you give us a hand? The integration code that we came up with for the satellite communication just isn't able to keep up with the translation."

"Gladly," Wes said with a chuckle. He stretched his arms, popped his knuckles, then took a seat at the operations station. He immediately began rearranging lines of code and moving files at a blinding pace. "And, that should do the trick." He stabbed his index finger against the control console. The viewscreen flashed to life with the image of a long red, cylindrical object that loomed over the nearby asteroids.

"Woah," everyone said with a unanimous gasp.

"How far away is that thing?" Doug cautiously walked forward without taking his eyes off of the screen and sat in the captain's chair.

"Fifty thousand klicks if the readings are right. Wait," Wes tapped at the control console. "Fifty thousand klicks from this particular satellite that we're tapped into. Looks like it's one of the guidance beacons out in the asteroid field."

"That doesn't tell me much." Doug impatiently drummed his fingers on the armrest of the captain's chair. "How far away is that beacon in relation to us?"

"Hold on, I'm working on it," Wes said.

Trae stepped forward in front of the viewscreen. He stared at the image of the massive alien vessel on the screen. "What's it doing? Are those cables or arms coming out of the nose of the thing?"

"Make sure that you're recording all of this, Wesley," Lizz said, nudging him in the shoulder. "I'm sure that someone will want the footage of mankind's first encounter with an alien spaceship."

"All sensor data and video feeds are being recorded." Wes grinned over his shoulder toward Lizz. "Okay, so that beacon is on the far side of the system." He tapped at the control console and brought up an overhead layout of the system that appeared in the lower right corner of the screen over the image of the ship. "Right now, it's about one AU from our current position, smack dab in the middle of the debris field and upspin of the ecliptic."

Doug scratched at the stubble on his chin. "Can you get a better view of it? Maybe it has some kind of markings on the hull or something that we can use to identify it at least."

"Oh wow," Wes looked up at Fergus and Trae. "How did you guys tie these satellite things into the ship? This is crazy." He scrolled through the readout on his console. "We have full access to," he said, pausing for a moment, "over one thousand individual satellites along with the sensor packages on three different mining stations positioned throughout the system."

Fergus chuckled and smiled proudly. "Well ya see, I connected the…"

"Wes," Doug interrupted, "Can you get us a better view of the ship?"

"It looks like it might be near one of the mining stations," Wes said. He tapped at the controls and the image suddenly flashed to a close up of the alien craft along its starboard bow. The hull was almost seamless along its octagonal length. White markings that resembled Norse runes stood out in contrast to the dark reddish-gray of the hull.

"Oh shit," Trae gasped. "Those are grapplers coming out of the nose. See there at the articulation points," he said, pointing at the nose of the ship.

"Hang on. I think I can get a bit better view." Wes adjusted the image on the screen, then switched the view to a sidelong perspective of the alien ship. "That should do the trick," he said. A measurement icon appeared on the viewscreen that quickly tagged either end of the vessel. "If these measurements are right, that thing is over a thousand feet long."

Fergus joined Trae on the forward portion of the bridge near the viewscreen. They studied the ship in fascination as the nose of the craft separated into eight segments that spread out to twice the diameter of the hull. Eight grappling arms protruded from the forward section of the alien ship, angling to capture one of the large rocks. The arms maneuvered the rocks into the maw of the beast, like a Kraken devouring a ship. They watched as in minutes, dust and debris formed a cloud near the rear of the vessel as it was expelled, just forward of the propulsion system.

Fergus looked up from his watch. "Okay, so that's about five minutes from the time a rock entered into the crusher until it started to shit out the gravel."

"And that thing is radiating some serious heat along its midsection," Wes said. "Thermo is picking up steady temps of around four thousand degrees Kelvin."

"Damn, that's hot enough to boil plutonium," Fergus said.

"If that's the case, then what the hell is that thing made out of?" Trae stared in awe at the image on the screen.

Doug leaned forward in his seat. "It's a mining vessel like the *Betty*. It's just bigger and the layout is a little different. But it runs on the same process. Grind up rocks, smelt down the good stuff and then dump the slag."

"They must be running with a butt-ton of ceramic lining inside the smelter to run those kinds of temps," Willy said. "Nearly everything on the interior of the *Betty's* foundry system is coated in an inch or more of ceramic or refractory liner." Willy half sat on the corner of the operations station. "That damned grappler must be some kind of special material as well to take the beating that it's getting. I wonder what kind of propulsion system they are using to move that hulk that size? You said it just flashed into existence?"

"Hell, for that matter, I don't see any external turrets or gun ports," Trae said. I wonder what kind of weapons they have aboard?"

Fergus turned and looked between Big Willy and Trae. "Maybe they are all internal and only deployed when needed?"

"Possibly, but how quickly could they deploy them if they needed too?" Willy scratched at his bushy beard. "Maybe they don't even bother with deflecting stray rocks like we do on the

Betty with the gauss turrets. Maybe they just rely on their armor plating to protect them from the rocks?"

Fergus snorted. "Oh come on, Willy. No one in their right mind is going to go out, let alone into deep space without some sort of defensive system. You're going to have pirates."

"Um, hey guys. I hate to interrupt your sausage fest," Tiff said. "But does this mean that at some point we get to kick some alien ass?"

Trae turned and gave Tiff his sidelong *are you shitting me* look. "That thing is at least three times our size. Do you really want to tangle with it?"

Andy stepped forward, poking at the image on the main viewscreen as he examined the image of the alien vessel. "Ya know, I betcha if they are the sort that are penny-pinching cheapskates, the only armored part of that ship is the nose section where all the action is at. See the hull lines," he said as he pointed at the difference in the hull. "It looks thicker on the front third of the ship."

"Wait," Trae said turning his glare toward Andy. "Are you seriously siding with her?"

"Arrg! Yo ho ho," Wes shouted.

"You aren't helping," Doug said.

"See, Wes is on my side," Tiff said as she pointed toward Wes. "That means we get to be pirates again." She clapped and happily bounced a happy dance in place.

A sudden repetitive beeping drew everyone's attention. Wes tapped at his console. "We have a new contact. Downspin and hauling ass. It just appeared out of nowhere." He brought up a new readout on the main viewscreen that overlaid the live feed, then looked back toward Doug in surprise. "The new contact is making a B-line for Big Red."

Doug scootched forward to the edge of his seat. "Can you get a visual on it?"

"Hold on." Wes swiped through a myriad of screens, tapped one and expanded the feed of the new wedge-shaped ship on the main viewscreen with the image of the red mining vessel. "Okay, cool, recorders are still running. I'm picking up transmissions from both ships, but I'll be damned if any of it makes sense to me." He flicked the readout of the transmissions onto the main view screen from his console. "Each of them are transmitting on different frequencies."

"Any idea what they are?"

"My guess would be communications, but that's just a guess," Wes said. "I'll have to analyze the data later to know for sure."

The hull of the new craft looked as if it were covered in mismatched, pieced together sections of hull plating. Two tubular sections protruded slightly to either side of the ship's underbelly. The mining vessels main engines powered up, propelling it forward. Its grappling arms retracted into the forward hull as it began its retreat.

"The new contact is on a collision course with the first ship," Wes said. "They are adjusting their trajectory to match Big Red's course change."

"Oh sweet, we get to watch a space battle." Fergus sat cross-legged on the deck in front of the viewscreen. "Someone tell Mel to make some popcorn.

"There's a massive power build-up coming from the new ship," Wes shouted. "The new contact is still holding course."

Trae laughed. "Are they seriously going to ram them? All of this fancy alien tech and no pew pews?"

Wes chuckled and looked over to Trae. "Seriously? No pew pews?"

"This is really starting to be a bit disappointing," Tiff said. "I expected an alien space battle to have pew pews. So far there aren't any."

"I'm not sure what this energy signature is, but it's radiating out from the nose of the wedge-shaped ship," Wes said. It's like a blanket. It's not focused or anything."

"Shields! They have freaking shields!" Trae disbelievingly shook his head.

The wedge-shaped ship became a sudden blur of multihued light. The red alien mining ship split into two nearly equal halves.

Trae snorted a laugh. "God, I hate it when I'm right." He laced his fingers together behind his head and wrapped his arms around the sides of his head. "They just seriously used their ship as a freaking battering ram," he shouted in astonished disbelief.

"I have the second ship back on the scope." The viewscreen panned upward. The two halves of Big Red listed aimlessly away from each other among an expanding field of debris and escaping gasses. "They are upspin, off to the port of Big Red and changing course to intercept the debris field. Looks like they are heading for the aft end of the ship."

"What the hell kind of drive system could move a ship that fast and not kill everyone aboard." Doug stared slack-jawed at the screen.

"Something with a lot better compensators than we have, to start with," Big Willy said.

"Are you kidding me?" Wes turned to look at Doug. "What we just witnessed was a classic science fiction warp drive in action. If I had to guess from what Trae and Fergus said about how Big Red showed up," he said as he thumbed behind himself toward the viewscreen, "I'd say they are using some sort of dimensional FTL jump system."

"Um… Okay," Tiff stammered, then clapped her hands together. "English, please. Not all of us non-nerd-geeks understand your native language."

"F...T...L...," Wes said deliberately slow. *"Faster than light."*

"I'm not stupid Wes," Tiff said crossing her arms she glared at him.

"What he means, Tiff," Trae said with a groan of frustration, "is that the ship passed into a higher dimension in which it was able to travel at an insane velocity and reappear at a chosen point at a fraction of the travel time or fuel involved."

"Our Kamikaze friend has come to a stop just above the drive section of the Red," Wes said. Everyone's attention turned back to the viewscreen. Tentacle like appendages exploded from the wedge-shaped ship and captured the wreckage. Torches at the ends of the tentacles began cutting away sections of the Red alien's hull.

Willy stood and shifted his weight. "I'd bet they are going after the fuel core."

"Why do you say that?" Andy plopped down on the deck next to Fergus and leaned back on his elbows, stretching his legs out in front of him.

"That's what I'd go after first," Willy said. "It would be the most valuable and volatile thing on board any ship. Especially if they're using antimatter." Willy stepped forward in front of Andy and Fergus. "Ya see, once the containment bottles loose power, or the magnets get out of sequence or any other number of things that can possibly go wrong on a starship," Willy said then took a deep breath. "Boom! You lose everything that you were possibly about to salvage."

"What sort of power source would you need to pull off either of those types of drive systems?" Doug asked Willy.

"Not the slightest clue, Cap," Willy admitted. "If I knew, I'd tell ya. Now If I were to take a guess, I'd probably be wrong and just be blowing smoke up your ass. Once we have time to look over those derelicts in the hanger, we might have a better idea of what is possible versus what we only know as theory."

Trae took a seat at one of the port auxiliary stations. "There are so many theories that I have to agree with Willy. Until we can look at it, I wouldn't want to take a guess."

"Can you get us a better view, Wes? That's not the best of angles," Doug commented. "Most of the ship is in shadow in this view."

"Let me see what I can't do," Wes said.

"Now that they are sitting still, maybe we can learn something else about these new arrivals," Lizz said.

Tiff let out a frustrated growl. "Since you tied into those satellites can't you just lock on and fire a nuke or something from one of them? I mean, it's like the perfect opportunity man. They are just sitting ducks right now and we don't know if they are friendly or if they are face sucking rapist aliens or whatever."

"Tiff," Trae said, glaring at her.

"Just saying is all." She loudly popped a bubble with her chewing gum. "I'm sure that I'm not the only one thinking about it. I mean, really, what have we gotten ourselves into here?" She turned her gaze toward the deck and started to nervously pick at her nails.

The view on the screen suddenly exploded in an array of video feeds, each trained on the alien vessels. Everyone stared at a myriad of video feeds. Gaping at the scene unfolding before them.

"I've got something, Cap." Wes expanded a view from the bottom left of the screen to the full extent of the screen. It showed the vessel from a forward port profile, just above the central axis.

"Can you zoom in anymore?"

"Yeah, one sec," Wes said as he tapped at the control console.

The screen jumped again to a close up of the vessel. Missing sections of hull plating along her sides and top exposed inner bulkheads and the ship's superstructure to the vacuum of space. Multi-colored chunks of plating covered the nose section. Odd bits and pieces that didn't fit with the main lines of the vessel protruded from different points along the hull. One of the ship's tentacle-like appendages maneuvered a cut section from the remains of Big Red over one of its own open holes while two other appendages began to attach the section of hull plating.

"Would you look at that, Cap," Trae awed.

"Wow," Willy gasped. "She looks like a patchwork quilt of ship parts."

"*So…,*" Andy started. "Are we dealing with pirates or just scavengers? Maybe it's a territorial dispute? I mean, they could even be on a galactic quest to rid the universe of the *red menace,*" he said, accentuating his words with air quotes.

Trae glared at Andy. "Well how about we just hail them and see what their intentions are. I'm *sure* that they'll welcome us with open arms and invite us to join their *blessed* galactic union or empire or whatever fucking communist agenda that they are pushing on to the citizens of the galaxy."

"Fucking face-huggers, man, I'm telling you," Tiff muttered under her breath. "Ooo, or maybe they're body snatchers or black-market organ thieves."

"Shut up! Every damn one of you," Lizz said.

"Pan the view back out, Wes," Doug ordered. "Are there any markings on the original hull anywhere?"

"It's really hard to make out anything that's original," Fergus said. "I think it's more patches than original."

"Hey, what about that section, port aft just off from center," Rachel pointed. "No dummy, to your left a little more, zoom it in right there," she said pointing with an impatient finger.

The view zoomed in closer and paned to the left slowly.

"There?"

"Yeah, stop it right there." Rachel got up from her station and approached the view screen. "Can you get it in any tighter right here," she said as she motioned at an area with wide circular arm movements.

"Hold on," Wes said as he adjusted the view. "That's the best that this camera can get. Let me see what else we have available." He brought up the array of other views and quickly tabbed through them. "Here. This one is upspin of the ship."

The view shifted to an overhead view of the alien vessel. The camera zoomed in and refocused, revealing an hourglass-shaped profile. On either side of the waist section of the ship was a white emblem that stood out from the gray of the main hull. It looked like a massive white upper case I, rounded on the top and the bottom with a downturn on each leg.

"Bi ömnö ni üüniig katabümruu kharj baisan. Ene ni manai khümüüsiin dür törkhiin ard khana deer baina. Aguu khanan deer baigaa ene burkhad ni belgedliin khanand naaldaj," Casraownan chittered loudly. He rushed over and shook Lizz by the shoulder, pointing at the viewscreen.

Lizz looked at Cass, half scared. "What? Have you seen this symbol before?" She pointed to the image on the screen.

"Oh no," Fergus blurted out with a laugh. "What's that girl? Did little Jimmy fall down the well? Oh my gosh, golly gee willikers, what will we ever do." He laughed.

cHAPTER 26

Unknown Red Giant System
2nd planet / Alien Starport
Catacombs
July 2nd, 2176 / Late Afternoon (Betty Time)

"It's a bloody cruise liner advertisement," Lizz said with an exasperated huff. "At least we know what it looked like before the patchwork repairs."

"Sure looks like it to me," Doug said as he brushed away dust from the painted wall. "I'm not really all that surprised, honestly. I mean, we did set up shop in an abandoned starport, after all." He took a step back and adjusted the beam of his flashlight to a wider spread. A large, faded mural stretched across the wall of the terminal transport tunnel. What must have once been a fully functional moving sidewalk quietly stood sentry over the starport's lower catacombs. One of the cat creatures stood tall and proud in a dark blue flight suit. Pins and gold trim decorated the uniform. Behind the figure loomed a large gray wedge-shaped ship shown orbiting over a blue-green planet on a blue-black star-filled background. The same odd-looking upper case I symbol decorated the lower right of the mural.

"Why do you suppose these guys attacked the other ship?" Lizz asked as she gently touched the ancient mural.

"Bi chamd yuu gej khelev? Ene bol khanan deer baigaa züil deer belgeddeg shig." Casraownan pointed at the mural, then mimicked the stance of the cat creature painted on the wall. Jouqon let out a slight giggle and duplicated his father's stance.

Doug and Lizz both let out a laugh at the pair.

"Maybe you should make learning their language a top priority, Lizz," Doug suggested. "If that cruise liner is crewed by Cass's people, it would be extremely helpful if we could communicate with them, especially if they are going to be lurking around the system. If we can't communicate with them, then any time that we go into orbit, we could be a potential target until we can find out what it is that they want."

"Here's a thought, Doug," Lizz said. "Do you think the planet was originally attacked by the Reds? Possibly that's why the other ship attacked?"

"I wouldn't think so," Doug said. "All of the damage that we've seen so far looks like it is from weather and age. We haven't found any massive areas of radiation or signs that the planet was nuked or bombarded from orbit."

"It would be nice if we had some kind of timeline to work with. Maybe we should hire a few scientists when we get back to Earth," she suggested.

"Agreed," Doug said with a nod.

"Cap, come in Cap," Rachel said over the comms.

Doug keyed his mic. "Go ahead Cheezy, what's up?"

"You'd better get back up here. That rat rod ship sent security codes to the SATNET and is now on the move. Looks like they are on a trajectory for orbit."

"Don't do anything until we get back up there. Sending you an image." Doug detached his comm unit from his belt and handed the flashlight to Lizz. "Hold this up for me please." He snapped an image of the mural and sent it across their private network. "Image uploading to you now. Looks like that ship originally came from here. If Cass's people are on board, we don't want to do anything to provoke them."

"Copy that, Cap," Rachel said. *"Don't do anything to piss off the space kitties."*

cHAPTER 27

Unknown Red Giant System
2nd planet / Alien Starport
The Hans Landa / Bridge
July 2nd, 2176 / Evening (Betty Time)

"**S**he's a very old cruise liner, from what Cass just showed us," Doug said as he took a seat in the Captain's chair. "Wes, can you bring up the image I took and show it next to the video feed?"

"Sure, Cap, just one sec," Wes said.

The image of the mural appeared beside the live video feed of the cruiseliner as three umbilicals extended below the vessel down into the planet's atmosphere.

Lizz curiously squinted at the screen. "What are they doing?"

"Either they are refueling, which means they may have a power plant similar to ours," Willy said, "or they are refilling their oxygen tanks. Either way, it means that they can't run indefinitely, they have to stop and resupply."

A warning alert binged from the operations console. Wes quickly tapped at the controls. "We have a new contact, bearing 62.35 mark, 10.66 to our alignment axis from the star at a distance of 0.88 AU from our position. Oh shit, it's another Red and they popped in near the wreckage of the other ship."

"Well shit," Trae said. "That's not good."

Fergus chuckled. "No, that's just great. We get to watch another kick-ass space battle." He hurried over and took his seat on the floor. "I just wished I had some popcorn to go with it. Hey hon..."

"No," Rachel barked. "You can get it your damn self!"

"Okay, okay, I was just asking. You don't have to bite my head off."

"Hey guys, shut up," Wes interrupted. "The new Red is inbound on our position." A new video feed suddenly appeared and slid to the upper left corner of the viewscreen.

"That's not a surprise," Fergus grumbled. "It's a classic set up. Don't do it! You're rushing right into their trap!"

"Bad Fergus, bad. Down boy!" Rachel reached deep into her flight jacket and threw a rubber chicken at Fergus's head. "Be quiet, the adults are talking."

"Hey now!" Fergus turned and scowled back at Rachel.

"Cool it, all of you," Doug said.

"Looks like the cruise liner has spotted them too. They are reeling in their umbilical's." Trae took a seat at one of the gunner's stations. "Hey Wes, did you get the SATNET tied into weapons yet?"

Wes looked up from his console with a perturbed glance. "No, not yet. When the hell have I had the time to tie it in?"

"Just checking, man," Trae said defensively. "Are you picking up any odd energy signatures this time?"

"I don't know. Hold on." Wes swiped right on his control screen and brought up two new displays. With an upward flick, the windows appeared on the main view screen. A chart of frequencies and magnitudes appeared.

"There are all kinds of signals and energy readings," Wes said, "but I have no idea what I'm looking for here."

Trae walked toward the front of the bridge and examined the readout. "Right there would be my guess. All of this up here and those couple of emissions in the lower band should be output from the star," he pointed at a number of lines on the chart. "But that one right there, I'd be willing to bet would be cruiseliner. They are close enough for us to pick them up. Can you set a warning or something, so we know when a new emission appears?"

"Yeah, that's not a problem," Wes said as he tapped away at the console. An odd warble warning began to sound.

"What the hell is that alarm for?" Doug shouted.

"That's the SATNET warning system," Wes shouted over his shoulder. "Looks like we have a new contact that broke off from the Red. It's tiny in comparison."

"Missile," Doug blurted.

"You're probably right," Trae said.

Fergus stood from where he sat on the floor ahead of the control stations. "In the red corner, weighing in at over one hundred and fifty thousand metric tons, Big Red!" Fergus cheered and hooted.

Fergus," Doug barked.

Fergus groaned a huff. "Fine."

"The cruise liner is on the move," Wes reported. Looks like they are...oh shit, never mind, they are just ... um … gone."

"What about the Red," Doug asked.

"They are still inbound on our position, heading…and never mind. They just blinked out." Wes let out an exasperated sigh. "There has to be a way to set up early warning alarms now that we're tied into the network and we have those energy signatures on file."

"Go ahead and dig into the SATNET and see what you can figure out," Doug said. "That network will be invaluable to us later. We have a lot of prep work to do before we can go Earthside. Trae, take Casraownan and finish mapping out all of these tunnels and the upper levels. We need to know what we have available to work with."

"Really?" Trae turned to Doug with an unblinking grin. "How in the hell is that going to work?"

"It'll work because you're a smart cookie and he'll at least be able to point out where not to step or go where anything else that might want to eat us would be."

Trae let out a frustrated sigh and started off the bridge. "Good point. Come on kitty face, we've got work to do," he motioned for Cass to follow, then stopped and looked down at

Jouqon. He looked up at Cass with a serious stare, then pointed at Cass. "You and me," he pointed to himself. "Are going to explore," Trae turned his fingers into a walking stickman on the opposite palm. "But I don't want to take the boy with us," he pointed at Jouqon with a shake of his head.

Cass stared at Trae with an unbelieving wide-eyed look, then nodded and muttered something in his native tongue.

"Good, that's settled then," Trae said. "Let's get him home and get to it then." Trae motioned for them to follow as he marched off the bridge.

cHAPTER 28

Unknown Red Giant System
2nd planet / Alien Starport
Basecamp
July 3rd, 2176 / Lunchtime (Betty Time)

"Ya see Cap," Willy said. "I think we're perfectly fine building another unit. Fabrication of the parts will just be time-consuming since we have the full manufacturing schematics in the database. No researching to figure out what does what. The materials will be easy to pick up back on Earth. I just don't know about the resonance crystals." Willy poked at the bits of gravy covered meat on his plate. "I really don't want to take the thing apart just yet, and that's exactly what I'd have to do in order to take a sample to do a full analysis on it."

"Any thoughts on how long it might last or what might happen if it broke down while we were passing through a flux?" Doug pushed his plate away.

"Not the first clue about either, honestly," Willy said. "My first thought about the flux system breaking down while passing through is that it would be bad. Very bad," he laughed. "My guess is that we'd just wink out of existence or maybe we'd forever be trapped between the layers of space-time. It's really hard to say." Willy pushed his plate away. "Ya know, this stuff wouldn't be so bad if we had some hot sauce or something to go with it.

Doug grinned. "I know, mystery meat surprise is always better with something that you can identify."

"Pay attention dipshit," Fergus shouted. "Hey Cap, where did you want these kegs?"

Doug turned in the direction of the voice. Fergus stood at the bottom of the *Betty's* loading ramp as Andy eased a pallet stacked with beer kegs down the ramp.

"How about you actually help instead of standing there like you're too good to help," Andy said.

"And if I did that, then how would you ever learn the value of a hard day's work?" Fergus chuckled.

"Fergus," Doug shouted over his shoulder. "How about you learn the value of a hard day's work and let Andy take a break for supper."

"Ha!" Andy engaged the parking brake on the pallet jack and walked away.

"But, Cap..."

"Don't even start, Fergus. Get it stowed," Doug ordered.

"Shit," Fergus said, grumbling under his breath as he trudged up the *Betty's* loading ramp.

"Now that that's taken care of," Doug said then took a sip of sweet tea. "Could you get a material list together so when we get back to Earth, we'll be able to get what you'll need to build a second unit or at least to make replacement parts?"

"Oh yeah, Cap. That won't be a problem at all. I can have that for you by tomorrow, easy."

Melanie walked up next to Doug and crossed her arms. "Ya know, I can hear y'all over here making all of these wonderful plans and all."

"Okay…" Doug turned to Melanie. "Why does it sound like you're about to throw something?"

"Oh, I'm about ready to," Melanie said with a wide-eyed nod. "If I'm going to set up any kind of proper cafeteria for the number of people you are talking about, I'm gonna need more than two pots and a fire pit. I can barely keep enough cooked at one time to feed everyone before starting the next meal," she said with knife-hand emphasis. "I really need a good stove set up with a bunch of new pots, pans, utensils and the whole lot.

Cooking on board the ship is one thing, but if we're not relying on ration packs that you run through the hydromaster 3000, then you gotta do something or I'll just let your asses starve for a few days. I am not going to work my ass off and get bitched at for not having it all done on time."

Doug stood and took a step back. "Mel, calm down. We'll get what we need. We just have to make do with what we have for the time being."

"You say that now," Melanie growled. "But I'd bet money on the fact that I'll end up cooking for a crew of thirty or more without an extra hand or a pot barely big enough to piss in."

"Hey Melanie, are there any more of those little biscuit things you made for breakfast? I never got any of them," Andy shouted from across the bay.

Melanie gestured toward Andy, "See what I was just fucking saying? I can't keep enough made at one time!"

"Okay Mel, okay. Duly noted," Doug said. "We'll make sure to get what you need."

Melanie turned and rushed off at the sound of metal lids clattering to the floor. "What in the everloving hell are you doing in my kitchen, Andy! Git! Git out now or I'll cook your ass next!"

"What? I just wanted to see what was in the pot," Andy said defensively.

Doug and Willy watched as she stomped away in pursuit of Andy.

"Oh my God she's on a rampage today," Doug whispered to Willy as he sat back down at the table.

"I know. I'm not sure if I should feel sorry for Andy or feel sorry for Mel."

"Right." Doug flashed a cheesy grin at Willy. "Okay, so where were we?"

"Materials list," Willy said. "I'll see what I can come up with. It won't take me long to put together. With what we have available here in this system and with the foundry equipment on the Betty, I think we could produce most of the raw materials ourselves. The problem will be with that liquid metal in the gyro and then acquiring the crystals themselves."

Rachel suddenly appeared from nowhere behind Doug. "Hello, my Cappie Cap," she said cheerfully into his ear, then ruffled his hair. "You *are* going to love me." She flashed a wide cheesy smile as she rocked on her heels.

"This had better be good," he said in an annoyed tone.

She stepped around to the side of the table and leaned against it, then scooped two fingers worth of gravy from Doug's bowl and slurped the thick goop from her fingers.

"What the hell, Rachel? Really?" Doug looked up at her with annoyed disdain.

"*I know where we are... I know where we are...*" She wiggled her hips in an odd shuffling dance to the beat of her sing-song.

"Okay. So where are we then?" Willy interrupted.

"Was I talking to you, Willy," she snapped a glare at the large engineer then turned back to Doug and smiled.

"If the computer is right and the stars that I identified are also correct, we are in the Eltanin, or Gamma Draconis star system. One hundred and twenty-seven or so light-years from Earth and in the Draco constellation. So that means that we are on Eltanin 2, unless you want to name it something else entirely. And since I was already taking a look around, I sent a few probes out to scope out the rest of the system. There is this super Jovian around 2AU and two other gas giants that are about the size of Neptune. Now, the really cool thing that I found is that the Jovian has its own little system of moons or planets or whatever you want to call it going on. So far, the computer has identified around seventy or so moon-sized or larger objects in orbit. Spectral analysis on three of the moons shows a breathable atmosphere. I went ahead and took the liberty of logging the planetoids as habitable and named them, Auel, Asimov, and Koontz, respectively."

Willy scratched his head. "Why did you use those names?"

"They are some of my favorite authors," she said with a shrug. "Ya know, we really should get a bonus for finding habitable planets."

"But wait…," Willy said. "What if after closer inspection the planet is too hostile for one reason or another to sustain human life? Now someone has spent a lot of time and effort to only find that it was crap."

"Adding a hefty fine for filing crap claims would be a good way to deter that sort of wildcatting," Doug said. "Let me think about it. You did the work, so you've got dibs if we decide to work it like that."

"But that's pretty cool, hu? Four possibly habitable worlds in one solar system." She shrugged, scooped another two fingers of gravy from the bowl and happily skipped away toward the *Betty.*

"Well, *okay* then. At least we know where we are now," Doug said.

"Better than not knowing, I'd say," Willy added.

"Hey Cap," Tiffany said from over Doug's shoulder.

Doug laid his head down on the makeshift table and buried his head in his arms and groaned. "Yes Tiff?"

"Hey, I was just wondering. How long do you think Trae will be gone for? It's been a few hours and I'm starting to get worried." She nervously picked at a fingernail. "I mean, it's not just me you know. The pups are whimpering and whining, and they won't listen to me like they do with him."

Doug turned slowly to look at her. "He'll be back when he gets back."

"But what if something happens to him, Cap? I mean, the last time he went wandering out there in the tunnels he ended up fighting with that great big dirt dog."

Doug turned around, fully facing her and took her hands into his. "Tiff," he began, sarcasm slathered thick in his voice. "Trae is a big boy. He knows how to take care of himself. It'll be alright."

"Seriously Cap. I don't know what I'll do without him. And he's so much better at handling the pups than I am. I won't be able to keep them under control. They actually listen to him," she whined.

"So, we put them down and carry them to Mel to make mystery meat surprise," Willy said jokingly. "Though at that point would it really be mystery meat?"

"Oh my God, Willy. Seriously now. You'd go and eat my babies?"

Doug took a deep frustrated breath. "Tiff, he'll be fine. Cass is with him."

"But Cass doesn't speak like a regular person. What if he can't get Trae's attention in time?"

Doug glared at her.

"I'm just saying, man." She defensively waved her hands in the air. "You never know what else might be out there. It's like, literally an alien world that we just unlocked out there and we've just barely started to level up and explore any of it."

"Tiff," Doug said with a perturbed glare.

"Okay, okay. Just saying, man."

Doug turned back toward Willy and placed his elbows on the table. "Okay, where were we again?"

"Hey, Cap, um…Are you sure?" She whimpered under her breath.

"He'll be fine, Tiff. I promise. How about you go see if Mel has anything you can help her with. She was just talking about needed extra hands."

Tiff lowered her head, her lower lip poking out and on the verge of quivering. "Alright, as long as you think he'll be fine."

"Trust me, he'll be fine, now go on and stay busy so you aren't thinking about it."

Reluctant, she slunk away heading toward Mel's cooking area.

Willy stifled a chuckle. "I'm sorry, I can't help it," Willy said holding up an apologetic hand.

"It's all right. Now where were…" Doug's comm chimed with an incoming message. He stiffened at the sound and rolled his eyes. He snatched the small Procom personal communicator out of his pocket. "What already? This had better be important because I'm about to keel haul someone."

"How about the two of you old ladies stop it with all the hemhawing around and get things in order," The chief growled over the speaker. *"It's bad enough listening into some of the things coming from those witches of yours, but you two need to seriously learn how to pull rank and tell your subordinates to fuck off, do as your told and move on."*

Doug and Willy stared at each other with confused looks.

"If you would just take the time to read up on the ship's manual for this new bird, then you'd know what you needed in order to resupply the damned thing. First, you'll need to find or learn how to grow your own Kyanite crystals for the resonance generator. Second of all, you'll need to mix up an alloy of primarily steel, manganese and thallium. Now if it were me, I'd toss in a pinch of uranium and arsenic to thin out the mix a bit and help to lubricate the system. If I'd had y'alls attitude back in my day, you damned pups would still be struggling to survive back on Earth. So quit your God damned bickering, quit making bullshit excuses and just get it done already. Chief out!"

"Well alrighty then," Doug said.

"Ya know, he does have a point, Cap."

"I know he does. He's right. I just hate to be that guy, you know."

cHAPTER 29

Gamma Draconis system
Eltanin 2 / Alien Starport
The Betty / Witches Quarters
July 3rd, 2176 / Afternoon (Betty Time)

“I seriously don't know what the hell Doug is thinking sometimes,” Krista said as she forcefully folded a shirt, then placed it in the worn wicker basket that sat on the floor next to her.

“He's just trying to make a better life for all of us,” Maggie said. “Maybe instead of struggling day to day, we'll have a chance to thrive. Not only that, we are establishing the first intergalactic human colony. One day someone will write about us in the history books. Just like the original pioneers that established the Moon and Mars colonies.”

“Do you remember any of their names?” Krista glowered toward Maggie as she picked up a stack of folded clothes.

“No, not really.”

“See, that is my point, exactly. No one will remember us.” Krista tucked the clothes away into an ancient wardrobe at the back of the compartment. “I'm going to kick his ass if the only reason he's putting us through all of this is so that he can leave some sort of a legacy behind.”

Maggie fluffed out a towel and folded it over. “You mean you would rather go work for some big company where your boss wouldn't even know your name?”

Krista blanched at the thought, scrunching up her nose. “Blegh, hell no, not that. I'd rip out my identification chip before I ever thought about going to that extreme.”

“Then can you blame him?” Maggie looked at her matter of factly. “I think it's absolutely genuine. He wants to build something here that will be better for all of us and our children. We'll be independent and won't have to rely on what scraps are tossed to us for all of our hard work."

"Maybe you're right," Krista said then sighed. "I've known Doug for most of my adult life. He's never been so gung-ho about anything before. I just don't know."

Amanda burst out into hysterical laughter. "That is so classic!"

"What in the hell are you going on about over there?" Krista scowled over at Amanda.

"This book I downloaded from Project Gutenberg before we left Earth. The visual in this one scene is classic *Sara Brooke*. A hot and steamy sex scene that ends horribly for the character."

"And you're holding back on us? What the fuck, man," Krista said with an exasperated huff. "That's not cool. So, what's the name of it?"

"*The Bed*," Amanda responded.

"Oh hey, this might be good after all." Krista tossed the towel she had just picked up back into the basket and quickly trotted over to the ancient sofa. She tucked her skirts and flopped down next to Maggie, who fell over into Krista's lap from the bounce of the cushions. "Well okay then, I guess if that's how it's going to be, we might as well be comfy." Krista wrapped her arms around Maggie as the two wiggled into snuggle positions.

"Well come on then, spit it out already. Don't hold back on us," Maggie urged.

"Alright, hang on," Amanda said as she sat up and swiped the pages backward on the datapad. "Okay, here, this is the good part," she said, then took a deep breath.

Opening his eyes, he saw her standing in the center of the living room. She was the most beautiful woman he'd ever seen, though he was not normally a fan of redheads. He liked her, because she had sensual lips and dark eyes. Her red hair flowed down her back and her round pert breasts were set perfectly apart. Rosy nipples pointed in his direction, like two mounds of strawberry ice cream. Ted felt his penis throb, harden and lift as she approached him. The sensations running through his body were delicious rivers of melted chocolate that sent sweetened sensations to every nerve ending.

The strange woman sat on his lap and straddled him. As she wrapped her fingers around his neck and brought her face to his, he could feel the warmth of her crotch against his pants and moaned, pushing himself against her as they kissed deeply. The kiss seemed to get hotter and hotter until Ted thought he might explode in his pants. When their faces parted after a perfect kiss, the woman stared at him with a meaningful look, then opened her mouth as if to say something. But her mouth continued opening until it filled her face and the darkness of her mouth filled his vision.

"Oh wow", Krista squirmed. "That just gets me all tingly and hot inside."

"No shit," Maggie agreed with a laugh, fanning her reddened face. "That was, wow. I don't even know what to say."

Krista laughed, fanning herself as well. "I know right? You got anything else good tucked away in there?"

"Um...Maybe," Amanda said with a guilty grin.

Krista and Maggie both beamed at each other.

"She's been holding out on us," Maggie said.

"I know," Krista said, her voice heavy with sensual innocence. "She's been a bad girl."

"I think she needs to be punished, mistress," Maggie said, fighting back a giggle. She snorted, then choked on her own breath.

"Oh God, don't die on me." Krista patted Maggie on the back. "You aren't allowed to die. I need help with her punishment. Oh, oh oh, I know! We need jello shots!"

Maggie composed herself, took a deep breath and swallowed hard. "That's perfect," she squealed with glee and sprinted around the coffee table to stand in front of Amanda.

"Wait, what?" Amanda looked at the pair in complete confusion.

Maggie put on her best innocent pouty face, hands behind her back while rocking on her heels. "Our mistress, the fair and great green Earthbound Goddess has requested her favorite refreshment. But since you are new to this secret witch's ritual, you get to have the first six all to yourself."

"But...," Amanda thought out loud, "I thought we were supposed to turn in all supplies for inventory?"

"Oh, don't go and worry yourself about that," Krista said waving her hand nonchalantly. "What Doug doesn't know won't kill him. I'll get the door, you two get started on the shots!"

Maggie smiled wide then quickly grabbed Amanda by the hands and pulled her out of the chair.

Gamma Draconis system
Eltanin 2 / Alien Starport
Hans Landa / Captains Quarters
July 3rd, 2176 / Afternoon (Betty Time)

"One datapad, locked," Doug said into a small medical-style micro recorder. "One handwritten notebook containing Captain Dieter's personal log, one bottle of what looks like a prescription of little blue pills of something spelled out in German," Doug dropped the items into a small plastic container. He sorted through Captain Dieter's desk, dividing the personal items from the useful. A knock came from the doorway.

"You busy Cap?" Trae leaned against the thick bulkhead doorway.

"Nope, just finishing up. Did you find anything interesting?"

"Plenty. With a little bit of backache, we could get most of the upper layers cleared of sand and make them usable again. Though the outer areas will need some sort of cover since the glass or whatever they used is long gone. This place is massive once you get into the outer service areas. Looks like there are smaller repair bays, office spaces, and storage areas that we could use as warehouse space or maybe as workshops. Plus, there's lots of junk to salvage. There's no telling what we might find under the sand once we start clearing it, but I'd be willing to bet that it'll be preserved like things back in the Sahara Desert back on Earth."

Doug leaned back in the uncomfortable station chair and laced his hands behind his head. "Did you run into any new creatures that we should be worried about?

"No, nothing but a few more of those tater squid things, though Cass was cautious the entire time we were out. I don't think that things like the pups wander in here too often."

"How'd he do out there with you otherwise?"

"He was fine. We really couldn't speak as such, but he understood me, and I understood him well enough just with hand signals and body language. He seems to know most of this place like the back of his hand. But he's extremely cautious in certain areas. My guess is that's where they've run into things like the pups before."

"It'll be nice once we can get their language figured out. I'm sure there will be glitches along the way in translating things, but we'll have a better chance of knowing when there may be something going on."

"Yeah," Trae laughed, then looked up quickly, deep in inner thought. "I just remembered. I want to take some samples of the structural metal used in these buildings and from a few of the abandoned ships in the hanger. Our analysis gear is limited. I'd like to dig a little deeper and see what exactly that we have to work with here. Even if we're just salvaging the material from one of the collapsed buildings to haul back to Earth and sell."

"That's not a half-bad idea. Get whatever samples you want, and we'll get them inspected."

"Alright. What's the next thing on the list? I've still got a bit of juice left in me."

"Have you been to see Tiff yet?" Doug asked with a raised eyebrow.

"Not yet," Cass just left, and I came hunting you as soon as we got back."

"Then how about you go take a break for a bit. I think you've earned it."

"Are you sure Cap? I mean, there's still plenty to get done."

"Yeah, I'm sure. I sent Fergus, Rachel, Andy, and Kara with the three new Martian recruits up in the Betty to mine and load out the hold. Should be able to fetch a pretty penny when we get back. I've got Wes working up some want ads for new crew that he can spread on the net once we get back into the Sol system. The witches are doing whatever the witches do, Willy is going over the ship's systems on this heap and everyone else is working on their things. So, I think we're covered. Go spend some time with your wife, she's been worried to death about you."

"Alright. Thanks, Cap," Trae said as he grabbed an overhead conduit near the door and stretched. "I'll catch you in the morning."

cHAPTER 30

Gamma Draconis System
Eltanin 2 / Alien Starport
Base camp
August 8th, 2176 / Late Morning (Betty Time)

"I wish that you didn't have to go," Tiffany said sadly as she gazed up at Trae. Her arms draped around his neck. "It's bad enough worrying about you when you go off to wander the tunnels. I don't know what I'm going to do, knowing that you'll be light-years away."

"Don't worry, Tiff, you'll be fine," Trae said. He smoothed back her black mohawk. "You have the pups to look out for and there's plenty still to do around here to get things set up." He picked her up by the waist with ease and brought her lips to his. She wrapped her legs around his waist. Kissing him deeply she let out a half-moaned gasp.

"Hey, how about you two get a room." Fergus slapped Trae firmly on the left butt cheek as he brushed past the intertwined couple. Trae grunted. His eyes shot an irritated glance from the corner of his eye toward Fergus, then quickly closed as he returned his attention to Tiffany.

"It's really no wonder that the Reds were mining in this system when you think about it," Fergus said to Doug as he approached.

"And why would that be?" Doug looked up from his datapad with a quizzical smile.

"Well, we managed to harvest, smelt and process enough ore to fill the holds of both ships in just a few weeks. Granted, we don't have an extremely detailed spectral analysis report, but that's just over thirty-five hundred metric tons of refined titanium, vanadium, nickel, tungsten, and molybdenum. That we know for sure. Then toss in some gold, silver, palladium, iridium and some scandium just for good measure. We are fixing to have the biggest payday any of us have seen on a single run. I'm seriously starting to think that you were right about all of this, Cap."

Doug nodded, "Yeah, but the unfortunate part is that we'll be spending most of it on new recruits, supplies, and equipment. At least for the time being. There's no telling what we'll be able to salvage planetside once we really start to explore this place."

"Oh hey." Fergus perked up suddenly. "If we're getting supplies, does that mean we can pick up about, oh, I don't know, maybe a hundred or so pounds of fertilizer?"

"Actually, yes," Doug said grinning wide, "but not a few hundred." He looked back down at the datapad scrolling through a list of supplies.

Fergus shifted nervously, uncertain how to continue. "Well, how much are we actually talking then? A few bags maybe? I could make a few bags stretch for a little while."

"More like a few hundred," Doug said then stopped, thinking. "Well, really more like a metric ton of high-grade fertilizer if I'm figuring right."

"An actual ton?" Fergus's jaw dropped in astonishment.

"How else are we going to prep and condition the soil here for crops?"

Fergus snapped back to reality with a hurt look on his face. "Crops? Wait. What?"

Doug held out the datapad for Fergus to see. "How else will we be able to establish a colony if we can't support our own needs? Most of the credits earned on this run will be reinvested into the project."

"Wait, what about our pay?"

Rachel dodged around Doug and slipped a kiss onto Fergus's cheek. "See ya fuck face, wouldn't want to be ya."

"What the hell," Fergus yelled, "that's all I get?"

"Yup, be grateful you got that much." She carelessly waved at him as she continued toward the loading ramp of the Martian ship.

"Not even a reach around?"

"Nope, sorry," she yelled back as she excitedly continued up the loading ramp, a duffle bag slung over one shoulder.

"Love you too," he shouted back, stretching out on his tiptoes.

Doug curiously stared at Fergus. "You guys alright?"

"Yeah," Fergus sighed. "She's just been in a mood lately."

"Well don't worry about the money. You'll each get your cut, but it'll be at some point down the road. Lizz has been working out exactly how to go about paying everyone since we're in an entirely different star system."

"Do you think there's any chance I could acquire a little bit of that fertilizer for a personal project at some point?"

"Sure," Doug said. "Just don't do what I think you plan to do with it inside of the complex. I'd rather not have the roof coming down on top of us.

"Fair enough, Cap." Fergus quickly stood at attention, holding up two fingers on his right hand. "I solemnly swear to not blow any of us up or to bring the roof down on top of our heads."

"Okay, good," Doug said then leaned to the side, peering around Fergus. "Hey, what's wrong with Rachel?"

Fergus turned and saw that Rachel had stopped and stepped away from the ship. She stared upward; her gaze transfixed on the side of the ship.

"Rachel!" Fergus shouted. "Everything alright?"

"We can't go," Rachel said quietly as she stepped backward. "It wouldn't be right if we did. She's let me touch her, play with her. I've tickled her innards without so much as even a thank you."

Doug and Fergus turned to each other with looks of confusion then back toward Rachel.

"Um, hon," Fergus said softly. "You haven't been eating the lithium grease again, have you?"

"No, you dumb shit," Rachel retorted. She turned, dropped her duffle bag and sprinted toward Fergus. She gripped him by his flight suit and shook him violently. "We can't go!" She breathed heavy; a deep feral growl began to rumble deep in her throat.

"Okay, okay, we can't go, I got ya," Fergus said. "But why can't we go?"

Rachel breathed deep; hyperventilation imminent. "She needs a name!"

cHAPTER 31

Gamma Draconis System
Eltanin 2 / Alien Starport
Base camp
August 8th, 2176 /Early Evening (Betty Time)

Casraownan led the way for those of his people that wished to visit the strange tailless ones. They covered their eyes to block the at the bright lights of the base camp as they approached, and their eyes adjusted.

"Whoa," Jouqon said. "What is that, Father?" The young Chinchanssin sat perched atop Casraownan's shoulders and excitedly pointed ahead at the scene before them as they entered the outer edges of the base camp.

"That, my son, is some sort of vessel," Casraownan said. The words rolled oddly off his tongue. "Like the ones told of in the ancient stories of our people and the ancient vessels that I have shown you within these very caverns."

"So, they fly, like in the stories?"

"Yes son," Casraownan said. "They float and fly about on their own. I have watched as one of them, the larger of the two, lifted from the ground amid a great fiery windstorm."

"And you say that they come from the stars? They are not from the above?" Mapharye, the young gray and white female clung closely to Casraownan's arm.

"From what I can gather, yes," Casraownan replied. "They are the same stars that our ancestors once visited, long ago. The one that I have been speaking with, Lizz, has said that they are travelers and their home is a very very long way away."

"What are they doing now, Father? Why is the vessel covered like it is?" Jouqon pointed toward the nose of the gray vessel.

A wide section of material draped over a section of the nose of the ship, concealing it from view.

"I do not know," Casraownan said. "Perhaps it is a custom of their people?"

"Didn't you say that some of them were returning to their home?" Mapharye looked up at the young hunter.

"Yes, they are," Casraownan said. "If I understood correctly, they were preparing to go back and gather supplies and workers. But I do not know what this is about." He motioned at the scene before him. All of the tailless creatures were gathered around and seemed to be impatiently waiting for something.

"You mean they intend to invade," Ceiwo coughed and stumbled backward.

"Father, are you alright." Mapharye released Caraownan's arm and gripped her father's arm as he regained his balance.

"No, it isn't an invasion," Casraownan said. His gaze locked onto the large tailless one and he pointed. "That one is known as Trae. He is the one that killed the Kaowla mother, then took in her litter as if they were his own. And that one," he pointed at a large-breasted female of their kind that followed behind Trae. "She is his mate, to the best of my knowledge and known as Tiff."

Behind the pair, the three Kaowla pups hurriedly scrambled across the stone floor of the chamber. The small group of Chinchasan's cringed and huddled together behind Casraownan as the creatures barreled headlong in their direction.

"You have led us to our deaths, Casraownan," Ceiwo cried out. "They have unleashed the Kaowla upon us!"

Jouqon began to sob. "Father!" He squalled.

Trae bellowed something that Casraownan didn't understand. His shouted words echoed throughout the chamber. The pups backpeddled as they slid on the dusty stone floor. With a whimper, all three of the beasts wandered away into the darkness.

Another of the furless creatures yelled into a cupped hand toward the covered section of the vessel.

"Who is that one," Mapharye asked.

"That is Cap..ee..tan Doug," Casraownan slurred. "He is their leader, I think."

"You think?" Ceiwo scoffed.

Casraownan scowled back at Ceiwo, his mate's father and Jouqon's grandfather. "I am not completely sure yet. It seems that both he and the one called Lizz share in the duties of leadership."

"So, they are a mated pair then? That would not be strange, that was once how things were with our people, were they not father," Mapharye asked toward Ceiwo.

"That is vague memory from a long ago past, Daughter," Ceiwo replied.

"They are not…," Casraownan paused. "I am not sure if they are mated or not. I will find out soon, though. I have been working with the one named Lizz," he said, pointing toward the short blond among the tailless creatures. "That one is known as Wesley," he said pointing at a large round male among the group. He has also been helping me to learn their language."

Doug shouted upward once more.

"What do you suppose he is shouting about father?"

"I do not know, son," Casraownan replied.

"**R**achel!" Doug impatiently bellowed. "Are you done or not? Let's get this show on the road or I'm leaving without you!"

"Keep your pants on Captain pushy," Rachel shouted in reply. "You can't rush perfection."

"Well everyone is waiting. Hell, even the cats are here waiting on you," he thumbed over his shoulder toward the gathered aliens.

"Okay, okay. One last touch," Rachel said.

"Cheezy," Trae shouted through cupped hands. "Get on with it already. I want to go!"

Tiff latched onto Trae, burying her head into his chest. "But I don't want you to go."

"Yeah, hon. Hurry the hell up, already," Fergus said. "We've been standing here for over an hour and I gotta go pee. Don't make me piss on cat boy, again. You know I'll do it."

"Fuck it, alright, I'm done," Krista fussed. "Y'all can just go on and do this without me. I have other shit to get done." Krista quickly walked away from the ship toward the main base camp area.

"Okay, okay, I'm really done this time." Rachel appeared from behind the curtain at the top of the motorized scaffolding. "Wait, shit, hold on. One last touch." She ducked back behind the curtain.

The gathered crowd groaned.

"Rachel! Enough," Doug yelled. "You can touch it up later. We're loaded and ready to go."

"Fine," Rachel sighed. "If that's the way you want to go about half-assing everything that I do."

"Get on with it!" The crew yelled in unison. Hisses and spits started in the crowd of cat creatures as they joined in the harassment.

"Fine! There, I'm done." Rachel re-appeared from behind the curtain and tossed her paintbrush to the floor. "I Had to add a shadow that I forgot." She cupped her hands, "Krista! You may want to stay for this! It's important!"

Krista turned and glared up at Rachel. She crossed her arms and glared back with a perturbed look. "This had better be damned well worth it. Time's ticking and I got things to get done."

Rachel beamed at the crowd below. She stood tall, proud of what she had just accomplished. "Ladies and Cats. By Earthen tradition, may I present the newest, in what we hope to be a long line of vessels in the new Earth empire fleet…"

"We are not the Earth empire, Cheezy," Wes interrupted.

"We're just renaming her, remember," Doug added.

"Oh, right. Um...where was I," Rachel asked. "Wait, that's right, I remember what I was going to say." She took a deep breath and began with a flourish of her hands. "By Earthen tradition, we ask for blessings for her crew, for luck and for favorable winds during our voyage. I present to you, *Veronica*!" Rachel pulled on a rope that hung loosely nearby and the curtain fell away to reveal a vaguely familiar pin-up girl over a dark blue background that winked over her left shoulder to the onlookers. Veronica was stenciled in bright white lettering along the bottom edge of the image in stark contrast to the ship's bland gunship gray paint. The figure was completely nude, save for thigh high stockings and leather gloves that came above the figure's elbows. The figure knelt, legs tucked under her and slightly to the side. An exaggeratingly plump derriere was accentuated with the defined lines of her waist and two small, but very pronounced back dimples. The profile of one very large, round, and impossibly perky breast, almost as if it housed an antigravity device within its supple curves, distracted and drew the eye. Long black hair hung down to the middle of the models back and framed a very familiar, Native American shaped face. The crew all turned and looked at Krista.

Krista gasped at the sight. "What in the…"

"We love it, Rachel," Doug interrupted. "Now can we get underway?"

"Hey now, hold on just one damned minute here," Krista said, motioning toward the painting. "I think I have a right to get a say in this."

Rachel hooted. "Oh, great Goddess, as you have said on more than a few occasions, just let it happen." She snorted a laugh. "Oh shit, wait, no we're not done." Rachel ran down the scaffolding to a worktable littered with paint, brushes and miscellaneous odds and ends. With the speed of a lame jackrabbit, Rachel snatched a small black bag from the table, then turned and ran back up the scaffolding. Carefully once at the top, she removed a squarish, black labeled bottle from the bag. "I christen thee, *Veronica*! May you sail straight and smooth!"

"Wait, no! That's my whiskey!" Trae sprinted toward the scaffolding just as Rachel swung. The glass bottle smashed into tiny fragments as the amber liquid splashed across the side of the vessel and rained down upon the dry, cracked earth.

cHAPTER 32

Sol system
The *Betty* / Bridge
August 8th, 2176 / Late Evening (Betty Time)

"Vsphere network connection confirmed, Cap," Wes reported. "Transmitting on all outbound frequencies."

"Good," Doug replied.

"Well, crap." Wes blew out. "Our data transfer rates just tanked."

"Is the transmitter down again?"

"No, we still have a strong signal. Hold on." He tapped at the controls. "Oh, no freaking wonder. Everyone's accounts on game servers and such just auto logged in and started doing automatic updates, plus the downloads that I already had in the cue from before we left the system."

"Wait. Why was there anything active in the first place?"

"It's stuff that was already in progress or just left logged on before we went through the flux." Wes cycled through a number of screens on his console.

"Hey, come on, you gotta at least let the game updates roll,' Trae said. "There should be new patches and firmware updates by now. Tiff will be pissed if you kill those off."

"Tiff can go on and get over herself. We need the bandwidth," Wes said as he tapped at the console. "There, I think I stopped all of them."

"So, we're good?"

"Yup, I think we're good."

"Good," Doug said. "Send out the job ads and get our flight plan logged with the I.A. and Luna colonies, then send the director our cooked-up data."

"Aye Cap," Wes replied.

"Now hail the *Veronica*."

A short, but low tone indicated the open channel.

"And you're on," Wes said.

"Alright Rachel, we're good here. Get yourself and the Veronica into position upspin and go dark. We'll let you know when we're ready to do a transfer."

"You know this would be a whole lot easier if I just flew in with you," Rachel replied.

"I know it would," Doug said, "but that's a no go. We need to get the *Veronica* registered as derelict salvage with the Commonwealth and Luna before we bring her anywhere near Earth. I don't want to chance the I.A. stealing her from us when we have people still on the other side."

"Copy that, Cap." Rachel let out a heavy, frustrated sigh. *"I'll just go wait, way over here, in the dark. No one to talk to or to keep me..."*

"You'll be fine, Rachel," Doug interrupted. "*Betty*, out. Alright, Trae, get us to Atlanta as fast as you can," he ordered.

cHAPTER 33

Earth
Independent Alliance / Atlanta Headquarters
August 9th, 2176 / Morning (Betty Time)

"Sir, we have them," a young agent said as he frantically burst through the office's double doors. He intently tapped at a datapad cradled in the crook of his left arm as he walked.

"What is the meaning of this interruption?" Director Lepetomane glared at the young agent.

"Sir, you wished to know when the *Betty* or any of her crew re-emerged onto the net. The ship reconnected to the Vsphere network last night around 2300 hours and began to upload an encrypted priority message that was directed to you." The agent scrolled through the information on the datapad. "It looks like it is addressed to you from one Elizabeth Trower."

"What?" Color crept up the director's neck, reddening his ears. "Why was I not informed immediately? If it was sent last night, then why am I just hearing about it now?"

"They initially logged back into the system via a repeater satellite on the outward side of the asteroid belt, on the opposite side of the solar system," the young agent said. "That very large upload traveled from one repeater to another until it reached our servers back here on Earth. It was just a matter of time and file size in this case."

"Well, then show me," the Director ordered.

"Yes sir." He tapped at the datapad and the room exploded with holographic display windows that hung like ghostly portals in the air. "It looks like they came through on the contract, sir." Schematics, data outputs, and assembly break downs hovered in mid-air above the Director's desk.

"Good," the director crooned to himself. "I had my doubts but knew she could pull it off in the end." He let out a long sigh of relief. "Is there any other activity?"

"One moment sir." The agent sorted through the information on his datapad. "It looks like there were some personal messages outgoing." He continued through the information. "They have also connected to a number of gaming and entertainment servers and a number of Illegal download server...Oh my," the young agent stammered.

"Oh, my *what*, agent?" The Director glowered at the young man. Impatient consternation lined his face.

"Um...Well, sir. There are a number of download search strings that have initiated since the ship reconnected to the net."

"Downloads?" The director stared blankly at the young agent.

"Yes sir."

"Are they downloading classified information? Is there anything to be concerned with?" The director's tone was cold, plain and straight-faced.

"Well, no sir. Nothing classified. I'd say concerned would be subjective, though."

"Then what is it already? Spit it out, agent."

"Well, sir." The young agent nervously swallowed. "These look like automated download search strings that re-initialized for girl on girl, girl in fox suit, girl on girl in fox suit on cephalopod, midget grannies, granny zombies, and midget granny bukkake, sir."

"Bukkake?" The word rolled oddly off the Director's tongue.

"Trust me, sir. You really don't want to know," the agent insisted. "There is also a video being uploaded to a popular sharing site that has been linked to dozens of other sites." The agent tapped at his datapad once more and brought up a holographic window with a video that he moved to hang in front of the director.

"Well hello my dear, Elizabeth. It seems there is more to this than they have willingly reported." He longingly watched the video feed. "Monitor all of their communications and assign an agent to follow each of the crew members once they land. Ensure complete discretion," he waved a finger at the agent. "I also want to know what was in each of those outgoing transmissions."

"Yes, sir. Right away, sir." The holographic screens vanished in the blink of an eye as the agent tapped at the datapad and quickly turned to leave the room.

"Also, agent, please write up a full report for me on this, bukkake topic."

"Yes...yes, sir," the agent stammered.

cHAPTER 34

Earth / South Atlanta
Atlanta International Spaceport
August 13th, 2176 / Mid-Morning (Betty Time)

"I appreciate you coming along to the office with me, Bob," Lizz said thoughtfully. "I can usually handle myself, but this isn't exactly the best area of town to wander around on your own. It's comforting to have an extra set of eyes along with me."

They walked along a dirty, trash-strewn sidewalk in the shipping and receiving area of the Atlanta Spaceport, south of downtown at what was once the old Jackson airport. Tractor trailers and containers of all sizes filled any available spaces within the fenced-in shipping yards. Cranes worked and trucks scurried about moving containers and materials in a choreographed mechanical ballet.

"It really isn't a bother, Elizabeth," Bob said. "It's the least I can do until I can find my place within the pecking order of the crew. Nothing wrong with the position of whipping boy, in my personal opinion." He winked. "It's the best way to learn the down and dirty truths of a situation."

Lizz turned and looked at Bob with a sidelong, wry smile. "You'd best be careful. I may just take you up on that position, literally." She returned his wink.

Bob blushed. "I find that proposition both terrifying and exciting at the same time." He chuckled under his breath.

"That's the point, isn't it?" She smiled up at him and laced her arm through his. They turned right down a side street and stopped abruptly at the strange sight before them.

What was once a multistory mini storage facility had been converted into a micro-office complex a little less than a century ago. During the asteroid mining boom that began shortly after mankind had established its first colony on Mars; hundreds of mining companies sprung up overnight. In order to register with the I.A., these companies were required to maintain a physical address, but no one wanted the enormous overhead of office space when they might physically be in the office for one or two days a year. Lizz gawked at the line of waiting people that wrapped around the building and ended only paces away from where she and Bob stood.

"What in the bloody hell," Lizz blurted.

A man at the end of the line turned and tipped his thread bear green cap, "Ma'am." Sweat ran down his face as the warm summer sun blazed down from high above.

"What in the world is with the line?"

"You haven't heard?" The man asked with wide-eyed surprise.

Lizz and Bob glanced at one another then turned their attention back to the man in the green cap. "No, we haven't. We were here on some personal business. What would have so many people waiting like this under a baking sun?"

"They're hiring for the new expansion," the man said excitedly. "Don't rightly know if it's government-funded like the last time, but I don't see where that matters as long as there's good-paying work.

"The new expansion?" Lizz's eyes went wide with terrified knowing.

"Yeah, they are planning a colony outside the solar system or something. There hasn't been a new colony in nearly seventy years. Not to mention a chance for real exploration." The man's gaze drifted off to inner thoughts.

Lizz looked up to Bob as panic began to well up inside her breast. "What company?"

The man chewed at a hangnail on his crusty looking right thumb for a moment. "I'm not entirely sure, to be honest."

"Oh, hell." Lizz darted ahead toward the office complex.

"Okay, we're running then." Bob trotted after Lizz, nodding to the man as he passed. "Thank you kindly, sir."

"Not a problem at t'all. Y'all have a good'in." The man called after Bob as he jogged ahead to catch up to Lizz.

Shouts of line jumper followed them as they hurriedly made their way forward. They pushed their way into the building and up the stairwell. Angry fists pumped in the air as they forced themselves through the crowd. Lizz stopped and caught her breath at the fourth-floor landing. The line turned left, then disappeared midway down the corridor to the right, directly toward the micro office of Lizzco.

"This cannot honestly be happening," she gasped then took off her heels.

"What can't be happening?" Bob asked, dryly panting.

"I have always operated with a high level of discretion. Always under the radar."

"And this is anything but discreet," Bob said, finishing her sentence.

Lizz nodded, then straightened and smoothed her skirt. She brushed an errant strand of hair from her face as she composed herself. "What will be, will be I suppose. We will adapt and overcome," she reassured herself, then continued down the corridor.

Bob loomed just behind her as they continued to follow the line around the corner to the right, where it stopped at office number 442. Just above the small roll-up door, a screen displayed the latest in Lizzco advertisements.

"Didn't you say something about being a businessman before, Bob?" Lizz asked, her eyes locked on the video screen.

"I did," Bob said, catching his breath. "Why? What are you thinking?"

"Considering the results of Wesley's video there, I think we've outgrown this little space," Lizz said, nodding at the display screen.

"Ah, I see. The proverbial Pandora's box is open for business, but it needs a facelift?"

"Something like that." Lizz took a step back and looked down the line then back to Bob. "I need you to find something a little more suitable. Something that will look more professional and help draw in more than just roughnecks and space jocks. We need curb appeal. If we do this the way we are talking about, we'll need applicants from all walks of life."

"That I can do," Bob said. "But I wouldn't feel right leaving you here to deal with all of this on your own."

Lizz glanced over the line of potential employees, then quickly entered an access code into the door's keypad. The door rolled up to reveal a tiny closet-like space. A small bar table, two bar stools and a file cabinet all but filled the small office space. "You, sit," Lizz pointed at a petite, out of place young woman at the head of the line. She wore a bright yellow sundress, cowboy boots, and a denim jacket.

"Yes ma'am," the woman said and quickly leapt onto the nearest bar stool.

Lizz looked over the line once again. "You, the big guy," she pointed at a large black man with long, thick dreadlocks in oil-stained overalls. "What's your occupation?"

"Mechanic, miner, you name it I can do it," the man stated proudly. His voice was a deep heavy bass that resonated within the small corridor.

"What's your name?"

"Chico, ma'am. Chico Michaels," his voice boomed.

"Alright Mr. Michaels," Lizz said with a smile. "You're hired. I want you to help me corral this mob if things start to get out of hand. Think you can handle that for double the standard pay for the day?"

"*Absolutely*." The large man happily stepped out of line and stepped forward; his hand outstretched toward Lizz. "Thank you, ma'am." He shook her hand then stood next to the office door. Crossing his arms, he scowled menacingly at the crowd.

Lizz turned back to Bob. "Is that acceptable?"

Bob gave the large man a sidelong glance. "I believe that will do, my dear."

"Good, then on to your assignment." She stepped into the office.

"On it boss." Bob turned and hurriedly disappeared down the corridor.

"What's your name, miss?" Lizz sat on the second stool and straightened her skirt.

"Jenny Reynolds, ma'am."

"And what are your qualifications?"

The young woman quickly opened and handed over a neatly organized portfolio. "My primary skills are in linguistics and translation of business documents."

"Really," Lizz said with a surprised look. She took the offered portfolio and began flipping through the pages. "How are your organizational skills?"

"Well," she snorted a laugh. "You can't do translations without being able to organize the sentence structures from one language to another."

"Close enough, you're hired." Lizz handed the portfolio back to the young woman. "Now, if you would please step over here, I'll need you to help document all of the other candidates." Lizz motioned to the filing cabinet on her left.

"Next!"

cHAPTER 35

Earth / Atlanta
Georgia Tech
August 13th, 2176 / Afternoon EST

An image faded slowly into view to the soft metallic twangs of a dobro guitar accompanied by a melodic bass beat of a hand drum. Silhouetted against the dark sunset shades of red and orange, a distinctly female form emerged from the darkness on the screen. She stood tall and proud atop a mountain crag as if she looked ahead, far into the future. Insignificant bursts of wind tousled her hair and skirt before the painted scene of heavy storm clouds in the distance. The image brightened as it orbited slowly to the left to reveal a shapely, but mature looking blond, dressed in a light gray dress suit. Large winding curls hung over her shoulders and teased at a peek of lace and the pert, but ample mounds which presented themselves from the button-down portion of the outfit. Experience glimmered within her eyes. Confidence played along the crook of her devious smile.

"Our future as a species is out there," a narrator's deep voice boomed. The view continued to orbit the image of Lizz. She shaded her eyes and gazed longingly into the distance.

"Beyond our limits of sight and understanding lay countless unknown opportunities." The music grew heavy with the thump of a muted bass drum.

A bright red star faded into existence and replaced the shapely figure.

"Job opportunities await you within the Dragon's Lair."

The image panned right, revealing a dense asteroid belt and a bright sandy world beyond.

"Travel to exotic new locals. Help to establish mankind's first colony beyond our solar system. LizzCo Industries Unlimited needs you. All professions are welcome. Dishwasher, engineer, geologists and more are needed to colonize and create mankind's new Eden beyond the stars."

The planet slowly changed color to a deep dark green with large areas of blue.

"Think of your future and ours. Humanity needs you! Do your part. Join today. Lizzco needs you!"

Doug looked up from the datapad. He rolled his head to the left and took in the sight of Wes's beaming cherub-like face. He scowled at Wes, concern lining his tired face.

"So, what do you think?" Wes waited; his hopeful wide eyes begged for an answer.

Doug wrinkled his nose and sniffed at the air. "Is it just me or does the place smell mildewy?" He looked around for the faint hint of mildew that clung to his nostril hairs. They sat in the newly renovated waiting area of tech tower, the administrative hub of Georgia Tech. Dark hardwoods mingled with glass and stainless-steel accents around the room. He thought the uncomfortable chairs resembled something he'd seen in an ancient 1960's television show once. White, egg-shaped and lightly padded with bright, eye-straining colors.

He turned back to Wes. "Do I smell?"

"I don't think so," Wes said then sniffed at his shirt.

"Are you sure? Since we've been back on Earth, I keep smelling this mildew like smell and I can't figure out where it's coming from. It's not like my clothes have been wet for days or anything. I can't figure it out."

"Oh yeah. I caught a whiff of that too, but couldn't remember where I'd smelled it before. So, what did you think of the promo video?" Wes beamed with hopeful delight.

"I think that Lizz is going to kill you if you're lucky." Doug handed the datapad back to Wes and stretched. "Hopefully we won't have to wait much longer. Our appointment with the Dean was at one o'clock. What time is it anyway?"

"Twelve thirty-two in the afternoon," Wes replied.

"Really?" Sarcasm dripped from the squint-eyed look that he gave Wes. "The sun is out dufus. I think I could have figured that part out myself."

"Ya never know. We've been in the G.D. Lair for so long you could have Dragon Lag."

Doug yawned, then looked back at Wes in total, unamused confusion. "What? Speak English. G.D. Lair? Dragon lag?"

"It's just like jet lag, but because we were on G.D., er, wait. Gamma Draconis time, the lag is that much worse."

"You're having fun with this aren't you?"

"Absolutely! Who wouldn't want the chance to name all of these new places and things? That is some serious bragging rights, not to mention a chance to get into the history books."

Doug wrapped his arms tightly around himself and stretched. "Hopefully it won't take the Director of the I.A. too long to fulfill his part of the bargain. Lizz has already sent them the info and our doctored schematics on the *Veronica*. We'll need every penny that we can get to set things up. Then we might have a damn good chance to make it into the history books."

"Well, we could always make it into the history books as the first spacer crew to turn into the Donner party."

"How about we don't and just say we did?"

"Mr. Rackham," a high pitched, nasally voice interrupted from behind where the pair sat.

Doug stood and turned to find a plump but seductively curvaceous young brunette blandly staring back at him. "I am."

Wes turned in his seat and gasped. "Whoa."

Doug snapped his fingers without breaking eye contact with the young woman.

"Sorry." Wes averted his eyes.

The young woman quickly turned to conceal a blushing smile and walked away, but called over her shoulder, "Doctor Walker will see you now." Her short-legged quick pace caused the pleats of her short orange skirt to audibly swish and sashay as she walked.

"Thank you." Doug grabbed Wes by the shoulder of his jacket and tugged. "Come on Geek, let's go." They followed the young woman down a narrow hallway that abruptly turned to the right. She quickly disappeared into a small alcove that was set up as a secretary's station next to a thick wooden door with a heavy bronze plaque that read, Dr. Ronald J. Walker, Dean of Students.

She opened the door with a wide, inviting smile aimed toward Doug. "Please let me know if you need anything at all." She teased with a sidelong smirk as she brushed past the pair and took a seat at her desk.

"Well alrighty then." Wes stepped aside and motioned Doug ahead of himself. "After you, Captain Rackham."

"Down boy. Let's do this thing." Doug slapped Wes on the shoulder and continued into the room.

A tall, pot-bellied man sat behind an antique wooden desk that looked as if it had been in the office since the day that the college had been established. He quickly stood to greet them. "Gentlemen, please, come in and have a seat." The large goiter on his neck bobbed as he nervously swallowed.

"Thank you for seeing us on such short notice, Dean Walker." Doug sat in one of the plush antique chairs that matched the look of the desk.

"Oh, it is my absolute pleasure to meet with you, Captain Rackham." Dean Walker excitedly dabbed at his partially bald head with a handkerchief, then sat back down. "I have to say that these are indeed exciting times that we are living in. I have been instructed by the board of directors and other interested parties to entertain any reasonable offers that you wish to negotiate."

Doug opened his mouth to reply, then quickly snapped his mouth shut. He studied Dean Walker for a moment, then glanced toward Wes with a deep, contemplative sigh. Doug leaned forward and sat on the edge of the chair, fingers interlaced in front of his mouth. "All of a sudden, I'm not so sure that we really want to be here." Doug coldly glared at the Dean. "It was everything that I could do to get this appointment with you when I began to contact the college yesterday morning. Now all of a sudden, you're visibly shaken and directed to be compliant to any offer that I might make?" Doug sat back in the chair and propped his feet up on the Dean's desk. "So, what gives Dean? Something smells fishy to me."

"I thought you'd said it smelled mildewy earlier," Wes said jokingly.

Doug looked to Wes with a squinty-eyed glare. "Yeah, that too," he said with a nod then turned back to the Dean. "So what's the deal, Dean?"

Dean Walker nodded with a nervous smile. His face twisted with pain as he forcefully swallowed a mouthful of bile. He motioned with a finger for the pair to wait a moment, then reached into a lower drawer of the desk. Shakily, he poured a handful of antacids, popped them into his mouth and began to chew. He replaced the bottle then began to gulp from a bottle of liquid antacid to wash down the chalky, dry mess.

"You know that isn't exactly healthy. Should we go ahead and leave?" Doug thumbed toward the door, "There are plenty of other colleges in Atlanta that would be willing to speak with us."

The Dean swallowed hard and gasped. "No no no, please don't do that." He dropped the bottle back into the drawer and gulped back a burp. "Excuse me," he said as he patted his chest lightly. "For the record, you are Captain Douglas Rackham of the mining transport, the *Betty*, aren't you? Part of LizzCo Industries Unlimited?"

Taken aback, Doug suspiciously glared at the Dean, then slowly turned his gaze to Wes.

"What?" Wes said defensively.

Without a sound, Doug covered his ears with his hands, then his eyes followed by his mouth. Wes nodded in wide-eyed understanding and immediately tapped at the SAPP implanted into his forearm.

Doug turned back to the Dean. "Yes sir, that is correct."

Dumbfounded at the scene before him, Dean Walker continued. "Then as I previously stated, I will gladly entertain any offers that you wish to make."

"Clear," Wes interrupted. "This office is bugged for sure. I just can't tell exactly what kind of gear they are using, so I'm broadcasting on all frequencies. Stay within twenty feet of me and no one will hear or see anything except *the cat came back*."

Doug snickered, then stood and leaned onto the Dean's desk. "Please explain to me who in the hell it is that is pulling your strings."

Dean Walker leaned back in his seat. Heavy tears filled his eyes. "I'm sorry. I didn't have a choice. They threatened my family."

"Who are *they*?" Doug demanded.

Dean Walker let out a fitful sob. "But if I tell you, they will kill me."

"If you don't tell him, life might not be worth living after he finishes with you," Wes said.

Doug drew his pistol, cocked the hammer and placed it on the desk. "Who," he quietly demanded.

The Dean sobbed uncontrollably. "The I.A. They approached the board of directors just shortly after you contacted us."

"Shit."

"Big brother is all over it," Wes sighed.

"Yeah, no shit." Doug holstered his revolver, then sat on the edge of the desk. "Did they say what they wanted?"

"No, they didn't."

Doug sat quietly for a moment in thought, then turned his attention back to the Dean. "Alright then, since Wes let the cat out of the bag already, here's the deal. We have established a colony in the Gamma Draconis or Eltanin system. But to fully support our efforts, we need funding for supplies and equipment. In exchange for funding, we are offering your top researchers the opportunity to study and document the planets and alien life forms within this system. We have already made first contact with a sentient species on the second planet and have documented a number of alien vessels. The planet is covered in the ruins of a civilization that once inhabited it and I for one would really like to know what happened to them. We will offer transportation and on-site support to your people, to include meals, lodging, and medical care. In exchange, we would like a flat rate of five hundred thousand credits per researcher biannually, plus full access to all data and findings."

Dean Walker stared blankly at Doug. His eyes darted back and forth in thought as he tried to comprehend what was just said. "You're serious, aren't you?"

"As serious as a heart attack." Doug produced a small datapad from his jacket and placed it on the desk in front of the Dean. He activated it and a video began to play that showed Casraownan.

"H...h...hello from Eltaaanin," the cat-like creature in the video said in horribly broken English.

The Dean gasped, then smiled wide as the realization hit him like a lemon wrapped about a large gold brick. "Do you know what this means? This information alone will turn the research community upside down. I could get you," he stammered as he tapped at the side of his nose, drifting off in thought. "I can get you a physicist, three sustainability researchers, and a microbiologist almost immediately. Possibly a structural engineer and more with a few days."

"That would be excellent," Doug acknowledged. "Though I would like to have an archeologist on permanent assignment to document things before we move or possibly destroy evidence."

"I'm sure that I could find someone with a few calls," the Dean said.

"Good." Doug smiled. "You have my contact information. Please submit a short overview of each team member for approval by tomorrow evening. As for the I.A., if they want to slip one of their people into the mix, then I say we let them. Just make sure that you mention *peanut butter* in that person's file. That way I know they aren't one of your researchers."

"Agreed, Captain Rackham." Dean Walker stood and extended his hand. A hopeful smile painted his face, "These are indeed, exciting times."

Doug happily took the Dean's hand and shook it. "Indeed, they are."

cHAPTER 36

Earth / Atlanta
Corner of Peachtree & 7th Streets
August 14th, 2176 / 0600 EST

" I really don't know what to say, Bob. This is perfect." Lizz marveled. "Thank you for going the extra mile on this one, but how did you manage to find this place, let alone purchase it so quickly?"

"It was my utmost pleasure Ms. Elizabeth," Bob assured her. "It just so happens that after a little digging, I found out that I personally knew the previous owners of this building. A few phone calls and strings later, I managed to pick up the entire building at well below the market value." He winked at Lizz, then produced a deed and a heavy-looking set of keys from his jacket pocket. "You just have to complete the paperwork to purchase the property from me for the same price and it is owned by LizzCo Industries Unlimited."

"Wait, did you say the entire building?"

"Yes, I did." Bob smiled proudly. "All nine floors of it. Now hear me out. We can easily utilize the current coffee shop space as our main face to the public. There are currently five other businesses renting space within the building. We can keep them on or evict them and utilize the space as we see fit. That depends on what you wish to do with the property. In order to cover all of the overhead and make this headquarters self-sufficient, I'd say we should leave the existing businesses and fill the empty offices as quickly as we can. As you can see," he gestured with arms flung wide, "Peachtree Street is booming. By putting your name up there, you will only make LizzCo a household name to all of those passing by. That is something that we can easily build on for the future." Bob took her hand and proceeded across the street.

"Is the coffee here that good or are they just that slow at serving the customers," Lizz asked, pointing at a line that had begun to form.

"I also took the liberty to contact Wesley last night and had him update the contact information on the promotional video and all of the other ads that he put out there on the net. Most likely, that line of people are waiting for you." Bob looked down and smiled at Lizz.

"Hi, hello," a well-dressed woman in the line said in a sweetly soft Boston accent. She waved as she stepped out of the line toward Bob and Lizz. "You're Elizabeth Trower, aren't you?"

The pair stopped as they reached the sidewalk in front of the building. "I am," Lizz cautiously replied then looked up at Bob and whispered. "Please remind me to contact my old friend, Hiram, later this evening. I might need to hire some security while I'm at it."

"Hi, my name is Camiel Lewis," the short brunette said as she approached. She beamed a smile at Lizz and enthusiastically held out her hand to shake. "Listen, I know how important first impressions are during the interview process, but I really need to get going. I'm already late for my regular job and if I could, I'd like to leave you a copy of my resume and the completed job application that I downloaded from your site." Camiel produced a neat black folder from the depths of a massive leather purse that hung across her chest and handed it to Lizz.

"Hey lady," a voice from the line interrupted. "How about you wait till they open the doors like the rest of us working stiffs."

Camiel suddenly became rigid, her face went blank of all emotion, then just as suddenly she smiled wide. A gleam of mischief twinkled in her eyes. "Please excuse me for just a moment, Miss Trower," she said in a chipper, but utterly annoyed tone. Her heels clicked loudly as she did a flawless about-face toward the voice in the line.

"That's right honey, get your tail back in line like the rest of us," said an overly tall man in a worn, one size too small blue suit.

Lizz watched with amusement. Camiel's gaze locked onto the complainer who she quickly stepped to and stood toe to toe with. She brushed an annoying hair from her mouth and adjusted her black, horned rimmed glasses as she craned her neck upward to look into the man's eyes.

"Do we have a problem here mister? I need to get myself to work so that I can pay the bills and feed my kids and myself since my deadbeat of an ex-husband was worthless enough to stop paying his share of the bills and land himself in prison. You want to knock me for trying to push ahead and better myself and my situation while still remaining responsible for the fact that I need to hurry so that I can clock in and earn my paycheck?" She took a deep, nasally breath.

The man waved his hands at her in defense. "No ma'am, I didn't mean anything of the sort. I just meant…"

"You meant that you didn't have the balls to do the same, did you? Not a surprise. I know your type. Men like you are all the same." Her glare burned a hole into the man's soul.

"Miss Lewis," Lizz shouted. She flipped casually through the extensive resume.

Camiel turned to Lizz with a smile. "Yes, Miss Trower?"

"You filled out an application for general accounting. We are not in need of a general administrator. I am terribly sorry, but I can not accept your resume."

"Oh, okay." Camiel drifted off in thought for a moment. "I could fill out another application for another position and get it to you by this evening at the earliest."

"How about instead of filling out an application, you go ahead and open up the office for me and let's start processing these applicants."

"Wait, really?" Camiel gasped, "but what is the pay and position?"

"I am in need of a ballsy, go get em kinda gal for the office manager's position. Five hundred credits for today. We can negotiate your salary tomorrow. You interested?"

"Absolutely!"

"Then let's get started." Lizz handed the ring of keys to Camiel. "It looks as if we are going to have ourselves a long day ahead of us."

"Yes ma'am." Camiel turned to face the line of applicants. "You heard Miss Trower. We're going to move this line along and get on with it. First person in line behind me and keep em rolling!"

Earth / Atlanta Spaceport
The *Betty*
August 14th, 2176 / Morning EST

"**M**ake sure that all of the current market info is up to date in the system. See what you can do about finding us a small storage facility nearby. Prices will never stay constant. We may have to packrat a load or two away Earthside until we can get a good price for it." Doug strode up the *Betty's* loading ramp.

"Copy that, Cap," Wes replied and continued into the ship.

"How are we looking…" He stopped in mid-sentence; a look of constipated consternation knotted his face. "Just about done with loading, Cap," Trae said. He ratcheted a cargo strap over a pallet of used microwaves. "We should be ready to leave by this evening. Maybe a little sooner if you or Wes give me a hand loading and tying everything down."

"Um… Why is there a pallet full of junk microwaves on my ship?"

"Radaranges actually," Trae replied. "These are industrial versions as powerful as some of the original ones developed after the Second World War."

"Alright, Radaranges," Doug agreed. "But why is there a pallet of them on my ship?"

"There, that should do." Trae closed the ratchet and straightened, massaging his still-healing hand as he walked over to Doug. "Why are they on your ship you ask? Well you see, they are on your ship because I purchased them and loaded them onto your ship."

"Okay, but how and why did you purchase them and load them onto my ship?"

"The how was easy. I agreed on a price, then let the vendor scan my credchip and boom, I purchased them. I didn't want to leave them behind. They might have felt lonely and abandoned if I had."

Doug forced down a laugh, then composed himself. "You're enjoying yourself, aren't you?"

"Yup." Trae laughed.

"Okay, so what's really up with them?"

"Parts, parts, and more parts. I can reuse the waveguides, capacitors and the magnetrons for a number of repairs. And these are a whole lot cheaper than trying to buy replacement parts for the ship."

"Fair enough then," Doug said. "Did you find out anything about the alien alloy that we brought back?"

"Actually, yes. And you aren't going to believe it." Trae said excitedly. "I took the samples to my buddy, Tim, at Lafarge Industries. He ran a full battery of materials testing and spectral analysis on them. It turns out that it's an odd mix of silica, beryllium, and zinc. He said it presents itself with a lot of the same properties as a silica bronze, but the tensile strength of the material is triple that of steel and its weight is half that of titanium. It isn't so much the base materials, but the process used to produce the material. So, he put me into contact with a Foundry up in Pennsylvania, who is highly interested in the material."

"Well of course they are," Doug scoffed. "If they are the only ones with the material, then they can corner the market and dictate their prices." He paused in thought. "We might have to sell it out to a number of foundries to keep them all honest. We can cross that issue later. I still have a few things to get done, so grab Wes and finish the loading. Once you're done, we'll rendezvous with the *Veronica* and take her cargo to Luna station."

"Planning to pay Sven a visit?"

"It has been a while," Doug thought. "And a little of the raw material might ease things over between us."

"You collapsed one of his mines," Trae reminded him.

"No! That's not what I was talking about. And besides, he can't hold me accountable for his shoddy construction methods."

"Then what were you talking about?"

Doug smiled. "The less you know, the better."

cHAPTER 37

Lunar Orbit
The *Betty*
August 14th, 2176 / Late Evening, (Betty Time)

A weak warbled beep radiated from the helm control console. "Sounds like we're in range of Luna." Trae quickly reconnected a thick duct-taped tangle of wires and cables to the side of the main view screen. "Try the screen now, Wes."

The view screen hummed with static as it powered up and Earth's moon faded into view.

"See, I told you we wouldn't have to replace it," Wes said.

"Now if we can just keep Rachel from doing any percussive maintenance, we can make it last a while longer." Trae hurried and took his position at the helm. "Luna station, Camden Control, this is the *Betty*. Spaceframe registration number MT00001242 CFT-82-0033-C. Point of origin, Atlanta, Georgia, American Commonwealth. Requesting permission to land."

"Hey," Wes said to Trae. "Do you think we should call Doug?"

"No, just let him sleep. We can handle landing and cargo transfer."

"Betty, this is Camden Control, we have you on visual," a generic sounding, even-toned voice replied over the comm. *"Transponder squawking clean. Welcome to Lunar air space. What can we help you with?"*

"We have a belly full of ore and some supply stuffs from Earthside. Looking to do some business, then get back out to the dark. Those rocks aren't going to mine themselves."

"Copy that Betty," the controller replied. *"Anything fresh would be appreciated up here. Follow transponder frequency 27.2 Gigahertz to docking bay three. Your assigned access to the Lunar data net is Tango, Kilo 421."*

"Copy that Camden Control. Tango, Kilo 421." Trae switched off the comms and looked over to Wes," You got it? Are we into their systems?"

"Hold on," Wes sighed. "They have some new firewalls in place this time." He tapped away at the touchscreen display. "Ha! There we go, we're in."

"Sweet," Trae said. "Make sure that all three of us have as high a security access as you can get us."

"One thing at a time," Wes argued. "I'm already working on that, but it looks like to set us up with anything more than epsilon access clearance, we'll need a three-part authentication code. I'm not sure we'll be here long enough for my crack software to run that sort of encryption crack. Man, they've really changed up all of the security protocols in the last year. The last time we were here it wasn't anything for me to hack into their systems."

"What does epsilon give us?" The view screen displayed the moon's surface with a projected flight path in amber and their current flight path overlaid in green. Trae fired the ship's maneuvering thrusters to adjust their flight path, aligning the overlays.

"This would be so much easier if the different moon colonies used the same systems," Wes groused.

Trae chuckled. "What would be the fun in that? At least this way things stay interesting."

"It would at least be convenient. Oh hey," Wes said in surprise. He flicked his finger across his console and a new display window appeared on the main viewscreen. "How about epsilon alpha clearance? It's for facilities maintenance access."

"Does that get us access to Director Garland's office?"

An orthographic view of the colony, from domed surface structures to the lowest levels slowly flashed up on the main view screen. "It'll give us access to basically everything but main control and a few of their military facilities."

"That sounds perfect," Trae said. "Garland may shoot us on sight when we waltz right into his office, but we can wing it and figure something out at that point. I'm sure that Doug would approve. Go ahead and flash our data chips with the clearance codes."

"Way ahead of you. I'm flashing the updates now." Wes sucked in a suddenly surprised breath. "Oh my God! Dude! You are not going to believe what I just found."

Trae glanced over with a look of annoyance at Wes. "You found definitive proof of Bigfoot and the Loch Ness monster?"

"Yes, wait, no… What the hell?" Wes glared at Trae.

"What? You just make it way too easy sometimes. So what did you find?"

A huffed whistle escaped from Wes's nose. "Fine. I found the current municipal equipment inventory for Camden Station."

"Okay, so? I'm sure that Doug could use it to his advantage when he goes to talk with Garland, but that isn't exactly as exciting as you might think it is."

"Oh, but it is." Wes grinned. "This is the *full* inventory for Camden Station, from office computers to assigned vehicles. It just so happens to include a full inventory of everything in the Lunar orbital boneyard on the dark side of the Moon."

"Wait, what? Oh, that is just perfect. Maybe Doug will really be able to cash in on the favor that Garland owes him then. Firing retro thrusters in three, two, one." Trae adjusted the glide path of the Betty as the retro thrusters engaged. Momentum suddenly shifted forward, forcing them to lean forward.

"Put together a shortlist of interesting items in the boneyard. Drop ships, orbital foundry ships, or any mining vessels. Maybe even a few decent shuttles. The fewer repairs needed the better."

"Aye aye," Wes agreed. "Doug is going to flip when he sees all of this."

cHAPTER 38

Lunar Station Camden
Over the moon Cafe
August 15th, 2176 / Morning, (Betty Time)

"So, you got the appointment scheduled with Garland?" Doug took a seat at a table toward the rear of the coffee shop as he landed from a long bounce.

"Yeah, scheduled and confirmed," Wes said. "I also posted the job listings, pushed the ad video and posted the cargo onto the Camden data net."

"Ok, so how am I supposed to get into his office without being recognized?"

"I used one of the lower level maintenance guys credentials and flashed your data chip. If they scan you, you'll show up as one Sean Maggert. He's the sector twenty-four maintenance shift lead who has waste processing issues that need immediate attention. You shouldn't have a problem getting into the office."

"You know," Trae interrupted, arriving at the table. "You'd think it would be a whole hell of a lot harder to get into the Colonial Regent's office than this. It's almost absurdly easy and convenient." He pulled up a chair to the table and sat on it backward.

"That may be, but I for one won't look a gift horse in the mouth," Doug said.

"Here are your drinks, gentlemen." The young barista sat a tray with four coffees down on the table. "Please enjoy your…" Her words were abruptly cut off by the tinny sound of tiny cymbals accompanied by the slow beat of a flat drum. "Oh my God." The barista sighed and rolled her eyes upward. She glared back over her shoulder toward the main entrance. Those around the table followed her gaze to a group of disheveled individuals dressed in brown, burlap-like robes at the entrance of the establishment. "Weren't you guys saying something about hiring new crew when you placed your order at the counter?"

"We were." Doug smiled back at the short, young woman. Her mousy brown hair created an odd halo around her head in the low lunar gravity. "But I'll leave you to these two. I have a very important meeting to attend to."

The young woman slid into the seat as Doug stood to leave. She extended her hand to shake. "Hi. My name is Rebecca. Where do I sign up," she said with an anxious smile.

Doug picked up two of the coffees and slowly bounced away. "Don't you guys have too much fun while I'm gone."

"Have fun yourself, Boss," Trae said with a nod, then turned his attention to the young woman. Cautiously, he took her hand and shook. "Don't you want to hear what we're offering before you jump in headfirst?"

"Honestly no," she said matter of factly. "I don't care what the job is or how much the pay is, as long as I can get off of this rock and away from those freaky coffee cultists." She leaned her head in the direction of the entrance.

"Um...Okay," Wes stammered. "So, what sort of skills do you have? We have everything from cook's helper to engineer available."

"Oh, you have cook's helper available. I can do that." She smiled wide. "So can my sister. Then there's my husband and my sister's husband. They both do some mechanicing every now and then. So, sign us up."

"Wait, whoa, hold up now," Trae said. "You can't just sign up three other people onto the rosters. We're conducting interviews to weed out the undesirables."

Rebecca leaned up on her elbows. "Actually, yes I can. You see, once upon a time my husband took it upon himself to sign the four of us up for the Lunar colonies. He thought that he could come up here and make a fortune with barbeque. It would have been a great idea, but nothing tastes right on the moon. Something about the low gravity and how your body chemistry changes. I'm so freaking tired of it. I'm tired of this freaking place. I'm tired of those freaky Java Crucians that come in here *every* single day. I don't want to go back to Earth. There isn't anything back there for us, so you're the next best option. Sign us up." She tapped a finger firmly on the table.

Trae and Wes glanced to one another, unsure of how to proceed.

"Okay...sure," Wes said and placed a datapad onto the table.

"You'll need to get the others in here in the next few hours so that they can sign for themselves," Trae added. "What I can do is tentatively add them to the roster to hold their places."

"Good enough for me, so where do I sign?"

Wes slid the datapad over to her. "Please enter all of your information and you'll be good to go."

cHAPTER 39

Lunar Station Camden
Regent's office
August 15th, 2176 / Morning, (Betty Time)

Doug shoved open the hatchway to the Camden station Regent's office hard enough that it bounced against the wall, swinging closed behind him as he stepped through the doorway.

"Holy shit!" Lunar Regent Garland McDonald fell backward in an odd slow motion out of his seat behind a large, ordinary-looking metal desk.

"You don't mind if I come in, do you Gar?" Doug bounced over and sat one of the coffees down on the desk, then took a seat. He took a long, satisfying sip from his cup. "It just so happened that we were in the neighborhood on business and I thought to myself; hey, it's been forever since I saw my old buddy Garland. Maybe I should be courteous and pay him a visit while in port. So here I am." Doug motioned with open arms.

"You must either have a death wish or you have some seriously big steel balls to just walk in here like this." Garland sat his seat upright and straightened his uniform jacket. He glanced down suspiciously at the coffee cup in front of him.

"It isn't spiked if that's what you were thinking." Doug laughed, took a sip from Garland's cup, then place it back onto the desk. "See? You act like you don't trust me or something. Would I be stupid enough to spike it and then take a sip myself?"

"Possibly. It depends on if," Garland paused, then leaned forward and whispered, "if *him* is with you."

Doug flashed Garland a questioning look. "Him?"

"Yes him. That tubbo of chaos that you call a sidekick. I wouldn't put it past that cronie of yours to be just outside the door ready to break through at the mention of a code word." Garland visibly braced himself for the door to be kicked open.

"I wouldn't do that to you after what happened the last time we were in port." Doug leaned back in the uncomfortable metal chair and propped his feet up on the corner of the desk.

"He nearly destroyed the colony the last time you were in port!"

"Now hold on," Doug said. "Wes was just trying to lend a hand. Your guys asked him for an opinion and let him look at the equipment. It was an honest mistake when he closed off the relief feed for the atmo recyclers. It wasn't properly marked, and that falls back onto your maintenance guys."

Garland closed his eyes and shook his head in frustration. "That's all in the past and beside the point now. You want something, otherwise, you wouldn't be here."

"Really? A guy can't visit an old friend without wanting something in return?"

"No," Garland said with a sneer. "A guy like you doesn't have friends. You have acquaintances."

"For the record, you are right though, I am after something," Doug admitted.

Garland's face melted from anger to an expression of upset realization. "You're finally going to cash in on that favor I owe, aren't you?" Garland sat down in his seat.

"Ding ding ding," Doug said, tapping the tip of his nose. "That's it exactly. I'd say ten years is plenty long enough to wait. Wouldn't you?"

Garland leaned forward; his fingers laced together on the desk. "Alright, let's get this over with. What do you want," his voice cracked with a dry and serious strain.

"We have had an opportunity of galactic proportions fall into our laps. To make a true go of it and make it happen, I need a ship."

Garland tilted his head in confusion. "That's it? You need a ship," he said in a disbelieving tone. "You already have a ship."

"Actually, I have more than a few ships now if you count the ones abandoned in the hanger. But those won't serve the purpose that I currently need."

Garland slammed a fist down on the desk so hard that the coffee cup bounced away and began to spill in mid-air in the low lunar gravity. "Then spit it out already. Cut the bullshit, Doug. Let's get this over with. What do you want!"

Doug leaned forward, eyes ablaze with a gaze of daring confidence. "On the dark side of the moon in the Lunar orbital boneyard, there is a Brynhildr class foundry ship that has been rotting away for decades. Per the maintenance logs that we were able to obtain, she's still intact, for the most part. I want her." Doug flashed a predatory smile at Garland.

Atlanta Georgia
Peachtree Street
August 15th, 2176 / Morning, (Betty Time)

"I am dead serious when I say this," Lizz said to Camiel. She squared off with the young brunette and gave her a deadpan look. "Operate this office as if it were your own. We will be off-world most of the time and I need someone here that I can trust to do the job." Lizz turned and continued down Peachtree Street, heading south toward the new offices of LizzCo Industries. The click, click, click of their high heels on concrete echoed from the faces of the close-packed buildings.

"But…," Camiel started then swallowed hard. "But what if something horrible were to happen? Like a full-blown war or alien invasion or something?"

"It's as simple as this. Keep the doors open, keep investing and keep making money," Lizz said plainly. "If you or anyone else working here is in danger, then use your best judgment. You are getting a partnership percentage of all profits. So, the more successful contracts and investments you make here, Earthside, the larger your paydays will be. Bob reorganized everything last night in preparation for our return to Eltanin. I have no doubt that you can take the reins here and thrive at it."

"I sure hope you're right," Camiel looked down and said under her breath.

"Stop it," Lizz demanded. "We'll have none of that destructive self-talk. Chin up, positive attitude. Ah, speaking of Bob." Lizz tapped Camiel on the arm to bring her attention back.

Bob burst through the front door of the new LizzCo office. His suit jacket and decorative tie were a flurry of motion as he rushed to hold open the door for the approaching pair. "Welcome back ladies. You both had an enjoyable lunch, I hope?" He smiled wide and bowed. "You have two...um," Bob cleared his throat, "gentlemen waiting in the lounge for your return."

"Oh, well then let's not keep them waiting," Lizz said and hurriedly stepped through the door, pulling Camiel along with her.

Two very muscular men in combat harnesses stood as Lizz and Camiel entered the building.

"Well now, would you look at what we have here," Lizz said in a sultry tone. She stepped into the waiting area and stopped, admiring the well-built male specimens. Lizz thoughtlessly chewed on her lower lip as she ogled the pair. "Hiram didn't just send us muscle, he sent us some very pretty muscle. Wouldn't you say so Camiel?"

"Um…" Camiel nervously gulped, forcing herself to take a stuttering breath. "You could say something like that." Her face melted with a warm daydreaming numbness.

"We were told to ask for Elizabeth Trower," the large blond-headed Viking looking mercenary said.

"And you have found her," Lizz replied. "Did Hiram fill you in on any details?"

"No, ma'am," the shorter, dark-haired man answered with a deep, gravelly voice. "He just said to report directly to you as soon as possible and the details would be sorted out afterward."

"You will report directly to our office manager, Camiel," Lizz said while gesturing behind her. "What she says is as good as my own word," she said with a stern glare at the pair. "I'm sure that Hiram has filled you in on that little tidbit before you left."

"Yes ma'am, he did," the large Viking like one gruffly answered.

"Oh, now, I don't know about all of this," Camiel argued. She drifted off in dreamy thought. "I mean, look at them. What am I supposed to do with them? And good Lord, what in the world do I feed them?"

"Their primary duty is to protect you, secondary is to protect the business." Lizz took Camiel by both hands and looked her levely in the eye. "You do whatever you see fit. These two are on indefinite loan to me from Hiram for whatever I want or need to do with them. Consider them yours to do with as you wish." She quickly turned to Bob and straightened herself. "I believe that we have a ship to catch. Are you ready Bob?"

"Yes ma'am. Shall we?" Bob offered his arm to Lizz.

"Gladly." Lizz looped her arm through his and they walked out the door.

"Well, alright then." Camiel nodded nervously and began to wring her hands. "Fellas." She admired the tall blond-haired man, stopping herself short as she reached out to caress his heavily muscled and tattooed arm.

The large blond-haired biker smiled. "It's alright. Go ahead. You can touch it," he said in a tone so soft as to be impossible for his size. He flexed his right tricep and presented his arm to her.

"Oh, my," Camiel said as she exhaled heavily. She caressed the chorded line of muscle down the side of his massive tricep. She gasped, then yanked her hand back and snapped her fingers. "I know what we're going to do." She hurried toward the doors and stopped just as she pushed the door open. "Well, what are you waiting for? Let's move it," she shouted in a tone reserved for drill sergeants and angry mothers.

The pair looked at each other and shrugged. "Okay," said the larger of the two. "Where are we going?"

"Shopping," she said matter of factly. "The battle rattle biker look may work for you on a normal day, but not here and not on my watch. You can put the battle rattle back on later tonight," she said with a wink. "Now let's move it!"

cHAPTER 40

Sol system
Asteroid Belt / Flux point Alpha.
August 18th, 2176 / Mid-Morning, (Betty Time)

"Betty, come in. This is the Veronica," Rachel's voice cracked. *"I have you on radar with a positive return on the IFF transponder, but there are three other contacts riding in your wake."*

"Oh hey, hold on," Trae flipped on the main view screen. We have you on visual Rachel."

"It's okay, Cheezy, they are with us," Doug said.

"Oh...Okay then? Well, while you guys were off doing whatever the hell that you've been doing, I decided to tinker around a little with the flux drive," she said, then proudly smiled.

"You what?" Trae gasped and began to hysterically laugh. "Oh, my God, we are so screwed."

"Oh, no," Wes shouted. "Cheezy, no! Bad Cheezy! Bad girl!"

Doug slowly massaged the bridge of his nose. "Please tell me that you didn't use Willy's wrench."

"Guys," She shouted. *"Oh my God, will you shut it already! I think I figured out the finer details of how the system works."* She huffed with exasperation.

"Alright. Fair enough then. Everyone shut it," Doug ordered. "Let's hear what you've got, Cheezy."

"The standard drive system on the Veronica is way more efficient than the ancient, first-generation drive on the Betty. But why does the Veronica burn so much more fuel you ask?"

Everyone on the Betty's bridge blankly stared at the viewscreen, waiting on Rachel to continue.

"Well, I'll tell you!" She excitedly continued, wagging her finger at the viewscreen. *"If I am right, then we could possibly cut the amount of fuel required per jump in half! That's right! Save half of your fuel costs with a simple procedure that even a geek could accomplish."*

"What the fuck ever," Wes said.

"With a simple tweak. A minuscule adjustment. A…"

"Get on with it already," Doug interrupted.

"By simply fine-tuning the frequency output of the flux emitters to more closely match the frequency of a specific nexus point, our required power output to maintain a stable aperture will be significantly lower than it had on previous portal penetrations."

Wes exploded with laughter at Rachel's cheezy and toothy salesman like appearance.

"You practiced that for a while didn't you," Doug asked.

Uh-huh," she mumbled through her still bared teeth.

"That's a good find Cheezy," Doug said. "I only assumed the other ships could pass through with us. That might actually give us more flexibility in what we can bring through."

Doug questioningly looked over at Trae who sat at the side engineering station.

"Shoot over the data," Trae said. "Let me and Wes give the numbers a look over first, then maybe we can give it a shot."

"Sounds like a plan to me," Doug said. "Let's get it done and get back to the Lair."

cHAPTER 41

Eltanin 2 / Dragon's Lair
August 19th, 2176 / Lunch-time-ish (Betty Time)

Secondary power turbines whined as they arrived at a steady-state idle. Bob and Lizz appeared walking arm in arm down the *Betty's* boarding ramp as it lowered to the ground.

"Welcome home," Willy greeted.

"William!" Bob enthusiastically waved with his free hand in greeting. "How have you been my friend."

"Busier than mustard trying to ketchup." Willy grinned.

Bob and Lizz laughed. "So, we've arrived at the horrible puny condiment portion of our relationship, have we?"

"Eh, yup." Willy snorted a laugh then continued. "I suppose so. I have been going nonstop since you all left. The new machine shop and fabrication bays are all cleaned out and ready for whatever new toys you managed to bring back for me. How was the trip? Uneventful and productive I would hope."

Lizz chortled. "From a business perspective, it was an extremely productive trip. Much more than I could have dreamt of. I'm sure that Bob will fill you in on all the juicy details later. But for the time being, I need to speak with Melanie about setting up our new hires." Lizz rose up on tiptoes and kissed Bob on the cheek. "You boys play nice and don't get into any trouble." She seductively sashayed away from the loading ramp toward the basecamp area.

Willy turned back toward Bob with an accusatory grin. "Didja get all of your personal business squared away while you were Earthside?"

"Yes, fortunately. I even had the time to visit my old watering hole and pay off the tab that had lapsed into collections status."

"Anything interesting happen?"

"Oh, you know how it goes." Bob nonchalantly waved at the question. "A little extortion with a touch of blackmail on the side for good measure. Oh, and Lizz managed to arrange some dedicated security personnel at both the new offices and here, plus extra hands to get things off the ground. Apparently, she has some very close ties with the National President of some motorcycle club or something. I'm not quite sure about them myself, but I've never really had dealings with that type before."

"They wouldn't happen to have been from the Wings of Odin MC, were they," Willy asked.

"Yeah, that's them. Elizabeth said something about calling in a favor that the club president owed her."

"Wow." Willy crossed his arms and stared at the ground in thought. "If Lizz called in the favor that Hiram owed her, then she's dead serious about this place. She's going all-in or bust I guess."

"You make it sound like this is really serious," Bob said.

"The job that we pulled to earn that favor had gone sideways, upside down and backward six ways from Sunday. It nearly got every one of us killed. It was in no way the easy job that Hiram had promised. Lizz was pissed and threatened him with something from way back when. Like back when they were kids or something. I don't know exactly. That was totally between the two of them. All I do know is that she had some sort of dirt on him from way back that she used as leverage. He promised her a no strings attached favor. No questions, no argument, no matter what it was, he would honor their agreement when and wherever that she wanted it."

"Wow?"

"Yeah. Exactly." Willy looked back over his shoulder in the direction that Lizz had gone. "If she called that in, then she is all in on this." He motioned at their surroundings.

"What's the word, Willy?" Doug eagerly bounced down the *Betty's* loading ramp and stopped dead in his tracks. He, Bob and Willy all glanced curiously toward the sudden sound of Fergus shouting.

"Damit devil woman! You took off and forgot your wifely duties! Get over here and give me some lovin'!" Fergus trotted toward the *Veronica* as Rachel sprinted down the length of its ramp. The spacesuit he wore slowed his progress.

"Come over here, you hairless monkey man!" Rachel leapt into the air and wrapped herself around his encumbered form. She wrenched her legs around his torso and pushed herself upward. Grasping his head, she repeatedly kissed his forehead over and over again.

Willy turned back to Doug and Bob. "I'll catch up with you in a bit, Bob. Mel should have dinner ready by now."

"Captain." Bob graciously bowed to Doug. "I look forward to the conversation, Willy. I have a few things that I should attend to also. Oh," he said as he stopped in his tracks. "I made sure to add extra sugar and tea to the shopping list while we were Earthside," he said as a sidelong comment then continued down the ramp.

"You said dinner," Doug said to Willy. "What time is it here?"

"1730ish hours, Gamma Draconis time," Willy said.

"At some point, I suppose we'll have to establish a full calendar for this place too." Doug stepped aside as new faces began to disembark the ship. "Just head over toward the base camp and Melanie will set you up with accommodations." He waved the new crew members onward then turned his attention back to Willy. "Sorry. You were saying, Willy?"

"Well, like I was saying to Lizz and Bob. I have the machine shop and fabrication bays cleared out and ready for any equipment or materials that you brought back. I took a full inventory of those two bays and a lot of other cargo that I could identify as valuable from the other cargo bays. From what little exploring that I did in town, it looks like we could easily salvage a few loads of that structural material from the rubble. But we'll have to haul it all to orbit to smelt it down in the *Betty's* ore processors. We need the cold vacuum of space to operate that system properly."

"Hey, Cap, you don't need me for anything right now, right?" Wes hurriedly trotted down the Betty's loading ramp.

"No, you're good Geek. Take the night off and spend some time with the wife."

"Awesome. Thanks, Cap." Wes leapt forward, then stopped dead in his tracks. He hesitated momentarily, then slowly marched forward.

Doug followed Wes's gaze toward a roof support pillar that lay in the direction of the makeshift base camp. Flip Winston leaned against the support, casually watching Wes as he descended the ramp.

"You guys shouldn't have too much trouble unloading the ships. All of Mel's foodstuffs and kitchen supplies are on the first dozen pallets here on the *Betty*." Trae held out a datapad toward Willy as he strolled down the ramp. "All of your machinery and materials are on the Veronica. The rest of the load is general supplies, some real furniture, things like that. Oh, and I have a few pallets of scrap stuff. They can go into the fab shop for now and I'll strip them down later."

"Wait? You brought back scrap?" Willy looked at him questioningly, then looked to Doug.

"Don't ask," Doug replied.

"You seen Tiff?"

"Yeah, she was cleaning out one of the upper spaces for your quarters. Take that ramp up one level to the concourse area, hang a left and down two doors," Willy said.

"Gotcha, thanks, brother," Trae said with a quick handshake then turned to Doug. We good, Cap?"

"You're good. Take the night off," Doug said.

"Copy that." Trae presented a slack armed salute and proceeded off into the darkness of the bay, then stopped abruptly. "Oh, Willy. There are like a half dozen pallets marked fragile. Those belong to Sullivan and Rampkin. I'll tell you right now, there's no pleasing either one of them. I understand that the equipment the universities sent with them is delicate, but there's only so much you can do with a skid loader. It is what it is. But if you try to explain that to them then you'll have both of them bitching in your ears.

"I'll have to remember to drop one of the pallets then," Willy chuckled.

"Hey, it's your funeral, big man. I've got nothing to do with it." Trae continued on his way down the loading ramp.

"If you've got a handle on things, I'm going to see what Mel has cooking and give her a heads up on all the new folks," Doug said to Willy. "Oh, and we have a load of cots to temporarily bunk everyone until we can get full quarters set up. Found a bulk deal at this old Army-Navy store out near Cartersville. You might want to get those off and set up somewhere fairly quickly. Get Richie, Flip and Andy to help you. As soon as you can get the loads swapped out, we'll head back on another run."

"Yeah boss, I've got this," Willy replied.

"Good, I'll leave you to it then," Doug said as he strode away down the *Betty's* loading ramp.

Eltanin 2 / Dragon's Lair
August 19th, 2176 / Lunch-time-ish (Betty Time)

"Well hello there little fella," Krista cooed. "You look like you need a nap. Want me to hold you?" She squatted and held out her hands to pick up Joquon, the young cat creature, son of Casraownan. "I know, that big bad sun is bright up here, isn't it? It'll be alright little one. Come here, let Aunt Tata hold you and we'll go sit in the shade." She reached for the small cat creature, stretching to grab him up as he entered the upper concourse area of the complex.

Cassraownan and Mapharye followed close behind the young Chinchassan. Jouqon blew past Krista and ran straight to Amanda with his arms held out, he leapt and wrapped them around Amanda's neck.

"He loves me more," Amanda teased. She stuck out her tongue toward Krista, then hurried over to a shaded camp area that was set up away from the outer walls of the primary concourse of the ancient starport.

"I see how it is. I'll remember that the next time I make something sweet." Krista slicked back sweat-soaked wisps of hair from her face.

Cassraownan and Mapharye nodded a bow, fists across their chests, then both suddenly extended their middle fingers toward Krista.

Krista stared at the cat creature couple in utter disbelief.

Maggie burst out in laughter. "I guess they have been hanging around with Fergus, haven't they?"

"It is good to meet you once again great Earthbound Goddess," Mapharye said slowly in a cat-like yowl that heavily accented her words.

"Oh, well now. Doesn't that just sound absolutely lovely," Krista chortled with delight.

"Don't let it go to your head, sadist," Amanda said.

"Will you two stop the petty bickering for once." Maggie moved her crate of tools forward and began to drive another stake into the ground. "I get so sick and tired of hearing you two go back and forth about nothing."

Casraownan sniffed with a curious curl of the nose at the air, then continued. "Our people still fear the surface, but we wish to learn," he said slowly, careful to pronounce each heavily accented syllable.

"Well, um." Krista glanced around, unsure where to start. The concourse area was tall and open to the outside world. The glass or what the ancient Chinchasan's had used like glass had broken and deteriorated ages ago. Sand littered the floor in small drifts and dunes. Remnants of preserved fixtures and furniture poked out from beneath drifts of sand. They had been driving stakes into the ground and marking the areas with string in preparation for building raised bed garden boxes. "I'm not sure if any of this will interest you or not. We're just leveling and marking out garden spots at the moment. Once we get that done, we'll use what we have at hand to build the beds and prep as much soil as we can. Willy is working on a pump system to get water up here from the underground spring that you showed him. That might be more interesting to you."

"I am very interested to know how you will grow food." He nodded and smiled. Pleased with his progress of the English language. The sour smell of fermented waste wafted in on the breeze. He wrinkled his nose again and turned to Mapharye. "Ene ni yamar ünertej baina?"

"Look out, toxic waste coming through," Fergus announced through the speaker of his containment suit. He guided a self-propelled wagon into the concourse area. It carried a large

cylindrical tank that was secured to the wagon deck with cargo straps.

"Oh good, the fertilizer is here." Maggie quickly leapt to her feet and dusted off her hands. "Just put it back there in that old shop area. It'll work great as a compost." She pointed in the direction that she wanted Fergus to go.

"If for some reason that you run out or that you need more, there shouldn't be a problem. We have plenty more where this came from. Just make sure that you specify to whoever gets stuck with the shit detail," he emphasized with air quotes, *"that they make sure to transfer it from the untreated tank. Anything from the treated side will most likely poison the garden since it's packed full of processing chemicals."*

"Blegh," Krista gagged. "My God, do we really have to have that here?"

"Yes," Maggie quickly replied with an annoyed glance over her shoulder.

"There is still over six months' worth of shit from the Betty's waste recycling system available," Fergus informed. *"No one bothered to turn the thing back on and it completely slipped their minds to empty the tanks when they were back Earthside.*

"Blegh," Krista gagged again.

"You'll be fine," Maggie admonished. "It's the best chance that we have to get a good crop started in this sandy soil. Suck it up, buttercup," Maggie laughed, then returned to marking the garden spots.

cHAPTER 42

Eltanin 2
Dragon's Lair / Mel's Diner
August 20th, 2176 / 0900 (Dragon Time)

Large stockpots toppled from their pallet and clattered across the concrete floor of the ancient alien warehouse. "Set down everything in your friggin' hands right friggin' now before I cut them off!" Melanie ran shaky fingers through her hair with a frustrated huff. "I swear to God. If I wanted kids, I could so easily have them. I promise you, I really could. All of these here parts still work." She waved her hands about her torso like a game show prize girl.

"But Willy told me to come over here and give you a hand," Andy said.

"I couldn't give a shit what Willy said." A small saucepan flew in Andy's direction and bounced off of one of the many pallets of supplies that littered the area. Melanie firmly cupped her right breast. "Hell, these things might even produce some milk if I ever decide to drop a living human being out of the dusty leathery sack I call a womb. But that's on the rare off chance that I actually have sex and manage to get pregnant. Get out of my kitchen!"

"But I'm supposed to be helping," Andy argued as he dodged a large copper plated frying pan.

"I'll do it my friggin' self. If you do it, I'll just have to go back behind you and do it all over again."

"But…" Andy started, then ducked behind a stack of boxes.

"Go hang on Willy's skirt tails for a little while so I can clean up this mess you made." She carelessly picked up and chucked one of the large stock pots through the doorway of what was to become the kitchen and food prep area.

Andy ducked behind a pallet stacked full of cooking equipment, boxes of utensils and packages of supplies as he escaped what had been designated the Dragon's Lair cantina, or better known as Mel's diner. "Look out, coming through!" Andy shoved his way past four individuals at the entrance of the cantina and made a hard right. His boots clanked on the metal grating of the catwalk style steps as he raced to the platform of the levels above.

The new arrivals gazed about in awe at the nearly empty three stories of the space.

"Are you Melanie," a quiet voice asked.

Melanie turned to the four individuals at the entrance of the Cantina. "That all depends on who you are and what you want. I haven't had time to cook anything more than some stew, so if you don't like stew, I guess you're just shit out of luck. If it's anything other than that, then I don't know what to tell you." Another pot soared through the kitchen entrance and clanged against the back wall.

"Hi, I'm Becky," the young woman said introducing herself. "This is my sister Sabrina, my husband Perry and my sister's husband Chris," she said as she pointed in a quiet, mouse-like tone. "My sister and I were sent over to give you a hand. We were told that you needed kitchen helpers when we signed up." She nervously picked at a jagged fingernail.

"And what about those two? I suppose they are just here to do the heavy lifting for the two of you?" Mel glared at the two men.

"Oh no, nothing like that at all," Becky said.

"Willy said for us to wait over here for him," the pudgy, dark-haired man added in a strange mouth breathing accent. "He's got things for us to do, but he had other stuff to sort out first. So, we're supposed to be helping you out for right now."

"Oh, so I'm supposed to babysit you is what you're saying?" Melanie scowled at the small group.

"Nope. That's not what I said at all. Alright, let me break this down to you in words you can comprehend." The dark-haired man said, accenting his words with a slow-motion of his hands. "Me Chris. You Melanie. Big man Willy," he puffed himself up to look bigger, his chest out and chin tucked, "tell to me, come help you. Me Chris help you, Melanie," he pointed to her as he slurred the words. "We work hard. We get job done." Chris pounded his chest and grunted.

Melanie stared at him in consternation. "Well bless your heart. Your momma must have dropped you on your head a few times, or ten, didn't she? Or did you eat too many paint chips when you were younger?"

"Ya know, with all of the space that you have here, there's plenty of room to expand the menu to include some specialized Earth favorites. I bet if you give me and Chris the chance, we could build you a smoker that will be the envy of the galaxy," the orange-haired man said. "Have you ever had true southern applewood smoked barbecue? Delicious, melt in your mouth flavor. And I'm not even talking about just Texas-style barbecue. We could set aside a few smokers specific for Carolina style or Jamaican jerk. It just depends on what folks would want."

Melanie angrily glared at the orange-haired man. Her left eye began to twitch ever so slightly in the span of a single breath. Another large stockpot effortlessly soared through the air into the kitchen entrance. "I have days and days' worth of work ahead of me just to get things in this kitchen set up. Crates full of supplies to inventory, stack and find a home for. Pallets of cots to assign to all of the new personnel and no one has even told me where all of the crew quarters will be located. Then you want to come in here and start adding shit to my list of things to do or be responsible for when I'm already stretched way too thin as it is. I swear that I've had it. I've had it up to here!" She motioned with a knife-hand above her head.

"I'd leave if I were you," Andy said, shouting down from the second-floor catwalk.

Melanie's glare shifted upward toward Andy. "Andrew Lee Kleszinski!"

Andy sprinted down the stairs for the open doorway.

A frying pan sailed in a high arc across the length of the cantina to connect with the main entrance door frame, inches away from Andy's head.

"Do we need to have another talk about maiming the hired help, Mel?" Doug asked as he entered the cantina.

"No. We don't. I just don't know what else you expect from me. You have me cooking and cleaning and putting all of this stuff away and assigning quarters for the new people when we don't even have any quarters for them to be assigned to and…"

"Mel!" Doug interrupted. "I expect you to use the resources that I give you to your advantage. Work smarter, not harder." Doug looked away toward Becky. "Have you ever worked in a hotel or anything in the service industry? Anything to do with serving the public. Fast food would especially count in this situation."

"Yeah," Becky replied. "I was the barista at the java bar on Luna station Camden when you guys found me."

"Good, then you understand how to prioritize your orders and organize? At least minimally I'd hope? Oh, and a side thought now that you mention the java bar. If we picked up the equipment would you be up to setting up a coffee shop here?"

She gave Doug a suspicious, sidelong glance. "Yes, I do and okay, sure, I guess," she said suspiciously slow.

Doug redirected his questioning, "Mel, you prefer to just cook and keep everyone fed, right?"

"I'd be much happier to just deal with the cooking and nothing else," Melanie said.

"Then that's what you do. Consider this kitchen and cantina as your personal little kingdom and run it as such." Doug turned back to Becky and Sabrina. "I need someone to run general services around here. You'd be assigning quarters, arranging community functions, group movie night or any other creature comfort sort of thing. The little things that will help to make this place home to folks. Temporarily, we need barracks-style arrangements for all of our workforce. But eventually, we'll need to set everyone up with their own places. Especially the ones that have no want to return to Earth and would rather call this place home. Then we'll eventually have to look at the prospect of people having babies and starting families. Do you want the job?"

Rebecca's throat bobbed as she attempted to swallow. Her eyes narrowed to a suspicious glare as she let out an exasperated huff. "You're screwing with me, aren't you?"

"Nope, not in the slightest." Doug grinned, then continued. "Everyone that we bring in will need to learn how to be flexible and do more than a few jobs initially. Well, at least until we get the Lair fully functional and self-sufficient. We have brought back twenty-eight new crew members, including the four of you," he pointed to each of them, "plus four light-transport crews. Mel will be busy keeping everyone fed, which includes menu planning and supply orders for two or three months at a time since we don't have a regular schedule for Earthside trips as of yet. When you aren't working directly on planning or assigning accommodations, I would expect you to help Mel in the kitchen and with service, at least until we hire in a few others."

"I could handle that, I guess," Becky said.

"You guess, or you know?"

"I know I could handle it and do the job. Do I get to choose who works for me," she excitedly asked.

"That would be one of the perks of being in charge of something," Doug replied.

"Good, then my sister Sabrina is working with me." She pulled Sabrina in for a sisterly side hug.

"What about these two?" Doug nodded toward Chris and Perry.

Her face crinkled in a snarky, disgusted visage. "Are you kidding? I wouldn't hire them if I had to. They are your problem."

Perry shrugged his shoulders and chuckled. "What can you say to that? There's no real argument worth arguing there."

"Do you two have anything to do?"

"Oh yeah yeah yeah, we're good," Chris stammered. "Willy sent us to help in here temporarily till he was ready for us."

Doug looked back at Becky, "If you can use them in the meantime, then go ahead. It all depends on what Mel needs, but I'd make getting bunks set up a top priority.

Doug turned back to Mel, who had busied herself with inspecting the contents of a large container. "Now, back to the reason that I came here. We're heading back Earthside just as soon as Willy and Trae can get us loaded. I need to know if there's anything else that we missed on this load that you immediately need. The next load we were going to focus on equipment as much as possible. But if we need something for you then I'll make sure it gets into the ship's manifest."

"Can you take Andy with you and just leave him there while you're at it," Melanie suggested.

"Um...No. Not really, Mel."

"Then there isn't much you can do for me, now is there." Her glare could have burned a hole through a six-inch steel plate.

cHAPTER 43

Earth
Isla Escudo de Veraguas
The northern coast of Panama
August 28th, 2176 / Afternoonish (Local Time)

"I really don't know, Cap," Wes said as they walked along a sandy boardwalk. It gradually led the way from the shore up a small rise to a Spanish style beach house. "I mean, the thing is huge compared to the *Betty*. Is Willy absolutely sure that the flux drive can handle something as massive as a Brynhildr class foundry ship along with the *Betty* and the *Veronica* passing through the flux? What happens if the opening collapses while we're halfway through the flux? Do we just cease to exist? Do we snap to one side or the other? Are we divided between the two points of space?"

"He said that drive could easily handle the aperture diameter and the mass involved," Doug replied. "I had him and Trae both review the data and they are both certain that the flux drive will be fine. He said it isn't a matter of how big something is when passing through the flux, but more of how wide that you can expand the opening. They both did say that the flux drive can only channel so much energy through the emitters, which is what limits the aperture opening. But right now, we're good."

"*Okay*? I'm still skeptical," Wes said.

Doug stopped momentarily, lit a cigarette and took a long draw. He turned to take in the beauty of the picturesque, tropical beach, then exhaled slowly through his nose. A comfortably warm breeze carried the scent of the sea and tropical flowers across the island toward the beach where they stood. Doug closed his eyes and inhaled slowly. "It's like something you'd see on a postcard, isn't it?"

"Yeah, it really is," Wes said as he looked around then turned back to Doug. "So, then the limiting factors are power and the ability to focus that power."

"Yup," Doug said with an annoyed glance. "Which is why we'll have to keep that fact in mind when Willy starts fabrication on a flux drive for the Betty. I want to be able to drag rocks and more through those holes with her if I want. If we can bring back any claims or salvage to our system, then that minimizes the number of personnel that we have to send out for recovery."

"Wow, you're really getting into this aren't you?" Wes smiled at Doug.

"What do you mean?"

"I mean that you've been laying out some seriously long-term plans. Not just a few months ahead like we've been doing for what feels like forever. You're making plans to homestead and make something of all of this." Wes smiled proudly.

"Just doing what feels right. And it isn't just for me, but for all involved. If I make a bad call, any of you can get hurt or killed like it was nothing." Doug took another long drag from his cigarette. "I'm trying to make the best decisions that I can, using the least amount of effort for the largest gain. Simple business math."

"How the hell is that simple business math," Wes asked.

"Because we want to turn a profit with minimal losses and expenditures," Doug replied. "The less effort, time and material that we put into any endeavor the better. It will only increase our bottom line."

"Oh wait, so now we're just numbers hu? I see how it is," Wes said jokingly. "Maybe you've been spending a bit too much time around Lizz."

"Maybe," Doug said with a shrug. He field-stripped the burning ember from the end of his cigarette and continued up the path. He could see that the path led into a secured patio area at the back of the house. A tall stucco-clad wall topped with wrought iron spikes formed the perimeter of the small, but plush beachside manor house.

"Um...Cap," Wes nervously said. "What sort of business did you say your friend was into?"

"A little of this and a little of that. I'm not exactly sure what he's currently into," Doug admitted. "He managed to score a small fortune when he was younger with stocks or commodities or something like that. I'm not exactly sure, but I do know it was stock market sort of stuff. Why?"

Long tanned legs adorned with black stiletto heels appeared from behind the wall and stood in plain sight as the gate opened. Attached to those well-tanned legs was a fully nude brunette of Hispanic or possibly islander descent. Full, round breasts swayed and jiggled with the few steps that she took to step into view.

"Master Barrington wished for me to welcome you to his island sanctuary," she said in the scripted tone of a quickly memorized the message. "He also wished for me to inform you, that he will be with you shortly. He is currently engaged in hostile negotiations with our Swedish diplomat. Please, come in, take refreshments and relax while you wait."

"Are you sure that's what his current profession is," Wes asked. He struggled to not stare at her shapely, but completely nude body.

"It is perfectly fine to look or to do really anything that you'd like," she said with a contemplative eye roll, then winked at Wes.

"I have no honest clue at this point," Doug admitted. "It's been years since I've seen him. But in the end, does it really matter? We need funding to get everything established."

"You wouldn't want to be funded by blood money, would you? Cash earned on the backs of innocent women and children, for example," Wes said.

"True, you have a point there." Doug proceeded through the gate as the brunette motioned for the pair to enter.

She led them to a marble-topped patio table that rested next to a crystal-clear plunge pool. "Please, sit and relax gentlemen," she urged. "Should there be anything that you desire," she giggled, "please speak and it shall be yours if it is within our ability."

Three other nude female forms decorated the landscape. One skimmed the pool with a long-handled bug net. Another, a cute, perky looking redhead quickly removed the bottle caps from two clear bottles, inserted a lime into each and placed them on a small tray. The third nude female, a thin, small-breasted blond with a cute pixie style cut quickly rushed over to the bar to retrieve the tray.

"Oh man, I could really go for an ice cream sandwich right now," Wes innocently blurted.

The hostess's eyes got wide with surprise and she smiled. "I will see what we have available." She nodded a bow, then turned and left. The *click click click* of her heels on the tiled patio accentuated the sway of her hips as she walked.

"Are you really sure that we should be here asking him a favor?" Wes turned to Doug, worry lining his face. "I don't like to question you on your decisions but, damn. A personal island full of naked slave girls," Wes argued. "Really? That's like epic level drug lord status or some shit."

"Don't jump to conclusions, yet. They don't look as if they have been abused. They all look well-fed and um...very, very healthy," Doug said sideways as he ogled the curves of the cute little blonde with the tray of beers.

"Please feel free to enjoy yourselves, gentlemen." She placed the beers on the table in front of them.

Doug took a nervous breath. "Curiosity has the better of me. I have to ask. Are all of you girls free to leave whenever you want? You aren't being forced to stay here, are you?"

"Oh no, not at all," the blond giggled from behind a cupped hand. "We all willingly work here. Master Barrington pays us extremely well for our services."

A pair of French doors at the back of the beach manor flew open as Maximus Barrington strode onto the patio. "Bom Dia meu amigo! Dougie," he shouted with a heavy Brazilian accent. "It is so good to see you again, my friend!" He tugged and straightened an untied silk robe that very loosely covered his otherwise naked form. Maximus's long legs made short work to cover the distance from the house to the patio. "Oh, my goodness, Dougie. You haven't changed a bit, my friend. Please, stand, let me get a good look at you," Maximus animatedly motioned for Doug to get to his feet.

"Dougie?" Wes pointedly asked through the corner of his mouth.

Doug glared back at Wes. "It's probably better if you don't ask." Reluctantly, he stood, held his arms out to the side then spun around where he stood. "Is that better? You don't look like you've aged a day, Max. How have you been? Um, I don't mean to be rude, but you did know that your robe is untied, didn't you?"

"My robe," Maximus thought for a moment. "Ohhh…. No no no no my friend." He grinned, then waggled a finger at Doug. "I just like the way it feels when it slides across my ass cheeks." He grabbed the loose edges of the robe and demonstrated how easily the robe slid across his rear. "See. Simple. Does this robe make my ass look big?" Maximus momentarily posed, smiled, then burst into a flurry of motion and picked Doug up off of the ground in a manly chest to chest bear hug. "Dougie! Oh, my goodness it is so good to see you again after all of these years! I have so missed you, my friend!

The times that we've had in the past! I couldn't believe it when you contacted me! This makes me so happy, Dougie! It really does!"

"Oh, my dear God and blessed mother Mary," Wes snorted and shielded his eyes from the disturbing display of masculine security.

"Um, hey Max," Doug said uncomfortably, struggling to breathe from the tight hug. "Could you put me down, please? It's good to see you too, Max, but we're a little pressed for time. Could we get to the business at hand? On my next Earthside trip, I promise that I'll return to catch up?"

"Yes, yes, yes, of course. Early bird gets the worm and all that. I completely understand. Please, sit," Maximus motioned at the seats. "He really hasn't changed at all. Always so serious this Dougie," Maximus said to Wes. Leaning against the table he smacked Wes on the shoulder and thumbed the air in Doug's direction. "We never could get him to cut loose."

"Um… I don't mean to seem rude, but could you put your little friend away, please. He's starting to look at me funny." Wes blindly waggled a finger in the direction of Barrington's crotch as he glanced the other way.

A wide, mischievous grin crossed Maximus's face. "You mean this little friend?" He bunched the robe behind his back and waggled his member in Wes's general direction.

Wes glanced toward the movement and instantly regretted it. "Oh, dear God! Yes that! Put it away please!"

"Is this how you American's dance about for your lady loves," Maximus writhed and undulating in Wes's direction.

"Max," Doug barked.

Maximus sighed. "You Americans. Always so uptight about things. Always so serious. That and fried everything is why you don't live as long as other nations. Cheeseburgers, constipation, and too serious." Maximus wrapped the robe back around himself. "Still the same old stickler." He took a seat at the table with the pair. "You know, when we first met and started hanging around on the streets of Atlanta," he said, looking to Wes, "we couldn't even get him to loosen up and have a drink. Everyone in the street crew tried. Even the girls." He gasped in memory. "Remember that night when Evie insisted that you be held down and forced to enjoy yourself," he said to Doug.

"*Max*," Doug said in an admonishing tone.

"Eh! See he does remember," Maximus laughingly cheered.

"Max."

"Six girls. And not just girls. No, no, no," Maximus waggled a finger at Wes. "These were not girls in any sense of the word. These were six, beautiful bombshells. Six unadulterated women," he emphasized while cupping large invisible breasts, "that you may only witness in person once in a lifetime."

"And? What happened?" Wes leaned forward; his tone sounded interested.

"Nothing," Maximus said in a long, drawn-out breath followed by a disappointed sigh. "Not a damned thing happened. He'd gotten so frustrated and pissed off at all of us, his buddies, his amigos, that he'd went numb and, well nada." He shrugged his shoulders. "He was always planning and thinking about the next job."

"Max," Doug said as he began rubbing at his temples.

"Wait," Wes said. "You said something about a street crew?"

"Yes," Maximus gleefully hissed. "Do you not know who you are working for, amigo?"

"Yes, I was part of a street crew," Doug reluctantly admitted, "and that is part of the *ancient* past." Doug glared at Maximus, his jaw muscles clenched slowly, then released.

"Alright, alright." Maximus threw his hands over his head in defense. "As you wish, Dougie. To the business at hand then." He snapped a finger which elicited immediate action from the redhead behind the bar.

"Do you at least like what I have done? The effort of all of those petty scams and schemes when we were younger have finally paid off."

"You've done very well for yourself," Doug admitted. "I've lucked into some land myself recently, which is why we've come to pay you a visit. I was hoping to work out a long-term plan to develop this property." He gave Wes a knowing, sidelong glance.

"What sort of investment opportunity is this?"

"Currently?" Doug closed his eyes and mentally thought through what they had been recovering. "Raw minerals, new exotic alloys, and other materials, artifacts, new advancements to current technology just to start with. The end potential is something enormous that we are only now scratching the surface of."

Maximus leaned forward and rested his elbows on the table, then placed his head in the palms of his hands and drifted away in thought. He sucked in a quick breath. "Did you find a crashed flying saucer of some ancient race on this property or something? You make it sound like something from one of those horribly bad American science fiction movies."

"No. Not exactly," Doug hesitantly said. "And I'm not at liberty to go into the full details of the situation either. You just have to trust me when I say that after we get things set up, we'll be making money hand over fist."

"How much," Maximus skeptically asked.

"Five Million," Doug stated plainly. "At our current rate of production, I can repay that in say, two months."

"Without knowing what I'd be investing in, how can I make a properly informed decision?"

"Faith, Max," Doug said. "Blind faith. Have I ever lied to you before? I just need a short-term investment in order to fully establish our operations."

Maximus let out a long, nasally sigh as he contemplated Doug's words. He looked Doug dead in the eye. "Fifty percent interest per month for the first month and seventy-five percent interest for each following month just because I'm feeling generous between old friends."

"Holy shit, that's highway robbery," Wes blurted.

Doug threw up a hand in Wes's direction without breaking eye contact. "For fifty percent, I could get double my asking price from Cragwall or Hyder."

"Ah, but borrowing that amount from them also comes with a high risk of slowly losing body parts," Maximus said coldly. "They still prefer a centimeter at a time over the course of a few days, in case you had forgotten. I'll just take that wreck that you call a ship as collateral against the account along with anything on board."

Doug slid back his chair and began to stand. "I'll tell you what, Max. If you come to some sane sensibility, then give me a call. I expect our good fortune to last quite a while longer. So, there may be other investment opportunities in the future. Should I let you know if that happens?"

"Wait, sit!" Maximus slapped the marble tabletop. His mouth twitched in frustration as he tried to form coherent words. "You said minerals. So mining, no? If I know you, then this is really important, otherwise, you wouldn't be here." He gently rubbed at his temples. "What sort of equipment are you after?"

"Asteroid mining equipment, lathes, mills, preferably all automated. Transports, shuttles, really any ship and crew willing to go off into the black without knowing where they are going or how long they'll be there." Doug smiled a triumphant smile.

"Repay me as soon as you can, plus fifty percent on top of the original amount. But I want to send my own ship and crew to help with the effort," Maximus pointed a finger at Doug. Doug glanced to Wes, then back to Maximus.

"Consider it my own little insurance policy," Maximus said. "My men will do everything in their power to ensure your success."

The young blond returned, placed a napkin on the table followed by a tall, slender drink glass topped with a colorful paper drink umbrella.

"Thank you, Jillian," Maximus said to the young blond servant. He took her hand and gently kissed her knuckles. "I believe that I'm starting to get a headache my dear." He rubbed furiously at his temples.

The petite blond giggled, feigning shyness. "Of course, Master." She smiled and quickly knelt. "It would be my greatest pleasure, Master." She disappeared beneath the table.

"Oh, yup," Maximus squirmed. "That may just do the trick, my dear."

"What the…" Wes's eyes bulged with surprise.

Doug cleared his throat.

"Oh, I am such a terribly horrible host. Where are my manners?" Maximus snapped his fingers twice more. "I am so sorry for my rudeness. Please, accept my own personal prescription for headache relief." He winked at Doug.

"That is completely alright, Max," Doug assured him. "We were here for business, not pleasure."

Both the redhead and the brunette appeared by Maximus's side. "Yes, Master," they said in complete synchronicity.

Maximus let out a frustratingly disappointed sigh. "You're sure?" Frustrated disbelief showed on his face as he looked from Doug to Wes and back again.

"Yes. I am very sure," Doug said.

"Alright, alright," Maximus waved a dismissive hand at the two young women, then relaxed and adjusted himself in his seat.

"Five million plus another two point five million when I can," Doug reiterated. "Have your crew contact me as soon as possible." Doug stood and extended his hand across the table toward Maximus.

Maximus leaned forward ever so slightly, and reluctantly shook hands in agreement. He flashed a disappointed smile at Doug. "It is a shame that you are in such a rush that you refuse hospitality, my friend. But promise me one thing, Dougie."

"What's that, Max?"

"At some point, you will slow down and enjoy some of what life has to offer before it all passes by," Maximus said with a distracted smile. "But for now, safe journeys my friend. We will make up for it when you return." He slid down in his seat, leaned his head back and closed his eyes.

Gamma Draconis system / Eltanin 2
The Dragon's Lair / Power Pit
August 28th, 2176 / Lunchtimeish (Local Time)

"So, if Trae picks up both of the squat cages that I had on the list, they could fit into this corner, which means that the bench press and butterfly machines can go over into that corner and I should have plenty of room for a heavy bag in the center of the room, right about here." Tiff held out her arms in an approximation of the diameter of the punching bag. "That should work pretty damn good, man," she muttered to herself. She chewed on the left corner of her lower lip as she mentally measured the space around her. The space was surprisingly empty of containers or shelves, unlike most of the other areas in the lower level of the ancient spaceport. A thick layer of dust covered the floor except in the areas where she had been pacing, or where the existing gym equipment from the *Betty* had been brought into the room.

"Well now, ain't this some sort of coincidence. Just the person we were looking for." Tiff turned to see a gangly wisp of a man standing in the doorway. He brushed back oily strands of dirty blond hair behind his ears.

"Oh sweet," Tiff said excitedly. "Did Lizz send you to give me a hand down here?"

"Yeah, that's it. Lizz sent us to...um...help you." Empty spaces stood out in the creepy snaggle-toothed grin that he flashed toward Tiff. He looked back into the passageway, then casually strolled into the room. Two other figures followed closely behind the first man.

Eerie shadows danced across the far wall as the men crossed paths with the drop light that illuminated the room. The largest of the three men was tall, bald and wore a pair of gray miner's coveralls. The other was short and looked as if he'd missed more than a few meals during the course of a short but very precarious lifetime. The first man continued forward toward Tiff as the other two began to pace in a wide circle around her.

"Well, I tell you what. If you guys would like to start with that stack of containers in the back corner, I can set that space up for a few treadmills. But that's if they actually pick up a few treadmills for me," she said as she drifted off in momentary contemplation, tapping a painted fingernail to her lips.

"Now there's a thought that sounds mighty tempting," Snaggle-tooth said. "Everyone loves a good cardio workout, now don't they. What do you guys think? Think she could give us all a good cardio workout?"

"Uh-hum," the large bald man said with a devious leer.

"I believe that you are right on the money with that thought, Brody. I think that she'll do just fine," the skeletal looking man said. He wiped away a dribble of drool on the back of his sleeve.

"Oh no, that's just it. We don't have the cardio equipment yet. We have to clear out the space to put it. You'd think that Lizz would have…"

"Heh," the large bald man laughed. "Are you fucking kidding me? She doesn't get it, Brody."

"Yeah," Brody sighed. "I can see that, Jake. I'm not a fucking idiot. Don't matter none though noways. She ain't gotta be all there for what I need her to do."

"Hang on one-sec, y'all," Tiff interrupted. "Lizz didn't send you down here, did she?"

Brody snarled as he reached for Tiff's flight jacket and yanked her off balance, toward himself.

"What the fuck bro? Let me go!" She struggled to pull away, but she was too far off balance and toppled forward.

Brody grasped the collar of her jacket, picked her up off of the floor and slammed her against the wall. "You're going to do exactly what I tell you to do or else you might just happen to stop breathing there, doll face. Now we wouldn't want something like that to happen, would we?" He adjusted his grip around her throat. Tiff gasped from the impact and struggled as he held her in place.

The skeletal man chuckled, "You just hold her steady, Brody." He sprinted over and began working at the buttons of her pants.

Tiff squirmed and inched her neck this way and that in an attempt to breathe. She clawed at the vice-like hands clamped around her throat.

"Hurry the fuck up and get those pants off of her, Jessie," the large man demanded as he unzipped his coveralls. He wiped away beads of sweat from his bald head with the back of his hand.

The warm embrace of darkness engulfed her. At the edges of her senses, she could hear the heavy breathing of the skeletal man named Jessie. The smell of an alcoholics sweat enveloped her from the one who held her in his vice-like grip. She kicked. The animalistic need to survive found the strength to fuel her fight for life. She kicked and felt the numb impression of her right foot impact upon something soft. The dry, dusty air of the underground base never tasted so sweet as it did in that first gulped gasp that rushed into her lungs as she fell to the ground.

The unmistakable scent of alcoholic vomit filled the surrounding air as Brody doubled over, coughing and gagging.

"Jessie, get hold of her," Jake demanded. Jessie fought through her feeble slaps. He grabbed for her, but only grabbed shirt fabric, lifting her. She dropped back to the ground, ripping a large section of the shirt away. Jessie positioned his arms around her in a full nelson hold and dragged her to her feet, lifting her off of the ground.

Jake ripped the pants off of her legs with a few violent jerks. He tossed the unneeded garment aside and grabbed at her flailing ankles.

A hoarse crackle escaped her throat as she attempted to scream.

"Hold her…," Jake had started, then went suddenly silent at the sound of a heavy thud then limply slumped to the floor. In his place stood a man with a dreadlock tangle of stark white hair. The man's face looked strangely young. He wore a ragged, grease-stained flight suit and well-worn leather flight jacket. He dropped a metal pipe that clattered as it fell to the concrete floor.

"Let her go!" The white-haired man growled through clenched teeth. He drew a pistol from his side and aimed it toward the man named Jessie.

"Like that matters," Jessie argued. "You got a gun. You'll just off me as soon as I let her go."

"I promise. I won't kill you," the white-haired man said. He held his pistol up into the air and let it dangle by the trigger guard on his index finger. "See, I'm not going to hurt you."

"Bullshit! You'll shoot me in the back!"

"Listen, pal, I'm not about to shoot anyone in the back. That's just not something that I'd do. And in reality, it's only a matter of time before someone comes looking for either of us. Do you really want to wait for her husband to come looking and find you here holding her prisoner? He knows ways to keep a man alive in the face of agony."

"You may have a point there," Jessie nervously huffed.

"Yeah, I just might at that. And listen, just between me and you. I wouldn't blame you if you went ahead and got the hell out of here. Letting these two take the fall for this doesn't hurt anyone. It was their idea, anyway, wasn't it?" The white-haired man nodded toward the two unconscious men on the ground. "Nobody's got to know no different, ya know?"

"Yeah, and it would serve them both right, too," Jessie agreed. "They are the ones that dragged me into this. It wasn't my idea. This is exactly what they both deserve." He let Tiff drop to the floor and sidestepped her disoriented form. He swiftly kicked the unconscious form of Jake as he passed the motionless mound of flesh and bounced past the white-haired man en route to the doorway. "Thank you, brother. I ain't never gonna forget this," Jessie said as he skipped out the door.

In one blindingly swift motion, Jessie's leg erupted in a shower of red droplets as a .45 caliber round from the white-haired man's pistol penetrated deep into the flesh of Jessie's leg. He collapsed to the floor, crying out in excruciating pain.

Dazed, Tiff mumbled in a low, half moaned tone. "Thank you," she said under her breath.

He holstered his pistol and quickly moved to Tiff's side. He removed his flight jacket and draped it over her bare shoulders. "It's alright Tiffany. They aren't going to hurt you again. I promise you that." He held out a hand to help her to her feet.

"Thank you," she quietly stuttered. She took his hand and stood, uneasily.

Quickly the white-haired man tore the sleeves from his flight suit and bound the three men. He took the radio from Tiff's belt. "Elizabeth. Someone needs to come down here to Tiffany's proposed gym area. She's alright, but there was an attack. The three attackers have been neutralized and detained."

"Who is this," Lizz responded over the radio.

"Does that really matter?" He said into the radio.

A wet squishy thud came from behind him. "Tiff! No!"

Tiffiny broke down in tears as the bloody pipe clattered to the floor next to Brody's lifeless form.

"Shit," he mumbled, then keyed the comm again. "Um...Lizz. Make that two would-be rapists and one body."

cHAPTER 44

Sol system / Asteroid field
Near flux point Alpha
Bridge of the *Glorious Mouse*
September 2nd, 2176 / Evening (Betty Time)

"**D**id the boss say anything against working side deals while we're on this job?" Jeffrey, the young helmsman tapped away at the ship's controls. "I'd bet I could get a few card games going or something like that once we're on station."

"Don't forget about the cases of whiskey down in the hold," Terry added. "There's always a demand for good whiskey."

Captain Wills laughed. "Are you certain that there is anything left in the hold, Terry? How do you know that it wasn't ransacked during an impromptu midnight rendezvous with a pair of Javacrucian fugitives?" He winked at Terry with a wide, cheesy grin.

Terry turned in his seat at the engineering station. "Wait? Are you talking about the two tweakers that we dropped off last week at *Luna station Oberon*? Seriously, Wills. You'd better not have wasted all of that good whiskey on a couple of tweaking hookers. I don't care if Barrington put you in charge on this mission or not; I'll toss your ass out of an airlock myself and blame it on a bad flux capacitor or some shit."

Ashtin's nearly constant head bobbing and under the breath vocals suddenly ceased. She locked her console controls and turned in her seat, lowering the headphones that had left permanent impressions on the side of her head. "Did you just say something about tweakers? I swear to God y'all had better never bring any tweakers on this ship again. You can't trust those kinda people. Every bit of our shit will grow legs and walk away. I can't believe any of you let them on the ship in the first place and I don't care if they were paying customers or not. You just can't trust people like that. What if they blew an airlock while we were all asleep just to steal the ship or they poisoned the ration packs? Hu? Did any of you ever stop to think about that? See now, I didn't think so. That right there is the problem. None of you even thought about the possibilities. Y'all just all willy nilly let them on the ship because they had the money to pay for passage. Maybe you should do a background check on people before letting them on board." She quickly replaced her headphones and turned back to her console.

"Alright then." Captain Wills clapped his hands together and snapped his fingers. "I gotcha. Doesn't mean that I'm going to listen to any of it, but I hear you," he replied to the back of Ashtin's head.

"We're receiving a transmission from the *Veronica*," Terry announced.

"Put it through," Wills ordered.

"Glorious Mouse, this is the Veronica, come in please."

"Glorious Mouse here. Go ahead *Veronica*," Wills replied.

"Rachel is sending over the flight plan now. Since we aren't sure what our actual effective range is, make sure that you stay within one hundred meters of the Betty."

"Course transmitting now, Cap," a female voice added over the comms.

"I've got it," Jeffrey said.

"Captain Rackham," Captain Wills continued. "What is it... that will happen should we deviate from the prescribed flight path? Is there some... sort of debris or some other hazard that does not show up on the charts? We have nothing showing on our sensors."

"Honestly, Captain Wills, we aren't completely sure ourselves," Doug said. *"We still have a lot of testing to carry*

out on this ship's systems. You'll have a better understanding very shortly. If you'd like a front-row seat with clear skies, please have your helmsman take up the point position when you lay in your course."

"Copy that, Captain Rackham. We'd be honored to take point... and continue on course. *Glorious mouse...* out," Captain Wills proudly stated.

"Course laid in, and we are now in the lead. But this is strange," Jeffrey said. "The course takes us hard upspin and in approximately fifty thousand klicks it just ends. There's nothing at all out there on this course per the charts. No asteroid or comet or anything. Or, well, at least nothing that we know of."

"That doesn't matter in the end," Captain Wills stated coolly. He stood from the captain's chair and propped his foot on the helm console, his crotch uncomfortably close to Jeffrey's face. "You see Jeffrey... Master Barrington wanted us to keep a close eye on this bunch and find out any juicy intel that he could use to his own advantage. We'll quietly play their game until we have what we need and the opportunity to return presents itself. But in the meantime... we have a mission. Turn on... the recorder, Terry. I'm feeling... inspired."

"Uh-huh," Terry grunted at Wills. "Go ahead and knock yourself out, buddy. The recorder is running."

Wills returned and stood behind the Captain's chair. "Captain's log," he began. "We are... on a mission of chance and glory. Our benefactor... Master... Barrington has handpicked each of us for this mission. His trust... in us will not go unrewarded."

"More like we were the only suckers available on short notice," Terry said sarcastically.

Wills scowled at the back of Terry's head. He straightened his flight suit, crossed his arms and continued as he began to slowly pace about the bridge. "Success in this... could mean fame... fortune... even recognition for myself, and my... crew of loyal servants."

"Loyal servants?" Terry turned in his seat and glared at Wills. "Do you believe this arrogant jackass, Jeffrey? Why we ended up under his command on this run I'll never understand." He turned back to his console and angrily tapped at the controls.

Wills cleared his throat, then continued. "Disheartened mutiny... is always a risk with such an endeavor. With a high... priority mission such as this... tension will be high... nerves will become frayed. I can only hope... that it does not come down to execution of executive order Gamma Phi. Truly... that would be the act... of a desperate man. Captain out."

"Do you even know what all of that meant that you just puked out of your mouth?" Terry and Jeffery both turned in their seats, scowling at Captain Wills.

"Captain," Ashtin shouted. "There's something really strange happening. I think the Veronica is producing a variable layer high-frequency field."

"Maybe this is part of what they were talking about," Terry said.

"Possibly. Keep...a close eye on the instruments... and record all data," Wills ordered. "Should we be worried about radiation...with this new field?"

"It's acting really weird, Captain. I've never seen a field like this before," Ashtin shouted as she continued to head bob to the tune of her own drum.

Terry leaned over and pulled one side of Ashtin's headphones away from her head. "You're shouting at us," he shouted then let go of the headphone.

"O, M, G, what? Rude much?" She glared at Terry as she cringed away from his invasive touch.

"Is there radiation or such that we should be worried about," Terry shouted.

"What," she screamed as she removed her headphones.

"Is there radiation or such that we should be worried about," Terry repeated.

"Oh, um." She looked taken aback. "Why didn't you say that in the first place?" Quickly she tapped out a series of commands on her console and reviewed the data. "No, not that I can tell. But there is a strange anomaly just ahead that we are going to impact within, three..."

"Anomaly?"

"Two."

"Impact?"

"One."

In the space of a fractional second, the image on the main viewscreen suddenly shifted from a perfectly normal starfield to an asteroid field orbiting within the glow of a red giant.

"What...just...happened," Wills gasped.

They all stared at the viewscreen with amazed wonderment when suddenly the eerily alien panorama vanished. Replaced by the patched and red-painted belly of an extremely large craft that filled the view as the collision klaxons screamed at the crew.

Sol system / Asteroid field
Near flux point Alpha
Bridge of the *Betty*
September 2nd, 2176 / Evening (Betty Time)

"That wasn't such a bad run," Wes said. "We accomplished a lot this trip, Cap." Wes turned in his seat at the *Veronica's* operations station. "We picked up ten new general contractors, a licensed doctor, a few of those Ph.D. science types plus three complete salvage crews and ships to top it all off.

"Don't forget about the foundry ship that we're towing," Doug said.

"That too. Ooo, I want to name her!" Rachel locked her controls and turned in her seat.

"What? No!" Wes scowled at Rachel. "You named the last one. I've got dibs on this one."

"Nope, you aren't special enough to name a ship properly. It takes a special finesse to connect with the soul of a ship and see what her name is." Rachel dreamily stared off at nothing in particular.

"*Doug,*" Wes said softly. "You're going to let me name this one, aren't you?"

"Sure Wes. Knock yourself out," Doug said.

"She's a Brynhildr class foundry ship, isn't she?"

"Yes. A Brynhildr class, G2 model to be exact," Doug said. "I don't think there was much difference on any of the G models other than the extenders."

Wes grinned. "We should call her the *Ethel.*"

"*Ethel?* Why on Earth would you choose *Ethel?*" Rachel tilted her head and glowered at Wes from across the center console that divided their stations.

"Because it was my grandmother's name," Wes said. "She was this big, beautifully ugly woman that no one in their right mind would mess with."

Doug hummed his acceptance. "That sounds like the perfect name for her. Update her transponder to reflect the new name. What was the name of Maximus's ship?"

"*The Glorious Mouse,*" Wes answered.

"Alright. Open a channel and hail them."

"Copy that, Cap," Wes said. "Channel open."

"*Glorious mouse,* this is the *Veronica,* come in please."

"Glorious mouse here. Go ahead Veronica," Captain Wills replied.

"Rachel is sending over the flight plan now. Since we aren't sure what our actual effective range is, make sure to stay within one hundred meters of the *Betty*."

"Course transmitting now Cap," Rachel said.

"I've got it," a male voice confirmed.

"Captain Rackham," Captain Wills continued. *"What is it... that will happen should we deviate from the prescribed flight path? Is there some... sort of debris or some other hazard that does not show up on the charts? We have nothing showing on our sensors."*

"Honestly Captain Wills, we aren't completely sure ourselves," Doug answered. "We still have a lot of testing to carry out on this ship's systems. You'll have a better understanding very shortly. If you'd like a front-row seat with clear skies, please have your helmsman take up the point position when you lay in your course."

"Copy that, Captain Rackham. We'd be honored to take point... and continue on course. Glorious mouse... out," Captain Wills proudly stated.

"We'll be at the flux point in a few minutes, Cap," Rachel said. "*The Glorious Mouse* is moving into position at the head of the convoy."

"Hail the other three ships and give them the rundown."

"You don't want to talk with them," Wes asked.

"No. I'm not too worried about the other ships and crew," Doug said. "We'll need to keep a good eye on Max's people, though. They are here for more than to just work. If anything happens to them, it wouldn't be good."

"Copy that, Cap. Transmitting instructions," Rachel said.

"It's entirely too quiet on this ship. She just doesn't sound the same as the *Betty*."

"Right? I know what you mean," Wes agreed. "I have full access to my database. Want me to turn on some music?"

"Yeah." Doug sighed as he stretched and relaxed into his chair. "That's what's missing. We need some tunes."

"Ah. Here's a classic."

The unmistakable guitar rift of Jimi Hendrix's', *All along the watchtower* blared through the ships internal speaker systems.

"That's much better," Doug shouted, "but can you turn it down to a level that doesn't paralyze my brain's ability to think?"

"*Sure*," Wes said as he turned down the volume.

"Coming up on the flux coordinates," Rachel shouted

"Alright." Doug drew in a nervous breath. "Fingers crossed that *Ethel's* ass isn't too damn big for this. Initiate the flux drive."

"Gyro core engaged, spin detected on all axes," Wes reported.

A low, cyclic hum resonated throughout the ship's bulkheads.

Rachel hummed along with the tone and swayed in her seat. "*Veronica* is singing her siren song before plunging us through the looking glass."

"Looking good, Cap," Wes said. "Steady-state achieved, and the flux field is forming."

Rachel cycled through a series of screens, then adjusted a 3-D representation of the ships on the main viewscreen to show an overhead view. "There you are, you little thing. Time for you to grow up big and strong." She pinched her fingers together over the display and moved her fingers outward. A glowing amber mesh that surrounded the ships on the display grew larger beneath her fingertips. She spread her fingers as if to zoom and changed the shape of the flux field, expanding it to encompass the entire convoy. Rachel grunted in a surprised, but frustrated tone.

"What is it?" Doug asked.

"Well, I've got everyone in the field, but I think I just found the limit," Rachel said. "It won't let me make it any larger and it's showing an instability region around the designated field area.

"Instability warning?" Wes curiously said.

"Just this weird instability in the field," Rachel said. "I don't know how to describe it otherwise," Rachel admitted. "It just looks all wibbly-wobbly."

"Maybe that's where you don't want to be if you're at the system limit," Wes said. "Maybe it'll tear apart anything in that region?"

"Just keep an eye on it," Doug ordered. "Make sure the system recorders are on so we can go back and review the data later."

"Got it, Cap. Recorders on, ready or not, here we go," Rachel happily said.

The viewscreen switched to show the nose of the foundry ship, *the Ethel*. Just above and a few hundred meters ahead of the *Ethel's* bow cruised a tiny transport, *the Glorious Mouse*. Amid the black nothing of space, the small ship vanished as if it had been suddenly devoured by an invisible space beast.

"Into the breach once again," Doug muttered under his breath.

Wes squee'd. "I don't think that I'll ever get tired of watching this."

The nose of *the Ethel* began to vanish as it passed through the flux point. The veil of the looking glass sluiced by in a fractional moment as they crossed over to the other side. A ball of plasma fire and debris hung just above the bow of *the Ethel* where the *Glorious Mouse* should have been. The massive underbelly of a red alien mining vessel raced upspin from their position in the direct path of emergence from the flux portal. The flaming debris of *the Glorious Mouse* tumbled and scattered in an upspin direction with the flight path of the Red.

"The cat cruise liner is back!" Wes shouted. "They are engaged with three of the red mining vessels."

Cannon turrets flashed from the two closest red vessels. Chunks of the cruise liner exploded; sections of the ship's hull vaporized instantaneously with impact. The third red vessel continued its upspin maneuver while it fired two volleys of missiles.

"There's a power surge coming from the cat cruiser," Wes announced.

"Is there reactor going critical? Looks like they are taking a pounding out there."

"No, it looks like they are going to jump," Wes reported.

The image of the cruise liner abruptly blurred across the view screen through to the opposite side of one of the Reds. The alien starship split in two, the nose and tail sections drifted uncontrollably apart in opposite directions. The cruise liner reappeared from behind the Red, its nose a mangled disaster of twisted metal. The ship's spine looked disjointed and broken as if the space frame had attempted to accordion itself. She listed lifelessly. Gouts of flame erupted from the otherwise, lifeless ship.

Doug keyed the comms. "Willy! Cut the cables and set the *Ethel* adrift. Get high and turn the rumblers on the Red that grazed our nose. We'll take care of the other one. *Days of Ore*, *Aurora Tetra*, and *Pollux*, just get clear of this. You're too small to do any good. If you want to do anything, latch onto the *Ethel* and tow her out of the action."

"You got it, Cap," Willy said over the comms.

"Punch it, Cheezy," Doug ordered. "Get us over to that other one as quick as you can. Wes, fire up everything we have."

"Oh, hell yes!" Wes eagerly tapped away at the console. "Aye aye captain! Point defenses and defensive countermeasures, online. Gauss capacitors charging. Holy shit

Cap. Did you know that we have nine dual gauss turrets on this thing."

"What else would you expect from a heavy frigate," Doug said.

"Goddammit," Trae shouted over the comms. *"Andy, give me a Toro!"*

"What in the hell makes you think that this ship can handle a Toro," Andy argued.

"Oh hell, I see what you're thinking," Willy added. *"The Betty can handle the strain. Just do it!"*

"Is Willy right, Rachel?" Doug asked. "Can the Betty hold up to a Toro at that speed?"

"Maybe," Rachel said in a questioning tone.

"All weapons online, Capacitors charged," Trae reported.

"This is insane," Andy said. *"In a shuttle or a fighter maybe, but in this hulk? No way, it's suicide to pull that maneuver."*

"Just fucking do it!" Willy ordered. The sound of something snapping under a heavy fist crossed the distance of the transmission.

"Fine," Andy said. *"What the fuck ever. It's not going to be my fault if we all die because the ship breaks apart."*

"Here's a funny concept," Doug added to the transmission. "Don't break my ship."

They watched on the viewscreen as the nose of the Betty pulled up hard, the main engines fired at full power, causing the ship to tailslide as it accelerated upspin in chase of the Red vessel.

"A ship that big should not be able to move like that," Wes said with awe.

"Are you kidding? The Betty can take it," Rachel said proudly. "That only looked like ten G's or so at the tail of the ship."

The Betty's nose pointed at the remaining red vessel just as the landing thrusters fired, propelling the Betty into an orbiting maneuver around the massive alien vessel. Thrusters fired adjusting the ships angle of attack, keeping her nose pointed at the red vessel.

"Oh my God we're going to die," Andy cried.

"Really," Trae said, exasperated. *"Just shut the hell up and hold her steady, man. We may not get another shot like this. Molecular density is approximated. I have a target lock,"* Trae announced. *"Fingers crossed boys and girls."*

The Betty's massive forward-mounted maser cannons rumbled to life, instantaneously burning a gash around the circumference of the Red ship as the Betty orbited it.

Doug pounded his fist on the arm of the captain's chair. "Come on Cheezy! Get us into the fight!"

"I'm giving her all she's got, Cap," Rachel giggled.

The *Veronica* bobbed and weaved as they entered into firing range of the remaining alien ship.

"Stay on the move, Cheezy. We're a lot smaller than that cruise liner was. That should make us more difficult to hit."

The *Veronica* sickeningly lurched nose down and left as something smashed into the hull.

"Get us in close," Doug shouted, "Don't let them have a chance to lock onto us."

Rachael maneuvered the *Veronica* high and toward the aft of the Red. She side slid the ship with a falling back roll and slipped into a close, parallel course with the alien vessel, racing along its hull. She rolled the ship to the left, presenting the best target to the starboard cannons.

"Fire at Will," Doug ordered.

Wes giddily laughed, "Yo ho ho!" He tapped the controls of his console and pressed a big red button marked *fire* on the display. "Booyah!" Three of the ships dual 502mm rail turrets fired into the dull red belly of the alien ship. The port bank of cannons fired as Cheezy rolled the ship to deliver the second broadside.

"Cap," Willy yelled over the comms. *"We took a missile up the tailpipe and the reactor casing is cracked. She's venting plasma. Had to shut her down before we lost containment. We're dead in the water and we still haven't taken this one out yet. I think we did manage to piss it off. They are lining us up to get us into their ore processor."*

Umbilicals suddenly shot outward all around *the Veronica.*

"Shit," Rachel shouted as she pushed forward on the control yoke and kicked the rudder pedals hard to the left in a sudden attempt to avoid the mass of tentacles. The ship jerked and all forward momentum ceased. Wes slid from his seat, then quickly scrambled back into it, buckling his harness over his shoulders. "They got us, Cap!" The ship awkwardly rocked forward to the clang and clatter of tentacles passing the Veronica toward the nose of the alien vessel.

"Cap! We're being pushed toward the Red's crusher. They're going to chew us up and spit us out." Rachel tapped at the controls. "Thrusters aren't responding."

"It doesn't look like the reactor took any damage," Wes said. "I don't understand why aren't we moving?"

"We have plenty of power. We just aren't moving because those umbilicals are physically restraining us in place. They use those to maneuver asteroids into the maw of this thing. Do you really think our little ship will be a problem for them to hold?"

"I need options people," Doug shouted. "We're outgunned, backed into a corner and about to be devoured by a big red space beast."

"Cap," Willy said over the radio. "We might have one shot left in the capacitors for the rumblers. Trae thinks he's got the frequency tuned in better than before. It'll either work or it'll blow every relay and waveguide on the ship."

"Show me the *Betty,*" Doug ordered.

The viewscreen immediately switched over to reveal the *Betty*, being pulled into the maw of the massive red alien ship by the ships umbilical's. From their angle, it looked as if a space Kraken was about to devour their home. Bright flashes of static discharge indicated that the *Betty's* maser cannons were firing. Molten slabs of the alien ship began to flake and float away into the vacuum as explosive gouts of flame and atmosphere burst forth from the hull of the alien ship.

Cheers erupted across the comms. *"We got the bastards Cap,"* Willy said resignedly. *"But we're dead in the water. I have no clue what it'll take to get her fixed back up."*

"Life support and thrusters are out, too," Andy added.

"And well, there's that too," Willy added.

Trae snorted a laugh. *"It'll be easier to list what still works. The rumblers shorted out systems all over the ship. Oh man, I'll have to rebuild all of those relays again."*

"Hey Cap," Wes interrupted. "What if we can get loose and get back to the flux point? Maybe we could shake them on the trip through?"

"Oh, hell no," Doug said. "Are you crazy? Do you really want that thing tearing through the Sol system? Besides, we'd have to get loose first."

"Hey Cap," Rachel interrupted. "It looks like we're only a few dozen klicks away from another flux point. What if we can get them to that one?"

"Well, we did tow the *Ethel* through the other flux point. That Red isn't much bigger than the *Ethel*."

"Yeah, but the *Betty* was towing with us," Wes added.

Doug clapped his hands and rubbed them together. "Let's do it. We've got a brand new, military spec frigate that hasn't even been broken in yet. Take all nonessential systems offline, even life support. Funnel everything that we have into the engines."

"Have you ever been fishing and had a catfish snag your bait?" Doug asked.

Rachel wrinkled her nose in confusion. "Um... No. The only place I've ever seen a real fish is on a plate."

"Me either Cap," Wes said.

"When you get a catfish on the line, they become masters of leverage and maneuvering. If we kick over max thrust and roll the ship to an odd angle, tangential with the umbilical's holding us we might be able to break free. Disengage the safeties with a full forward Woodward shift."

"Why not? Not like we have anything to lose at this point." Rachel disengaged the artificial feedback actuators from the control yoke. "Strap your asses in and hold on."

Wes pulled his harness straps as tight as they would go.

The ship leapt forward less than a second after Rachel slammed all six throttle levers to the full forward stop.

"Disengaging all automated safeties. I hope y'all are ready because this is gonna hurt!" She slid the control yoke fully forward to the detent stop. The *Veronica* sickeningly lurched forward, then jerked to a halt like a dog on the end of its chain. The large alien ship fired its forward thrusters in an attempt to counter the *Veronica's* pull but began to creep forward.

"Alright, here we go," Doug cheered. "When I tell you, I want you to nose her over and flip a complete one-eighty. If we can get the Red leading ass first into the hole, we might have a chance. At a thousand meters out from the event horizon, I want you to go full burn to slow us down. As soon as the Red crosses the line, kill the flux drive."

"Oh, this is gonna be good," Rachel said with a laugh. She eagerly checked her systems and prepared for the maneuver. "Gotcha Cap. I'm ready."

"What the hell? Are you sure we won't be sucked through the flux with the Red?"

"No, but I don't have any better plans. Do you Wes? I'm all ears if either of you has any ideas." His tone was sarcastic and final.

The ship creaked and groaned from the strain.

"Come on girl, hold together. I know you can do it," Doug mumbled to himself.

"Woo hoo!" Wes gasped with terrified excitement. "We're moving and really picking up speed. Twenty thousand kilometers per hour and climbing."

A relay control cover panel from overhead the auxiliary port station popped and buckled outward under the strain.

"Hold together baby." Doug crossed himself and said a quick prayer.

"Thirty thousand KPH and climbing," Wes reported.

"Core temp is going critical," Rachel announced. Warning alarms sounded with a low whup whup whup. "She's in the red on most systems and overheating. I don't know how much longer they can maintain this output."

"We have coolant leaks in engineering," Wes reported. "Initiating emergency containment. Forty thousand KPH and still climbing."

"She'll hold together. Just keep it full bore! We've got this!"

The high-pitched warble of the flux warning resounded over the ship's creaks and groans.

"Flux warning dead ahead," Wes reported. "One hundred klicks off our bow. Fifty thousand KPH and climbing."

"Now Cheezy! Now," Doug yelled. "Flip that hog on its back!"

"Engaging full thrusters! Flux drive is hot to trot!" Cheezy chopped the throttles, rolled the yoke and arched her back as she pulled with all of her might, nearly touching the yoke to her chest. She held the yoke collective back then slammed the throttles to full power. The ship lurched and pulled a hard nose up roll. Every section of plating, conduit, covers, and bulkheads onboard rattled from the sudden G load that twisted the *Veronica's* space frame. The force of the turn crushed each of them deep into their respective seats.

Rachel let out a half-screamed shout like a berserker battle cry. "Woodard field is fluctuating, but it's holding! Any more G's and we'll all pass out."

"Hold what you have!" Doug's grip on the command chair arm slipped and he collapsed over the left arm. Pain shot through his side as he was pressed deeper into the seat. "Get that ship where we want her!"

"I can't feel my legs," Wes cried out.

"Just hold! It's going to work!"

Rachel growled, shouting out in pain and began panting. "My fucking leg just broke! Cap? The bone isn't supposed to be on the outside, is it?"

"Oh God, oh God, oh God, I don't want to die," Wes cried.

"Hold it together Geek! We've got this and you'll hold," Doug ordered.

"Boosters engaging in three," Rachel shouted over the noise.

"What boosters," Wes worriedly said.

"Two."

"Whip them into flux, Cheezy!" Doug ordered.

"One." Rachel reached beneath the helm console, pulled a yellow and black striped handle, turned it ninety degrees then shoved it back into the console. The ship lurched forward again. "Alien ship is on target," Wes reported.

"Shut down the flux drive," Doug ordered.

Cheezy flipped open another side panel and slammed her fist down on a big, red button. "Flux drive disengaged!"

A sudden shudder ran through the length of the ship and the *Veronica* eerily floated free.

"Give me a visual," Doug ordered.

The viewscreen shifted to a rear-facing perspective. The alien ships umbilical grapplers floated listlessly about the bisected shell of the ship's hull. A third of the ships aft section had been severed away at an odd angle only a few hundred meters away from the *Veronica*.

"We're gonna die," Wes gasped and slumped over in his seat.

"Rachel, bring us to a full stop. Re-engage all of the safeties," Doug ordered as he unstrapped and leapt forward to check on Wes. He gasped for breath and collapsed to the deck. Pain radiated throughout his torso. He tucked his left elbow close to his side and stood.

"Aye Cap," Rachel replied. "Are you alright?"

"I'll be fine," he replied. "Just a few broken ribs most likely." He fought through the pain and approached Wes's station. "We'll get you back to base as quickly as we can, buddy." Doug looked Wes over, but couldn't find any obvious wounds. He keyed the comms from Wes's station. "Rackham to any ship. Mayday, mayday, mayday, Dragons Lair, do you copy?"

"Cap," Rachel slurred as she slumped over her controls. The ship slipped sideways with an odd roll.

Doug rushed around the console to the pilot's position. He pushed Rachel back into her seat and let the controls return to neutral. Dark blood soaked through the leg of her flight suit. Blood splattered all over the seat and control console. Without hesitation, he whipped his belt through the loops of his pants in one yank and strapped it around her leg, above the exposed bone fragment.

"Does anyone copy? Mayday, we are in need of immediate assistance! Goddammit! Someone fucking answer! Geek and Cheezy are seriously injured."

"Cap," Wes wheezed. "Did you turn out the lights?"

Doug looked up at Wes in somber silence, his face washed blank of emotion. He swallowed hard. "Anyone. Please hurry," his voice silently cracked.

cHAPTER 45

Gamma Draconis / Asteroid field
Mobil Foundry ship, *The Ethel*
September 3rd, 2176 / Early Morning (Betty Time)

Piping hissed and rattled throughout the *Ethel's* main docking bay as stale, sterile air equalized within the airlock.

"Goddammit Doug, can this thing go any slower?" Krista complained over the airlock comm systems.

"It's going as fast as it can," Doug said. "You have to be patient and wait."

"Well it ain't fast enough," she complained. *"Wes and Rachel could both be dying while I'm trapped in this damned transport."*

"Calm down. They're not dying," Doug said, reassuring her. "Our new doctor has them both stabilized and doing well. She's watching over them right now."

"What sort of unspeakably arcane methods are they being subjected to? Those are our people, Doug," Krista said. *"You really went and let some...doctor, do whatever he wanted to do to them? How could you, Doug? Maybe he was even nice enough to go ahead and install trackers for the man while he was at it?"*

"No Krista. *She*," Doug emphasized, "managed to get both of them stabilized so that they didn't die. Her name is Doctor Janey Fillmore and she came highly recommended by more than a few people for her work in the Middle East and Africa. She's worked most of her career in third world underdeveloped countries and has successfully saved lives."

The docking bay's airlock clanked and groaned as the locking mechanism released its grip and allowed the door to swing freely open.

"She?" Krista shouted as she exploded from the airlock into the corridor that led to the docking bay control room. Maggie and Amanda stoically followed close behind as the witches three entered the docking bay control room. Krista stood toe to toe with Doug and glared upward at him. The fire of a hateful spell burned behind her eyes. "So what, you're replacing me now? Is that it? You went out and got you some hot young thang to play doctor with? Is that it? Am I so old and worn out that you traded me in for a younger model?"

"Krista, we need *people* from all walks of life to give this hodgepodge colony of ours the best chance of success," Lizz said.

Krista pointed a sharp finger and hissed in Lizz's direction. "I don't want to hear one word out of you." She glared at Lizz. "This is between me and him, you got that?"

"What? No, I didn't trade you in on a younger model," Doug said defensively.

Krista hissed a laugh. "And you expect me to just believe that? Is she a blond or a redhead, Doug?"

"Yes, I do," Doug said, "and she is a strawberry blond if you must know."

"Ha!" Krista slapped her knee with victorious satisfaction. "I knew it! And not just blond or red, she's a *strawberry blond.* You had to go exotic with this one, didn't you?

"With the number of people that we have been bringing in, it only makes sense to have medical personnel on staff." Doug ran a frustrated hand through his hair. "It not only makes sense, but it's just a smart idea all around. And why are you complaining? We aren't even paying her salary."

Krista crossed her arms and pushed out her naturally swollen chest. "Oh, well now that's just lovely, now isn't it? So exactly how good is she if she was *free*. Did you pick her up at the Nunnery while you were in town? Are there any other strays on board that we should know about?" Krista sidestepped Doug and hurriedly continued out into the main corridor. Maggie and Amanda silently trailing behind her.

"I managed to get a university to fund her cost and a stipend for the trip," Doug shouted in Krista's direction.

"Don't care," Krista replied with a wave of the hand and a highly raised middle finger as the witches three exited the control room.

"She's overly stressed, Doug," Lizz said.

Doug looked up at the ceiling with a sideways glance as he patiently listened. He held up an index finger in Lizz's direction.

"Doug, which way do we go," Krista shouted from down the hallway.

"Keep going the way that you are, the third passageway on the right, up one deck and you'll be at the medical bay." Doug turned back to Lizz. "You were saying?"

"I said that she's overly stressed, between the fight up here and the attack back at the Lair."

"Whoa, attack?" Doug snapped concerned look toward Lizz. "Did the Reds attack the base?"

"No Doug, it wasn't the Reds," Lizz reluctantly sighed. "A few of the miners decided they wanted a little more of Tiff than she was willing to share."

"Wait? What? Is she okay?" Anger flushed up Doug's neck as his jaw reflexively contracted.

"She's okay. A little shaken, a few bruises, but otherwise, she's fine. Someone was watching out for her that day. She described him as young looking, but his hair and beard were a mass of tangled white dreadlocks. I don't remember them coming back on the previous Earth run, but in my defense, I did meet a lot of new people that week."

"He doesn't sound familiar to me either. He had to be from one of the smaller vessels that we brought through." Doug nodded toward the door. "We might want to get to the medical bay before Krista has time to string up the doc."

"You might be right," Lizz said with a laugh.

"So, what happened?" Doug asked as he led the way out of the door.

"You know how Tiff can be. She was bored and dying to get a gym set up. We'd agreed on a space near to where the new witches lair will be. She was down there getting measurements and trying to figure out the best layout for the space when three men entered. She initially thought that I'd sent them to help her, but according to her, that changed pretty quick. They overpowered her and managed to get her partially undressed before her white-haired angel stepped in and changed their minds."

Doug stopped in mid-stride as his entire body went rigid. "Do we know who these men are? Has she identified them?"

"The ghost tied up two of the assailants after he called me on the comms. Tiff crushed in the leader's skull pretty good with a pipe. He's alive and conscious, but not by much."

"Alright," he said, nervously rubbing his face. "One more thing to take care of. Not a problem. It's probably time to establish a few written rules anyways. We have a lot of new names on the roster."

"Unfortunately, you're probably right," Lizz agreed. She continued down the corridor. "How's everyone from the ships?"

"Everyone that was aboard *the Betty* was fine. No real injuries other than a few bumps and scrapes. The ship took a beating, but otherwise, they were good. I managed to walk away with four broken ribs and a dislocated collar bone. Wes has a number of pinched nerves along his spine, some fractured vertebra, and a few ruptured disks. Rachel managed to break one leg so badly that the bone shot through the skin and her flight suit, plus fractured her other leg in three places. The smaller transports that came through with us didn't see any action except for the *Glorious Mouse*."

"*Glorious Mouse*," Lizz said with a questioning shake of her head.

"Max's ship. She had an unceremonious meeting with the underbelly of one of the Red's as we passed through the flux. None of her crew made it."

"That'll need to be dealt with as soon as possible," Lizz reminded.

"I know, but it'll wait," Doug said. "That's the least of our worries right now. Once I show Max the telemetry, it'll be fine. It wasn't anything to do with us. Shit just happened. My main concern at the moment is these alien ships. We haven't had a chance to explore the wreckage yet. I put the *Days of Ore*, *Aurora Tetra*, and *Pollux* to work policing the wreckage and towing the *Ethel* into position near the old mining station in the asteroid field. They'll bring it all to one location and established parking orbits so we can go through the wrecks when we have the opportunity."

"I have this feeling that the cat cruiser was the last of its kind," Lizz said. "But the Red's will most likely continue to return."

"This system is rich in minerals and the design of the Red vessels screams mining vessel," Doug said. "I have to agree, they'll continue to return."

"Maybe the cruiser was trying to defend the system from invaders?" Lizz pondered.

"Possibly," Doug said. "I just don't like the idea of waiting around for another Red to pop in before we can find out if they are friendly or not."

Lizz gasped. "You can't possibly be thinking of chasing them down."

"That's exactly what I'm thinking. We may not be able to read or understand anything from their computer cores, but star charts are star charts. Once Rachel is up to it, I planned to put her on the task of updating our charts. Then we send a team of volunteers out in *the Veronica* to start mapping out other flux points. Not only will we be able to establish trade routes, but we may get lucky and find a Red out there."

"I can't say that I like the idea a whole hell of a lot, but you're probably right," Lizz admitted. "We'll need to eventually establish trade routes to other places besides Earth if we're going to make this work. And I don't see that we have many other choices to find a Red, other than to wait."

"Are you people insane? Get out of my medical bay right now!"

Metal trays clattered against deck plating and echoed down the corridor. Doug and Lizz glanced to one another with a look of surprised terror. "Krista," both murmured under their breath, then quickly sprinted up the stairs to the next deck.

"Who in the hell are you people? Get away from my patients!"

Doug slid to a stop in the doorway to the medical bay as Doctor Fillmore swatted a surgical tray in the direction of the witches three.

"Y'all keep that pill pusher over there while I get *our* people saged off," Krista said as she fanned at a bundle of dried herbs. "There's no telling what kind of evil juju she's brought along with her. Amanda, yank that damned line out of Rachel's arm," Krista ordered. "There's no telling what kind of poisons or mind control kool-aid that this witch is pumping into Rachel.

"It's best for everyone if you just listen and do as the Goddess requests of you," Maggie said to the confused doctor. She stood stoically, arms crossed and unmoving between her and the patients.

"Don't you dare take that I.V. out," Doctor Filmore shouted. "She needs to finish that bag to help fight off the infection that is sure to come without it. Do you even know how bad her injuries were?"

"It doesn't matter," Amanda added. The monitors buzzed with warnings as she pulled the leads free from Rachel's skin. "Krista will do what Krista wants to do when Krista wants to do it, and nothing is going to stop her."

"You can just go on back to where you come from. We don't need your kind around here," Krista said with a snarl, then hissed at the woman in the white lab coat.

"Krista," Doug shouted as he stepped into the medical bay.

"Doug, will you please tell this person that we will not be in need of her or her services and that she can go on back to wherever she came from," Krista growled. She finished fanning the smoldering sage and stood protectively at the foot of the beds. "Did you see what she'd done them? What she did to *our* people," she said with a pained pleading to her voice. "Needles and hoses unnaturally penetrating their bodies. Did she even ask them first if they wanted to be poked and prodded by her medical malpractice?"

"Medical malpractice?" Janey gasped, taken aback. "How can you even say that? You're the one acting like a damned witch doctor from the bush."

Doug bravely stepped between the two practitioners, holding up an open palm toward each. "Doctor Fillmore, you'll have to excuse Krista. She is our resident healer and practitioner of alternative medicine." He turned his gaze and glared at Krista. "Krista, you need to back down. We are bringing in all of these new people and not everyone will be willing to come to see the resident...," he giggled under his breath, "witch doctor." He smiled wide. "Ya know, I like the sound of that. I might just have to start calling you the witch doctor or shaman woman, maybe? No, I like witch doctor better."

"That's Goddess to you, mister," she waggled a pointed finger in his direction. "Now what are we going to do about all of this? We can't have this happening all the time."

"Good point, no we can't have this happening all the time," Doug replied. "Which means you need to mind your own business and tend to your own patients. Folks will be able to see who they want to see. And I do have plans to put a regular doc down at the Lair. So, you'll just have to get over yourself. We are getting entirely too many people for you to handle alone."

"Who the hell says? Hu?" Krista crossed her arms defensively. "How do you know that I can't handle more than a few at the same time?" She cocked a challenging eyebrow at Doug.

"Oh. Well now," Lizz gasped with a sidelong smile.

Doug awkwardly cleared his throat. "Sure, you go for it then. In the meantime, you'll tend to any medical issues that crop up planetside. Janey will handle things up here. For now, this is her medical bay, which means her word is law."

"Bullshit," Krista coughed.

"You expect me to work with her? I don't think that even a jackal could work with her," Janey said.

"You may be the earthbound Goddess, but she's now the sky Goddess," Doug said in a serious tone. "You are sisters of healing and you both need to work together for the good of the people."

Krista blushed slightly. "Oh, well now. I kinda like the sound of Earthbound Goddess when you say it like that," she said. "I could get used to that." She smiled and rocked back on her heels.

"Until these two get back down to the ground," Doug said, pointing at Rachel and Wes who silently slept, "you'll keep your hands off of them."

"And what if I don't," Krista said, sticking out her nose as if to challenge.

"Then I'll hog tie you and throw you into the brig," Doug said matter of factly.

"Ooo...I might like that too. Can we do that later?"

"Maybe. If you behave and remind me," he quickly replied. "Take a few minutes to check on these two, then get back down to the Lair. When they are stable, I'll have them sent down to you."

"Hey…," Krista started.

"Shush," Doug interrupted. "No argument, just do it. We need to get everyone together, probably in Mel's diner, so I need you to head that up before I get back down there." He turned to Janey. "I need these two stable enough to travel because I need everyone down there for a gathering. No exceptions. What I have in mind is important and involves everyone."

cHAPTER 46

Eltanin 2
The Dragon's Lair / Mel's Diner
September 5th, 2176 / Evening (Dragon time)

"Alright, give it one more shove," Danny, the newest engineering mechanic said. He stepped back and stroked his long, white goatee.

Big Willy put his shoulder into the massive, antique jukebox from the *Betty's* rec room and pushed.

"That's perfect, Willy. Just enough cord." Danny plugged in the colorful machine. Lights flashed and bubbles flowed upward through the liquid-filled sides of the flashy machine. "We can't have a proper intergalactic truck stop without a jukebox, now can we?"

"Ooo, that's a good one," Willy said, pointing at the glass-enclosed catalog.

"Oh no, here's the one we need." Danny tapped in the code for the track he wanted, one, nine, eight, four, then trotted off to a nearby table. "Oh yeah, baby! Here we go!" He climbed onto the table, wiped the sweat from his shaved head, straightened his goatee then clapped in anticipation. His arms shot skyward in praise as the song began. He sang along with the opening vocals, *"Ahhhhhh, yeah!* Come on everyone," he shouted between the verses then continued to sing along with the song.

The crowd clapped and stomped their feet to the beat of Queen's, *Fat bottom girls*. He clasped his hands behind his head and began a pelvic thrust to the time of the song.

Kara, Krista, and Maggie all tore small strips of napkins began to resemble ancient paper money and waved it in Danny's direction.

"Now you see…," Chris started as he turned in his seat and spoke to Rachel at the next table. Drawing her attention away from Danny. Lizz and Tiff leaned in to hear over the music. "My brothers used to hold me down and try to torture me when we were younger. They'd use duct tape, or rope, or hell, just about anything they could get their hands on to tie me up with. Then they'd heat up the ends of paper clips with a lighter and use em' to pierce my nipples."

Lizz and Tiff both gasped at the thought, rubbing their own, now erect nipples. Rachel leaned in closer and placed her elbows on the table.

"See, then one day, they had this bright idea to get a set of gator clips. Ya know, like jumper cables, only smaller. Ya know the kind that you use with a multimeter for checking wires for current. Well, they'd take turns hooking them up to different batteries or little generators, or they'd just plug them into the wall. They always wanted me to scream for mercy, but I never would." A look of inner reflection washed over his face for a moment, then he continued, snapping out of his daze with a snort. "I'm not sure when it happened, but at some point, I really started to like it." He grinned a rotten, crooked tooth smile and casually set a battery on the table along with a set of alligator-clip wires.

"Oh, hey now," Tiff said as she sat back.

"Wanna try it?" Chris's unibrow wriggled with hopeful anticipation. "My wife won't hook me up, but she's fine with me being hooked up by someone else." He smiled a hopeless smile.

Rachel blankly stared across the table at him.

"*No?*" He asked in a hopeful tone. "Ya' really don't know what you're missing. I'll tell ya what, how about you catch me later if you change your mind." He gathered up the clips and put them back into his jacket pocket.

"Ya know, I joined up for the cheap beer and the chance to blow some shit up," Danny shouted as he leapt down from the table. "But I have yet to blow some shit up." He took his seat and poured another beer from the pitcher.

"This one time," Andy started, then took a sip of his beer. "I managed to blow out an airlock using only a can of lubricant and a nine-volt battery."

"Well this one time we put cherry bombs in the courthouse mailbox," Chris said, making the motion for an explosion.

"Oh hell, that's nothing," Danny bragged. "Have you ever seen what a quarter stick of dynamite will do to a cop car's exhaust?"

"This one time," Andy said, "my father in law had me climb under the house to figure out why the drains kept clogging up. Nothing I did seemed to help. The pipes were this old cast iron looking stuff. So, I opened it up at a y junction, lit and shoved one of those fountain things into it and then closed it back up. Figured it would burn it all out. Turns out the fountain was one of those kinds that had aerial rounds built-in that explode way up in the sky. By the time I came back out from under there, I was covered head to toe in sewage."

"That's a pretty shitty situation if you ask me," Danny said, in an uninterested tone.

"Shit," Chris slurred. "That's still nothing, man. I tell you what," Chris stammered as he uncomfortably rocked in his seat. "You should have seen what happened after my brothers shoved a Whistlin' Bunghole up my bunghole and lit it."

. "Hell, this one time..."

"Doug," Lizz shouted, catching a glimpse of the Captain as he entered the cantina. She snatched up her drink and hurried behind him as he headed for the stairs to the upper level.

"What are you smiling about?" Doug asked Trae as he approached the load-masters perch on the upper level of the cantina.

"Oh, I'm just watching for the moment that the paradox forms around those three from the high levels of bullshit they are throwing at each other," Trae said pointing at Danny, Andy, and Chris. "I figure it'll hit critical mass any time now and a singularity will form, then collapse and wipe out all of reality."

Doug blankly stared at Trae as he fought to hold back a laugh.

"You ready to get this over with?" Trae asked with a sidelong glance. "It's only right that the community knows what happened."

"Then you know what I have to do," Doug reluctantly sighed.

"Yeah," Trae said, nodding. He stared down at the people below. "I talked it over with Tiff. She doesn't like it, but she knows for the grand scheme that it's the right choice." Trae straightened and stood square to Doug. "We're both good with it. You do what you need to do," he said resignedly.

"So, you have my back? No questions asked?"

"Nope," Trae said. "I'm all in, boss."

"Alright then," Doug said. "I'll get this shindig started if you want to go ahead and bring them in. Take Willy and Fergus with you."

"Aye, Cap," Trae said then made his way down the stairs and out of the cantina.

Lizz approached and placed a gentle hand on Doug's shoulder. "It's what needs to be done, Doug. Don't doubt yourself or your decision."

Doug took a deep breath and stepped to the edge of the railing. He watched the people below with interested delight. Cheerful conversation, laughter, and haughty challenges all mingled with the melodic tones of Black Sabbath's *War Pigs* from the jukebox.

"I'm not doubting," he whispered. "I just don't like that we've come to this so quickly. I'm starting to wonder if we even belong out here in the stars. We are so self-destructive on our own as it is, what's going to happen when we add alien tech and influence into the mix? Or what if they find out about Earth? What happens then?"

"You're doubting yourself, Doug," Lizz quietly comforted. "Stop it. You cannot control the actions of the people under us. You can only lead by example. Set the standard for everyone to follow and hope. At that point, all you can do is hope. Otherwise, we move forward and plan for the future. Those who wish to be part of this will be. Those who are out for something else will eventually fall by the wayside and go their own direction or be forcibly removed from our path."

"I suppose you're right," he sighed. "Guess I should get this show on the road." He cupped his hands and took a deep breath.

"Listen up!"

The entire cantina went silent and turned to look upward in Doug's direction.

"If someone is missing, it is all of your responsibility to fill them in on all of this later." Doug nervously cleared his throat. "We are trying to establish and build something here, that will outlive all of us. It could possibly even outlive our children or even our grandchildren. We are the first humans to colonize a world outside of our home star system. For those who haven't been informed yet, you are on the only habitable planet in the Gamma Draconis star system, which just happens to be over one hundred light-years from Earth in the Draco constellation." He proudly looked down at all of the faces that stared back at him. "I had the final say on hiring each and every one of you. I was the one who brought you all this way from Earth, and therefore I am ultimately responsible for each and every one of you. All that I really ask is that you do your jobs and that you use some common sense." He glared about the room and slowly started for the steps. "We will work as a community," he continued as he started down the stairs. "We will work together to build something great; something that future generations will be proud of because we are now the pioneers of mankind. We *are* the new explorers. We are on the edge of the great unknown!" He quickly made his way to the bottom of the stairs.

"We have in our possession, proof of alien races and have even made contact with the ancient race of this planet, the Chinchassin's," Doug nodded in the direction of Casraownan and the other few cats who attended the gathering. "Their people have managed to survive some cataclysm that we have yet to ascertain." He smiled at the gathered crowd as he reached the bottom of the steps. "Unless someone back on earth attempts to hide the facts, we have already made the history books, people! And all that pass through these halls will be listed as such. We will document and record every name for posterity's sake. I promise each of you that. You have created a legacy that will continue for all time."

Doug glanced sideways as movement from the main entrance caught his eye. Trae led a bound and hooded man into the doorway. Doug nodded for him to enter.

"Up until this point, we have been flying by the seat of our pants. We haven't had a need for rules or laws beyond the standard shipboard rank structure. Up until now, everything has been perfectly fine, flowing along fluidly as it should be," he said as he paced.

Trae, Willy, and Fergus led the hooded figures into the cantina, stopping just inside the doorway. "Prisoners, on your knees," Trae ordered. The three figures complained but knelt.

Doug forced his eyes away from the prisoners and focused on the gathered crowd. He took a deep breath, then continued.

"That being said, we have had an incident." Doug ripped the hood away from the figure led by Trae. One side of his face was deformed from swelling and bruising. "Brody Blackford,"

Doug said loudly, then ripped away from the hoods from the two other prisoners. "Jessie Sharpe and Jake Hansen. You have each been implicated and charged with the attempted rape of Tiffany Crowley." Doug's nostrils flared.

"Rape is *not*...and will *not* be an acceptable option! I don't care who you are or what you do. It will ... *NOT* ... be ... tolerated!" Doug's face turned an odd shade of plum red. "I hired each and *every* one of you. I am responsible for every soul here. I am the *Captain*," he said, scowling about the room.

So many new faces stared back at him. Some scared, some anxious, while others grinned in anticipation at what was about to happen to the prisoners. Doug walked around and stood in front of the three men. He angrily sucked on his teeth.

"Before this community of gathered souls, do you freely admit to the charges of attempted rape of Tiffany Crowley?"

"Fuck you dip shit." Brody spat at Doug. A bloody yellow, puss scented wad landed on Doug's left pant leg.

Doug sighed, then turned his gaze to the other two men who knelt on either side of Brody. "The both of you stated, to Lizz, the Overseer, that Brody instigated and initiated the rape. Is this correct?"

Both men quietly nodded with mumbled yes sir's from under their breaths.

"Fuck all of y'all," Brody shouted. "Guy can't have a little fun every now and then?"

Doug's face stretched in a grin that seemed wider than a clown's painted smile. "Don't get me wrong, gentlemen. I can completely understand the need to get lucky. Hell, I want to get lucky. I'd love to be getting lucky right the fuck now. How about everyone else?" He spread his arms wide to include the crowd that filled the cantina. "Anyone else in here wishes that they were getting lucky right now instead of being here?"

Whoops and cheers mingled with the silent replies of raised hands and murmured yes's from the crowd.

"Rape is not the way!" Doug glared at the crowd. His gaze bore into each individual present. "Find someone willing or take matters into your own hands. It's as simple as that, and no one gets hurt that way." Doug quietly squared himself off in front of the man named Brody. His eyes burned with rage as straightened before the prisoner. "Any last words before you are sentenced, Mr. Blackford?"

Brody looked around, confused. "What the hell? Are you fuc..."

The echoing report of Doug's now smoking, antique revolver cut the convicted man's words short. A rivulet of blood trickled down from the entrance point of the 0.45 caliber round that suddenly appeared between Brody's eyes. Doug holstered his weapon before the still-warm body unceremoniously slumped to the floor. He quietly stood quiet for a moment, breathing deep, centering himself. He removed his long leather trench coat and covered the now motionless form.

Individual gasps and whispers became quiet sobs and tear-filled coughs among the crowd.

"By ships law, I am the Captain and I have the final say. If you're hired on, then you're hired on. That's that. You follow my rules, which aren't many, and merely common sense. But rape, WILL...NOT...be tolerated, and henceforth will be punishable by an early grave." Doug looked up and nodded to Trae and Fergus then looked to the other two prisoners. "Would you two please be so kind as to pick up your friendly fellow there and carry him to his final resting place," Doug said to the prisoners. "Trae and Fergus will show you where."

Trae and Fergus grabbed their respective prisoners by their shoulders and forced them to their feet. "Pick him up and let's go," Fergus ordered.

The two men slowly lifted the body and shuffled from the room.

"As you all know by now, we have a possible threat to what we are building here. If anyone wishes to back out, you can. Contracts can be nullified. We are not unreasonable and know that there must be an allowable amount of flexibility when unforeseen circumstances arise. If you wish to cancel the agreement and go back Earthside, then you'll be on the next run back, whenever that may be. However, if you decide to stay, then the contract stands as is. You were hired to do a job, so do the fucking job. It's that fucking simple."

He casually sat on a nearby table and grimaced as he stretched his sore, broken ribs. "I promise, things will get better. Right now, we are just beginning to establish our colony. So, bear with us and I promise, it will get better."

"What about the aliens," an unfamiliar voice in the crowd asked. "I mean, will we be safe here?"

"Stand up or come forward or something. I can't see who I'm talking to," Doug said, craning his neck about.

"I'm sorry. Excuse me," a tall, dark and clean-cut man said as he pushed his way through the crowd.

"There are so many new faces that I just don't recall you," Doug said apologetically. "What's your name?"

The clean-cut young man nudged his dark-rimmed glasses up his nose in that nerdy, Clark Kent kinda way. "Benjamin sir. Benjamin Tyler Swanson," he said proudly. "You negotiated mine and my wife's contracts with the University of Pennsylvania in exchange for archaeological research rights."

"Oh... I remember now. You were excited to begin studies on the Chinchassans and their ancient culture."

"Yes sir. I am very interested to learn everything that we can about these Chinchassans," he slowly pronounced. He glanced toward Cass and the few other cats who had decided to attend.

"They will be the first spacefaring alien race documented by mankind. It's amazingly fascinating." He nervously pushed his glasses up the bridge of his nose again, "But what do you plan to do about these new aliens? The Red's, I think I heard someone else call them?"

"To start with," Doug began, then motioned to Mel for a drink. He cleared his dry throat, then continued. "Fergus and Wes have been working to arm and reprogram the existing satellite network for our use only. They may not be fully armed yet, but we do have some defensive capability available to us. There will also be a team assigned to salvage whatever we can from the defeated alien vessels and incorporate it into the *Ethel*. Not only will she be an orbital factory ship, but she will also act as a defensive platform. That team will be determined after the new, primary mission roster has been filled."

Doug smiled with a sigh of relief as Mel delivered a glass of golden amber to his hands. He took a long draw from the glass, then continued.

"We need a team of volunteers to hunt down the Red's. We are going to find out who they are and what they want. If at all possible, perhaps we can negotiate some sort of agreement with them or at least figure out how to stop them. Additional to that, we will be mapping the flux points. The team will take the *Veronica* and jump from one point to the next, mapping out possible trade routes that we can use in the future."

"Do we get hazard pay?" Someone in the crowd shouted.

"Yes," Doug replied without hesitation. "Contracts of the volunteers will be adjusted to reflect an additional two percent for the duration of the voyage. Otherwise, I have some special assignments for a few of you that, *will not*," he emphasized, "be going on the hunting trip. Geek and Cheezy fall into this category for obvious reasons. Anyone that wants to throw their hat in the ring, step right up and sign away your soul," he said with a flourish, pointing toward Lizz."

"Very funny, Doug," Lizz laughed sardonically. "Remember, volunteers only. Do not feel pressured or obligated in any way."

Doctor Fillmore pushed her way through the now dispersing crowd and eagerly stood before Lizz. "I'd like to sign up, please."

"Only just arrived and ready to leave us?" Lizz asked.

"No." She searched her mind for the proper response. "It just sounds like it would be much more exciting than patching up scrapes and burns on dirty old miners."

"It does, doesn't it," Lizz agreed. "Unfortunately, I'll be here attending to plans to make this place into something.

"Goddammit! Let go of me," Amanda shouted. She jerked her arm out of Krista's grasp. "Maybe for once, I can be useful. Maybe for once, I will be able to earn my keep. And maybe, just maybe I might learn something useful from a real doctor instead of some rainbows and butterfly's charlatan." She stomped over and stood next to Doctor Fillmore.

"I take it you'd like to volunteer?" Lizz handed Amanda the datapad.

"Absolutely. Anything has to be better than being here with her," Amanda said with a backward glare toward Krista.

"**W**hat do you mean, Casraownan?" Mapharye grasped Casraownan by the back of the arm and held fast. "You can't go with them," she quietly shouted.

"Don't bother arguing, daughter," Ceiwo said. "If he wishes to throw away his life and abandon us, then let him." The elder Chinchassan adjusted himself on the odd seat and watched the crowd of hairless ones as they ate and chattered. He picked up another piece of meat from the platter that sat on the table. "What did you say that the *hoomans* called this?" He examined the sauce covered meat. "*Barrrbeeqoo*, was that it? It is exquisite." He nibbled slowly at the sauce covered meat.

Casraownan stopped and glared back at his mate's sire. "And why shouldn't I go with them. I know I don't fully understand their language, but I wish to learn more from them. I spoke with Lizz a few moments ago. If I understand correctly, they are in search of the ones that battled our ancestors in the skies overhead."

"Lizz, Lizz, Lizz," Ceiwo spat. "Has she befuddled your mind, Casraownan? We still do not know their intentions."

"No, we don't," Casraownan said. "And we never will if we don't actively seek out the knowledge." He pointed in the direction of Lizz. "Do you see those of their kind lining up before Lizz? They are volunteering to go out into the great dark above and search for those who may do us all harm."

"Look at all of this around us," Ceiwo said with a nod. "Have they not already invaded us? Are we not being harmed by their presence?" He picked up another piece of meat and sucked at the dripping red sauce.

"You make them out to be evil invaders, but yet you adore all that they have brought into our lives," Casraownan said, motioning at the food on the table.

"Why is this so important to you, Casraownan?" Mapharye soothingly stroked the large Chinchassan's arm. "Why not stay, with us and learn from them, here?" She said pleadingly, leaning her head against his muscular arm. "And what about Jouqon? Would you leave him without a father?"

Casraownan looked down a Mapharye and turned to face her, taking her face into his large hands. "I do this for all of us, Mapharye. For you, for Jouqon, for all of us. Before these people arrived, we were barely surviving. Everyone, even the younglings knew the pains of hunger all too well. Our bellies have never been as full as they are now. They offer us food, knowledge, and skills freely. That debt alone must be paid if for no other reason than to give back in thanks for what they have done."

"What they have done is befuddle your mind, Casraownan," Ceiwo said as he nibbled at another piece of meat.

"You should talk," Casraownan said with a growl.

"I'm going to sign up too," Jouqon said. He quickly climbed into his father's arms. "I'm going to explore the black with you, father!"

"I'm afraid not, Jouqon." Casraownan peeled the youngling from him, handing him to his mother. "I have a feeling that our people are on the verge of something great. Just you wait and see. Then, you will make your own stories out there in the black."

Casraownan bent down and placed a gentle kiss on the youngling's head, then Mapharye, his mate. "For our people," he said then turned and headed for the table where Lizz sat.

cHAPTER 47

Gamma Draconis system
Near flux point Beta
September 8th, 2176 / Morningish (Dragon time)

“One gauss turret on line. Two, two gauss turrets online, ah ha ha ha,” Fergus yelled in a horrible imitation of Count Dracula. “Three, three gauss turrets online,” he continued to count.

“Did you figure out what that pressure fluctuation in the coolant pumps was about?” Trae looked up from his console toward Willy, who sat stoically in the command chair.

“Nope,” Willy replied. “I tapped on the transmitter, wiggled a few wires, but nothing. We'll just have to see how it goes; I suppose.” He cocked his head and shrugged.

“Okay, I think I have an idea of how this system works,” Jenny Reynolds, the newly acquired linguist said. “It looks a lot like the old Babeltron 1500 that I trained on in college. She tapped a thin finger on pursed lips as she contemplated the controls of the communications station which sat on the forward port side of the bridge.

“The Geek supposedly fixed it up so that even a monkey like me could run the thing,” Fergus said, then continued counting to himself.

“All sensors online and fully functional,” Trae said out loud to no one in particular. “We’ve also received images and details on the Reds. Holy shit!”

“What? Fergus looked up from his console.

“You aren’t going to believe what the Reds look like,” Trae said, then sent the image from his console to the main viewscreen.

“Well I’ll be damned,” Big Willy said.

"Who'd have ever guessed we'd find an entire race of cryptids out here in the black."

The main doors to the bridge slid open with a woosh as Janey and Amanda stepped onto the bridge and suddenly stopped in the doorway, staring at the viewscreen. Casraownan closely followed the pair, then abruptly turned, making a B-line for Trae.

"What is that?" Janey asked.

"That, my good doctor, is what we like to refer to as, a mythological creature," Trae said as he looked up at Casraownan. He nodded to the Chinchasan, who took up a position behind and to the right of Trae's station, behind the command chair.

"I can see that, but why is it on the screen?"

"Because what you are looking at is, in fact, the aliens that we have been referring to as, Reds," Trae continued, then glanced back over his shoulder at Casraownan, who stood stoically, his hands behind his back. He eagerly watched, observing Trae's every movement.

"Hi," Trae said to Casraownan and smiled.

"Hhhhi," Caraownan said, then flashed a toothy, cat-like smile.

"Hu, well I'll be damned," Janey said, then continued to her station.

Fergus leaned over close to Trae. "Think he likes you, Trae," Fergus whispered. "Didn't anyone ever warn you about feeding strays?"

Trae pushed Fergus back to his side of the station. "Will you shut up."

"Oh hey, I know," Fergus said excitedly. "Let me see your laser pointer."

"What? No," Trae said with a scowl. "I'm not going to give you my laser pointer. I know what you're planning to do with it." Trae glanced back over to see Casraownan still staring at him He nodded again.

"Nope, not creepy at all," Fergus said with a chuckle.

"Did you find the Medical bay to your liking," Big Willy asked Janey.

"Very much so, actually," Janey said, spinning her seat to face Willy. I half expected it to be a closet, to be honest with you. We have all of the medical supplies inventoried and stowed. I wish we had more on the medication side of things, but we'll just have to make do with what we have."

"I'm sure if we needed something particular for the mission, Krista would have given us the herbs to use," Amanda said.

Janey let out a sarcastic giggle as she activated the bridge medical station, positioned on the starboard side of the bridge. "I believe that Krista would let everything fall apart out of spite, just to prove me wrong in some way.

"Yup, the coffee is hot, bitter and could strip the paint off a house." Denise propped her feet on the auxiliary console and took a slow lip-smacking sip. "Just like my ex-mother-in-law," she added. Everyone looked up in her direction.

"What does that have anything to do with preflight checks," Trae asked, shaking his head wearily.

"Not a damned thing," Denise said. "Everyone else was tossing out this or that so I figured what the hell, why not join in the fun."

Andy loudly tapped at the helm console, passing through one readout after the next. "What in the hell? That doesn't look right and it sure isn't going to do us any favors either," he said more to himself than anyone else.

"What's wrong," Willy asked.

"I don't know," Andy replied. "Can't you hear that hum?

"It's just the engines man," Trae said without looking up from his console.

"No," Andy argued. "I know what the engines sound like on this boat. It's not the engines."

"Does anything show up on a diagnostic," Fergus asked.

"No," Andy said. "I've already ran three different system scans."

"You're just imagining it," Trae said.

"It could just be something specific to this ship that you aren't used to yet," Fergus added.

"No, it isn't," Andy huffed. He continued through system readouts, initiating additional diagnostic scans.

"It'll be fine, Andy," Willy said. "Whatever it is, I'm sure that it'll work itself out as break this ship in."

"But what if it is something and we fly apart going through a flux or something craps out at the perfectly wrong time like when we're being chased down by an alien fleet bent on the total destruction of the human race," Andy argued.

"I just pulled the diagnostics," Trae reported. "Everything comes up within parameters."

"I don't care what the diagnostics are showing. I'm telling you, something is off," Andy continued to argue.

"We don't have time to sit here chasing gremlins," Willy said. "Let's get to the flux and get this shindig started."

"Your commanding officer gave you a direct order, Andy. Are you going to follow that order or do I need to remove you from this ship," Fergus threatened.

"Fine," Andy said with a huff. "But I don't want a damned one of you bitching at me when something flies off or shorts out for no apparent reason."

"Just go," Willy shouted.

"Fine." Andy input the destination coordinates for the secondary flux engaged the Woodward drive and rolled the two primary throttle controls to fifty percent. "There, are you happy now?"

Willy growled under his breath. "Would you just shut up and fly this thing."

"It's flying itself right now," Andy said. "I'm going to piss and get a drink real quick, y'all want anything?"

"Sure, I'll have a beer and some nachos, heavy on the cheese," Denise ordered.

Willy's growl grew louder.

"Just stay put," Amanda announced. "I'm not doing anything important right now. I'll go down to the galley and get drinks for everyone."

"Oh, would you look at that? That's a fucking brilliant idea," Trae said in a heavily sarcastic tone aimed at Andy.

"Oh, okay. That works I suppose. Um...thank you," Andy said then reluctantly sat back down at his station.

"Leaving the perimeter of the secondary system defensive grid," Trae announced.

"Hey, didn't you guys say something about rearming those things," Andy asked.

"The satellites?"

"Yeah," Andy responded. "Since they still worked and all, that would be a major benefit to the colony. And actually," he stood from the helm station and walked over to the forward most starboard auxiliary station. He tapped at the controls and cycled through screens on the console. "Don't you think we could duplicate a few of the dud torpedoes that were left in orbit?" He suspiciously gripped a plastic cover for an overhead relay junction and wiggled it. *Squeak, squeak squeak.*

"Leave it!" An angry red flush crept up Willy's neck.

"See," Andy said. "Didn't I tell ya I heard a noise?"

The high-pitched warble of the flux alarm sounded. Andy sprinted back to the helm. "Approaching flux point. Flux drive engaged."

"Alright, here we go." Willy took a deep, soothing breath.

"All systems ready," Fergus reported.

"Event horizon in five," Trae said. "Four, three, two..."

"Hey," Andy broke in. "What if the tail section of that red is still sitting on the other side of the flux?"

The entire bridge exhaled a unanimous sigh, "fuck!"

cHAPTER 48

Gamma Draconis system
Eltanin 2 / Dragons Lair
September 9th, 2176 / Evening (Dragon time)

Danny leapt upon a dimly lit alien stairwell that led to the newly designated command center. "Hey Doug, hold up for a second," he shouted as he sprinted ahead to catch up.

"Make it quick," Doug said, impatiently waiting on the stairs. "I was supposed to have already been in a meeting with Lizz about our overall progress."

"Oh good. I'm heading to operations to give our lovely Overseer my assessment of the alien ships. Mind if I walk with you?"

"Not at all," Doug said, then slowly turned and continued up the steps.

Danny looked over the odd but sturdily constructed columns that lined the open area below. "Looks like those things could hold up to a nuke if they had to," he said, nodding toward the columns.

"They were probably designed for just that," Doug said. "We've set up our new operations center in what we think may have been the space port's main operations center. The layout along with control consoles and large wrap-around view screen looks like something we would have built."

"I've been tossing around some ideas with Flip, Chris, Perry, and that other new Engineer, Cara Cutillo," Danny said. "You brought her back on the last Earthside run. We took a jumper out and did an up-close and personal inspection on the alien hulks."

Doug stopped and glanced back at Danny with a hollow-eyed stare. He dug out a cigarette, lit it, then kicked back a boot and leaned against the wall amid a thick cloud of smoke. "Okay so give me the details. How many souls were on board each of those ships?"

"Cats or Red's?"

"Let's start with the Cats," he blew smoke out from both nostrils.

"Too many," Danny said reluctantly. "I'm sure that we'll never know how many were sucked out into space when the hull breaches happened, but what was on board was a lot." He sighed heavily, then continued. "Over half of those on board were females and children. It looked like they had been living on the ship for generations."

"Dammit," Doug took a long draw, fighting back tears. "Not exactly the sort of thing that I wanted to hear right now, but alright. What else do you have? It can't be any worse than that."

"After seeing the, um… kittens..." Danny said then dryly swallowed. "I figured that you'd maybe want to bring them down for burial or something. We made sure that they were all secured and couldn't float out of any holes in the ship's hull."

"That's good. Thank you for that," he nodded while he fought to blink back tears. "We'll have to get with Cass's people and see what they would like to do. I hate to sound like a vulture about to pounce on the dead, but we could use the parts and materials. What about their ship? Can any of it be salvaged?"

"Well, she is running an antimatter reactor similar to ours. We haven't dug deep into the system yet, but we may be able to salvage and adapt a number of components from her to use on the *Betty*, *Veronica* or any of the other ships running that type of system. Power ratings will be critical to test, though. We don't know what the output is on their reactor, yet."

"Wes thought they were using an energy shield of some sort when they made their kamikaze runs. Look into that and see if it couldn't be adapted to work with our tech."

Danny smiled wide. "Already way ahead of you Cap. I left Chris and Perry up there to begin digging through their systems. Also, it didn't look like the cruise-liner had any offensive weaponry, only defensive batteries. You'd think after all of this time they would have put into port somewhere and tried to add some weapons to her."

"Maybe, maybe not. Maybe whatever had happened to their people had them too scared to set down on any planet," Doug speculated.

"It's possible I guess," Danny said.

"Alright, so what about the Reds then? Those ships are bound to have something we can use," Doug said.

"Each of the Red ships had roughly two dozen crew members on board, maybe. Each of those ships took heavy damage with multiple decks exposed to the vacuum of space." Danny clapped his hands together and began to rub vigorously. "Now this is the best part. Are you ready for it?"

"Alright, I guess," Doug said.

"You'll never guess what they look like." Danny's face brightened like a child waiting to tell a secret.

"Like little *green aliens*?"

"Nope," Danny giddily laughed. "Try seven-foot tall, ironically covered in reddish-brown fur and smells like three-day-old roadkill. Well, more like a skunk that had been dead for days."

"Smell? Wait? How the hell did you smell them when they were exposed to the vacuum of space?"

"We brought one back to *the Ethel* for that new doctor chick to look at. It stunk something fierce. She was driving us crazy wanting a specimen to *study*," he said, exaggerating with air quotes. "So we obliged her." He forcibly rubbed at his nose. "It'll take me weeks to get that scent out of my nose."

"So, what you're saying is that they look like interstellar Sasquatch," Doug said guessing.

Danny flashed a cheesy used car salesmen grin. "Ding ding ding, we have ourselves a *wiener,* ladies, and gentlemen! Congratulations and thank you for playing! Most everyone that was over there with us said they looked like Bigfoot or those big hairy aliens from that classic space flick where the dude had all of those daddy issues. We also took it upon ourselves to pass on the info to the expedition team before they left the system."

"Okay…," Doug sat quietly in thought. "That's good, but what about the ships?"

"They look like they are running fusion reactors similar to the first-generation fusion reactors that the I.A. run on their battle cruisers or larger. But the reactor aboard the Red ships is half the size of the Betty's antimatter reactor. We aren't quite sure what types of weapons that the Reds have on board yet. They have an energy weapon of some kind; we know that for sure from the battle. But any more detail than that will take some time to figure out."

Doug took one last drag from his cigarette, stripped the ember and pocketed the filter as he continued up the stairs. "Unless something important here in the Lair or onboard the *Betty* happens to break, then you should focus on fixing up the *Ethel* and upgrading her with whatever you can salvage from the wrecks. Surely there should be something useful from four Reds and one Cat cruise-liner. But great work so far, Danny. Keep me up to date on any other major finds."

"You got it, Cap," Danny said as the two continued up the darkened stairwell.

cHAPTER 49

Gamma Draconis system
Eltanin 2 / Witches Den
September 10th, 2176 / Morning (Dragon time)

Rachel quietly rolled herself into the Witches Den, the colony's new medical bay. She brought her makeshift wheelchair to a sudden stop, examining her target. In the center of the circular bay stood a large table that resembled a medieval torture device. Comfortably fastened to the device's slightly tilted surface, Wes snored lightly. Cables ran from a large wooden hand crank at the head of the device through a series of pulleys, securing its occupant in place. She slowly rolled forward.

"*Wesley*," she quietly sang. "Hey *Wesley*. I have your favorite cookies." She waved a ration pack chocolate chip cookie in the air. "Come on boy, dance for mamma. You can do it, buddy." She glared at the sleeping Geek and let out a frustrated sigh. "Dammit, guess I'll just have to wake him, then." She wheeled herself over next to the strange bed, removed a carefully tucked away comic book from the depths of her flight suit and slapped it down onto his husky midsection with a loud smack. "Hey! Wake up! What's up homeslice?"

Wes jerked to incoherent awareness with a coughing snort. His eyes darted about, attempting to focus in the dim light of the Witches Den.

"What the hell, Cheezy? Don't you think that I'm in enough pain? Are you trying to give me a heart attack too?"

"Awww. Did I wake the wittle baby?"

"Go away," he looked upward at the dark, blank ceiling. "I'm not in the mood for you right now."

"What the hell man? Fine, I'll just take this back and leave you to suffer in your own self-pity." She snatched the comic back and carefully tucked it back into her flight suit.

Wes gasped with astonished horror. "Wait...what... Is that what I think it is? Where did you get that from?"

"Doesn't matter now, does it? You want to be an ass about it, so I'm taking my comic book and going home." She begrudgingly wheeled herself around the table and started for the exit.

"Unnnggghhh," he heavily sighed. "Fine! I am *so* very sorry Rachel. I am an ass and did not mean any disrespect," he said slowly and concisely, making sure to pronounce each word precisely.

"And?"

"Really? You want more than that?"

"Oh yeah, big daddy. You know what I want. Let me hear those secret little words come out of your mouth," Rachel said in her sexiest voice.

"Fuck me. Fine," Wes said with a sigh. "I am so sorry for being such a diaper baby that clung to my mother's tit for too long and for smelling of elderberries."

"That's it, big boy," she chortled. "You know what mamma likes. Now that wasn't so bad, was it?"

"Yes," he growled then glared at her in a seriously annoyed tone.

"Well. You see," she retrieved the comic from inside of her flight suit. "I happened across this little gem many many years ago. I figured that it might come in handy at some point, so I sweet-talked the kid out of it for the cover price."

"Wait, what?"

"Well, more like I demanded that no matter how old it was, the price on the cover was the price on the cover and the little shit finally gave in."

Wes Gasped. "You have a first issue Betty and Veronica comic book for the ten-cent cover price?"

"Yup," she smiled. "And I even paid that little shit with an honest to God Mercury dime that I'd carried in my pocket for years."

"Wait? You what? Never mind, I don't care. Can I see it?"

"Oh no, that dime probably matters more than trading the comic for a dime. It took all nine hundred terabytes of my porn collection to get that damned dime. But that's alright. I'd loved to have been a fly on the wall when the guy I got the dime from started watching the elephant porn videos. He'll be scarred for life with that." She snorted a laugh. "Did you know that an elephant's penis is prehensile? They can like, scratch their bellies or swat at flies with the thing."

"Oh my God, that's not something that I ever needed to know."

"How can you say that, Wes? Now, think about the possibilities with an appendage like that."

"Dammit, Cheezy. Will, you just shut up and let me see the comic?"

"Oh, you mean this?" She teasingly held up the ancient comic book in his full view. "See, I knew how much you liked your comic books, and how much you especially loved your Archie comics. So I got it and held onto it. Now seemed like it was the best time to show it to you. I thought you might could go for a distraction to take your mind off of everything else."

Wes struggled to glance at the cover, his head immobilized in a clamp, unable to turn. "Dammit, I can't see it and I can't freaking get loose from this contraption."

"You had better not get loose if you ever want to walk again," Krista warned. She emerged from the inner depths of the Witch's Den dressed in a green leather dress and a heavy black velvet cloak covered in runic symbols.

"Eh, legs are overrated," Rachel said. "See? Look what I can do!" She spun the chair in circles as fast as possible. "Oh man. That doesn't feel so good." She stopped the spinning motion and sickly wavered in her seat. "Ungh, maybe that wasn't such a good idea," she groaned. "I'm gonna puke."

"You'll be fine. Now get out of here and let him rest," Krista said.

"Wait, no. Don't go Cheezy," he begged. "What about the comic?"

"You can do without it for now," Rachel said.

"But I'm so freaking bored sitting here like this."

"Aww, poor baby," Krista chided. "You do realize that you were the one that agreed to let me tie you up like this? Right?" An evil, conniving grin stretched crossed her face. Her hand gently glided across his chest. "I could do anything that I wanted to and there isn't a damn thing that you could do about it." Her finger found the ridge of his erect nipple poking at the fabric of his undershirt. She teased at his nipple as her finger circled it in slow, steady strokes.

Wes flushed. "I have to say that is an intriguing thought, but I don't know how well that Kara would take to the idea."

"Good, then that's settled." Krista flicked the tip of his nipple then turned the hand crank attached to the side of the table without hesitation.

Click, click, click, POP! Something within the depths of the Geek's torso exploded with a loud release.

"Oh, dear God! I don't know if that was good or bad." He gasped heavily, trying to catch his breath.

"Ooo, ooo, ooo, Can I crank it next," Rachel asked.

"What? You're still here? No, you can *not*," Krista said gruffly. "Medical professionals only."

"Fine." Rachel wheeled herself in the direction of the exit. "I'll come by later and read it to ya."

"No, please don't leave me here with this crazy woman. I'm starting to think that she likes inflicting pain."

Krista cackled. "Maybe I do and maybe I don't. Either way, you still need your rest. Now scoot," she waved Rachel from the room.

"See ya, wouldn't wanna be ya," Rachel cried as she rolled out of the room.

"Alright big boy. Now when I tell ya, I want you to turn your head and cough," Krista directed.

"Wait, what? Oh my God, Cheezy, please help," Wes begged.

Krista forced her hand beneath his back and ran her fingers across his spine. "Looks like we're going in the right direction." She forcefully pulled her arm out from under him, then pulled a small pin from the sleeve of her cloak. "Tell me if you feel anything." With a flourish of the pin in her outstretched hand and a flare of her cloak, she began her invocation. *"By steel and sting, for guidance, I sing,"* she harmonized as the runes of her cloak glowed a bright silver. She systematically began poking the tip of each of his toes. "Anything at all yet?"

"What in the everloving hell?" Wes stared at her in confused disbelief.

Krista grinned wide. "You like it? I had it made years ago, but never had much reason to use it."

"It's a bit over the top don't you think," Maggie said as she entered the treatment area. She sat down a wooden box on a makeshift side table near *the Den* entrance.

"I don't think so," she said with a pouty faced grin. "I think it's just perfect for the witches three. We'll have to get you and Amanda similar one's made up."

"It's too flashy." Maggie unenthusiastically stared. "We're supposed to be healers, not stage performers. You look like Liberace with oversized tits."

"Hell no, it isn't. At least I don't think it is," Krista said. "I happen to like it. You'll see, you will too. I'll get two more made up the next time we go back to Earth, and you'll just love it, trust me."

"What if I don't want one," Maggie argued. "What if Amanda doesn't want one? Did you ever consider that or think to ask first?"

"Why wouldn't you want one? It's so cool and glows, see." Krista pressed the hidden button causing the runes to illuminate their bright silver glow.

"Just stop," Maggie pleaded. "You keep pushing and pushing and at some point, you'll push too much." A tear rolled down her cheek. "You may have already pushed Amanda too far and we won't know until the expeditionary crew returns." She sucked in a sobbing breath. "You can be a selfish, cold-hearted bitch sometimes, you know that."

Krista stepped up toe to toe with Maggie, locking eyes with her fellow witch. "What if I don't care if it's over the top? What if I don't care what anyone else thinks? Maybe I want to push people's buttons. Did you ever think about that?" She held out her hand and once again pressed the tiny red button sewn into the sleeve of her dress.

"Really!" Maggie said with an exasperated huff. She rolled her eyes and wiped at a new stream of tears.

"Oh, just shut the fuck up." Krista wrapped her hands around the back of Maggie's neck and pulled her close. The pair kissed deep between short gasps for air. Maggie pulled her closer, deeper into the magic embrace. They both let out soft, sensual moans as they kissed.

Wes whimpered, trying to see what the two were doing.

"Eh hem," Doug loudly cleared his throat.

"Oh shit...um...I'm sorry," Krista said, taking a step back. "I have no idea where that came from."

"Cap," Wes forcefully whispered. "You can go away now."

"No need to be sorry," Maggie said. She gripped Krista about the waist and pulled her close. She leaned down and lightly placed another kiss on Krista's lips, then turned back to the Captain. "Did you need something, Captain?"

"Um...Not particularly. I was just stopping in to check on Wes."

"Oh, well he's just dandy as you can see," Krista motioned in Wes's direction. "He's making progress for sure."

"Good," Doug nodded. "I could use his help on the data cores from the other ships as soon as possible."

"Oh, that won't be a problem," Krista said with a nonchalant wave of her hand. "He'll be back on his feet in no time."

"How are your ribs, Captain?" Maggie asked, then nuzzled the edge of Krista's ear.

"As good as they can be," Doug said. "Broken ribs are broken ribs."

"If that's all that you needed Captain, would you please excuse us." Maggie giggled to herself. "We have a few buttons that need a good push." She grabbed Krista by the hand and led her away into the depths of the *Witch's Den*. Both playfully giggled as they drew the heavy drapes shut.

"Dammit Cap," Wes grumbled. "You scared them off. They were getting ready to put on one hell of a show, too."

"Eh, you'll live. I need you back on duty as soon as possible. That means do whatever they tell you to and get well. Kara should be back from her run to *the Ethel* soon. I'll send her to save you as soon as she's back in *the Lair*."

"Ya know, I had a thought, Cap. What if they don't make it back?"

"You mean the Expeditionary crew," Doug asked.

"Yeah," Wes said. "What if they don't make it back? What if after everything else that we've been through that now we're stranded here for good?"

"I already have someone working on that," Doug said. "With the design schematics that we pulled from the *Veronica's* computer, we're going to build a flux drive and retrofit the *Betty*."

"Is that possible," Wes asked. "I mean, the Martian krauts are as good as any of the German engineers back Earth-side. But with the extremely tight tolerances and no room for error, how will we pull off that sort of precision in these conditions?"

"You let me worry about that. Big Willy found this idiot savant, for lack of a better term, from Lower Alabama on the last Earth run. When it comes to machining and fabrication, the krauts can't even touch him."

"So, we might have a pretty good chance of pulling this off?"

"Yup." Doug smiled proudly. "We might just have a chance, Geek."

cHAPTER 50

Location Unknown
September 17th, 2176 / Evening (Dragon time)

The *Veronica* rocked violently as they emerged from the event horizon of the flux. Someone on the bridge screamed as the ship yawed awkwardly to the left from another hard-explosive impact.

"Status report!" Big Willy yelled over the cacophony of alarms.

"Mines," Fergus shouted. "We came out of the flux in a minefield. Active sensors are picking up hundreds of small objects that are roughly four cubic meters in size and surrounding us."

The sound of something heavy and metallic bounced along *Veronicas* outer hull. All present on the bridge tracked the sound of the object as it bounced along overhead and aft.

"Oh shit," Denise gasped.

"That doesn't sound good," Amanda said with a whimper.

"Nope," Trae said in agreement. "This is probably going to hurt."

The *Veronica suddenly* lurched upward, ass first and slid sickeningly left.

"God Dammit Andy," Big Willy shouted. "How about you miss a few of those fucking mines!"

"It's kinda hard to miss them when you fly blindly into a hornet's nest!"

"Come about to 56.9 by 225.4 by - 99.45 degrees. There's an opening in the field that we should be able to fit through if you can hit the hole," Fergus said.

"What?" Andy shouted. "Which way is that?"

Denise laughed out loud. "Ha! He said hole. Haha!"

"Really?" Trae glared over at Denise. "Could you for just one second, be serious? Our lives are in serious peril and you want to make gutter jokes?"

"Yup. You betcha." Denise propped her feet on the auxiliary console and continued to sip at her coffee.

"Nose up, roll to the right and kick the rudders slightly left," Trae said to Andy.

"Well hell, why didn't you say that in the first place?" Andy chopped the throttle. "Hang on!" He pulled the nose up, hard, gunned the engines, rolled to the right with a slight tailslide to the left. From somewhere toward the aft end of the ship the distinctive metallic thwunk of a mine impacting the hull could be heard. The ship shook again from multiple nearby explosions.

"What in the hell do you think that you're doing? You're going to kill all of us!" Jenny screamed. She desperately clutched at her console.

"No, look out! There's another one to your left," Amanda screeched, then covered her eyes.

"Ta nar alakh gej baigaa bükh burkhduudaar bin chini," Casraownan said with a yowling hiss as he clung to the bridge's rear auxiliary station.

"Are you stupid or something," Denise added. "Go under it. See the hole is right there!" Released her restraints, she leapt from her seat and ran forward, tapping at the viewscreen.

Another mine detonated somewhere overhead, but at a distance. The concussion of the blast jostled the ship.

"That one was not my fault," Andy shouted. "Actually, none of these would be my fault if I had good directions. Crap! Everyone hold on to something!"

The ship suddenly nosed up and jinked right.

Denise fell to the deck and tumbled haphazardly to the port side of the bridge.

"What was I even thinking? I just wanted a little adventure," Janey shouted toward Andy. "I never wanted to get blown up in the middle of nowhere!"

"What the hell?" Denise struggled to peel herself from the deck. "You made me spill my coffee! Dick!"

"Can't you slow this thing down a little," Jenny cried.

"I just want to go home!" Amanda sobbed as she desperately wrapped herself around the back of Janey's chair.

"Goddammit, Andy," Big Willy roared. "Just get us out of this field!"

"Preferably in one piece, please," Trae added.

"I'm working on it! It would be easier if there weren't a bunch of back seat drivers yelling at me!" He glanced angrily around the bridge.

"Eyes on the road, Jeeves," Denise said, snapping her fingers at Andy as she hurried to return to her seat.

"You almost got this! Clear in ten seconds," Fergus said.

Willy pounded on his chest and sucked in a deep, reassuring breath. "Woo! Are there any other signals out there?"

"Not that I can find," Trae replied. "The mines are giving off some major interference."

"Jamming signal maybe?" Fergus suggested. "Clear in three...two...one. We are out of the field."

Willy slumped into his seat. Slinging his head back against the headrest he pressed the heel of his hands into his eyes. "Oh my God, that was intense. Park us a safe distance away from the field and let's figure out where we are."

"Already on it," Trae said. "It doesn't look like we are anywhere near to a star system. I've got nothing on visuals and the sensors are not picking up any major gravity wells nearby. I am picking up a few nice sized rocks floating nearby along with, hu, looks like there's wreckage scattered all over the area."

"I'm coming up with something and nothing all at the same time," Fergus said. He examined his tactical display with unsure curiosity. "Here we go. It looks like a massive minefield surrounding the flux point. Oh wow," he gasped. "Scratch that. A massive minefield surrounding five flux points. Wow. Now like Trae said, there are wrecks and debris scattered all around. No power signatures or anything. They are all cold and dead."

"There's no telling how long some of these wrecks may have been out here," Trae said.

"What about location?" Willy asked.

Trae laughed. "No clue," he said, then continued examining his display.

"Oh, well this is just great," Denise huffed. "You spill my coffee, nearly blow us the hell up, and now you're saying that we're lost in deep space? Does that about sum up the situation?"

"We're lost?" Amanda began to whimper. The color-washed from her already pale complexion.

"It's just the way it works," Trae said. "Until we can map out these fluxes, we won't know where they go. And for me to get our location, we need to scan the sky, compare the stars that we see with the stars we have already Identified from Earth and from Gamma Draconis. Then from that information, I can approximately triangulate our position in the galaxy."

"If we plan to use any of these points on a regular basis, we might want to send through some cleanup crews first," Andy added. "I sure don't want to do that every time I fly through one of these points."

"Well shit," Fergus said.

Big Willy turned in his seat to look at Fergus. "What?"

"Andy actually came up with a good idea for a change," Fergus said.

Janey released her seat harness and quickly leapt to her feet. "If no one is injured then I'm heading to Medical to check for damage."

"There isn't any damage showing on the damage control readouts," Fergus said.

"Maybe so, but that doesn't mean that my Medical bay isn't a disaster from all the shaking," Janey said and quickly left the bridge.

"Not a half-bad idea," Willy added. "We did take a few good hits back there. Jenny, Denise, Amanda, start deck by deck and look for any damage. I'll head down to the engine room and check out the reactor and flux drive. I want to see how well the alignment is holding up, anyway." Willy released his seat harness and rolled himself out of the captain's chair. "Trae you have the bridge."

"There had better be some real aliens out here somewhere or someone is going to get my foot in their ass," Jenny threatened. She stood and straightened her skirts. "I didn't sign up for this shit to get myself blown up!" The loud glump of her cowboy boots echoed as she stomped off of the bridge.

"Yeah yeah, just after I finish my coffee," Denise said dismissively.

"Seriously," Trae said in consternation. He glared at Denise with an astonished shake of his head. "We're out here to figure out what the hell those aliens want in order to save our colony. We are on our own and have to work as a team or else we'll be absolutely fucked in the ass while getting raked over the coals, and you want to finish your morning cup o' joe?"

Denise looked directly at him with a narrow-eyed glare. "Ya think, bubba?" She took another slow sip of her coffee and opened a game of solitaire on her console screen.

Gamma Draconis system
Eltanin 2 / Witches Den
September 17th, 2176 / Evening (Dragon time)

Wes belted out the lyrics to *Jukebox hero* as the song blared through his headphones, singing along horribly off-key. His wireless earbuds abruptly flew out from his ears.

"The things that those two witchy women did to each other in there," an unfamiliar voice said over the sound of the headphones. "My God, man. I didn't know that the human body could stretch and bend like that. I'm not so sure that some of it was legal in some countries."

"What in the hell?" Wes struggled to see beyond the restraint that held his head in place. "Chief? Go away you cockroach."

"Slow, sensual kisses," the Chief continued. "One started at the toes and worked her way up the other's body until the two of them merged into one." He gasped in remembrance. "They took my breath away just watching..."

"Oh wow, really?" Wes nervously swallowed. "Did they... wait, you fucking perv!"

"Hehe, yup," the chief said, quietly chuckling. "It is amazing what people do when they think they are alone."

"Wait? What?" Wes's eyes bulged with surprise. "What do you mean? Have you been spying on everyone?"

"Shush. You've got company coming, boy."

Wes could hear the quiet retreating shuffle of feet on the dusty floor.

"Hey butt face," Rachel shouted. "I almost forgot something totally awesome that I think you can appreciate. I've gotta make it quick though. Don't want the witches to catch me and turn me into a newt." Rachel wheeled herself next to the traction table and placed a small data recorder on the table next to Wes's restrained hand. A fast, evil metallic chomping rhythm blared out from the device as soon as she hit the play button. "A little something to help your recovery, brother."

"That is so sweet..." His compliment was cut short as she grabbed his left nipple through his undershirt and twisted.

"God damn you, you evil bitch! I hate you, Cheezy!"

"Love you too, Geek. Enjoy the tunes!" Rachel spun the chair around and stopped abruptly in her tracks. "Oh hi, Kara. He was just crying out in loneliness for you," she laughed.

"Awwww. My big fluffy hubby missed me?" Kara sauntered up to Wes, "I have traveled to the stars and back in aid to our comrades. How dost my handsome knight fair? Be he well or be he dead?" She leaned over and carefully kissed him on the cheek.

"What's up, bro," Tiff said as she appeared behind Kara. "You gonna live, or what man? I call dibs on your classic game collection if you kick the bucket."

"Where the fuck did you get that," Rachel shouted at Tiff.

"What? Not my fault man," Tiff blurted defensively. "I didn't do anything man. I just got here."

"Oh, my," Kara crooned into Wes's ear. "I do fear that a dispute is about to erupt, my dear."

Rachel rolled herself over and grasped the leather flight jacket that Tiff wore. She stared at the patch on the jacket's right breast pocket and right arm. What looked like a triangle, the letter T and the letter X, the Greek letters Delta, Tau and Chi, stood out in bold red over a dark starfield that was surrounded by dirty, ragged gold edging on the sleeve of the jacket. The large mission patch on the right breast displayed the nose on profile image of a ship that resembled the *Betty*. Wrapped along the circular edge of the patch, over the image was a motto in a faded silver thread that read, Hellbound/Heaven sent. Under the image in the same bold silver embroidery was the name and the serial number of the ship. EAGLE / UCSS 82-0033. Above the breast patch was sewn a small ribbon patch, embroidered with the word, Ferryman. The name tape on the left breast of the jacket read, Thomas, John D. An additional, smaller name tape was sewn just under the first, and read Chief. Service pins for pilot, engineer, gunner and orbital para drop decorated the jacket. Rachel caressed the right breast patch of the jacket.

"Um...Hey Cheezy," Tiff said. "I don't think Trae would be cool with it anyway, but I don't exactly swing that way, ya know. No offense, you're cool and all. Just saying, ya know."

Rachel spun Tiff around to look at the left arm. The shoulder of the jacket sported the flag of the United Commonwealth, but it was outdated by at least one hundred years. It looked like the original Commonwealth flag. Only sixteen stars decorated the blue background. Rachel compared the patch to the one on the jacket that she wore. She gasped with excitement and began to yank at the jacket. "Take it off Tiff. I need you to take it off right now, please. I have to see the insides.

"Okay okay, geez man, you don't have to strip me," Tiff huffed.

Rachel immediately laid the jacket open across her lap to reveal a patchwork of mission and ship patches lining the inside of the jacket. Barely any of the original liner was visible any longer. Every usable inch of space had a patch sewn over it. Kara appeared next to the Rachel and leaned against the wheelchair, watching over Rachel's shoulder.

"There is no fucking way. This cannot be possible. Do you know what this is?" She looked between Kara and Tiff with pleading eyes.

"What the hell is it," Wes begged. "I can't see shit from over here."

Rachel tucked the jacket up onto her lap and wheeled herself over to the traction table. She held the jacket up, displaying the patches to Wes.

"What is it," Tiff asked.

"Holy shit," Wes's eyes bulged. "Those missions were over a century ago. At least one of those ships is hanging in the Smithsonian now. Where the hell did you get this from?"

"Jesus Christ, Wesley! What," Kara demanded. "What is it already?"

"John Thomas," Tiff pondered. "Why does that sound familiar?"

"Holy fucking shit Batman!" Wes sucked in a nervous breath.

"Because he's a legend." Rachel rolled her eyes and gave Tiff one of those, *really, are you that brain dead looks*. "He was one of the original boomers that explored and established outposts throughout the solar system. If it weren't for him and the rest of the Ferrymen, we might have gone extinct as a species because the Earth was still poisoned back in those days. They established habitats to save humanity while the cleanup from the war was being taken care of."

"That doesn't make any sense," Tiff pondered.

"No, not really," Kara replied. "It's gotta be a replica or something." She dug at the collar, "I bet it has one of those made in China tags or something."

"Or it could have been stolen," Wes said loudly, rolling his eyes in the previous direction of the Chief's voice.

Rachel bundled the jacket back onto her lap. "I'm taking this to the Captain."

"No, wait. You can't. The chief let me have it." Tiff pulled on the jacket's sleeve.

"Tough titty big bitty. I'm gonna find the Captain." Rachel yanked the jacket free from Tiff's hand and wheeled away as fast as her arms would carry her.

"Wait! Come back Cheezy," Tiff pleaded as she chased behind.

Kara quickly stepped to Wes, leaned over gave him a long, deep kiss. "Get well my love. I regret that I must leave you for now. There is a mystery afoot," she said excitedly as she sprinted away in pursuit of the others.

Wes let out a frustrated huff.

"That one has my jacket," the Chief said as he approached. "I'll tell ya what bud, I'll make a deal with ya. I'll give you all of the tasty details of what's going on over there in the witches lair if you'll just pass on the message that I want my jacket back. I've had it way too long to just give it up to big tits there. I only loaned it to her since her shirt got torn off. You understand, don't ya, son?"

"What? Why should I help you? You've been a constant pain in our ass since day one."

"You really think so, hu? You bunch of young pup hotshot flyboys think you are the most shit hot crew of any in the commonwealth? If you only knew, boy. If you only knew," the Chief laughed as he walked away.

"Wait, come back… hey! Old fart! Chief?"

"Think about it bud," the Chief's voice drifted off into the distance.

cHAPTER 51

Unknown Location
September 17th, 2176 / Late Evening (Dragon time)

"We are through the flux," Andy announced.

"What's this one look like? Picking up any signals or anything?" Big Willy asked, leaning against the console.

"It looks like we're on the outskirts of a system. Like, out in the Oort cloud of the system."

Casraownan peered around the large man, gawking at the display.

"Will you stop trying to sneak a peek and just come over here already," Trae said, pointing at the floor next to him at the auxiliary station.

"Namaig tend bailgakhyg khüsee yuu?" Casraownan's ears perked up, his eyes wide and hopeful.

"Yeah, come on," Trae said. "Come up here if you want to see what's going on."

Casraownan's face stretched in an odd feline smile as he took his place next to Trae.

Trae squinted back at the display. "Hu!"

"Crap. Why doesn't that sound good?" Big Willy sat back in the command chair.

"Oh no, it's not anything bad. Just weird," Trae said. "I mean, this is the first time we've seen a star system like this before. The system is made up of five stars and a number of planets. Spectrometers are classifying the main sequence stars of the system as a pair of A-class, blue subgiants. They are similar to Sol, just a little larger and almost out of hydrogen to burn."

He flicked readouts onto the main viewscreen from his console and cycled through a number of display readouts.

Casraownan let out an astonished breath as he watched Trae's every movement.

"The primary companion star is a G class yellow dwarf, nearly the same size as Sol and is the center of a trinary star cluster that orbits the two blue subgiants. Both of those stars around the G class are white dwarfs." He continued cycling through the readouts. "Damn that was fast," he exclaimed.

"What?" Willy asked with an impatiently anxious tone.

"I've got our location," Trae said.

"That's a first," Fergus complained. "So, where the hell are we?"

"The Sarin star system. We're in the constellation of Hercules. It's one of the few stars that you can make out from Earth with the naked eye. Roughly ninety-four light-years from Earth and," he paused as he double-checked the numbers, "around seventy-six light-years from Gamma Draconis and the Lair."

"Great," Denise said. "Now that we know the address, someone order a freaking pizza. I'm starving."

"Oh, hey now, that's new," Trae blurted. "I have a signal. Looks like we have a live one out there."

"Woot! Finally, we get some action," Fergus exclaimed. "It only took us a dozen jumps in the last week to find something."

"Wait? Did you just say there's something out there?" Jenny excitedly fumbled with her headphones. "I'm picking up all sorts of comm traffic in the system." She giggled. "Oh my." Her foot nervously bounced as she listened. "There are at least a dozen distinct languages in the transmissions that I'm picking up. Oh my, this is so amazing!" She let out an excited squeal. "Wait! Oh God, no, no, no." She quickly stood up and tapped at the upper controls of the station. "I have to record everything. I can't let this opportunity slip through my fingers."

"All stop," Big Willy ordered. "Let's hang here and see what we can learn before we go tromping through the middle of the system. Passive sensors only. Charge up the turret capacitors, just in case."

"Copy that," Trae and Fergus replied as one.

Willy keyed the comms. "We've found alien activity this time. Everyone be ready for anything." He switched off the intercom.

"Holy shit," Fergus exclaimed. "I just picked up a gamma-ray burst, fourteen thousand klicks off our downspin port aft."

"Can you get a visual on them?" Willy sat up excitedly.

"Already working on it," Trae said just as an image of a long, reddish colored ship appeared on the main viewscreen.

"Holy shit, it's a Red! Laying in an intercept course," Andy said.

"No, stop," Big Willy ordered. "Don't move this ship one meter." He stood and examined the data over Andy's shoulder. "Let's see what they do and where they go. Just keep a close eye on them for now."

"Ene bol minii ard tümnii sansryn ovgiig ustgasan ulaan chötgörüüd yum," Casraownan said with a growl.

"Calm it down fuzzball," Fergus said. "Don't make me go get a leash."

"Chill Ferg," Trae said then turned to Casraownan. "Don't worry, we'll get to the bottom of it all."

Doctor Filmore rushed through the main entrance and onto the bridge. "I don't want to hear the first complaint from any of you." She pressed an odd device to Denise's left arm.

"Hey now, goddammit," Denise shouted, swatting the device away. "I didn't say that you could go and low jack me."

"Fine," Janey said with a huff, moving to Jenny's station she tapped the linguist on the shoulder. "It's a, just in case cocktail that I've been working on. It'll give all of us a boost of vitamins, minerals, and a few extra touches to enhance our immune systems."

"Wait? A cocktail that you've been working on?" Denise growled. "So what? We're the mad scientist's guinea pigs now?"

"We have no idea what sort of pathogens any of these other races may carry or how they might react with our physiology," Janey said matter-of-factly. "I don't think that we can be too careful."

"Better safe than sorry," Big Willy added. "Alright, hit her then do me next." He held his breath as he looked away and grimaced.

"Don't worry big guy. You'll only feel a little prick."

"That's what she said," Denise cackled.

"Okay now," Janey said with a narrow-eyed glare back at Denise.

Jenny nodded and stood, pulling down the top of her skirt to expose her right butt cheek. She clenched her eyes shut.

Janey pressed the magnajet injector to Jenny's cheek and depressed the trigger. "One...two...three. That's it. If you don't want it, I won't force you. But I don't want to hear any complaints from anyone about being sick. You can just wait and see the witches when we get back if you want to refuse any of my treatments."

"If it isn't an I.V. of coffee, you can piss off," Denise said. "You ain't sticking me with any needles, Doctor Jekyll."

Trae let out a frustrated breath and shook his head. "Quit being such a whiny bitch and just do it already."

"Hey! If I wanted lip from you, I'd..."

"Shut up," Big Willy bellowed. "All of you! Come hit me next. If someone doesn't want it, then just move on. If they catch something communicable, the cure is just an airlock away."

Andy held his hand up as he glanced between Willy and Janey.

"What Andy?" Willy began to slowly grind his teeth.

"Would this have any side effects if mixed with alcohol or anything? I mean, it's not like I've been drinking or anything yet, but if I were to have a beer or something later after I'm off duty ya know."

"You're kidding, right?" Trae laughed. "We're always on duty on this run.

"It shouldn't have any reaction that I can think of," Janey said. "Is there a particular reason why you ask?" She continued around the bridge, inoculating each of the others.

"Oh, ok," Andy stammered. "Just curious is all. Forget I even asked about it."

Denise snickered. "So ya Irished up your coffee too, hu? Cheers mate." She held up her coffee mug in salute, then took another sip.

The grinding of enamel became louder as Big Willy grumbled under his breath.

"Picking up a new signal coming from that Red," Trae said. "She's changing course and speed."

"Transmission recorded," Jenny squealed. "This is so freaking exciting."

"Couldn't have been a refuel. Cargo drop maybe," Trae suggested.

"Depends. That just seems awfully quick, though," Fergus said.

"They could have been picking up or dropping off passengers, maybe," Andy added.

"I wouldn't think that there wasn't enough time to transfer crew," Trae said.

"Shit, it's gone," Fergus shouted.

"What? Where did it go?" Big Willy leaned forward, sitting on the edge of the command chair.

"Looks like they jumped," Trae said. "One second they were there, the next, poof, they are gone."

"Dammit! How the hell are we supposed to catch up to them if they can just disappear in a split second?"

"It wasn't just a split second," Trae argued. "I picked up an energy build-up. They must use some sort of capacitors or something that they have to charge before jumping. I bet they used this system as a navigational waypoint. That makes the most sense. They didn't drop anything or even stop. They appeared, cruised through the system then popped back out."

"That's as good an explanation as any other's we have right now," Big Willy said.

Jenny growled in frustration. "There isn't much more that I can do from out here. I have all of these transmissions being recorded and all, but until I can actually start speaking with someone and putting the syntax into place, it isn't going to do me much good. Is there any way that we can go check out the source of the transmissions? There seems to be one large and powerful transmission coming from the vicinity of the G type star with lots of other, less powerful transmissions from other sources. Maybe nearby ships? Until we can get closer that's the best guess that I have."

"Well, that's part of why we came out here, isn't it?" Big Willy scratched at his stubbly chin as he contemplated their options.

"Cap said that he wants to establish trade routes," Trae reminded him. "If this *is* a station, that would be the perfect place to strike up some allies and potential business contacts. There is something out there, I just can't tell what it is from here."

"A station is a station, right? Fergus said. "I mean, how many times have we stopped in at a Martian or Venutian station where we don't always understand what they are saying, but we are still able to conduct business? Business is business, no matter what you speak. You just need to know the currency and its base value."

"Yeah, that's true." Willy took in a deep breath and straightened in his seat, crossing his arms. "Alright, let's do it. Take us in, Andy. Lay in a course for the source of the transmissions."

"Copy that. Course laid in," Andy said to no one in particular.

"Take us in slow," Willy said. "We don't want them to think that we're on an attack run or anything."

"Will do, Willy."

"Jenny, go ahead and hail them. Let's see if they feel like chatting."

Warning alarms erupted across the bridge.

"We're being painted," Fergus shouted over the noise.

"It looks like a sensor or communications buoy," Trae said. "Twenty thousand klicks off our starboard bow."

"Well shit," Fergus said with a disappointed huff. "I was hoping for some action."

Trae turned and glared toward Fergus. "Seriously, man?"

"Um...We're being hailed," Jenny said in a surprised tone.

"Open a channel," Big Willy ordered.

"Channel open."

"I am Commander William Murphy of the..." He motioned for Jenny to cut the feed.

"We're muted," she said.

"We aren't technically part of the Commonwealth anymore," he said. "Who should I say that we're with?"

"We aren't with anyone. We're setting up our own planet for Christ's sake," Fergus said.

"Just say that we're an independent starship," Trae suggested. "That should be fine until Doug and Lizz decide on a designation."

"Open the channel back up."

Jenny nodded and Willy continued, "I am commander William Murphy of the Independent Star Ship, *Veronica*. We are new to this sector of space and you are the first people that we've come across."

"I'm getting a visual signal," Jenny announced.

"Put it up on the big screen," Big Willy said, motioning at the screen.

The image of a blue-tinted possum-like creature was suddenly staring back at the crew from the large view screen. A stream of unintelligible jowl slapping nonsense spewed from the creature's mouth. It's large, dark eyes intently looked over the bridge crew.

"I am Commander William Murphy ..." The creature abruptly cut him off with a long, drawn-out hiss. It reached down to the side and began fiddling with something. Willy continued." We're explorers and new to this region of..."

The creature held up one clawed finger toward the screen as it spit out more blubbering gibberish. The creature's shoulders visibly slumped as it exhaled in what looked like frustration. Electronic beeps and bloops muddled the transmission as the creature continued to mess with something offscreen. It spoke again pointing toward Willy with one hand while motioning with its other hand as if a sock puppet were speaking.

Trae coughed a laugh, desperately trying to catch his breath.

"Um…," Fergus said. "I think it just went stupid."

"No, I think it wants you to keep speaking," Jenny said.

"Possibly," Trae said slowly.

"Are you kidding? The critter is F'n wacko, man. Look at it, it's talking to itself," Denise pointed at the viewscreen.

"Can't we just be serious for a change," Fergus demanded.

Looks off blank confusion painted everyone's face as they turned to look at Fergus.

"What? These are the first aliens that we've encountered outside of the Chinchasa," Fergus said defensively. "How about we get down to business and make some allies out here?

Once we have that step taken care of then we'll know who the bad guys are, and we can start nuking some alien scum."

"Ah, there he is," Trae said. "There's the Ferg we all know and love. You had me going for a minute there, buddy."

"Ooo, ooo, ooo, I've got it," Jenny shouted and quickly stumbled over her own feet, making her way to the center of the bridge. She closed her eyes, took a deep breath, and began. "Greetings from the people of earth… We cast this message into the cosmos ... Of the 200 billion stars in the Milky Way galaxy, some – perhaps many –"

The creature excitedly flashed a wide snaggle-toothed smile and began to jabber. It sorted through a cluttered shelf behind its station then looked back at the screen and motioned for her to continue.

Perplexed, Jenny continued. "Perhaps many have inhabited planets and space-faring civilizations. If one such civilization intercepts Voyager and can understand these recorded contents, here is our message"

"Aaaaaa dra ta doo," the creature excitedly slurred. It returned to its seat, holding a golden disk that it proudly held out for the crew to see. It waved at her to again continue as it tapped away at its console.

"This is a present from a small, distant world, a token of our sounds, our science, our images, our music, our thoughts, and our feelings. We are attempting to survive our time so we may live into yours. We hope someday, having solved the problems we face, to join a community of galactic civilizations. This record represents our hope and our determination and our goodwill in a vast and awesome universe.

Denise scoffed. "What the hell kinda crap poetry are you reciting to the thing?"

"It isn't poetry," Fergus said. "It was a speech recorded by Carl Sagan and placed on the first voyager probe."

Everyone turned once again to Fergus with looks of surprise.

"What? I do know some stuff," Fergus said.

"That was impressive," Amanda quietly added.

Jenny blushed, color creeping up her neck. "Thank you. I memorized it after leaving Earth. Thought it might come in handy if an alien race had found the probe."

The creature waved wildly to get their attention.

"What the hell," Trae said.

The creature pointed at the crew, then pointed at its own ears.

Willy nodded in understanding. "Ok? You want us to listen," he asked. "So, what are we listening for?"

A recording of a man's voice suddenly played through the video feed, reciting the same speech that Jenny had just given. The creature held up the golden disk and excitedly pointed at it, nodding.

"Oh great," Denise huffed. "Now the thing wants to play fetch."

"How the hell," Trae gasped. "There's no way that the voyager probe could have made it this far out. Earth lost contact with it during the hell years, but back then, a random piece of space junk was the least of mankind's worries. Most just assumed it was lost forever."

"It could have been stolen or salvaged," Andy added.

"Really," Jenny huffed. "You want to accuse them of stealing a forgotten probe? Could you please be a little more courteous? We have no idea if it can understand us or not."

"Everyone just shut the fuck up!" Big Willy pounded his fists on the arms of the command chair. The bridge went eerily silent.

"*Shh,*" the blue alien possum began to strangely hiss. "*Shhh. Shuut. Shut daaa fooock up!*" It shouted, then pounded its fists on the console and pressed a button. The alien leapt to its feet and began to dance as *Johnny be Goode* blared from somewhere in the background.

"Um...," Andy said. "What the hell just happened?"

Trae rolled out of his seat as uncontrollable laughter overwhelmed him.

"Great first contact their buddy," Denise said. "You just managed to teach the fuzzy little Chupacabra how to say Fuck!"

cHAPTER 52

Gamma Draconis System / Eltanin 2
The Dragon's Lair / Mel's Diner
September 17th, 2176 / Late Evening (Dragon time)

"Cap," Rachel shouted as she wheeled herself through the entrance of the cantina. "Cap! You ain't gonna believe this shit!" The chair bounced as she gripped the wheels and skidded to a shaky halt.

"Slow down, Cheezy!" Tiff and Kara jogged behind the crippled pilot. They both bent over, hands on their knees, trying to catch their breath.

"Tough shit, catch up ya old hags." Rachel spotted Doug looking up from the far end of the long rectangular room. She maneuvered the wheelchair around the makeshift cantina tables that Willy and Andy had made from the ancient shelving units that once stood in this space. She wheeled herself onward toward the larger table at the back. Doug, Danny, and Chris stood around the table, leaning over a set of blueprints that were spread out over the table.

"What's up, Cheezy?" Doug glanced up briefly, then turned back to the drawings.

"I think that the Chief is actually *The Chief*, Cap. John D. Thomas kinda Chief and not just any swinging dick or regular old average John Thomas either. Look!" She excitedly held up the leather flight jacket for him to see.

"One sec, Cheezy," he said, motioning with a single finger. "What about rerouting all of the power inputs to be backups of all of the others? Redundancy wouldn't be a bad thing in this Frankenstein that you guys are building."

"Hell yeah, man. That shouldn't be a problem," Danny boasted. "Especially if we just run splice cables as needed.

There's no reason that we have to run conduit and tuck everything away just yet. We can run power from their cores and have a fully operational gun platform in a week, max. There's lots of good salvage on the Red hulks, all four of those reactors are still intact. The main drive engines on the cat cruiser are still in good shape, too. Same goes for their reactor."

Rachel laid the jacket onto the table without a word. Doug looked over, scowling at Rachel. "What? Just hang on for one more second. Let me get these guys back to work." He brushed the jacket aside and went back to making a note on the large drawing. "So, if we go this route, you think you could pull it off in a week?"

"And hell," Chris interrupted. "Once we figure out how their versions of jump and warp drives work, we could possibly start duplicating those too. Wouldn't hurt to have a secondary method of interstellar propulsion if the flux drive goes out. Well, that's also assuming that you want to put a flux drive on all of the ships. It just depends on what we want to use as a basis. The more uniform the design that we come up with down the road the easier fabrication will be. Once we lock down a standard, we could produce multiples to our specs." Chris straightened, stretching his back. "You just gotta tell me what you want and get me the people to make it happen."

"Perfect. Let's get to it, then." Doug held his ribs as he straightened with a groan. "I'm sure that you guys can handle this without me micromanaging it. You know what I want, and I trust you to get the job done. Use your best judgment. Get with Lizz to get crew assigned to you as you need."

"Freaking sweet, man," Chris cheered.

"You got it, boss man." Danny rolled up the drawings and mockingly saluted with the rolled tube. "If we just weld the space frames together instead of coming up with some mounting jig system, we could save tons of time," he said to Chris as they left the table.

Doug stretched with a groan, then turned back to Rachel. "Okay, sorry about that. What was it that you needed?"

Rachel let out a frustrated huff. "Do you know any of the of the *Betty's* history?"

"No. Not really," Doug said. "I didn't really think to ask when I bought her." He stretched in the opposite direction. "Why? What does it matter?"

Doug flinched as the jacket suddenly reappeared, brushing against his nose. "Okay," he replied. "I still don't know what you expect me to see. I've seen dozens of these jackets in spaceports, truck stops, and souvenir shops before.

"I think I know who the Chief really is." She threw the flight jacket back at him. Doug quickly snatched the jacket from the air, catching the weight of it with a painful grunt. He cradled his ribs and gave her one of his best fatherly glares. "I'm really not feeling up to one of your games right now, Cheezy. I just want to lie down, rest and take something for the pain.

"She's not lying cap," Tiff said as she and Kara approached, standing behind Rachel.

"What was it that you were saying about John Thomas?" Doug laid the jacket out on the table.

"Just look at it and you tell me," Rachel demanded.

"Okay. It's a flight jacket," Doug said with a shrug. "What's supposed to be so special about it?"

"Freaking seriously, Cap? You're killing me. Look at the patches, the name tape, the fight pins. Look at the Commonwealth's flag patch, Cap," Rachel pleaded. "The last ship that John Thomas was known to have served on, according to the history books was a Nova Star class transport, *the Eagle.* Service number UCSS 82-0033. What is the service number of *the Betty,*" she tersely asked.

"I don't know right off the top of my head," Doug said. "I've never had to worry about it before." He glanced over the jacket with confusion. "How in the hell could our Chief be *the* John Thomas? He'd be well over one hundred years old by now."

"The hell if I know, Cap," Rachel admitted. "Stranger things have happened before, I'm sure."

"He's got to be dead by now," Doug said. "Hell, I've visited his grave. There are statues of him all around Atlanta. There is a museum dedicated to *the* John Thomas, in Smyrna that has his flight jacket, his cherished harmonica and the first martian rock that he brought back to Earth."

"So that's where that went to," a hoarse voice whispered from the shadows behind the cantina's serving line. "Those fucking bastards stole my..."

Doug shushed Rachel and pushed her away so he could stand.

"Oh shit," the strange voice grumbled. A figured darted from behind the serving line, heading for the main entrance to Mel's diner. The figure tripped, falling flat to the ground among a pile of pots and pans.

"Chief! Wait," Rachel called out.

Doug sprinted to where the figure lay sprawled on the hard-concrete floor. Doug grabbed the figure by the arm as he arose, helping him to his feet.

"What? Hey, let me go. Get your grubby dick beaters off of me," Chief argued.

"Are you really John Thomas? I mean, *the* John Thomas," Rachel asked excitedly asked, rolling herself forward.

The Chief's eyes grew wide at the sight of his jacket in Doug's hand. "That is my property you thieving bastard! Hell, it's really my only property. Give it back!"

"So, you're the elusive Chief that's been busting our balls all of these years," Doug asked.

"Did you really drag that pirate ship through Saturn's rings during the Titan station rebellion? How did you survive the core failure during the Oort cloud mission?" Rachel pushed Doug to the side so she could see the Chief.

"Shit, you're one of those crazy chicks, aren't you?" The Chief panicked, flailing about as he attempted to break free from Rachel's grip.

"Rachel, calm yourself," Doug said.

"But Cap, what about a first-hand account of the Demios run, or the infiltration mission that the Chief and crew of the Eagle did into Phosphor station," she excitedly said.

"Rachel, enough!"

"But Cap," she whimpered.

"Enough," he said with an exasperated huff.

"You wait," he warned, then turned back to the Chief. "May I buy you a drink, Chief? Or should I call you, Commander Thomas?"

A look of disbelieving confusion contorted the Chief's face. "Why in the hell would you wanna do that?"

Doug smiled a knowing smile. "Seems to me that's the least that I could do for you, considering the number of times that you've saved our asses."

The Chief licked his lips at the thought. "Tell ya what. Keep the crazy lady away from me and you've got yourself a deal."

Doug turned back to Rachel. "Hey, Cheezy. You know I love ya, but go away for now and fuck off."

cHAPTER 53

Sarin star system
Unknown Alien Space Station
September 18th, 2176 / Morning (Dragon time)

"If I were a betting man, I'd bet that from the sound of that hum, there must be enough electromagnetic radiation in this room to be a health hazard to the people in it," Trae blandly said.

Blue phosphorescent lights wavered back and forth at a slow rhythmic pace throughout the compartment.

"But isn't that the point of a decontamination chamber? Kill anything that might be on you before you can enter a station," Big Willy said.

"Oh, shoot," Janey sputtered, frustratedly. She dug into the depths of her field medics satchel bag, its edges worn and stained from years of fieldwork. "I hadn't even thought about that possibility. If anyone notices any signs of radiation poisoning, notify me and get back to the ship immediately so that I can treat you."

Trae turned to the doctor with a questioning look. "Why would we need treatment for radiation?"

"We have no idea about this station or any other species that may be here," Janey said. "Didn't you say that there were at least fifteen different designs of ships that you counted docked at the starport?"

"Yeah, so?"

"Well there ya go, that's fifteen different alien species from fifteen different alien worlds and fifteen possible risks that we know nothing about," Janey pointed out.

Jets of steam like air burst into the room from ports mounted along the arched bulkheads of the chamber. Air hissed through airlock seals as the inner hatchway door released and opened into a long hallway like area.

Big Willy stepped cautiously through the open portal. "Damn, this reminds me of being put through a police lineup," he said, pointing at the mirrored wall to his right that ran the full length of the room.

"Fuck it, I'm done. I need out of here." Andy rushed into the long chamber, pushing past Big Willy. He rushed to the opposite doorway at the opposite end of the room, looking for a release.

The rest of the crew fell into line behind Big Willy in single file and stopped then habitually turned to face the mirrored wall. Denise stretched her foot through the doorway, carefully tapping at the floor of the long chamber.

Willy leaned forward to look past the others toward Denise. "What in the hell are you doing?"

"Something just doesn't smell right about this place," Denise fussed. "I don't trust it. Like...it feels like there should be some sort of booby trap or something in this room and I'm going to be the one lucky enough to roll a fumble and set the damned thing off."

"Really?" Trae said, shaking his head.

"But what if this is just some sort of elaborate trap that the aliens use to capture unsuspecting food," Denise said.

"Let's go already, Andy," Fergus shouted down the line. "What the hell man, you haven't figured out how to open the freaking door yet?"

"Did she just say that this was a trap?" Andy frantically dug at the edges of the door.

"Seriously," Denise said. "This doesn't scream trap to any of the rest of you?"

Willy clenched his fists, his knuckles turning white. "Just get in here already!"

"Fine!" Denise stepped through the portal and the hatchway slammed shut behind her. Locking mechanisms engaged with the sound of metallic clanks and bumps.

"See? No one *ever* listens to me," Denise said. "What the hell did I tell all of y'all? Now we'll be bagged, tagged and *anally probed*."

"But why would they trap us? They've seemed friendly enough so far," Jenny said.

Amanda buried her head into Janey's bosom like a scared child.

Trae burst out into uncontrollable laughter, rubbing his temples. He started to clap as he fought to catch his breath. "Oh my God...this is so freaking amazing...truly amazing," he said between gasps and chortles.

Casraownan started at the large man. His whiskers twitched with what looked like anxious uncertainty.

"Oh, hell no," Andy declared. "Ain't no one gonna be probing me with anything, dammit!" He pounded on the door.

"Shut up! Everyone just shut the fuck up," Willy bellowed. "And you," he pointed with a thick, meaty finger down the chamber toward Denise. "You especially, keep your mouth shut or so help me I'll help them with the probe by sticking my boot up your ass!"

"What the hell? That's my line," Jenny fussed.

Big Willy glared at the linguist and jabbed his meaty finger in her general direction. "Don't you even start with me!"

The long, mirrored wall suddenly went transparent. Two of the blue-tinted possum like aliens looked back at the crew. One held up the golden record and pointing excitedly at the disk. The other tapped away at the controls of a large control console, its lips moving in silent conversation.

Casraownan knelt down and curiously watched the blue creatures. His head tilted slightly to the side as he intently watched their every action.

"Aw hell, that ain't good," Denise said. "He looks way too happy for this to be a good thing for any of us."

Willy's eyes flared with anger. "That's it! Let me out of this thing," he roared. He pounded his massive fists against the transparent wall.

Trae fell to the floor, uncontrollably convulsing with laughter.

Andy began to pry at a cover panel next to the door with a plier-like multi-tool.

Jenny huddled in close with Janey and Amanda.

"Well, I guess there's no going back now," Denise said, then began to casually strip off her clothing.

The two possum-like aliens stared back through the transparent wall. Their brows furrowed with what looked like an expression of disbelief at the chaos inside the chamber. The blue-tinted creature holding the golden disk glanced at the other and shrugged. It flipped open a small yellow access cover that sat on the top of the control console and concealed a large red button. Its lips moved as it spoke to the other possum-like creature, then reaching forward it pressed the large red button. A yellowish blue mist hissed into the long, mirrored chamber. The actions of the crew slowed as they each drunkenly slumped to the floor as they succumbed to the effects of the tinted gas.

cHAPTER 54

Unknown

Amanda opened her eyes to near darkness. A light blue hue emanated along the edge of the nearly square ceiling. The cold permeated her body from the smooth plastic surface that she lay upon.

"Um...hello?" She sat up slowly, careful to otherwise be as silent as a mouse. She pulled her knees up to her chest and wrapped her arms around them. "Okay…, there must be an explanation for this," she whispered to herself. "We were in a hallway with a mirrored window, and now I'm here." She hiccupped a breath as she fought back a panic attack, forcing herself to take slow, deep breaths. "I can do this...I can do this," she told herself.

Carefully, she slid one foot from the cold surface to the floor where she tapped the tip of her boot, testing the distance from where she sat. She slid her hand along the edge of the bed-like shelf, tapping it with her fingernail. The distinctive tap, tap, tap of plastic returned to her ears. Slowly, she slid down from her perch and began to shuffle about in the dark dimness of the room. She felt about for anything like a light switch or door handle.

"Oh, that feels different," she said as she groped about. "That feels like it might be a button," she mumbled, then pressed the detented area. Light flashed across a large part of the wall as the room filled with the glow of blue incandescence. The image of what looked like a massive warehouse with bins overflowing with tentacled things appeared on the screen.

"Come on down to the Ryloprime discount Grig house. You'll find Griglings of all sizes fresh from the Rylosian badlands to pick from," said an unseen announcer.

The image shifted to that of a large flesh-colored worm-like creature with tall eye stalks. Six tentacle appendages extended from beneath a heavy robe type garment. Amanda watched with fascination as the creature tossed what she thought was a Grigling into a bin full of other lethargically slithering forms.

"Fresh Griglings caught daily! With only the choicest cuts of grig fat from the previous day's catch. All customers that purchase twenty or more Carnacks earn the chance to spin the wheel for a free choice cut of the day's special!"

The image shifted to another worm-like creature dressed in a long flowing cape that sparkled as it spun a large game show-style wheel.

"Come on down to warehouse row in Ryloprime right now for the freshest catch in thirty parsecs."

The salesman ripped the head off of a Grigling with its rows of needle-like teeth and spit the stripped piece of flesh to the ground.

"Trust me, you'll love it, and thank me later!"

The figure winked and gave what looked like the tentacle alien equivalent of a thumbs up, then turned up and sucked the juicy innards from the neck stump of the Griglings tiny, limp body.

The image shifted to an aerial view of a packed stadium. The crowd cheered and chanted.

"There it is! The score that we've been waiting for all season, Chip! Twenty-two Sarlcs in one charge through the midfield defenses. Flox Deb has completely decimated the opposition this season and left none of the opposing team's defensive line standing."

"So true Gleb, So true," Chip, the other announcer agreed. *"None of the visiting team look to even be breathing at this point. There are twelve skects left on the clock. There's still a chance, but I highly doubt they could pull it off!"*

"That's exactly it, Chip," the odd, orange and blue salamander-like figure said with a laugh as it appeared on the screen.

"Oh, it looks like the officials have made a ruling. Wait. What's this? Yes," Chip, the redish salamander-like creature said excitedly. *"This just in from the officials. Yes indeed, it is official. Flox Deb has slaughtered the entire santarian team single-handedly, Gleb! This match is officially over!*

"Maybe not Chip. Flox Deb does not look happy. What's this? Oh no, he's...he's turned on his own teammates, Chip. Flox Deb is not finished, ladies and gentlemen! He has turned on his own team and...Ohhhh!"

Both announcers cringed at the image on their screen. The display shifted, pushing the announcers into a corner of the screen while the main camera view zoomed in on a massive gray creature in a blue and yellow uniform with thick black horns that curled backward from the front of its head. It kicked the crushed corpse of one teammate out from underfoot then captured two others. It easily lifted the two smaller team members and smashed them into one another. Orange ichor splattered the massive being and oozed to the blue manicured field.

"That had to hurt, Chip."

"Indeed Gleb, indeed," Chip agreed. *"But not as much as the spear through the officials head. That is not going to go well with the gaming commission.*

Golden blue Warning lights flashed as alarm klaxons exploded throughout the stadium.

It looks like...yes, Gleb. They have issued an evacuation order for the stadium and the containment squad has been activated."

"The producer is urging us to go to break ladies and gentlemen. We will be right back with the results and the takedown of Flox Deb, after these words from our sponsors."

Amanda wiped a tear from her cheek. "What the hell is wrong with the universe?" She turned away from the screen and easily spotted the door on the far wall. She pressed a glowing blue button mounted in the frame of the doorway. It slid open to reveal a corridor in painted in shades of white. The five burning stars of the system were clearly visible through the clear paneled wall of the curving corridor.

"Hey! Watch where you're going," a robotic voice squelched from the floor.

Amanda glanced down, looking for the source of the voice. "Oh my God! What...what the hell is that!" She quickly stepped back into the doorway as a squat, fleshy creature turned toward her. It had a soft and generally triangular in shape. Three tentacles protruded from the corner of each pastey pink lobe. Jagged mandibles surrounded by smaller manipulating tentacles dominated the squarish side that faced her. Six beady black dots that must have been eyes protruded slightly from either side of the mandibles.

"I said to watch where you're going," the robotic voice said. It whipped a tentacle in her direction, striking her on the side of the calf.

She stared in befuddled disbelief as the creature continued down the corridor. Another alien, roughly four-foot-tall with a fish-like mouth, hummed a tune as it approached. Its eyes were large dark orbs and its ears looked more like a fish fins than ears. It smiled wide, showing off a mouthful of thick squarish teeth.

"Good morning. How are you?" It nodded. "I don't believe that I have encountered your species before."

Amanda stared, unblinking, then nodded back. "Um...good...I suppose."

The alien stopped. Its smiled turned to a look of concern. "Are you in need of assistance? You do not look well," it said.

"I'm...I'm not quite sure yet," Amanda stammered. "I arrived with friends, but I just woke up in this room."

"Ahhhh," the alien said with a gurgled. "Your companions maybe be at the bar, just down the corridor and to the left," it said, pointing in the direction it had come from. "You can't miss it. Just look for the compartment with all of the noise and lights."

"Um...thank you for your help," Amanda said.

Its large, fin-like ears perked up as it smiled an inhuman smile. Its large square teeth protruding from its retracted fish-like lips.

"It was my pleasure." The alien bowed slightly. "My name is Kissack, should you again require my assistance."

Amanda slowly backed away, with a curt nod she turned and quickly went in the direction that the alien had pointed. Turning the corner at the end of the corridor, she stood before a doorway to another world. A menagerie of creatures filled the room; drinking, socializing, and chattering within the large, semi dark room. Flashing artificial light of video screens sickeningly illuminated portions of the room.

"You must be looking for your friends," a soft voice said from behind her.

Amanda turned to find a tall, slender, and unmistakably female being standing behind her. She was dressed in transparent strips of silk-like material that attached to the collar and belt that she wore. She was a purplish pink-hued humanoid with a triangular nose and prominent cheek ridges that continued to the edges of her nose.

"It's alright," the alien assured her. "No one is going to hurt you here. Are you looking for others like yourself?"

"Yes...yes, I suppose..." Amanda reluctantly stuttered.

The alien female smiled widely. "Please, follow me. I'll show you where they are." She continued into the establishment, her silken strips floating about her as she walked. They passed by dozens of alien creatures gathered about the bar who were occupied by the overwhelming number of video screens displaying strange sporting events. She led Amanda around the massive bar that took up the center of the room to the farthest corner of the compartment.

Andy twisted and pulled at something behind Denise's left ear with his trusty multi-tool. "I will return shortly with a complimentary house special to commemorate your first visit to the Vespa. Please enjoy your stay," the alien female said.

"Can't you go any faster?" Denise complained.

"I just can't quite get at it," Andy said.

"Well then either get it or quit already. It freaking hurts."

"Hang on," Andy said with a quick twist. "I've got it! Hold on. I just have to get it out of you, now." He placed his knee against Denise's shoulder and pulled.

"You Goddamn asshole!"

"Almost there!"

An audible sucking pop overshadowed the noise of the bar as the implant pulled free. Andy flew backward and sprawled onto the floor.

"Fuuuuuuuuuu hu hu hu hu ck! Oh shit. That hurt!" Denise held the side of her head and slammed back her drink.

"What the hell is wrong with you two?" Amanda glared at Denise.

"Other than getting low jacked and roofied? Not a damn thing. Life is otherwise just peachy." Denise reached across the table and snatched an unclaimed drink, chasing down the first drink with it.

"Are you kidding?" Andy asked as he stood. "Here ya go," he said, dropping a minuscule metallic oblong shaped thing on the table in front of Denise. He snatched the empty glass from Denise and slammed it down on the table with a frustrated huff.

He turned back to Amanda. "Once we woke up and found each other I did a scan to see what the aliens had done to us. I started picking up high readings of cobalt nitrate behind each of our left ears. Apparently, they low jacked everyone after gassing us in that chamber. So, I poked around at it with my pliers and eventually dug out my implant."

Amanda stared back at him in shocked disbelief. "Okay..."

"Better to be safe than sorry, I always say." Andy waived for a waitress, holding up his empty glass. "What if it was rigged to blow a hole in our heads if we didn't comply with our new alien master overlords or something? Then what would you do? Hu?"

Denise dug a finger into her ear and shook it about violently. "Dear God, what is that horrible squealing?"

"I know, I hear it too," Andy said. He craned his neck, looking in the direction of the noise.

"What squealing," Amanda asked.

"Oh, my fucking god! You don't hear that?" Denise pointed toward a group of aliens a few tables away. "Really? You seriously can't hear that?"

"I don't hear anything besides some random conversations," Amanda said.

"Here you go sweetie, compliments of the house," the waitress said to Amanda as she returned with a drink on a tray. She placed a napkin in front of Amanda, then a tall glass that contained a smoking fluorescent lime green liquid.

"Thank you very much," Amanda replied. "But I think I'll just have a water for right now if that's alright."

"Well now," the waitress said, taken aback. "I didn't peg you to be a big spender." She flashed a surprised smile at Amanda.

Denise tugged on Amanda's sleeve. "What the hell is she saying?"

"Hu? What?" Amanda mimed that she couldn't hear Denise and turned back to the waitress. "What do you mean, big spender?"

"You're kidding me, right?" The waitress laughed with a roll of her eyes. "A glass of plain water alone is worth over one hundred Polsion credits. It's even more expensive if you splurge and go for the top shelf spring water." She pointed to a series of clear vessels perched on the top shelf of the bar.

"What...the...hell...is...she...say...ing," Denise growled.

The waitress glared at Andy and the tool in his hand. He quickly hid the chip and multi-tool behind his back.

"I said you two are ignorant asses for taking out your translator chips," the waitress yelled.

"Well, excu...se, me," Denise said sarcastically. She snatched Amanda's drink and sipped at the exotic drink.

Amanda turned back to the waitress. "Is that a bad thing, that they removed their chips?"

The waitress grunted with another eye roll. "Only if you don't want to pay a fortune to have another one installed. The Polsions install the first implant free of charge in hopes that the investment will spur new business and add to the local economy by making transactions easier to accomplish. The more transactions carried out on the station, the more taxes that they can collect."

"Well, that makes a lot of sense, I guess," Amanda said.

"It won't take long before the newness of you lot wears off from the locals," the waitress admitted. "Pulling a stunt like taking out your implant will only annoy the rest of the people on the station."

"The newness off us," Amanda asked, "I don't understand? What's special about us?"

"Everyone on the station has heard about your arrival," the waitress giggled. She looked over Amanda with a sidelong leer. "It's rare that a ship shows up with unplanted crew. Then to top it all off, an entirely new species." She winked at Amanda.

"Hu," Amanda mumbled to herself.

"Did you still want that water?"

"Um...no," Amanda replied. "No, but thank you for all of your help."

"You are very welcome," the waitress said with a predatory smile. "It's always nice to meet a pretty new face. Just let me know if I can get you anything." She turned and began clearing empty glasses from a nearby table.

"Rude ass bitch," Denise mumbled, then took another sip from Amanda's glass.

"Seriously? Can you stop complaining and being a rude bitch yourself for just one second." Amanda scowled at Denise. "She was being very helpful."

"Not to me, she wasn't. You'd think she'd be able to speak plain English if she's going to serve us, but nooo. She had to go on with all of that weird-ass gobbledygook of hers."

"Ouch, shit, get it off," Andy said. He leapt from his seat frantically shaking his hand. The tiny translator implant landed on Denise's sleeve. Dozens of hair-like appendages extended from the tiny cylinder and began to climb her arm."

"Uh, help!" Denise screamed in panic, swatting at her arm. "Get it off! Get it off!" The chip bounced and skidded across the table. It stopped dead in mid slide as the needle-like tentacles impaled the tabletop to arrest its momentum. The implant spun in place for a moment and once again began toward Denise.

"Die, tool of Satan!" Andy smashed the device with the heel of his boot over and over again. The entirety of the bar turned toward the commotion at the back of the room.

Amanda shook her head in disbelief. "Something is seriously wrong with the two of you. You know that don't you?"

"Eh, it's all good. I've got free drinks." Denise smiled and took another sip.

"Ya know," Andy interrupted. "That big blue guy is still staring this way."

Amanda and Denise turned to look in the direction that Andy nodded. A very large and bright blue alien in what looked to be a flight suit of some sort curiously watched their every movement.

"Eh, it's a free country. He can look all that he wants." She choked as she took another sip. "Oh hey, there's a thought. I wonder what color he'd turn if you strangled him. Would he turn flesh-colored since he's already blue?"

"Oh hey," Andy scratched at his stubble covered chin. "That's a mighty good question."

"Could one of you please tell me where everyone else went to?" Amanda crossed her arms with an impatient huff.

"How the hell should I know? I'm not their keeper," Denise grumped.

The waitress returned with a tall, frosted glass of bubbling blue liquid. Using a set of long tongs, she placed the glass gently down in front of Denise. "From an admirer," she said with a nod toward the bar, then returned to her duties.

Denise immediately looked at Amanda. "What did she say?"

"If you'd left in the translator, you'd know." She scoffed. "Apparently someone bought you a drink."

Denise pushed the bubbling drink away. "Did she say what it is? I'm not sure that I want to try this one."

"Just take a sip and taste it. See what color it smells like," Andy suggested.

"What the hell," Amanda shook her head. "Did you pull a wire loose in your head when you yanked out the translator?"

"What? No...It's a well-known fact that smell and taste are tied together," Andy defended.

"Well hell. You only live once, I guess." Denise gripped the glass with two fingers and carefully lifted the bubbling concoction toward her face. She puffed at the misty white fog, then blew it away from the top of the glass and inhaled. "Hu...It doesn't smell too bad." Cautiously, she sipped. "Hey, this isn't bad at all," she said through smacking lips. She smiled and held up the glass in salute with a thumbs up in the direction of her large blue benefactor.

The blue alien returned the salute and held his drink high in the air.

"Hell, that's a first," Denise said scornfully.

"What's a first," Amanda asked.

"No one has ever bought me a drink before," Denise said. She blinked away a stray tear, wiped her eyes on the arm of her flight suit, then gulped down half of the alien drink in one gulp.

"You never know," Andy mused. He placed a gentle hand on Denise's shoulder. "It could be love at first sight." Andy abruptly doubled over, gasping for air after Denise's elbow firmly made contact with his unprotected midsection.

Denise continued to sip at the blue bubbling liquid.

"Oh my god, will you two quit it," Amanda said. "Do either of you have any actual idea at all where the others may have gone?"

"I think Janey said something about checking out the medical facilities," Andy said coughing between gasps of air.

"Big Willy seems like the type to be the boy scout and offer our services to the station manager." Denise took another long sip.

"I'd bet you could find Fergus and Trae in the hangars checking out the ships or shopping for new equipment," Andy added as he slid into a seat at the table.

"What about Jenny?"

"No idea," Denise said between sips. "I do know that she got thrown out of the bar a few hours ago for harassing the customers."

"What? Why?"

Denise laughed, then looked at Amanda with those, do you really want to know eyes. "That crazy bitch was so excited about all the different species in here that she started harassing everyone in the bar for information about themselves, their species and their languages."

"Any idea where she might have gone after she got thrown out?"

"Don't know and don't care," Denise said. "I just wish she'd stayed long enough to get the free drink so I could have snagged it too."

"Are you really sure those free drinks are even suitable for humans? I mean, look at them, they glow," Andy said.

"Eh, they taste fine," Denise said. "This one kinda tastes like a light purple."

"Oh, like lavender or more of a mauve?" Andy asked.

"Neither," Denise said. "It has this slight tingle to it. So more like a," she smacked her lips together, "maybe an electric purple."

"I swear," Amanda huffed. She turned to leave and ran face-first into the chest of a large, leather-clad being. She craned her neck back to look up at a very large blue-faced alien that smiled down at her.

"Well hello there little one," the blue alien said in a smooth baritone voice.

"Hello," she said, smiling back.

He turned his attention toward Denise and smiled even wider. "Do you mind if I stare at you up close, instead of from across the room?"

Denise looked at the blue alien, completely confused, then to Amanda. "What did he say?"

"Um...I think I'll let you figure that out for yourself." Amanda nodded a smile at the blue alien. "Please, excuse me," she said, then sidestepped the large alien and headed for the bar entrance.

"Dammit! Traitor," Denise shouted after Amanda. She looked back toward the big blue alien. "What the hell do you want?"

"Blurrrrbb branthata groool bant." He raised an eyebrow and winked at Denise with a cheesy, big-toothed smile.

"Oh really? You really want to go there, do ya?"

"Duratha pa groooom," he whispered seductively as he sat in a seat at the table.

Denise held up her hand, rubbing her thumb and forefinger together, making what she thought was the universal sign for cash with an expectant gaze.

The large blue alien excitedly smiled and fumbled through the pockets of his flight suit. He produced a small golden-red bar of metal, stamped with strange hieroglyphic markings.

"Sure...Why not. What the hell do I have to lose," she said, then guzzled the remainder of her drink and snagged the bar of metal from the table. "Alright, papa smurf. Up and at em' if you want to complete this transaction then let's get the show on the road," she said, motioning for him to lead the way.

Andy sat quietly at the table, picking at a dark spot under a fingernail while watching the dozens of video displays around the room.

cHAPTER 55

Eltanin 2
Mel's Diner
September 18th, 2176 / Evening (Dragon time)

"I thought that was just a rumor," Doug said. "You seriously shut down the environmental systems for Mars station Alpha, to stop a riot? They must have known that their balls were in a vice just as soon as the circulation fans shut down." Doug blinked in amazement. "It had to be pretty bad for you to go to an extreme like that."

"Yup, it was," the Chief admitted. "It was the only way to shut everyone up and get them working together for a change. Sometimes an extreme measure is the only measure that will set things straight, but I think that you already know that." He sipped at a cup of dark coffee. "Granted, that was all before Sadowitz took over the place and turned it into his personal shrine to Hitler." The chief's brow furrowed. "It's strange...His fanaticism was so addictive and total to the colonists that it swept through the Martian colonies in under a year. In something like nine months to the day that he accepted office as the colony overseer, Mars declared their independence from Earth, the I.A. and all Earth governments. Even the damned Chinese colony signed on to be part of the Martian Reich."

"Did they willingly join, or do you think they were pressed into service," Doug asked.

"I really don't know, and I never had the care to ask," the Chief said. After all of that hard work that me and my crew put into establishing those colonies on Mars, they were useless to us and to the mission. The I.A. decided that it wasn't worth the resources to take over the colonies by force and they shifted my mission focus to establishing the Jupiter and Saturn satellite colonies."

"Are we late, boss man?" Danny and Chris trotted into the cantina.

"Good, I was hoping you'd be the first to show up," Doug said, then stood. "Help me to drag these tables together," he said as he moved the homemade chairs away from a nearby table.

"You got it, boss man," Danny said as he and Chris hopped to work.

"What in the friggin' hell do you think you're doing? I'll have work crews here in less than an hour for chow and you want to go and rearrange the place on me?" Mel glared at them from the entrance to the kitchen with her hands on her hips.

"It's only for a little while. The diner is the closest thing that we have to a meeting area, and it is by far the largest area with tables," Doug said.

"Ya know, at the rate things are progressing, it wouldn't be a bad idea to set up a real command center," the Chief added.

"We've already started on one, but it was put on hold because of the away mission. Lizz already has the beginnings of an Overseer's office. It'll just take a little time and extra hands to complete."

"What the fuck ever!" Melanie threw her hands up into the air and huffed back into the kitchen. "Just put it all back when you're finished," she shouted from the kitchen.

"Well now, would you look at that," Doug said, smiling.

The Chief turned to see Wes enter the cantina, cane on one side, Kara on the other with Tiff, Krista, and Maggie close behind as he shuffled forward one small step at a time.

"Wesley, you are looking strong and very much on the mend," Bob said as he and Lizz entered the diner behind the small group.

"Good, you made it," Doug said. "I'd like to introduce you all to our new senior crewmember." He stood behind the Chief and patted his shoulder. "He has had more experience establishing new colonies than all of us combined. His methods of solving problems and making things work may lean a bit toward the unorthodox, but they have worked well for him in the past. It might be a little bit of a shock to a few of you once you find out who he is, but after reviewing his experience and credentials, I think he'll be a great addition to our colonization efforts."

Rachel wheeled herself through the doorway and skidded to a stop behind Wes. "Come on already, man! Move it, gimp boy, you're holding me up. I've got a freaking meeting to get to. Beep beep mother fucker!"

"Cap, remember what I told you about that one," the Chief warned as he stood from the table.

"Relax, Chief. Rachel, mouth shut and stay where you are," Doug ordered.

"But Cap," she argued.

"Eh! Zip it Cheezy."

Wes laughed between snorts and gasping breaths. "He just told you!"

"Shush it gimpy." Rachel glared at Wes as he took a seat at the table.

"Alright then, back to business," Doug said. "I believe that you all know the Chief from his pain in the ass moments through the years," Doug motioned to the young, but white-haired gentleman seated next to him. "He is also known as John D. Thomas. The same John Thomas that established most of the colonies back home in the Sol system."

"Yes! I freaking knew it," Rachel cheered.

"Zip it, crazy lady," the Chief demanded. "If I walk, I'll personally make sure you live the rest of your days in paranoid hell, missy."

Doug cleared his throat and continued. "The chief will be assisting and advising on all projects to help establish our foothold in the Gamma Draconis system and especially here on Eltanin 2. Danny, Chris," he said, turning to the two mechanics at the table. "I especially want you two to work directly with the Chief to get the *Ethel* fully operational. The sooner that she's up and running at full refining capacity, the sooner that we can start retrofitting the other ships with flux drives. Geek, Cheezy, I need you two working to fully integrate our systems with the alien tech that we are salvaging from the Reds and the cat cruiser."

Rachel let out a muffled squeal through her clenched fists that were firmly planted to her face.

"Last chance crazy lady," the Chief warned as he stood again.

"Rachel! Please, we need him," Doug pleaded.

She pouted. "Sorry, Cap."

"Chief, please." Doug motioned to the empty seat at the table. "Kara, Lizz, I need you to put together a shift and delivery schedule. Set up a rotation for the research teams out in the field also. Work with Mel to make sure everyone has downtime and can get to chow without a problem."

"It would be an absolute pleasure to work with a living legend," Lizz said with a beaming smile. "Welcome aboard Mr. Thomas."

"Uh...Yes, welcome Chief," Bob stammered.

"Oh. Well now. I look forward to helping out in any way that I can." He nervously smiled back at Lizz.

Doug continued. "Tiff, have you made any progress on how to rearm or upgrade the satellite network?"

"It'll just take time," Tiff sighed. "We can easily build and replace the missiles from the satellites. But for the time being, there are some that are still armed."

"I made sure to disengage all of the defensive systems with unresponsive or inactive warheads," Wes added. "When Fergus and Trae get back, they can start pulling those for repair. Otherwise, we have a few hundred missiles still viable within the network."

Tiff smiled longingly at the Chief. "Thank you again for what you did, Chief. You didn't have to do anything, but you did it anyway."

"Wasn't nothing," the Chief said. "It just wouldn't be right to stand by and let assholes like them do whatever they wanted to do." He smiled.

"Still," Tiff said. "Thank you."

"Eh, no worries," he said shrugging it off.

"Alright," Doug started. "Witches...,"

"What in the hell do you think that you're doing?" A cooking pan bounced across the floor from the kitchen area. "I already told you, you little shit. You can't have any more cheese. You'll wait till chow time like everyone else."

"You okay in there, Mel?" Doug yelled toward the kitchen.

"Yes...this damn critter cat likes to help but she's munching more than she's freaking working."

"Okay...Anything we need to do to help?"

"No! Thank you. Sorry to interrupt," Melanie replied.

"You're welcome..." Doug looked at the faces staring back at him around the table. "Okay, where was I?"

Krista held up a finger in the air and waggled it with a smirk.

"Oh, right, Witches," Doug said, remembering.

"Oh, we are good to go, Cap. There's nothing that we can't handle on our end. It's all rainbows and butterflies all day long," she said nervously and smiled as she rocked back and forth on her heels. Maggie looked at her with an incredulous glare.

"Still," Doug continued. "The Chief helped to figure out how to grow sustainable crops in every environment possible back home. Our rations will only last for so long and the planet is limited on edible resources. Since we have no idea how long the away team will be, we have to ration and make do with what we have."

"Naw...It's all good," Krista waived as if it were nothing. "Me and Maggie have got this. It'll all be golden in the end." She bundled herself into her cloak and slumped down in her seat.

"We could use some help building additional planting areas," Maggie interjected. "The raised beds that we had already built were planted with...um..," she hesitated, "medicinal plants."

Doug glared beams at Krista.

"What," Krista said defensively with a shrug. "I didn't know we'd be stranded here. I was just working on restocking our medicine cabinet."

Doug gently massaged the bridge of his nose. "So, you haven't planted any of the food crop seeds that we brought from Earth?"

"Yes," Maggie excitedly volunteered. "We have garlic planted and thriving already."

Wes let out a hysterical cacophony of choking laughter. "Well, at least we won't have to worry about any sparkly vampires coming to get any of us."

Doug's fingers worked their way around to the sides of his head and dug into his temples. "So, what exactly do you currently have planted?"

"Like she said," Krista pointed toward Maggie. "It's all medicinal."

Doug abruptly stopped, glaring up past a furrowed brow.

"Oh alright...fine," Krista sighed. "Hemp, poppy, valerian, coca, peyote, jimson, motherwort, a few species of mushrooms and some other odds and ends."

Murmurs of *holy shit* and *what the hell* escaped from around the table.

"No worries Cap, I've got this," the Chief reassured. "Challenge accepted," he said with a self-assured, smug smile and a gleam in his eye.

"Should I recruit a narcotics officer on the next Earth run," Lizz mused.

"No," Doug said, letting out a long sigh. "At least not yet. There's no telling what we may need in the future, though."

"The hole," Rachel shouted.

Everyone at the table turned and stared at Rachel.

"Hu," Doug groaned.

"That's what we should officially name this place," Rachel said, slapping the tabletop for emphasis. "The boomer crews have already been calling it the Troll Hole instead of the Dragon's Lair. The Hole just rolls smoothly off the tongue in my opinion." She held her right hand as high above her head as she could. "I nominate the official designation for our underground base to be, *the Hole*. All in favor," she said in a hopeful tone.

"Aye," came a few voices from around the table.

"Aye," Doug said reluctantly. "Okay, are you happy Cheezy?"

"Yup," she said and happily bounced in her seat.

"Okay, anyway, back to the real business," Doug continued. "Bob, I'd like you to work with Tiff and the new girl, Becky. Take a few of the new grunts that we picked up on the last Earth run and see what you can come up with for permanent accommodations for everyone. We'll expand as we need to, but for now, let's try to keep things in as close to the core as possible. Let's use every bit of space to the best of our ability. We also want to make sure that we share everything that we can with the cats. This was their place first and it's only right to share anything we have with them. We aren't the British empire or the East India trading company."

The clatter of metal pots tumbling to the ground echoed from the kitchen. "That's friggin' it! That's it! Get out of my kitchen! You...are...done!"

"That is if Mel doesn't kill them all first," Doug said with a laugh. "Do we all know what we're doing?" He looked around the table at slow nods of yes or the occasional thumbs up and smiled. "Good. Dismissed, now get to work. Chief, Cheezy," Doug commanded. "You'll both be having a private dinner with Lizz and me on the *Betty*. Seventeen hundred hours and no excuses.

Jeers and catcalls came from the others as they exited the cantina.

"Yes sir," Rachel belted out, then wheeled herself away from the table.

"Aye Cap," the Chief responded with a brisk and cocky salute.

cHAPTER 56

Sarin star system
Polsion Space Station
Operations office
September 18th, 2176 / Late Evening (Dragon time)

"No, that's not it at all, sir," Trae said to the blue-tinted possum-like Polsion. We don't want to press charges or file a grievance. We're just trying to get into touch with this race." He held up a picture of a Sasquatch like alien against the thick glass wall that surrounded the station's security desk.

"So, then it's revenge that you seek?" The small Polsion hissed.

"No man, you aren't listening," Fergus said. "See these great big sasquatch looking, guys…"

"Pickup order number eleven," a voice boomed over the station intercoms. *"Pickup order number eleven, pikka glazed grig rolls is ready at the window."*

"Rohʙandī," the Polsion said.

"What?" Fergus looked at Trae.

"Their race is called the Rohʙandī," the Polsion repeated.

"Okay, now we're getting somewhere," Trae said.

"So, like I was saying, these Rohʙandī, have been lurking around Casraownan's homeworld and they attacked a ship full of his people…"

"Then I was correct. It is revenge that you seek?"

"No," Casraownan growled as he stepped up to the glass. "If you would shut your mouth and listen to what they are…"

"Whoa, hold on there, Cass, ol' buddy," Trae said, grabbing Casraownan by the arm. "Calm down. It's not worth getting arrested for."

"Naw, it ain't," Fergus said, grabbing Casraownan by the other arm. "Trust me. I've spent enough time in space station brigs to know."

"Listen, we are looking for them to find out what they want and what they know about Cass's people," Trae said. "If any of the Rohʙandī come to the station, could you please pass this on to them?" Trae held up a small data chip. "It has a message from our Captain to their people and includes all of the data that we have on them so far and the coordinates for Cass's homeworld.

The Polsion nodded and pressed a control on its station. A small panel on the front of the security desk slid away from the outside of the counter and opened to reveal an empty compartment.

"Please place the device in the tray."

Trae placed the data chip in the compartment and held up a folded piece of paper. "These are the electrical schematics for the data device. It might help you in accessing the data," he said, placing the paper in the compartment with the chip.

"We should not have an issue accessing your technology, but the gesture is duly noted." The Polsion officer nodded and pressed a control on its station, retracting the compartment. It turned and resumed watching the numerous feeds displayed behind the desk.

"There you guys are," Amanda said. "I've been looking all over for you. Please tell me that you didn't go brain dead like Denise and Andy."

"What does brain dead mean?" Casraownan asked, scratching his head.

"Oh my," Amanda said in a surprised tone. "You can talk."

"Well yeah," Fergus said. "He could talk before; we just couldn't understand him."

"Yes, Aaamanda," Casaroawnan said in a yowling cat-like tone. "I can understand you and speak your language now.

Thank you for all of the times that you have occupied my son, Jouqon, while his mother and I could learn your language from Lizz."

"I'm happy to lend a hand," she said shyly.

"These translators are some amazing technology," Trae said. I can't wait for the chance to take one apart and see how it works."

"Well, you might have a few to look at already," Amanda said. "Andy took his and Denise's chips out. The waitress wasn't too happy with them."

"As long as they don't get us kicked off the station I don't care. Now Big Willy, on the other hand, he might leave them behind just because they looked at him wrong."

"Oh…" Fergus laughed. "You mean like the time when Willy left Andy behind in Boston? That was hilarious."

"Bossston…," Casraownan said in a quizzical tone.

"Don't worry none about it," Fergus said. "Cap made us turn around and go back to get him, unfortunately.

"Have you found out anything on the Reds?"

"Rohʙandī," Fergus corrected.

"Ro..hu?

"Rohʙandī," Trae said. "That's what their race is known as. There are currently no Rohʙandī ships in port though. So, I left a data chip with a message for the Rohʙandī at this security desk," he said, thumbing toward the desk behind him. "Speaking of which…" Trae turned and knocked on the glass enclosing the security desk. "Hey, do I get a receipt for that?"

The station intercoms popped and suddenly came to life. *"Attention Bigmart shoppers! The store is now officially closed. You ain't gotta go home, but ya can't stay here!"*

Trae and Fergus turned to each other with looks of horror.

"Was that Denise?"

"Yeah, I'm pretty sure it was," Trae said as he began walking away from the security desk. He turned but continued walking backward. "Cass, Amanda, you two take a different route back to the ship. We'll meet you there."

"Wait? Why? What's Wrong?"

"Trust me," Fergus said, following behind Trae. "My spidey senses are pinging big time, man. I'm pretty damned sure that things just went sideways six ways from Sunday."

"Yup, I'm pretty sure that you're right," Trae said and turned to face the direction he was walking.

"But how do we get back to the ship?"

"Just follow Cass," Trae said. "He knows where the ship is."

Amanda looked up at Casraownan. "You know how to get to the ship?"

"I do," he said with a wide feline smile.

Sarin star system
Polsion Space Station
The Vespa Bar and Grill
September 18th, 2176 / Late Evening (Dragon time)

Denise collapsed into her previous seat at the table with Andy. She laid her head down on crossed arms and let out a painful moan. She cringed as a guttural alien voice boomed over the station's intercoms. "Have you even moved from here?"

"Nope." Andy barely glanced away from the multitude of alien sporting events displayed on the myriad of screens around the bar. "So, what happened to you," Andy asked without looking away. He crushed the paper-thin, magenta shell of an alien *bar nut* and fished out the meaty red chunks from the crushed shell.

Denise groaned as she slowly rubbed the back of her neck. "I could really go for a drink right now."

"Is that good or that bad?" Andy asked without looking away from the video screens.

"What happened to you?" Willy asked, taking a seat at the table.

"Papa smurf," she moaned.

Willy shook his head and looked at her questioningly. "What?"

Andy chuckled. "You really *do not* want to know, Willy. Hell, I didn't want to know. But there I was, minding my own business when this massive blue alien guy offered her a bar of something." He crushed another hand full of alien bar nuts and blindly fished for the tasty bits without looking away from the screens.

"Okay, okay, I can, unfortunately, see what you're getting at." Willy leaned back in the chair and crossed his arms. He shook his head in an attempt to shake the image loose from his mind.

"Excuse me, sir," an odd warbling voice said. Willy turned to see an anxious and disgustingly bulbous pig-faced individual approach their table. Wringing its hands, it smiled an ivory yellow smile.

"Oh my god, why does it sound like a pig is rooting around at the table?" Denise looked up in the direction of the noise. "Hu. Well, would you look at that."

"Can I help you," Willy said, turning in his seat to face the bulbous faced alien.

"Yes sir. I was wondering...or well, I was told...um..."

"What the hell is it saying?" Denise looked up through blurry, half squinting eyes then buried her head back into her folded arms.

"Why can't you understand him," Willy asked. "You got the same implant as the rest of us."

"Because I took out both of our implants," Andy said matter-of-factly through a pasty mouthful of the alien nuts.

Willy sighed, then turned back to the alien. "Listen, I don't have all day. Spit it out if you're going to."

"Um...Well, you see...um...well...I was told that the madam here was accepting new clientele and was told to offer her this as compensation." The alien held out a large gold bar that clanked heavily as he placed it on the table's metal surface.

Willy looked at Denise with a wavering certainty that the universe had lost all control of its senses. "That's it, I'm going back to the ship," he leapt to his feet and quickly walked away from the table.

The alien nervously cleared his throat.

"I think he's waiting for an answer," Andy said, laughing, then continued to loudly open mouth chewed the taffy-like nuts.

"Nada mas," Denise shook her head and grasped the golden bar, sliding it into her sleeve. "Nada, nein, no, zip, zilch, zero," she formed the shape of a zero with a hand then laid her head back down on the cool surface of the table. "Go away," she said into her arms, waiving away the alien.

The young alien grunted something in a snorting grunt, and she looked back up at it. "Hey buddy, what did I just say? I'm not talking just to hear myself. Fuck off." She gestured with a middle finger salute, then returned her head to its previously buried position.

The alien exhaled sharply, then spun on his heels and walked away.

"Um..." Andy stopped chewing as he watched the young alien speaking to others of its kind on the other side of the bar. "Um...hey, you," he nudged Denise. "Shit, what was your name again?"

"*Whaaaa*at, the hell do you want? I just want to rest," Denise groaned.

"I'm not sure but I think you might have pissed off that last guy's dad or something," Andy said.

Denise groaned "Why do you say that?" The words muffled through her folded arms.

"Do you hear what sounds like a pissed-off pig?"

"Yeah," she lifted her head and glanced around.

"Well, it's coming from that big guy over there that the last guy you told to piss off went crying too. He kinda looks pissed. And big. Really freaking big."

Denise looked up to see the young alien demonstrating her motion of flipping him off to the large alien. "Oh shit, he's coming this way. Time to go!" She jumped to her feet, snagging Andy by the collar.

"Hold on, wait, wait, wait." Andy pulled against her. He quickly grabbed the two bowls of alien bar nuts from the table and dumped them into the breast pockets of his flight suit.

"Fine. Fuck you," she released his collar. "I'm outta here."

The large alien bellowed something unintelligible from across the bar that caused others to scatter.

Denise pushed the waitress at the bar aside and leapt onto the counter, reaching for the announcement microphone. She gulped down a panicked breath. "Attention Bigmart shoppers! The store is now officially closed. You ain't gotta go home, but ya can't stay here!"

Andy ran by as Denise leapt back down from the counter and sprinted for the entrance. A roar rumbled across the room from the pig-like rhino alien. The pair turned the first corner in the corridor and took off at a full sprint.

"Make way," Denise yelled as she spotted Willy ahead of them down the long corridor to the docking ring.

"Willy!" Andy said gasping for air. "Big...Alien...probe."

Willy turned toward the commotion just as Andy and Denise sprinted past him.

"Stop them!" The massive rhino pig alien shouted as he rounded the corner and barreled into the corridor. Willy braced himself, standing his ground he crouched like a center on the offensive line. The large alien charged headlong down the corridor. Willy exploded forward in a blur of motion. His massively large sausage fist found itself wrapped around the thickly chorded neck of the alien creature. Willy leaned back and to the right using the alien's momentum. He vaulted the alien over his shoulder, choke slamming him to the deck. The alien's muscular body went immediately limp.

Two other rhino pig aliens rounded the corner, pointing weapons of some sort at Willy. The unmistakable electrical discharge of a mass thrower resounded through the corridor as slug crashed into the bulkhead just above Willy's head.

The charging capacitors of the alien weapons whined in the confined space.

"Time to go!" Willy turned. High stepping his way over the unconscious hulk he continued down the corridor. "Go," he shouted ahead to Andy and Denise as they rounded the next turn.

Willy skidded to the right at the next corridor junction, just missing two large Sasquatch-like creatures, crashing headlong into Fergus. His momentum carried the two of them across the open space where they impacted the far wall, denting the cover plates.

"See! I told you I didn't have to outrun a Bear," Trae said as he charged through the intersection at a full run.

"We might want to leave, like now," Denise yelled back over her shoulder.

"Dammit, Willy! You owe me a bottle of scotch," Fergus groaned.

"Just shut up and run, Ferg!" Willy pushed his massive bulk upright and continued behind Trae.

Andy stood at the docking hatch to the ship, pistol in hand aiming down the corridor. He lobbed a pump shotgun into the air in Trae's direction as he approached. Trae caught the sawed-off shotgun in flight, turned and slid to a crouched halt before the ship's airlock.

"Make way!" Fergus barreled around the final turn, bouncing off of the far wall.

Big Willy rounded the corner following close behind. The deck plating shook and rattled with each of Willy's heavy booted steps.

"Go get her fired up," Willy ordered Andy. "It's time to blow this joint."

Fergus snatched the pistol from Andy's hand just as he turned to run into the ship.

"What the hell did you do Denise?" Willy panted, glaring in her direction as he slowed to a stop.

"I didn't do anything!" She hid just inside the airlock.

"Bullshit! You had to have done something," Trae said.

"Wait," Willy started, "what did that one guy want that was at the table when I left?"

"How the hell am I supposed to know? I can't understand their pig snorting grunts," Denise said.

"She told him to fuck off," Andy said through the airlock speaker. *"Engines online, Willy."*

"Goddammit Denise," Willy yelled. "We're supposed to be making allies, not enemies."

"So fucking sue me," she grumbled. "I wasn't up for another round and he kinda looked like a disgusting, pimple-faced Quasimodo anyways. I know it's hard to believe, but I do have some standards!"

"Wait? What the hell are you talking about? Another round," Willy asked.

"Some big blue guy paid her a bar of gold or something earlier," Andy said.

Trae broke out into hysterical laughter. The barrel of his gun touched the floor as his knees gave way. He fitfully wiped tears from his eyes.

"You're fucking, serious," Fergus said. He straightened, pointing his pistol at Denise's head. "We go aboard our first alien space station and you start turning tricks? Who the hell does that? Seriously? Even I'm not *that* stupid." His face contorted as he shrugged and shook his head in disbelief.

A bulbous alien head popped around the corner of the corridor, then disappeared. Trae's laughter was instantly replaced by the cacophonous sound of a twelve-gauge double-ought round fired in the confined space. The emergence of buckshot coincided with the reemergence of the bulbous alien head around the corner. Purplish blood splattered across the junction and the body slumped to the deck. Trae racked the slide and loaded round. The second alien appeared, then stopped and blankly stared down at his companion as his own chest exploded in a gout of purplish ichor.

"Don't shoot," wailed a high-pitched voice from down the corridor.

"Hey now," Janey shouted, peeking around the corner of the intersection, opposite of the second alien.

"Come on," Fergus waved. "We gotta get!"

Janey dashed around the corner, dragging a sobbing Amanda behind her followed by Casraownan. "What the hell is going on?" She shoved Amanda ahead and through the doorway. "Get on board and don't argue." She turned back toward the alien bodies, knelt and checked their necks for a pulse. "Dead as far as I can tell." She produced tissues from her lab coat and wiped up some of the purple splatter from each of the aliens, then dashed for the docking hatch.

"Hurry up, everyone in," Trae ordered as he crouch walked backward. His gun pointed down the corridor. Fergus mashed the intercom button. "We're on."

"Getting clearance now," Willy replied over the comms. *"The bastards don't want to let us loose till we pay the docking fees."*

"Make way," a female voice yelled from around the corner of the corridor intersection.

"What in the hell is that," Fergus asked Trae.

"Someone please help! Stop this insane female," a robotic voice shouted from the speaker mounted to a hovering cart that appeared in the corridor. A man-sized willow tree in full floral bloom was firmly planted in the cart, its branches clawed and scraped at the sides of the corridor as the tree and cart barreled headlong toward the airlock. The cart bounced and bucked over the alien bodies that littered the intersection.

"I said make a hole! You big burly manly men could give me a damned hand with this thing." The calm and collected demeanor of Jenny, the ship's linguist now looked more like a wild-eyed maniac. Her neat and tidy schoolmarm bun had exploded into a frazzle of curly locks that floated about, framing her angelic, but strained face.

Trae and Fergus backed against the side of the corridor. They both sucked in their stomachs to allow the cart to freely pass. Three of the possum like aliens appeared at the far end of the corridor. They sprinted for the hatchway. "Cease and desist! Release the It'Vit ambassador!"

"Time to close it up, Ferg!" Trae turned and quickly sprinted through the hatchway.

"On it," Fergus shouted. He smacked the airlock close button then pressed the comms button on the control panel. "All aboard Willy. Get us out of here."

"Please help me," the willow tree begged through the cart's speaker. *"This creature has disabled my carriage and assaulted my person!"* Its whip-like branches shook with furious frustration.

"Sorry there Woody, but you're on your own for right now," Fergus said. He tucked the pistol into the back of his waistband and turned to leave. "We'll figure out what to do with you later.

"We've got bigger issues to deal with at the moment," Trae added, following behind Fergus. "Stay out of the way and we won't turn you into firewood."

"Oh my god, I forgot about that," Jenny forcefully slapped herself in the side of the head. "Do not tell me what it is saying," she pointed a threatening but shaky finger at Trae and then to Fergus. "I want to learn how it communicates on my own." She let out a laughing cackle. "Oh my...to learn the body language of a nonverbal species and to be able to carry on a full conversation without ever uttering a word." She excitedly sighed.

"You can't understand it?" Trae asked with an incredulous look.

"Oh god no," she shook her fuzzy mane with a look of utter disgust. "As soon as Mr. Andy said that he could remove the translator implant, I gladly let him remove it.

"Brilliant! Just fucking brilliant," Trae shouted at the ceiling. He laughed so hard that he began to cry. "Well you're just a great big ball of sane awesomeness, aren't you?"

"Hold onto something," Willy bellowed over the intercoms. *"Missiles inbound! We're gonna try to break loose from the station."*

Bulkheads creaked and popped as the vibration of the engines increased throughout the hull.

"Go! Out of the docking bay! Now," Trae ordered.

A dull tone rumbled through the framework of the ship. Something large impacted the outer hull. The momentum of the ship as she lurched forward countered the weak field of the anti-gravity generators. Trae, Fergus, Jenny and the alien willow plant creature soared across the compartment. They surged aft, impacting with a rear bulkhead. The *Veronica* suddenly jinked sideways with a violent explosion. They flew across the room once more as the nose of the ship dove and rolled downward, sliding starboard with a sickening lurch.

cHAPTER 57

Gamma Draconis System
Eltanin 2
Dig site Alpha
September 19th, 2176 / Early Evening (Dragon time)

Long shadows of early evening stretched across the parched desert of Eltanin 2. Pounding pulses of thrust propelled Doug and his hoverbike forward at breakneck speed. Dust billowed behind him in the form of a twenty-foot tall, swirling rooster tail. He dropped the throttle and the pulsing audibly slowed, lowering the tone as he approached the site. Doug lurched forward, bracing himself against the handlebars as the speed brakes deployed, causing instantaneous drag to slow the bike's forward moment to a crawl. He directed the bike alongside the ancient, but well-preserved station wagon.

"Hey there Mr. Rackham," Benjamin Swanson greeted with a wave. "I didn't expect to see you out this way." He sat on the open tailgate of his ancient, 1990's era Buick Roadmaster. It's white paint and plastic wood grain panels looked new and unblemished in the Draconian sun.

"How in the hell did you get that land barge this far out in all of this loose sand?" Doug lowered the landing gear and switched off the bike's pulse drive.

"Well, I had a few upgrades done to her to accommodate most possible terrains that I might find myself working in. She has a hover mode, deployable floats for river work, multiple options on the wheel treads. The upgrades have easily paid for themselves over the years."

"I'm sure of that, seeing as you're way out here." Doug removed his helmet and gloves then dismounted the bike.

Walls of the same concrete-like material protruded above drifts of sand in neat rows on either side of the area. "Hu..."

"I know," Ben replied. "Kinda scary how similar it looks to something back on Earth, isn't it?"

"Yeah," Doug gasped. "This is a suburban neighborhood, isn't it?" He turned back to Ben, who cleaned the dust from his glasses.

"Yes sir, that it is," Ben proudly answered.

"Well, I'll be damned." He slowly turned, taking in the extent of the neighborhood from this vantage point.

"Well, you didn't come all this way just to chit chat and take in the sights, Captain." Ben carefully slid his dark-rimmed glasses back onto his face and stood, tucking a handkerchief into his back pocket. "What can I do for you?"

"Honestly?" He grinned at the archaeologist's straightforwardness. "I just needed to get out for a ride to clear my head and your little operation just happened to be a nice, convenient excuse."

"I can understand that completely," he said, nodding.

"I did have one request for you," Doug said.

"Absolutely Captain. Shoot."

"The Cats have shown interest in everything that we have done so far," Doug said. "I'd like to include a few of them on your dig team if we can get them out on the surface. They have been underground their entire lives, so it will take time or some specialized gear to get them out here any time soon. That being said, are you up for the task otherwise?"

"I think that's a wonderful idea, Captain," Ben said. "I'd be happy to take a few of them under my wing to help them reconnect with their past."

"Good. I'll get Willy working on some goggles or something when he gets back," Doug said. "So, what directed your efforts all the way out here? We've gotta be a good twenty klicks from the hole," Doug said. He tucked away his helmet and gloves into a saddlebag.

"Well, Wes was able to do an aerial survey for us with the satellite network. We initially surveyed the area around the hole, but nothing really stood up and screamed at us. Once we expanded the search with the full battery orbital scans, we noticed that this area north of the base had an odd depression compared to the rest of the surrounding landscape. Come on, I'll show you," he said motioning for Doug to follow him. "It'll just be easier to show you what we've already found."

"How well are you and your team adapting to the environment," Doug asked, following closely behind.

"Things couldn't be better," Ben said excitedly. "Camille is an amazing champ on these outings. I couldn't do the work I do without her fine-tuning the operation from behind the scenes," Benjamin admitted. "And then there's my mother, Glenda. She keeps both of us in line and keeps track of the essentials so that Camille and I can focus on the data collection."

"Wait? Your mother is a member of your research team?"

"Absolutely," he smiled. "She's an essential part of the equation as far as I'm concerned." He nudged his glasses back up onto the bridge of his nose.

"Oh, hey there Captain Rackham," Camille said as she exited the field tent and waved. "What brings you way out here?"

"Just getting some fresh air and a change of scenery," Doug politely replied.

"We're having baked fish with fresh key lime pie for lunch if you'd like to join us," Camille offered.

Doug blinked in disbelief and looked around at the desolate, dry surroundings then turned back to Ben, and back to Camille. "Baked fish and fresh key lime pie?" He shifted uncomfortably and scratched at nearly a day's worth of stubble on his chin. "I know that it's only been a few days, but I have to ask. You have been drinking enough water and staying out of the direct sunlight as much as possible, haven't you?"

"Water," Camille said questioningly. "What's that Captain?"

Ben burst out in a full gut chuckle. "I'm so sorry, Camille," he pleaded. "That innocent look on your face had me and I couldn't hold it in."

"I just couldn't help myself, Captain," Camille said apologetically. "Yes, we have been staying hydrated and out of the direct sunlight as much as possible, and you did hear me correctly a moment ago. Glenda is making baked fish and fresh key lime pie. Or at least as fresh as vacuum-sealed and freeze-dried will allow her to use."

"Oookay then," Doug sighed. "That makes so much more sense now." He laughed and smiled back at Camille. "You had me worried for a moment there."

"Come on, Captain. Let me show you what we've found so far." Benjamin continued down the sand filled street for twenty meters and then turned left down a light slope, between what looked to be the remains of two residential homes. "What we found on the initial survey really struck me as odd. The other times that I'd seen a depression like this on orbital scans it had been an ancient trash pit or a collapsed section of an underground tunnel. Now, you have all of these structures that look like residential housing in this area," he said, pointing back up the slope toward the ruins. "And down here, you have this large, multilevel structure," he pointed off to the left to the ruins of a larger building. Two other researchers waived back at the pair as they continued their tour.

Doug waved back. "How goes it, guys?"

"We think this large structure may have been a community center or possibly even the equivalent of a church." Ben's shoulders slumped as he let out a long, frustrated sigh. "I have to admit that I've based my speculations of this area on similar Earth-based community layouts. But those are human designs on Earth. Really, until we learn more about the previous incarnation of Chinchassan society, we can only speculate."

"From what I see here, I think you are on the right track," Doug said. "My first guess as I rode in was that it was a neighborhood. It would make sense that a structure like that in the middle of all of this would be a church or other community type building. You're doing a great job that I can see so far." He put a hand on the young man's shoulder and squeezed in reassurance. "Anything that you find will help us to better understand what happened here and tell the Chinchasans about their past. So, what else did you find?"

"Oh, right," Benjamin said excitedly. He smiled and pushed up his glasses again. "This is the exciting part." He hurriedly made his way over toward a tarp, erected against the side of the large structure. "What we have here isn't just any old neighborhood. Something happened. Maybe it's only coincidence, but before we even set up camp I started poking around inside of the large structure and found this." He removed the lid on a wooden box to reveal a bright white, cat-like skull. He picked up the ancient collection of bones and held it out for Doug to see more closely.

"That is odd," Doug said slowly, taken aback. "When we first arrived, I sent Trae and Fergus to investigate the hanger doors. At the base of the section that they were clearing sand from, they found dozens of skeletons."

"Really," Benjamin gasped with delight. "Oh my, that will drastically change my base model for this excavation. I'll have to examine the remains if they are still available." His face contorted with a questioning look. "It almost makes me think that something really bad happened here a long time ago and time has just washed it all away."

"Yeah," Doug sighed in agreement.

Flux Point Foxtrot
Location Unknown
September 19th, 2176 / Early Evening (Dragon time)

"All clear Willy," Fergus said. "Nothing on passive sensors or in our immediate vicinity. I shot out an active sensor ping to make sure. But I keep picking up this insanely high frequency static. I'm not sure what it's about, but I'll hopefully know more in just a few. I started a full diagnostic scan on the communications and sensor package just in case we took some major damage."

"Damage report," Willy demanded.

"Looks like minimal buckling of the hull around the docking port and bulkhead section delta eighty-eight," Trae reported. "We managed to evade three of those missiles and the countermeasures took out the rest. I think we're good," he looked back to Willy.

"Alright, good," Willy said, letting out a heavy sigh. "How far is it to the next flux point?"

"At full thrust, about two hours," Trae said.

"Andy, set course, but only run her at about eighty percent," Willy ordered. "Let's give her a little shakedown just to make sure we didn't take any other damage."

"Oh! This must be the bridge," a strange electronic voice shouted. *"And I presume you to be the captain. Please, I beg you, sir. Save me from the prodding of this mad creature,"* the robotic voice begged. Jenny pushed the cart and shambling willow tree onto the bridge toward one of the starboard auxiliary stations. She grunted and strained with effort.

"Well hey there, Woody, ol' buddy ol' pal," Fergus laughed. "Enjoying your stay?"

"My name is K'etu, not Woody," the voice argued through the speaker.

"What in the hell?" Willy stared in disbelief at the shambling mound of whip-like limbs covered in blossoms. "What the hell is that?"

"It would really be nice if one of you strapping young lads would be so kind as to help a damsel in distress," Jenny panted.

"Captain," the willow tree shouted through the speaker mounted to the cart. *"I am an ambassador of the It'Vit people. Please, my people will pay handsomely for my safe return, sir. I implore you to release me."*

"Jenny," Willy said. "Can you not hear what it's saying?"

Trae began to chuckle under his breath.

"Well, you see, Willy," Fergus began, "our bat shit crazy schoolmarm here…"

"Had Andy yank out her translator implant," Trae finished the sentence.

"Andy! What in the hell would possess you to do something as idiotic as that?" Willy drove a clenched fist down onto the arm of the command chair.

"What? They asked me to do it. It's not like I went and forced them to let me take them out."

"You do realize that it's insanely expensive to have it replaced? The Polsions will only give you the first one for free."

"Dip shit here also took his and Denise's chips out as well," Fergus said as he thumbed in Andy's direction.

"Captain, please. Do you understand the words that I am speaking," the alien plant thing pleaded.

Willy frustratingly wiped a large meaty hand down his face.

"Get *off* the bridge!" Willy's finger firmly stabbed in the direction of the exit. "I don't care and right now I really don't want to know why there is an alien willow tree begging me for help."

"I will do no such thing," Jenny argued. "I need to document every movement in order to figure out this creature's language."

"Please Captain, please help me," it begged.

"Turn the damn thing loose, Jenny! What in the world would possess you to take a prisoner?"

"It isn't my prisoner, but it does not speak like we do," she said. "It communicates with motion only and I must know how it does this!"

"Get out!" Willy closed his eyes and breathed in slow deep breaths. He blew out a slowly through his nose. "We can figure out the details after we get back to the hole and talk to Doug. For now, get the hell off my bridge!"

cHAPTER 58

Eltanin 2
The Betty / Mess Hall
September 21st, 2176 / Evening (Dragon time)

"**C**ut the bullshit! You don't give a good God damn about me. You just want the prestige of knowing, *the* John Thomas," the Chief shouted as he jabbed a skinny finger at Rachel in emphasis. "You wouldn't know the real John Thomas if he bit you on the ass. And trust me, you wouldn't like him either, so don't go thinking that you know anything about me, girly."

"Chief, calm down," Doug said. "I wanted this meeting to be casual so that Rachel could tell you why she gets so spastic around you." Doug glared over at Rachel, daring her to get excited about anything at the moment.

"I don't give a shit why. She can keep her damned legs closed and stay the hell away from me. I know how you freaky deeky fangirls can be. I'm sure that I have great-great grandkids out there somewhere that are your age. Hell, this one time I had one chick try to cut my ear off as a fucking souvenir," the Chief shouted. He turned his head to the side. Pulling the hair away from his left ear he pulled down the tip of his ear to show off a ragged scar.

"You don't under...," Rachel started.

"No," the Chief bellowed. "You don't understand, princess!"

"Hey now," Lizz shouted at the Chief. "Calm yourself."

"Enough!" Doug threw a chair across the galley. "Sit your ass down now, Chief!"

"Or what?"

"Or I lock you in here with Rachel and leave you overnight."

"You wouldn't," the Chief gasped.

"I just want you to hear her out. It's something extremely important to her that she needs to get out, or she might explode." Doug nodded at Rachel. "Show him what you showed me."

Gently, Rachel opened her backpack and removed a heavy square object. It was wrapped in a layer of lightly oiled leather from an old military duffel bag and placed it on the table. She methodically unwrapped the package, one age-worn layer at a time. She lifted and folded down the last flap of material, revealing an aged leather-bound tome. Its corners and edges worn from years of attention and use. Scraps of paper, bits of this or that stuck out at odd angles in places.

"My grandmother gave this family heirloom to me years ago, just before she passed away. She had planned to give it to my mother, just as her mother had passed it to her, but my mother wasn't the responsible type and died very young because she brought me into this world. This," Rachel lovingly caressed the book, "is what inspired me to become a pilot and an engineer and to do whatever it takes to get the job done." She stared across the table at the Chief, tears filling her eyes. "You inspired me."

She flipped the large binder onto its front cover and flipped to the last filled page of the ancient scrapbook. Slowly, she leafed through the pages, wrapped in the warm, loving memories of her grandmother. "Unless we've missed something over the years, this should cover your entire career. All the way back to your days before flight school. The task has been passed down to the women of my family since its beginning. My grandmother passed it to me, her mother passed it to her, and my great-great-grandmother passed it down to my great grandmother." She smiled and pointed at a newspaper clipping. "See here, this was when they erected the statue of you in Atlanta." She looked up at the Chief and smiled. "You know, it's still there. Any time I go Earthside I make a point to swing by and leave a candle by it." She continued flipping pages.

Panic and a need to escape flashed across the Chief's face. "Besides being a family of creepy fangirls, what does this have anything to do with me?"

"See here," she pointed to a clipped magazine cover. "This is where you were awarded the humanitarian service medal after the incident on Venus station. And here," she flipped another page, "You took the top scores among hundreds of participants during the contractor testing."

"She was so proud of you." Rachel smiled wide as tears of joy trickled down her face. "And I get to tell you, her story." Rachel smiled and began to sob.

Lizz caressed Rachel's back with caring, motherly strokes.

"Do you remember Claudia Rose?" Rachel sniffled and sucked in a lip quivering breath.

"Claudia," the Chief gasped at the name. "I...I could never forget," he stammered. "But...h...how do you..." He swallowed dryly. "How do you know that name?"

Rachel flipped another page and removed a yellowed photograph from the scrapbook. "My great-great-grandmother is the one that started this scrapbook. That was back in the days before you were a hero. Before you even went off to flight school. She kept everything that she had from the earliest of days when the two of you dated in high school. She was so proud of you from the very start. She fell in love with your determination." Rachel lovingly smiled at the figure in the picture, then handed it to the Chief. "Her name was Claudia Rose."

"Claudia," the Chief shakily whispered. Confused, he took a ragged breath and tenderly accepted the time-worn photo. "Oh...my..." His slow exhale fractured into a face contorting sob. "My Claudia," he quietly wailed.

Doug clasped a comforting hand onto the elder space boomer's shoulder. The Chief reached up and thankfully patted the proffered comfort.

"She always wanted you to know that there was no one else," Rachel continued. "You were her one and only."

He leapt forward, grabbing Rachel's hands across the table. "But I came back! I looked for her," he growled.

"Claudia knew that you did," Rachel calmly said. She sniffled and wiped her nose on the collar of her flight jacket. "She even saw you from a distance one of the times that you tried to infiltrate the family's manor house. She was the first to notice you leaping over the hedgerow from the tree branch when you landed on your face."

The Chief sighed. "I remember that." He sadly giggled under his breath. "I managed to break my nose that time."

"You knew her family and how they were. It was all of her father's doing. After finding out that she was pregnant, her father, Marcus decided it would be best to keep her locked away and hidden. He hoped that you would just go away, which you eventually did. But please don't take that the wrong way. She did not expect you to wait for her. You had your mission and she knew how important it was to you."

The Chief's eyes bulged as the realization set in. "I'm a father." He glanced to Doug, then Lizz and back to Rachel.

"Yes." Rachel beamed, wiping away more of the happy tears. "You had a daughter." She flipped the pages of the scrapbook to a section that looked like a family picture album. Baby pictures, hospital bracelet, umbilical cord taped to the top of the page, scatterings of baby teeth all decorated the ancient family tome. "Her name was Ashlee, after your mother."

Location Unknown
Flux Point Charlie
September 21st, 2176 / Evening (Dragon time)

"We're through! The flux is closed," Andy said loudly as sparks exploded, showering the bridge from an overhead relay conduit.

"God Dammit! Damage report," Big Willy demanded. Control panel displays flickered as main lighting began to fail.

"We have a hull breach in aft engineering," Fergus reported. "Looks like emergency bulkheads are holding for now. The reactor is stable, but the power distribution system that is having issues right now. It's like that last hit was followed by an EMP or caused a surge in our electrical power supply system."

Purplish blue electricity arced from the forward starboard auxiliary station to the floor decking. The station suddenly exploded, sending circuitry, plastic, and Amanda flying across the bridge.

"Denise, help me," Janey ordered as she ran to Amanda's side, checking her for injuries.

"Comms and sensors are still working, but weapons are down. I'm getting faults in the main relay housing for the gauss capacitors," Trae said.

"Helm is a dead stick," Andy added.

"What about missiles?"

"Nada," Fergus sighed. "I'm not sure what the issue is, but the system is showing no missiles installed, but I know we have at least two dozen left.

"How's Amanda?" Willy turned, craning his neck to look around Janey.

"She'll live. Just scrapes and a few burns. Nothing serious. She got really lucky." Janey stood and held out a hand to help Amanda to her feet. "I'm going to take her to sickbay and patch her up."

"Alright. Bring us to an all stop if the thrusters will agree," Willy ordered. "Fergus, if sensors are up and running, try to find us a safe harbor so we can get these repairs knocked out. The rest of you, get to work. Andy, Trae, weapons, and helm are the top priority. Those bastards have hunted us down for the last three days. We can't afford to be sitting ducks again. I'm going for a walk to see how bad that hole is and to take a look around."

"Did you wake up and eat a bowl of stupid for breakfast or something?" Denise unlatched her harness and walked over to the command chair. "You're seriously going out there when those alien sons of bitches could show up at any moment without any warning whatsoever?"

"Absolutely," Willy said pensively. "I have a feeling that we've been tagged. It's the only thing that makes sense with how they keep finding us after we've gone through a flux point."

The alien willow tree rushed onto the bridge and zoomed up next to Willy in its hover-gator. Its tentacle-like branches whipped about in a flurry, striking Willy about the legs. *"You promised that you'd return me. You are as crazy as the female that captured me,"* the robotic voice of the translator frantically shouted.

"Okay, okay," Willy said, dodging the shivering bush's attack. "We'll get you back to where you need to be just as soon as we can. For now, you're just stuck with us. And if you want to live, I suggest that you go help look for damage before I make a toothpick out of your scrawny ass!"

The Willow's branches suddenly slumped and dragged along the ground behind the transport as it hovered toward the bridge exit.

cHAPTER 59

Eltanin 2 Orbit
The Ethel / Command information Center
September 24th, 2176 / Noonish (Dragon time)

"*N*ow *I tell you what, Captain,*" Chris said exaggerating his normally nasally southern dialect. He smiled at the camera mounted above the station in the engineering section. *"All of this zero-g welding and extracurricular spacewalks have left me feeling a might parched, Captain. We have been bleeding and sweating and working our asses off up here. Do you suppose that there is any chance that Miss Melanie would be so gracious as to work up a special batch of sweet tea for us when we set foot back down in the Hole?"* He flashed a crooked tooth smile over the *Ethel's* massive view screen.

"I'm sure that she wouldn't have a problem with that, Chris," Doug said. "Unless it's something special that we don't have in stock."

"Oh no, no, no, nothing like that at all, Captain. As long as she has the three main ingredients." He stuck up a finger and began counting them out. *"As long as she has tea bags, lots of hot water and the very, very most important ingredient of all,"* he paused, licking his lips. *"Pure white cane sugar."*

"There were enough people on the roster that drank sweet tea that I know we brought plenty of tea and sugar back with us."

"Maybe so Captain, maybe so. But let me ask you this. Does she know how to make true southern sweet tea?" Chris's large fluffy eyebrows comically rose with hopeful anticipation.

"I'm sure that she does," Doug replied. He began to rub his temples in a preemptive strike against the headache that he was sure was coming. "You just steep the tea bags in hot water and add sugar. I'm pretty sure that she can handle that, Chris."

"Ah, but I'd bet that's where you're wrong." He smiled and waggled a greasy black finger.

"Okay, how do you make true southern sweet tea then?" Doug crossed his arms and waited for Chris's earth-shattering reply.

"You see Captain, you mix in a great big ol' extra helping of diabetes into it. So thick and sickeningly sweet that you can feel yourself transcend upon a higher plane of existence." He closed his eyes and slowly licked one finger after another.

"Is Danny down there with you?" Doug said with an exasperated huff.

"Well yeah," Chris said. *"Why, what's up?"*

"Could you get him for me?"

"Oh hey, yeah, sure. Hold on just a sec there mon Cap-i-tan." Chris cupped his hands and looked away from the camera. *"Hey Danny! The Captain wants to talk at ya."* He turned back to the screen. *"Hang on, he's coming. He'll be over here in just a second."*

"What the hell are you doing man?" Danny joined Chris at the engineering station, walking into the camera's range of view. *"Did you get those injectors calibrated yet?"*

"Naw, not yet. I was fixing to get to it when the Captain rung me up," Chris said, pointing at the viewscreen.

"What? Get the hell out of here and back to work before I throw you out an airlock ya damn layabout." Danny threw the greasy rag that he held at Chris, then turned to examine the engineering console.

"Alright, alright," Chris threw his hands up defensively and backed away, out of the camera's view.

Danny looked up at the camera as he leaned against the console. *"What's up, Cap? You like our Frankenstein monster so far?"*

"So far, yes," Doug said. "What you've managed to accomplish the last few weeks is an impressive feat."

"She's nowhere near complete, but we have nine of the twelve reactors back online," Danny said as he untucked his shirt and wiped dirty sweat from his face. *"It was going to be such a pain in the ass to add struts and cut into the superstructures that we just said fuck it and welded the sections straight to the outer hull. Then we went back over it all with the extra bits and reinforced the design from the outside with an additional superstructure. So you now have the four Red engineering sections and eight of the twelve Red's reactors online and powering those systems. We still need to eventually cross tie the EPS system between those sections, but for now, we just worried about wiring up the controls and getting that routed to the Ethel's Command Information Center. This ship is so freaking big that it warranted a military-style CIC command center over a standard bridge. We managed to salvage the engineering section of the Cat carrier also and connected it to the ass end of the Ethel. Our old girl has a big ol' butt now,"* he smiled, cheesily. *"That Cat-carrier reactor is still operational, and it looks like it'll easily be compatible with our power systems without too much problem. But there again, we just worried about the control systems to make the connections. The forward superstructure of the Cat-carrier was good for scrap and that's about it, so we'll end up stripping parts and wires from her as we need to down the road."*

"So you have nine reactors online and powering this beast," Doug said. He shook his head in disbelief.

"Oh no." Danny giggled and grinned proudly. *"We have fifteen reactors total running onboard our prom night dumpster queen."* He lovingly stroked the nearby bulkhead.

"Holy shit," Wes blurted, then snorted a laugh.

"Maybe you two should get a room," Rachel said as she went over the helm console readouts.

"That is impressive, Danny," Doug said. "Will we be able to use all of that power?"

"Once we have all of the systems cross-connected, we'll be able to shut down reactors or turn them down to an idle state unless the power is needed," Danny said. *"We could also install battery banks and extra capacitors just because, but I think we'll be alright without them. She'll use the most amount of power once we fire up the induction furnaces, we're running material through her foundry. Hell, I'd be willing to bet that we could run the furnaces and all of the rest of the foundry gear plus push her to full speed while actively firing everything that we have. The biggest problem short term will be wiring it all up to be controlled from the CIC so we won't have to dedicate a body to each of these engineering spaces."*

"Now what about her defensive systems?" Doug looked down at a datapad. "Are any of the railgun batteries still operational?"

"None of us have really dug into them yet. We've been too busy with the structural bits. It looks like maybe over half of them were cannibalized for this or that over the years and a number of the turrets are just flat out missing," Danny said. *"Once we get these other items knocked out, we'll be able to concentrate on offensive and defensive systems. My primary goal is to plug all the holes and get the primary systems functioning again so we can start running the ore processors. Once we have all of that taken care of then we can produce any structural members or plating that we want or need."*

"Cap," Wes interrupted. "I'm picking up a distress beacon and flux point Beta just opened." He flipped through readouts that he displayed on the massive main view screen, pushing the video feed from engineering to the side.

Static erupted from the CIC speakers. *"Mayday, mayday, mayday,"* Willy shouted through the interference. *"Possible threat inbound...aliens...I repeat..."* The signal went silent.

"Open up all channels, Wes," Doug ordered.

"Attention all hands, battle stations," Doug said. "Attention all ships in the system. Possible threat imminent. All ships airborne and all weapons hot! Tiff, fire up the defensive grid."

"Calls coming in from the other ships, Cap," Wes announced. "Everyone has checked in, though the *Days of Ore* is heading back to the hole since she doesn't have any weapons."

"That's fine," Doug said. "Tell her captain to get with Lizz when they get parked."

"Tiff also reports the defensive grid is online and ready to go," Wes added.

"Cheezy, get us out to the *Veronica,*" Doug ordered.

Rachel turned in her seat and gave Doug a look of abject idiocy. "Are you sure that's a good idea Cap? I mean, one, is *Ethel* ready. Two, is she going to fall apart around us..." she continued.

Doug tapped the internal comms control on the arm of his chair then looked back up to the video feed from engineering. "Danny, let's give this old girl a little shakedown run. Do you think that she'd hold up?"

"Um...," Danny said as he stood upright at the station and crossed his arms, head bowed in contemplation.

"Well now, that doesn't fill me with any warm happy feelings," Wes said.

"Just hold on," Danny said. *"I'm still thinking. There's a whole lot of ship here and a lot of mismatched parts to consider. Remember, we've managed to pull off the greatest intergalactic redneck engineering feat known to man with duct tape and bailing wire. So just give me a minute to think."*

"I think I'd like to go home now, Cap," Wes said over his shoulder toward Doug.

"Shut it, wussy boy," Rachel growled. "We're all in and you know it. You can't back out now," she said with a cackle.

"Hey Danny," Doug said. "Is the Chief down there with you?"

"Yeah, man," Danny said. *"He's crawled back down the maintenance shaft for reactor one's injector manifold. He wanted to double-check the torque spec on the hardware before we fired her up."*

"Then we don't have time to wait," Doug said. "Your call, Danny. We need to get out to the flux point and pick up *the Veronica.* Can *the Ethel* make it or do we wait for *the Betty* to get airborne?"

Danny loudly sucked on his teeth as he nodded his head in slow contemplation. *"I think we'll be alright, Cap."* He looked up at the camera. *"As long as you don't try to pull any acrobatics with her, she should hold together. Keep her slow and steady and it should all be fine. No more than a quarter thrust for now."*

"Lay in a course, Cheezy. Let's bring our people home," Doug ordered.

Rachel powered up each of *the Ethel's* newly acquired drive sections. The hulking junkyard monstrosity creaked and groaned under the strain of her mismatched propulsion systems as they pushed her mass out of the planet's gravity well.

The crew rushed about, preparing for retrieval of the *Veronica* and their stranded family members. Hours later, the massive superstructure of the *Ethel* loomed over the drifting, lifeless form of the *Veronica*. Grapplers meant to manipulate large asteroidal chunks or salvaged debris extended from the *Ethel's* lower hull and captured the small Martian frigate.

"She's in and the docking bay doors are secured, Cap," Wes reported.

"Did you copy that, Danny?" Doug looked up at the video feed of the docking bay.

"I copy," Danny said. *"We're just waiting on the pumps to finish pressurizing the jetway and we'll be able to get inside."*

"Copy that, Danny," Doug said. "Rachel, get us back within range of the defensive grid."

"Cap," Wes said in a worrisome tone. "A new contact just appeared out of nowhere. It has a similar power signature to the Cat-carrier when it flew in on its warp drive. The contact is upspin and outward of our position but moving fast and heading straight for us."

"Danny, Chief, anybody in engineering. Give me everything we've got to the engines and weapons." Doug leapt to his feet, frantically staring at the two dozen empty duty stations scattered about the CIC. "Where the hell is the weapons control?"

Wes pointed to his right toward a raised platform area. "I think the main defensive controls might be up there."

Doug sprinted across the bridge and scaled the few steps leading to the platform in two long strides. "What the hell...," he cursed under his breath. Panels and console covers lay scattered and piled about the small platform area. Two seats remained mounted to their pedestals in front of the dozen defensive stations. Bundles of wires fell out or dangled haphazardly from the disassembled consoles. "Are the comms still open to Danny?"

"Yeah, go ahead, Cap," Wes said.

"Danny," Doug yelled. "Is there any way that you guys can run the defenses from down in engineering? The consoles up here are busted up something fierce."

"Yeah, we should be able to. Just give me a minute to get this door opened," Danny grunted.

"Door opened?"

"The Veronica's docking hatch is either jammed or not getting power," Danny said. *"So, we're opening her the old-fashioned way."* He screamed a grunt that was immediately followed by the sound of something heavy and metallic striking the deck plating. *"With a crowbar."*

"You sure are a sight for sore eyes," came Willy's voice over the intercom.

"Well don't fall at my feet or anything yet," Danny laughed. *"The shit is about to hit the fan."*

"Willy," Doug said excitedly. "Is everyone from *the Veronica* alright?"

"We've got some minor scrapes and bruises, but otherwise everyone's fit for duty. The Veronica on the other hand," Willy sighed.

"We lost communications and sensors hours ago, Cap," Trae said over the intercom. *"What's the skinny?"*

"Let me guess, we just made it into a cheezy B-rate sci-fi flick didn't we," Fergus added. *"There's this alien hemorrhoid that came from nowhere and is now heading straight for us, threatening to wipe out all life as we know it?"*

"Yeah, that pretty well sums it up," Doud said.

"Enemy hemorrhoid ETA, five minutes," Rachel added.

"Hey hon," Fergus shouted.

"Hey butt munch. Have yourself a good vacation? You know some of us actually have to work for a living around here," Rachel replied.

"We'll be right up, Cap," Trae said.

"Willy, can you give Danny a hand down in engineering and tell everyone else to get to their duty stations," Doug said.

"Can do, Cap."

"I have a visual on the hemorrhoid, Cap," Wes said with a laugh. "She's big and mean-looking."

"Put it up on the main screen."

The viewscreen suddenly flashed from the numerous readouts to show a heavily armored ship. It looked solidly built and compact. Weapons hardpoints bristled across its antique brass colored surface.

"That thing looks pissed," Rachel said.

"I'm picking up multiple energy signatures," Wes announced to no one in particular. "I don't recognize the output, but my guess would be that they are charging weapons."

"Hail them," Doug ordered.

"Channel open, Cap."

"This is Captain Douglas Rackham of the Dragon's Lair Colony…"

"See," Wes whispered to Rachel. "I told you it would sound cool."

"Please state your business," Doug said boldly.

The image of a large, bulbous headed rhino pig looking alien appeared on the main view screen. Its beady red eyes glowered down from the massive main view screen. The creature's mouth moved in time with an unholy ear-splitting squeal mixed with snorts and heavy guttural grunts.

Wes turned in his seat to look at Doug. Worry painted his face. "I've got nothing, Cap. The translation software hasn't even been installed in the Ethel yet, let alone updated for this thing's language."

"I'm sorry, but we do not understand your language. Please, if you can understand me, power down your weapons and let's discuss our options. Perhaps we may be able to learn enough of your language to negotiate the situation." Doug calmly motioned with his hands as he spoke.

Another painful squeal came across the CIC's speakers.

"Whoa! That looks like that big son of a bitch that was following us," Fergus said as he entered the CIC. "Hey there Quasimoto." He waived at the alien on the screen.

"Sorry pal, she's not available," Trae said to the image on the screen. "Like Willy told you before, we are sorry for the shame that she has brought upon your son, but she is part of our crew and you can not have her! Cut the feed, Wes," Trae ordered, then stopped and guiltily looked toward Doug.

"Cut the feed, Wes," Doug ordered. "What the hell was all of that about?"

"Where's weapons control on this barge," Fergus asked, looking over the empty stations across the CIC.

"Up there," Wes pointed toward the raised platform.

"We'll have to fill you in on the juicy details later because we've got other, more pressing matters at hand," Trae said as he rushed to the weapons control platform. "Those guys aren't going to take no for an answer, so we've gotta get ready for a fight. As for Denise, let's just say that she has been dutifully improving our relations with new and interesting species."

"Then see what you can do with the mess of scrap over there," Doug said. "Open a channel, Wes."

"Go, Cap."

"All ships," Doug firmly shouted, "draw them into range of the defensive grid and engage the enemy. Concentrate your firepower, but do not go toe to toe with these guys."

"Anyone got any duct tape handy," Trae shouted down from the platform as he balanced one of the disconnected fire control panels on the railing surrounding the raised platform.

"Are you kidding me," Fergus chided. "What respecting engineer uses duct tape in the middle of a crisis? Here, use this," he said as he pulled a small package from his pocket and tossed it toward Trae.

Trae caught the offered object in his free hand with ease. "Bubble gum? In all of this godforsaken mess, you toss me a package of bubble gum?"

"Yeah," Fergus said matter-of-factly. "If it works, don't fix it," he said as continued to sort through the tangled mass of wires and connectors.

Trae shook his head and began to nervously laugh.

"Picking up a new energy reading from the alien ship," Wes reported. "Wow, that's some serious output."

"How much," Trae asked, looking up from his disassembled panel.

"I don't know," Wes said. "Our scale stops at gigajoule."

Trae gasped. "They have shields," he whispered.

"What?"

"I said that they have shields," Trae said loud enough for everyone to hear. "We never really had a chance to scan them. This whole time it's been fight, run, fight, run. Which if they are capable of shields, that means what they were pounding us with must have been an energy weapon of some sort," he said with wide-eyed amazement.

"Oh my God," Doug said, wiping his face in frustration.

The ship jarred and rocked slightly underfoot as if from an almost imperceptible earthquake.

"Hu," Fergus huffed, "that feels a lot different."

"Well no shit Sherlock," Trae replied. "The *Ethel* is only about twelve times larger than *Veronica*."

"Damage report," Doug ordered.

"Alien vessel came in hot from upspin and strafed the upper superstructure," Wes reported. "I don't think that they hit anything important. It doesn't look like anything vital was affected, but it's really hard to tell."

"What's hard to tell," Doug asked.

"Yes," Fergus cheered. He placed the now powered control console face back onto the console frame. "I've got you now you sumbitch!"

Wes flicked the damage control window up onto the main view screen. Red blotches slowly pulsed across most of the *Ethel's* massive hull.

"Holy cow, it didn't seem like we were hit that hard," Rachel added.

"We weren't," Wes said. "The Ethel was already full of holes and missing parts of her hull plating. She just hasn't been fully repaired yet."

Heavy thuds of recoil suddenly reverberated throughout the ship.

"Whoo-hoo!" Fergus whooped. "That's right you alien bastards! Get some!"

"Mass drivers nine, fifteen and forty-two are on target," Wes reported. "All others are skewed."

"Remind me to boresight all of the turrets after this is over with," Trae said.

"They're coming around and are lining up for another attack run from downspin," Wes yelled. "Hang on!"

"There we go! Time for me to show you how it's done, Ferg," Trae barked. He placed the now illuminated face of a weapons control panel down on the activated console. "What's the current count?"

"Three hits in one barrage," Fergus said.

"Five it is then," Trae said as he pressed the fire button.

The deck of *the Ethel's* CIC bucked beneath their feet as if the ship had driven over an intergalactic speed bump at an unnecessarily high of a rate of speed. Ozone scented hums reverberated as blue arcs surged forth from newly ruptured EPS conduits. Sparks showered down from overhead relay panels.

"Port foundry compartments K, L and O have been hit, but I can't tell how much damage that attack caused," Wes reported.

"Haha!" Fergus shouted. "That's right! Run away, cowards!" Fergus fired the defensive turrets under his control at the enemy vessel as it shot away from the *Ethel*. "Four more hits! Hell yeah! Take that, sucker!" He danced a shuffling jig where he stood and flashed both of his middle fingers toward Trae.

"Uh, huh," Trae said dismissively. "I hope you're watching this." He flicked a display onto the main view screen. Twelve targeting reticles locked onto points across the alien vessel as it and its crew endured a high-g combat u-turn and came around for another strafing pass. "Behold a master at work with his craft," Trae boasted and pressed the fire button.

Purple ozone exploded from the control console and engulfed Trae in a blinding flash of light. His limp form soared in reverse and into the bulkhead by the force of the explosion.

"I've got Trae. Keep those guns firing," Doug shouted as he sprinted for the gunnery platform.

"Medic to the bridge," Wes shouted into the comms. "I repeat, medic to the bridge!"

"I've got you, brother." Doug skidded to a halt at the top of the steps, reaching down to check Trae's pulse. "Good, I've got a pulse! He's still breathing."

"What about butt munch? He alright?" Rachel punched her console. "Dammit, this thing moves and steers like a dead pregnant whale!"

"Don't worry, you're not rid of me yet, Hon," Fergus said.

"Hang on, enemy ship inbound for another pass," Wes announced. "I have five new contacts approaching on long-range. IFF identifies them as the *Betty, Aurora Tetra, Tsuro, Mauve Turtle* and the *Jabberwocky*."

"Tell them to engage at will,' Doug ordered.

"Copy that, Cap."

Hydraulic motors whirred to life as the doors to the CIC opened with a sickly groan. "Who's hurt?" Janey looked around as she entered the control center.

"Over here," Doug shouted.

Janey sprinted across the CIC toward the platform steps. The ship careened sickeningly nose up rolling left with a violent shuddered. Alarms erupted throughout the command information center.

"What in the hell was that?" Doug asked.

"I'm not sure," Wes said. "There's too much showing up as damaged, already."

"I've lost Navigational sensors," Rachel said.

"Comms are down, too," Wes added.

"Bridge, this is engineering. Who the hell's driving this train," the Chief shouted over the intercoms. *"We just lost the red section from the keel. Keep this up and they'll chew us up in no time."*

"Copy that, Chief," Doug replied, moving out of Janey's way. "I'm all ears if you have any bright ideas."

"You're on your own bubba," the Chief snorted. *"That last hit really did a number on us. We have coolant leaks all over the place. We have to abandon engineering."*

"Cap, we just lost the *Mauve Turtle*! The *Betty*, *Jabberwocky* and *Aurora Tetra* have been all been disabled," Wes said. "Holy crap, Cap! The Tsuro is standing toe to toe with these guys!"

"That's it! My guns are gone!" Fergus kicked his console.

"Get me something!" Doug hurriedly slid back into the command chair and pressed the comms button on the arm of the chair. "Everyone left on the ground, it's not looking good up here. I don't know how much longer we can hold them off."

"Cap," Wes interrupted. "Comms are down."

"That's right." Doug sighed. "Is there any chance that anything got through?"

"I really don't know, Cap."

"Um...guys. I hate to tell you this, but at this rate, we're screwed," Rachel added. "There's no way we'll make it back to the defensive grid before these guys rip us apart. *The Ethel* is one slow, fat hog. There's nothing sleek or fast about her."

The ship sickeningly slid starboard. The decking vibrated with an odd harmonic, then began to rattle the plating. Another gout of purple and blue arcs erupted from the rear of the CIC.

"Cut power to that EPS distribution node," Fergus shouted.

"I can't," Wes replied. "Most of the power distribution grid software was bypassed. Those systems are running on a default factory diagnostic program that I installed since the original was corrupt."

Distant explosions rattled through the *Ethel* from deep within her superstructure. New warning alarms sounded from overhead.

"We have a plasma fire on deck twelve and we've lost contact with two more of the added *red* engineering sections," Wes reported.

"She's a dead stick," Rachel announced. "I've got nothing up here, Cap."

"Cap...we're abandoning...," the intercom speakers crackled with static and distortion.

Doug slumped down into the command chair. "Well, at least we made a good run of it for a bit." He sighed as he watched the enemy vessel approach on the large main view screen.

Fluorescent green Plasma erupted from the nose of the alien vessel as it fired once again on the helpless *Ethel*. It slowed to a stop, what looked to be a short distance away in the massive display.

"Hu...they stopped firing," Wes said. "I bet they are hailing us and ordering us to surrender."

"Suppose they'll be boarding us next," Fergus said matter-of-factly. He helped Trae to sit up and supported him where he sat on the upper platform.

Five bright white flashes suddenly appeared on the screen in the darkness just beyond the alien vessel, replaced by five, very large and very ravenous looking *Reds*. Their grappling tentacles flailed out and their clamping maws opened wide. The alien vessel turned, zipping away off-screen before returning for a strafing run on the large alien mining vessels.

The *Reds* maneuvered together in a tight formation, their tentacles connecting to form a net between them. As the enemy ship maneuvered past the group of Reds, one of the manipulation tentacles latched onto the underside of the enemy's hull. It looked as if it were a fly struggling to escape a spiders web. It advanced, engines at full power, only to be pulled back into the fray by the numerous other tentacles that now attached to its hull. Slowly, the enemy vessel was directed to the front of the formation and entered the maw of one of the reds. They watched as the pack of alien mining vessels effortlessly devoured the alien warship.

cHAPTER 60

Eltanin 2
The Hole / Mel's Diner
September 25th, 2176 / Evening (Dragon time)

Leisurely stroked fiddle strings sang out in time with a rolling base beat and the whispered croon of a female voice as a song played from the cantina's jukebox.

"It's about freaking time that my song kicked on," Krista shouted from the far end of the cantina. She leapt to her feet and quickly pulled Maggie along with her. "See this is perfect. Just do what I do," she instructed as she began to rotate and undulate her hips in time to the music.

"What song is that, Krista?" Tiff asked from a few tables away.

"*The Story That Never Starts* by Abney Park," Krista said, then held her arms above her head and arched her back, doubling over backward.

Nearly all of the colony's inhabitants had gathered within the cantina. They sat scattered about the three stories of the open space as they ate, told stories and laughed at horribly bad jokes. The Chinchassa mingled among the colonists. Two of the younger-looking cat creatures wore white waitress aprons and happily delivered food and drinks to their awaiting customers.

"We should open our own orbital restaurant," Becky said through sloppy crunches of crushed ice. "Something to help draw in customers to the system. Make a real spaceport out of this place."

"Oooo," Sabrina said excitedly. "It should be a blue ship with these lasers that are really purple beams of light that you use like huge spotlights to act like a beacon for the customers."

"I could be on board with all of that," Tiff agreed.

"Ugggg…," Mel huffed. "You know that you're probably going to make my head hurt with this idea. It already sounds like something Andy would come up with." She pulled her hair back and smoothed the loose hairs back into place. "Ok, go ahead. I'm ready. So blue with purple energy beams. Now how in the hell are we going to talk the Captain into letting us set up shop like that? Where exactly do you crazy people come up with ideas like this that will never happen?"

"Oh, trust me. It can happen. It's all a matter of how we approach the Captain. But it has to be electric blue," Sabrina said.

Melanie groaned and vigorously rubbed her face, then took a deep, frustrated breath. "Okay, so any other bright ideas to throw at it? Should we give away door prizes or sell raffle tickets or something?"

"Oh, I don't know. I guess that could all work if we really wanted to do it," Becky replied.

"Ooo ooo ooo," Sabrina grunted, holding a hand in the air. "Can it have a panini bar? You can't kick alien ass on an empty stomach."

"What the hell is a panini bar," Melanie said.

"A station where you make Panini's, silly," Sabrina said, then drifted away in mental thought.

"That still doesn't tell me what the hell a Panini is." Melanie.

"Oh, they are these yummy grilled sandwiches that you serve with different sauces and dressings," Sabrina said.

"I like that Idea," Kara added. "It sounds perfect, especially after running a shuttle back and forth all day long."

Mel glared across the table at Kara.

"What? You can't tell me that you wouldn't want something like that on an ass-kicking ship?"

"Mmmmm," Sabrina and Becky hummed in unison. "Paninis," they chanted.

"See," Sabrina said, pointing at Becky and Sabrina. "At least I'm not the only one that knows how to have a good time in an alien star system."

"I couldn't help but overhear," Cara said, walking over to the table with her lunch tray. She flipped her shoulder length golden mane to the side. "There are lots of precautions you'd have to put in place for an intergalactic diner if you really start to think about it. Everyone knows you'd need a proton destabilizing laser net that is activated by the presence of foreign DNA."

"As long as it shoots out a purple laser thingy we'll be okay," Sabrina said.

"Well now, you'd need a special selector switch for your purple lasers, that way you could change it to blue or gold or even red."

"I'll tell you what," Sabrina said. "I'll come up with the pretty stuff and you worry about the smart engineering stuff.

"That sounds reasonable enough to me," Cara admitted, taking a bite of her baked potato.

"How about a shield that can pull enemies closer that also disables their ships so none of the weapons can be used?"

"You mean a tractor beam with an emp pulse?"

"If that's the smart way of putting it, then yes," Sabrina said. "Oh, and a thingy that can read the kind of tech they have even if it's more advanced and it can break down how it works, and the ship automatically updates itself by stealing the higher-tech."

"So, a side-scanning mechanism array, with electronic detection, auto modulation and an adaptable artificial intelligence interface to run the whole shebang," Cara asked.

"You two are way above my head," Becky admitted, then took a sip of her drink.

"I still think it should have a panini bar," Sabrina said. "Is there a technical way to say panini bar?"

"No." Cara sighed.

"Poor aliens…"

"Oh my God. Out of my dinner! All of you crazy people! Before you run off the paying customers! This is freaking insane. Becky, Sabrina, break time is over. Get back to work." Melanie huffed back behind the serving line.

"I guess if I have too," Becky groused, then turned and slogged her way back to the kitchen.

"You had me at Panini bar," Sabrina said with an exhausted yawn. "They sound yummy."

"Exactly…Aliens gotta eat too, ya know."

"For the love of God will you just get back to work already," Melanie shouted from behind the bar. "Enough about the panini bar. No one cares but you."

"Oh my god, what is that horrible smell?" Sabrina sniffed at the air, then sniffed at her armpits.

Becky sniffed at the air and gagged. "Oh man, that is foul."

"Eh, it's not that bad. I've smelled worse," Cara said, bragging. "Suck it up Chickadee. If you're going to run an intergalactic dinner, then you'll have different races with all of their oddities and weirdness to deal with."

"Evening Ladies," Doug said as he approached the bar. "I'd like to introduce Larrs'Neytee, Captain of the," Doug paused as he listened to the cooing growl of the seven-foot-tall Sasquatch-like creature. "Captain of the Nebula's Jewel. He owns the five Rohʙandi ships that came to our aid."

"Hey Larrs'Neytee," Cara said as she stood up and extended her hand toward the large hairy creature. "It's good to see you again."

The bigfoot like alien let out an urgent gurgling growl followed by what sounded like a high-pitched whimper.

"We will in just a moment," Doug said to Larrs'Neytee. "Are there any issues or allergies that we need to know about?"

"What did he just say?" Mel and the others stared wide-eyed at the massive alien before them.

"He and his crew would love to try our food, but also wanted to know where the restroom was in case things don't settle right."

Mel stared in amazement. "How the hell can you understand any of that braying?"

"The Rohвandi work directly for the Polsions, um…," Doug looked around the room. "The furry possum looking aliens over there are Polsions. They sorta run things and set the rules that everyone seems to follow, kinda like if they were the head of a galactic trade guild. They are the ones that produce the translator implant that allows me to understand them and them to understand me. It's based on some sort of ancient old empire technology from the way he explains it. Captain Larrs'Neytee," Doug looked up at the sasquatch looking creature to assure he was getting the name right, "Has agreed to supply our entire population with the implants, free of charge, in exchange for samples of our delicacies and a trade alliance since we have set up shop and laid claim to this system as our own."

Sabrina clasped her hands over her mouth. She convulsed with a restraining retch.

"Not in here," Mel yelled. "Out! If you're going to be sick, be sick someplace else!"

"Um Cap," Sabrina leaned over and whispered. "Nothing personal mind you, but your friend here may need a flea dip."

The massive potbellied Rohвandi grumbled and growled in Sabrina's general direction then grumbled something to Doug.

Doug leaned down toward Sabrina. "He can understand everything you are saying, crewman."

Sabrina quickly fanned herself with both hands. "If you would please excuse me," she gasped. "I have to go...um...powder my nose." She started to gag as she ran out of the cantina.

"I'm docking your pay!" Mel's glaring gaze turned back toward Doug and the massive alien captain. "If these guys can't follow the rules of my diner, I will forcibly remove every one of them myself. That includes using the facilities and not just finding a corner in here somewhere. You make sure he understands that." Mel jabbed a dishpan finger in the direction of the alien captain. "I am not cleaning up piles of alien shit! Got it!"

A perturbed look washed over Doug's face. "He and his crew are our guests and we'll need accommodations for approximately twenty of them." He turned to Captain Larrs for confirmation. The alien nodded. "It seems that one of the rating factors that they use when listing new trade locations is the quality of the food and its facilities. It doesn't necessarily matter if it does anything nutritionally for them because what they are really interested in is the new flavor profiles. I know our supplies are limited, but I'd like you plan a special meal for them with as wide a variety as you can."

"Really," Melanie sighed. "I'll do what I can, but no guarantees. It's not like I have a five-star facility here."

The large sasquatch looking alien chortled in agreement.

"How about we start with two beers," Doug ordered.

"Coming right up." Mel fished out two tall beer glasses and poured from an array of old tavern-style pulls. "So, they aren't upset about the four ships that were destroyed?"

"No," Doug said. "We've shown them the recordings of the encounters and they have basically chalked it up to a misunderstanding. The way that captain Larrs here puts it; the potential profits of a new trade alliance outweighs the need for retribution."

Melanie handed frothy drinks to Doug. He took a sip of the golden-yellow drink and handed the other glass to the large alien captain, who greedily accepted the tall glass into his massive hand. He drank, white foam clinging comically to the fur around his mouth. The large furry alien let out an obviously happy warbled grunting coo.

"You could easily take back gallons of this if you like it that much," Doug said. "We have a good bit currently in stock."

The Rohвandi captain happily smacked his lips and cooed again. He quickly drained the glass and handed it back to Mel with a pleading look.

"He'd like a refill," Doug said between sips.

"Hey now," Danny shouted from across the room. "My tunes! Bad walking carpet! You don't mess with a man's tunes, especially when Skynyrd is playing," he shouted at one of the large aliens that stood by the cantina's jukebox pressing buttons.

Doug laughed, then looked back up at the Rohвandi captain. "It'll take a little adjustment time, but I think once we get the mining operations in full swing, the crews will work well together."

Captain Larrs let out a scruffing grunt. He nodded and eagerly took the refilled glass from Melanie.

Jouqon raced past Doug in the direction of the juke box as Casraownan approached the bar and said something in his yowling Chinchassan language to Doug.

"Melanie, would you mind pouring another glass please," Doug said. "Cas would like to try a beer as well."

"*Sure*," she said, pouring another glass from the tap. "Let's just get the aliens drunk and have a shootout in my cantina. Just like in every freaking science fiction movie ever made," she sarcastically mumbled under her breath then placed the glass on the bar next to Cas.

Doug held his glass high, nodding to Captain Larrs, then to Casraownan. "To good health and a long, prosperous friendship."

ePILOGUE

Eltanin 2
Dig Site Alpha
September 27th, 2176 / Morning (Dragon time)

Ben looked across the vast open space between the ruins of houses and the suspected community center of this ancient neighborhood. He stood in the center of what looked to be a large depression from the satellite imagery.

"I just don't get it. Why would this be collapsed down like it is? The geologists didn't find anything strange about the area. The substrate is all granite and they didn't find evidence of caverns in the area." Ben connected a coax cable from his tablet to the radar unit. "We'll get to the bottom of this in just a few moments," he said to himself then happily whistled a cheery tune as he finished connecting the equipment.

"Ben," Camille shouted from the upper camp area. He turned to see the flapping orange tent material over the sandy ridge. Camille waved down at him. "Lunch is ready whenever you are."

"I'll be right there. Just let me test the sensors real quick."

"Be safe!" She gave him a thumbs up and disappeared back behind the rise.

"Alright," he said with an excited sigh. "Let's see what secrets you can uncover for me today old girl." He stood on the small platform of the radar ignitor and pulled the trigger. The unit, with him on it bucked and leapt a few inches from the ground. "That's always a fun ride, right there." He wiggled a pinky finger in an ear to clear the noise from the explosion as he checked the equipment readout. The obvious image of a skull and a scattering of other bones lined the area beneath the sensor pad. "Wait. That sort of resolution means it's nearly on the surface already."

Ben moved the sensor plate to the side and began to brush away ages worth of dusty sand. Quickly the bright white of bone revealed itself. He pulled a brush from his back pocket and skillfully brushed it away from the specimen.

"This can't be right." He frantically began to brush.

"Camille!"

Camille reappeared above the sandy rise. "Is everything alright, Ben?" Then her eyes caught on the unmistakable thing that he held high overhead. "Oh my," she gasped.

Two human eye sockets and a complete jaw jeeringly glared back at her from across the dusty distance.

The End